CHOSEN

D. T. Neal

NOSETOUCH PRESS

Chosen
Copyright © 2012 D.T. Neal

Cover Art: Christine Marie Scott.

ISBN-10: 1481127640
ISBN-13: 978-1481127646

www.dtneal.com

For Kit

ACKNOWLEDGMENTS

I would like to thank all of my readers, who offered their time, attention, and opinions to the writing and revision of this book. I would also like to thank Christine Marie Scott of Clever Crow Design Studio in Pittsburgh for her wonderful cover art and her invaluable assistance with the layout of these pages.

CHOSEN

D. T. Neal

PART
ONE

I.

Malcolm Travis Warner did not so much leap as slip into the slinking Mercy River, victim of a guzzle of apple wine that required too deep a tip of his head, upsetting his already tenuous balance while he sat alone atop one of the concrete and steel feet of the Mercy River Bridge, some twenty feet above the green-black water.

No one saw him fall because nobody else had been nearby. Mal had not been planning to commit suicide; he'd only been thirsting for a drink in private, in the railroad-shadowed, weedy no man's land between the tracks and the river, where trees grew wild and tangled amid globs of grease, where rusty bolts were thrown from railway cars like rings from dead giants' severed fingers.

All this clung to the rocky beach that existed between the tracks and the river, where nobody went except for drunks and potheads, and here Mal found his sanctuary. The remains of a stony structure hugged the shore, half-hidden by rhododendron bushes. It was this place that led the determined traveler to the Mercy River Bridge, and offered a kingly view of the barge traffic that lumbered up and down it, carrying coal, coke, scrap, and nameless crap to and from their intended destinations. The barges, like old society matrons, conducted themselves with an indolent yet stately grace, showing their age, but plodding onward with redoubtable determination to go about their own business.

The Perch, as Mal knew it, was like a reviewing stand for junkies, those few who knew about it, unafraid of the rusting skeletons of long-forgotten shopping carts jutting from the burlap-colored sand below. How they got there, no one knew, but they spoke to something in Mal, so he came there often. He liked to get drunk and watch things rust.

Rust was the coin of the realm in Ludlow, though one wouldn't know it from the slouching mountains that hid behind green trees and endless passing fogs. Up in those mountains, fortunes had once been made, and, like an industrial Valhalla, steel and coal barons had built mansion in those soft shale peaks, their houses invisible from the winding roads, their gateways announced solely by standing stones at the driveways, and a gravel path that led to parts unknown.

Steel was King in Ludlow; this was a point that none disputed, even if the King was long dead, the memory of his iron rule went on. However, in the valley, Rust ruled. Rust was what clung to everything, from darkened factories to decaying fences to railroad paths that led to no place, the rails themselves removed, to the husks of putrefying old cars that were anthropological signposts to lost affluence among working-class union people, a memory as faded as the piss-yellow and pea-green paint that still clung to the car corpses that lay along hunchbacked streets.

It was Mal who was the latest corpse in the Mercy River, falling with a soundless splash, still holding his jug, belatedly realizing his dire misfortune. He'd been stupid to get so drunk on the Perch, but it was stupidity borne of habit, the kind he was best at.

Down he went, after an abortive surface splash, where he tried, stupidly, to scream for help, only to drink down a mouthful of rotten river water. Above him, far out of reach, was the span of the Mercy River Bridge, protected by a lone blinking red light that watched him sink without expression. It bothered Mal to realize that he'd die unheralded, unnoticed, while far above, on that bridge, commuters were coming and going, heedless of his doom.

Blink.

Sink.

Blink.

Sink.

He flailed his arms as he tried to make for the shore, but his blue jeans held him fast, and, staring upward, Mal went down, watching that bridge light grow watery and insubstantial as he fell into the depths, praying he'd reach the bottom and could walk his way back out, his lungs burning and gobs of black dancing in his eyes until, unable to hold his breath a minute longer, Mal let go and began to drown properly, as God intended.

Down there, in the dark, he struggled, the water tasting of mud and rust and old river stones and broken glass worn pebble-smooth. It was this place where he'd come to die, and where he'd meet his Maker. He was angry at himself, angry at the world, angry at God, most of all, for letting it happen. And the Mercy River became his grave.

Until the Angel in the Depths came to him.

The Light in the Dark.

2.

Mal went into the water a drowning man and had emerged from it something else. He walked out of the water, choking on what he'd swallowed and inhaled, mindful of the passage of time, because he'd known that he'd died—he'd felt himself die, when the tickle of the last bubble gasps of air left his lungs and felt the agony as he drowned and his brain and body staged rebellions, sending him into spasms, then convulsions, until there'd been nothing left to do but die.

Therefore, he had died. Mal knew this, as clear as he knew his own hands, fingers wagging in front of his face.

He had died, and been born again.

It was as clear and undiluted as acid rain.

He had been reborn.

Born again.

Mal knew nothing of miracles, believed in nothing more steady than a paycheck, but he knew what he had experienced was a special thing. What was it?

A miracle. That's exactly what it was.

He knew it when he'd crawled out of the water, hands slick with river mud, knew it as his lungs, once cleared of water, had just as swiftly forgotten how to breathe.

Having died and been reborn, Mal no longer feared death. There was nothing a dead man had to fear, and realizing it, he laughed. Not a joyful laugh, the laughter of a child, but a hopelessly hard and hateful thing.

And something was better than nothing, and he laughed all the harder for it.

Mal saw that he was still carrying the wine jug, and, in disgust, he threw it away, finding fleeting joy in the smash of it against the biscuit-shaped river stones on the shore. He'd never need another drink so long as he lived. Though after smashing it, he'd felt a bit sad, for the wine had been the source of his deliverance, but he quickly strangled that thought where it was born, and walked out onto the sand, deciding to dry out right.

As he sat on the shore, waiting, Mal became aware of a pair of teens walking along the grass above and behind him, along the old stone precipice that paralleled the Perch. They looked like metalheads, one in an Army jacket, zitfaced and longhaired, the other in a worn denim jacket, mulleted blonde hair floating above pig eyes. They saw him at once, and froze in their tracks, like antelopes before a lion.

"You okay, dude?" Zitface asked.

"Never better," Mal said.

"You fall in?" Pigeyes asked.

"I sure did," Mal replied. "Went off the deep end."

The kids looked at each other, then back at him. No doubt, they'd been planning on getting stoned in the forest.

"You seen anybody else around here?" Zitface asked.

"Nope," he said. "Just me."

"Well, alright, then," Zitface said, and he and his friend disappeared into the trees.

3.

Drying off proved difficult, because Malcolm was cold—not chilly, but cold, like to the touch. He'd sat by the shore for quite awhile. He realized he'd have to bake in the midday sun, and he'd drowned at precisely 4:38 p.m., and though he didn't know what time it was, or what day, he knew a sunset when he saw it.

So, he got up, dusted the grit and gravel from his jeans, and walked home. Mal lived alone, worked at the Big Star Riverboat Casino. He'd wanted to be a dealer, but was unable to shake the smirk from his lips when he had a good hand, and he'd never been able to get far with card games, so he was a food runner.

He took a shower and tossed his stinking river-smudged clothes into the trash, and then decided what he was going to do next.

He'd looked at himself in the mirror, took stock of his face, and when he smiled, the smile didn't touch his eyes. His eyes, black eyes, were as dead as marbles, and he kind of scared himself when he looked directly in the mirror. He poked his face, and the skin gave way a bit, but was still pliant. It was weird.

"Lord, what have you done to me?" He asked himself in the mirror.

Same old Mal, and yet different. Long face, sharp chin, black hair, like it'd been dipped in shoe polish. Skin as pale as ever. Maybe paler. He didn't know for sure. He didn't know what he was.

What he wasn't was hungry or thirsty, which sort of messed with his mind a little, because he felt like he ought to eat something after what happened, but that thought came out stillborn and he was left sitting on the sofa in the dark, waiting for a heartbeat, but not hearing one. By then, he was definitely sure that he was dead, which made him walking around terribly confusing. He didn't feel like a zombie, but admitted to himself that he didn't know what a zombie felt like, anyway.

His phone rang, and it didn't startle him. He didn't know if he could be startled, after what he went through. He let it ring three times, then picked it up before the answering machine got it. It was Bernie Ross, his boss. Supervisor. Team leader.

"Mal, where have you been?"

"Huh?"

"You been out for three days," Bernie said. "We had to have Cleo fill in for you. I called the police, figuring something had happened."

Something had happened, alright.

"Nothing happened," Mal said. "Three days? You sure?"

"What the hell happened to you? You go on a bender or something?"

Mal tried to remember. It had been a weekday. A Friday. That's when he'd been on the Perch. He'd had the day off, and had decided to spend it getting drunk and watching barges.

"What day is it, Bernie?"

"You are drunk. It's Monday."

"Monday?" He'd been dead for three days.

"I'm sick, Bernie," Mal said.

"You said nothing happened," Bernie said.

"I meant nothing bad," Mal said. "I just got sick, is all. Look, I'll come in tomorrow, make up the shifts I missed."

"I'm still gonna have to write you up," Bernie replied. "For not calling in sick."

Not like it mattered, anyway; Big Star didn't pay out for sick days. Three days in the river. Wow. Mal had become aware of a certain leveling inside him, like a smoothing of emotional peaks and valleys to some kind of baseline—like the Appalachian Mountains of his heart had been eroded into a Great Plains. It wasn't a bad feeling; it wasn't so much of a feeling at all.

Just a sort of nothing.

"Yeah, you go ahead and do that, Bernie," Mal said. "I'll be in tomorrow."

It was a lie, but Mal didn't care about that. Maybe he'd be in, maybe he wouldn't. He didn't care. He hung up on Bernie and went to the television, turned it on.

TV helped him think.

Mal sat there, watching TV for twelve hours, staring at it in the dark, like a zombie.

4.

It was on the thirteenth hour that Mal stood up, got dressed, and decided he had been chosen to be a messenger. That was the only thing that made sense to him, why he wasn't dead-dead. That much he was sure of, even though he wasn't quite sure of the message, or who had sent it.

All he knew was that he wasn't dead.

Not alive, but not dead, either.

Undead.

That's what he was.

He knew that as sure as he knew a clenched fist.

He put on a necktie and a white shirt, and a pair of black slacks and some shiny shoes, and he went for a walk through town. The old part of Ludlow was trying to pass itself off as a genial little hamlet perched at the bed and breakfast base of the misty mountains, peering with crinkled eyes across the green river valley, wizened gaze benignly averted from the rotting steelworks.

Down Ash Street and First Street, along Church Street. Church Street held him for a bit, since it was home of the St. Vincent Cathedral, a pointy blackened church wrapped in wrought iron fencing. All the old buildings in Ludlow were black, at least those that hadn't been sandblasted to remove the soot that had come from the mills. It was like trying to wash away blood.

Mal stood outside the church for a bit, just staring at it, wondering whether or not he should go in. He took a step up toward it, then a step back. There wasn't anything in there for him—he wasn't a Catholic. He remembered his folks saying that the Catholic Church was a pagan institution, and that they weren't real Christians, like they were at the Second Coming Tabernacle of Ludlow. That old building had been a drugstore, once, but Reverend Willard Fisk had bought the building and evangelized in it. It wasn't very churchy, at least it wasn't like St. Vincent's, all fancy.

It was all dingy, held up by plain metal poles, floor old chapped Formica or linoleum, ceiling made of cracked asbestos-looking tiles. The Second Coming Tabernacle had shut down when Reverend Fisk had been caught sleeping with the daughter of one of the deacons. After that, Fisk went away, and took a lot of money with him.

Mal had always looked up to Reverend Fisk, with his hair slicked up and back and his thick ties and thicker fingers, like Vienna sausages. Fisk always had a good story, and his red face would shake when he talked, preaching about witches and devil worshippers and heavy metal. He'd get so mad, people thought he'd burst. But he could sure talk with the best of them, real syrup-sweet and gunpowder hot, when he had to.

And as for Anna Havilland, the deacon's daughter, well, people thought she'd been demon-led, tempting Fisk and leading a good man bad. She left Ludlow after that, for parts unknown. She'd been a classmate of Mal's, way back when. He'd always liked her and her blonde hair and Milk Dud eyes. He'd bought her a carnation, once, in secret. She'd even worn it, which was saying something, because she was a cheerleader, was popular, was always getting flowers. Mal couldn't remember what he'd had it say, as if a flower couldn't speak for itself.

Mal left the cathedral unmolested and decided just to go down to Tuck's, a pasty old bar down the block on Second Avenue, noted mostly for its fake brick vinyl siding that was slowly cracking and falling off, like the tavern had leprosy or something.

He walked up to the door and stepped in past the neon purr in the dingy windows, taking a seat by the television set which hung over the cracked old bar like a guardian angel. There were three people in there, two in a corner by the old blue vinyl booths, the third being the bartender, Vince.

Vince was heavyset, Polish-Italian, face like a haunch of beef that had been left out a bit too long, forever working on a ghost of a mustache that never quite came together. Still, he was an alright guy, quick with a drink. He'd had the TV set for sports.

"Hey, Mal," Vince said. "You want a beer?"

"Sure," Mal said, though he didn't. He sat down and pretended to watch the game while Vince poured him a draft and set it on the bar in front of him.

Mal watched the beer, willing himself to take it. He didn't feel a thing for it. That made him a little sad, cuz he'd spent so much time at Tuck's.

"Missed you on Friday, Mal," Vince said. "Jolene was looking for you."

"That right? I fell in the Mercy River," Mal said. "You believe that?"

"I sure do," Vince said. "Whereabouts?"

"Near the bridge," Mal said.

"You weren't jumping off or nothing, right?"

Mal shook his head. "I got too much to live for, Vince. Just lost my balance and fell in. Jolene, huh? What's she looking for me for?"

"That's between you and her," Vince said.

"Was she pissed?"

"Nah. Jolene never gets pissed. She's what you call 'even-tempered.' Went home with Stan."

Jolene worked at the Big Star as an attendant. She wore clunky bracelets and real tight jeans and had bottle-blonde hair that she sprayed up into a halo around her head. Mal never knew what she saw in him, but when he was there, she'd talk to him sometimes, when she wasn't busy playing pool. They had not been classmates; she'd gone to Whidmore High, further down the river. Whidmore was a Catholic school.

Thinking of Jolene, Mal picked up the beer and brought it to his lips, willed the glass to his lips. He'd never felt something like that—complete indifference. It might as well have been a paperweight he was hefting.

Vince was watching him.

"You alright, Mal? I know it ain't river water, but it's the best we got."

Mal forced the beer down, tipped it back and drank it down. His throat rebelled, like it had forgotten what the hell to do with a beer. He felt it fizzing down in his stomach, and then he felt something else, like he was gonna puke.

He set the glass down and threw a couple of bucks down with it, and walked out without another word, even though Vince said something cuz Mal could see his mouth moving, but he couldn't hear it. Mal just wanted to get out of the bar without puking.

And he made it. Just.

The beer spilled out of him, like it had no place to go but back from whence it came. He didn't even puke it out quite right—it just poured back out, spattering onto the sidewalk.

Made Mal sorta sad, cuz he liked hanging out at Tuck's when he wasn't working, but there was no reason for him to be in there if he wasn't able to drink. He could've played pool, maybe, or pinball. But after stomping out the way he did, he didn't think he should come back just yet.

So, Mal walked down Second Avenue, past the bakery and the toymaker's store and down past Flowers By Fran and the bridal store that had some mannequin brides waiting for Mr. Right to rescue them. Those caught his eye, the way they stared out sightlessly behind the display glass, looking blandly perfect in gowns of winter white, one pink blonde, one tan brunette, one black. Their faces were serenely aloof. Not like Jolene. Even-tempered, maybe, but never serene.

Mal thought all three would make fine brides. He could see his reflection in the glass, and thought maybe he was Mr. Right. But not just yet. A messenger had to deliver his message, and that's what Mal had set out to do.

So, he blew the brides a threefold kiss and went down to the River.

5.

Zitface and Pigeyes weren't around. Mal knew this cuz he had gone looking. Instead, there was a fat kid sitting on a hunk of concrete, not a kid, so much, but younger than Mal.

He was white, but had an afro of curly brown hair and a hunky nose and a weak chin. His T-shirt asked "Are We Having Fun Yet?" and was white, the letters in green. He'd been sniffing glue from a paper bag when he saw Mal standing there.

It was weird, the kid looking at him from around the bag, skin around his eyes purple-brown, half-lidded gaze. The kid took a long huff of the glue, then pulled the bag from his mouth. He was drooling.

"You a cop?" he asked.

"Not me," Mal said. "I'm an angel's messenger."

"Whoa," the Kid said. "That is fucked up. Am I dead?"

"Not yet," Mal said. "Do you believe in God?"

The Kid took another huff of the glue. Model airplane cement. Do not inhale. The orange tube of it was on a stone beside him.

"Does i'look lidoo?" The Kid laughed at this, cackling awhile. Mal took a seat across from him. "M'sniffin'glue, f'chrissake. You'a homo?"

"Not me," Mal said. "I'm a messenger."

The Kid took the tube and squeezed some more glue into the bag. Held it out for Mal, who waved him off.

"You said tha'already," the Kid said. "You come t'save me?"

"Yes," Mal said. "In fact, that's exactly why I'm here."

The Kid laughed, crinkling the bag and dropping it at his feet. He held his hands in the air, pointing to the bridge, far overhead. "I've seen the Light!"

Mal chuckled while the Kid laughed, though Mal was only faking laughter. He had already forgotten how it felt to laugh, though he remembered what it looked and sounded like. The Kid didn't seem to know the difference.

"What's your name, son?"

"Eugene," the Kid said. "How about you?"

"Mal," Mal said. "Do you really want to see the Light in the Dark, Eugene?"

Eugene stopped laughing, wiping spit from his lips. He reached down for the bag, but Mal kicked it out of reach.

"Hey, Fuckweed," Eugene said. "Tha's my bag."

"You won't need that, anymore. I'm going to save you."

"Huh?"

D. T. NEAL

Mal picked up the bag, and the tube of glue, and walked down to the River. Eugene was pissed off, yelling "Hey" and stumbling after him.

"Gimmeback my glue, Fucky," Eugene said, yelping as he turned an ankle on the rocks. Mal shook his head, grabbing Eugene, and dunking him into the water. First once, then twice, then a third time. Eugene flailed at Mal, but he wasn't nearly as strong as Mal was.

Mal marveled at how easy it was, holding Eugene under the water, letting him breathe the River. He held the kid underwater for twenty minutes, long after he'd stopped moving, grateful that nobody else had come along while he was doing it.

Then he realized he didn't know what to do next. He'd never converted anyone before. Did he leave him in the River, or was it the drowning itself that mattered? He didn't quite know for sure, so he decided to be scientific. If it happened once, it was an accident. If it was twice, it was something else. He remembered that from somewhere. Two men came back from the dead: Jesus, and Lazarus.

Miracles didn't happen twice; or did they?

Nobody knew what happened to Lazarus. He just got up and went his way. Mal could relate to Lazarus—he was in the right place at the right time, just like Mal was.

He stuck Eugene in an old shopping cart, weighing him down with slime-slicked river stones. Mal thought a lot about what he'd done, and what it meant. He didn't know if Eugene would come back or not. If he didn't come back, then maybe it meant he'd done it wrong. If that was the case, he'd try again and again until he got it right.

If Eugene did come back, then something really special was happening, and Mal would do what he could to spread the good news. He'd do more than that. A lot more.

He thought about this while he plunked stones atop Eugene's body, annoyed at how fat Eugene had been—he'd thought druggies were supposed to be skinny, but this kid had been fat. He'd not buried him deep in the river, but it took a lot of stones to cover him up.

He'd hoped it was enough, and that nobody would come along and spoil things. But he figured the river water was murky enough that nobody would see. Mal climbed out of the water and waited by the shore, dripping wet yet again.

He'd have to start a church.

Someplace close to the River, where he could conduct proper baptisms, without the police or bystanders getting nosy. It didn't have to be a big church; not at first. He'd call it the First Church of Lazarus. He'd call himself Mal Lazarus. He liked the sound of that.

Mal Warner was dead.

Mal Lazarus was undead.

It would take a lot of effort to set something like that up, however, so he'd have to get money, first.

Maybe he could go to the casino and get money from there. There had to be a way of making easy money. He chuckled dryly while he wrung out his shirt. It was funny—how did a dead man earn a living? He wondered if he needed to sleep. He hadn't slept, yet, hadn't felt tired. He'd sure save money on his food and heating bill. That was a plus. There were all sorts of things he could do. He supposed he could get a couple of jobs. That would do for starters, until he got more followers.

Followers made everything possible. It all depended on Eugene, on whether that fat kid would come out of the river in three days.

So, Mal waited.

And waited.

And waited.

And on the third day, Zitface and Pigeyes showed up, carrying a paper bag and some firecrackers. When they saw Mal sitting on a stone by the river, they ribbed each other and laughed.

"You fall in the river again, Dude?" Zitface asked.

"No, I walked in this time," Mal said. "Right in the deep end."

"You can't walk in the deep end, Dude," Pigeyes said. "You can only jump off."

"That's not true," Mal said. "I can walk right in."

"You're muddy as fuck, Dude," Zitface said.

"River's muddy, down under the stones," Mal said. "You boys want to see a miracle?"

They looked at him suspiciously, like he was crazy, but Mal wasn't crazy—Mal was dead. Zitface spoke up, while Pigeyes squinted disagreeably, crinkling the bag of fireworks. The water of the river lapped at the stones, little waves turning tiny cartwheels on the shore.

"We don't believe in nothing, Crazy River Man."

"Well, isn't *that* something?" Mal said with a smile, pointing over their shoulders, thinking the river was terribly big, and there was always room for a few more.

Lots more.

A helluvalot more.

A whole damned congregation.

Zitface managed a squawk, while Pigeyes just try to run, but Eugene had Zitface by the hem of his jacket, and Mal had caught Pigeyes in the stomach with a punch. Eugene watched Mal with black eyes, uncomprehending.

"Show them," Mal said. "Take them to the Angel."

Zitface screamed, but Eugene did as he was told, the fat kid with mud on his face and water pouring from his mouth, his brown curls caked with wet mud, his fat body pale, almost wormlike, but his strength undeniable. Zitface's scream was drowned out by the river flowing into his mouth.

Pigeyes went down without a sound, as Mal shoved the kid into the water, holding him down, while Pigeyes gazed up at him in horror, his face a blur of mud and watery ripples.

Into the river Mal and his first disciple went, taking their converts with them, deeper, where the shallows gave way to the deeper banks of the river. The kids thrashed, but Eugene and Mal weren't about to let go. Down, down they went, with the world none the wiser.

6.

The First Church of Lazarus opened for business at the riverside, as he'd planned, with Eugene, Zitface, and Pigeyes as his drowned deacons. Mal had made them put on black neckties and white shirts. They did it without question or complaint, their eyes as doll-dead as the rest of them. They had seen the Light in the Dark.

"I want you boys to bring a friend to the river," Mal said. "You bring them to me, bring them here."

"We don't have friends," Zitface said. "Nobody down here has friends."

His voice was flat, his face without expression. Mal looked at each of them in turn, realized they were, surely, hopeless.

Without hope. Without fear.

"Well," Mal said. "Find me somebody. Vagrants. Somebody. Bring me somebody, and I'll introduce them to the river. The three of you go find me someone."

And they went away, his three little missionaries, with their little mission, while Mal sat on the rocks, watching the water lap against the shore, waiting without breath, without boredom, without blinking. Just waiting. The sun had come up, rising over the nearby mountains, warming the rocks, even warming Mal, although he didn't feel the warmth touch him inside. Nothing touched him.

How did one start a church?

A real church?

There had to be a message.

He was obviously the Messenger, the prophet.

He thought back to Sunday school, the sermons, the passing of the plates. It was best to talk people into handing over their money, to willingly give it over.

He'd gotten the boys to give them whatever they had, and that was something, but between the three of them, it wasn't enough. He needed far more money.

He couldn't just go rob a bank; that wouldn't work one bit. No, a sermon was the best way to pick a pocket. It was like the car dealers, jittery, always talking too loud, the greasy guys with the hungry eyes selling cars to his mom and dad.

A sermon was like that, but sweeter.

Or maybe something with more fire. Brimstone, wasn't it? Sulfur?

Sulfur smog once filled Ludlow's skies. Sulfur he could understand. Mal remembered coughing on it, the horrible stink of it in the mornings. The way it burned his eyes, the back of his throat, the roof of his mouth.

Sulfur.

Brimstone.

Fire and brimstone.

Mal dipped his hands into the river, letting the water run through his cold hands. The water had no discernible temperature to him, he could not tell himself from it. There was unity there, communion. The sermon hardly mattered, with what he was offering.

Eternal life!

Freedom from fear!

Freedom from death!

Then he thought maybe he should watch how the professionals do it. That would help. Mal wasn't a natural speaker, but he wasn't afraid of doing it. There wasn't any need to fear anything again. He'd seen the bottom of the river, had drunk it down. He's seen the Angel. He wasn't afraid of a living thing. What did it matter to stand on a corner and speak his mind? What did it matter when contrasted with his divine mission? His church?

For that matter, what did money matter to him? Only as a means to an end. A church would let him gather a flock faster. That's what mattered. A proper church needed a cross.

Mal looked around, saw a rusty fencepost protruding from one side of The Perch. Long ago, there had been some kind of fence to keep bums away from the riverside, but it had long since gone to rust. The fencepost was a tall spar, taller than he was, with a slight crossbeam on it where it had once connected to another part of the old fence. There was barbed wire on it.

He thought it looked perfect, although his unbeating heart was unmoved by it. Mal walked to the thing and gripped the metal bar in his pale hands, tugged on it. He tugged on it and the thing would not move, wouldn't get free of the concrete it had sunk into. Mal tugged at the post and snapped it clear of the concrete, the old metal yielding with a clang. There was good metal in it still, beneath the rust.

The post was angular at the break, clean and shiny inside, where the elements had not touched it. It looked like the point of a hypodermic needle. Mal yanked the thing clear of the fencing, snapping the old barbed wire, which hung free from it like tendrils of hair. He walked the thing to his resting spot, where he'd been standing, and sank the thing into the ground, stabbed the earth with it, sinking it a foot deep in the soft soil. Then he grabbed handfuls of river stones and piled them at the base, to shore it up. Mal then twined the dangling barbed wire around the top of the fencepost, and stood back, looking it over.

The post was at a slight angle, forming a sloppy T-shape dressed with the bundle of barbed wire near the top. It looked crossy enough to Mal. He liked the cryptic message of it. Mystery was vital. There was power and mystery in this crooked cross. It was symbolic of Mal's salvation, taken in this place, from this sacred place. He watched the Sun cast the shadow of the cross, like it was a sundial, winding ribbonlike across the river stones. Perfect.

He was emancipated. The river had set him free. He didn't know why IT had chosen him as ITS messenger, but he was not one to argue. The message had been received, and Mal would do his best to convey it.

There was nothing else to do but wait for the Boys to return, and so Mal waited.

7.

Officer Don Ramsey wasn't sure what he was looking at: three kids accosting a bum. He'd read about those bum burnings in LA, but in Ludlow, there weren't so many vagrants, and kids weren't inclined to set them on fire. Almost instinctively, he found his eyes searching for the can of gasoline.

He chanced upon them near Third and Drexler Avenue, near the railroad tracks. Sometimes bums came through town on the trains, and there were always drug users and vagrants quite literally across the tracks, near the river.

Pulling up, it looked like the kids had latched onto the shaggy bum, the poor bastard greasy-bearded, stocking-capped, wearing about ten layers of filthy clothes. Two of the boys had the bum by the arms, while the fat boy was gesturing.

Ramsey toggled his siren to get their attention. The siren always sounded so loud, rebounding across the river valley. He took delight in that sound. It was like his cruiser was his dog, the siren its bark. Sometimes the siren alone did his job for him, got suspects to flinch or panic. He liked when they did that. However, the boys didn't do that. The bum jumped, but the boys just turned and looked at him, eyes dead pools gazing impassively at him. They looked pale, those three.

He called in to Dispatch, let them know what he was doing, where he was. Even though Ludlow wasn't exactly a high-crime community, shit still did happen, and he always erred on the side of caution.

Getting out, he put on his hat and nightstick and walked over to the boys, who had let go of the bum. The homeless man didn't look familiar to Ramsey.

"What is going on here, boys?" Ramsey asked.

"We were going to give this guy a bath," the fat one said. "Look how dirty he is."

The bum cursed out the boys. "They said they's gonna drown me in the river!"

The fat boy he didn't recognize, but the other two he knew: Brian Auckerman, and Drew Smith. Auckerman had a face shiny with grease, zits all across it, and Drew Smith was his equally greasy accomplice. Those boys were always getting into trouble in town. Usually petty vandalism and the like, but it hardly mattered how many times they had to scrub down some walls they'd spray-painted with swastikas; they'd be back at it a month or so later.

"Brian, Drew," Ramsey said. "I don't think the guy wants a bath."

"They was gonna drown me," the bum said, swaying on his feet. Ramsey thought the bum needed to dry out, certainly didn't need a dip in the river.

"What's your name, son?" Ramsey asked of the fat boy, who was watching him without expression.

"Eugene," the kid said. He didn't seem the type to really hang with Brian and Drew. If anything, he seemed like the type who'd be on the receiving end of whatever those two were dishing out.

"He gave me some glue," the bum said, brandishing a tube of model airplane glue. "Said I could have it. Then they grabbed me."

"We just did what Mal told us," Brian said. "Mal told us to bring him to the river."

"Who is Mal?" Ramsey asked.

"Mal Lazarus," Eugene said.

Ramsey took a mental note of that name. He'd never heard of any Mal Lazarus. Maybe a gangster? It was possible, although he doubted a gangster would waste time with these boys, and for sure not to brace a bum.

He took out his walkie talkie and inquired about "Mal Lazarus," to see if there was anything on such a character. It was surely an alias, but you never knew.

"He showed me the light," Eugene said. "The Light in the Dark."

"The Light in the Dark," Brian and Drew said, together, their voices devoid of emotion.

There was nothing on any Mal Lazarus. Ramsey told them he was going to look into it, said he had three kids trying to kidnap a vagrant. There wasn't much else he could say about it at the moment.

"Alright, boys," Ramsey said. "You're going to take me to this Mal Lazarus."

"Alright," Eugene said.

Ramsey went to his cruiser and opened the back door, gestured. The bum was walking away, gesturing at a passing tree, shaking his fist at it. The boys filed silently into the back of the car, and Ramsey shut the door. He was grateful his cruiser had the cage separating the back from the front, because the boys were just not right. Their shirts and ties made them look like Mormons, but their expressions were something else entirely. Not a lick of fear in their eyes, not even sullenness; just emptiness.

They should have been terrified, but they weren't. They weren't anything. Not a trace of emotion on their faces—not worry, or fear, or anger, or frustration. Just nothing. Like they were made of stone. Or on drugs.

Ramsey glanced back at the bum, who'd already rounded a corner past a concrete pylon, vanished from view.

He started up his car. "Which way?" he asked of Eugene.

"At the boat slip near the River Bridge," Eugene said. "That's where Mal is."

"Fine," Ramsey said, turning toward it. Maybe five minutes away.

"How many times do we have to do this, Auckerman?" Ramsey asked. "Your dad's going to be pissed off when he hears about this."

Brian didn't say anything. The boys didn't move in the back seat. Didn't squirm, didn't fidget, didn't even look out the windows. They were just sitting there, silent.

Ramsey wondered if they were on drugs or something. If so, it was far stronger than model airplane glue.

"Did you boys take anything? Did this Lazarus give you drugs?"

Silence. From his rearview mirror, it was hard to even tell if they were breathing. There was something about them that made him nervous, made him sweat.

"No," Eugene said, his voice like a tombstone, cold and hard. "He didn't give us anything. He's just the Messenger."

"Oh yeah?" Ramsey asked. "Who is he a messenger for?"

"The river," Eugene said. "The Light in the Dark."

It was late afternoon, and shadows were lengthening. Ludlow had slight mountains flanking it, so the light started to go sooner than later, as the sun would pass beyond the mountains, bathing the valley in darkness. It wasn't dark, yet, although Ramsey felt creeped out in his own squad car, felt like there was darkness in the car with him, those three kids staring silently at him.

The boat slip was one of many in Ludlow, which didn't have any proper harbor or piers, but had several concrete ramps where locals could launch their little boats. Past the tracks. He drove under the viaduct where the trains passed with their trucks full of coal and other things, parked his cruiser before it reached the fist-sized river gravel that comprised the shore. From here, there was only shadows, as the sun was blocked by the viaduct and the ribbon of gnarled trees that paralleled the railroad tracks and the river both.

There was a man sitting on a rock by the river, in a white shirt and black slacks, black tie, a black blazer draped across his knee. He looked kind of like a young Trent Reznor to Ramsey, pale skin, black hair. He looked like a creep. He looked up at Ramsey's cruiser without emotion, the same slack face the boys had.

"Is that him?" Ramsey asked.

"That's him," Eugene said.

Ramsey got out of the cruiser, took stock of the man. The man just sat there, watching him with the deadest eyes Ramsey had ever seen on a man. One time he'd seen a drugged-out nutball on PCP with eyes like that, just flat, like a shark's eyes. This Lazarus guy's eyes were like that.

"Mr. Lazarus?" Ramsey asked.

"Yes?" Lazarus said.

"Mr. Mal Lazarus?" Ramsey asked.

"Yes?" he said. Not a trace of anything. Just words, cold and empty, without a hint of heart behind them. This was a man capable of anything.

"These boys say you told them to kidnap somebody," Ramsey said.

"I told them to bring people to the river," Lazarus said.

"Why?" Ramsey asked, glancing at the fencepost sitting in the sand, hanging at an angle, bundled with barbed wire, stones piled at its base. What the fuck?

Lazarus seemed to look right through him.

21

"Why did you want them to bring people to the river?" Ramsey asked.

"To wash them clean," Lazarus said. "Ludlow is a filthy place. The river is clean."

That was a laugh; the river was polluted. There was way too much industry upriver for this place to ever truly be clean. Maybe once, when the Indians lived here. But not for the last few centuries. Ramsey wondered what it looked like back before the valley had been tamed, before Big Steel had come to this place, but the river was that murky green-black hue that seemed to plague most of the rivers he saw in the Rust Belt. Dirty river, dark and full of secrets.

"Funny," Ramsey said.

"I can show you," Lazarus said.

"No, thanks," Ramsey said. He was Roman Catholic, didn't take to those loony street preachers with their weird rituals. Dancing with snakes, speaking in tongues. Weird shit.

"Too bad," Lazarus said. "Your loss."

"You incited these kids to attempt an abduction," Ramsey said. "I'm going to need you to stand up. You're under arrest."

No reaction. Lazarus just stood up.

"So, arrest me," Lazarus said. He was tall, but skinny. Don Ramsey was a human cinderblock, a full head taller than Lazarus, a great big man. He glanced back at the boys in the cruiser. They were sitting like three bowling pins, pale and pointless.

"Is this some kind of church?" Ramsey asked.

"I am the church," Mal said. "I am the Messenger."

"I'm going to have to ask you to put your hands on top of your head. Go ahead and knit your fingers together."

"No," Mal said. "I'm afraid that's not going to happen, Officer Ramsey."

The coldness of his refusal clearly took the policeman off-guard. He was a man used to getting his way, both professionally and personally. Although his eyes looked dead to Ramsey, he'd seen the officer's name tag clearly enough.

Ramsey's hand went to his belt, the mace. "Mr. Lazarus, you're under arrest. So I'm going to ask you again to put your hands on top of your head."

Lazarus didn't comply.

Out came the mace, a squat black cylinder with a red cap, the little nozzle pointed at Lazarus.

"Last warning, Mr. Lazarus."

"Do what you have to do, Officer," Lazarus said, without blinking.

And Officer Don Ramsey did, spraying the mace into the man's eyes. He unloaded the thing, aiming it right at him, right in his face.

Tears of mace ran down the man's face, but he was unaffected by the stuff. Ramsey couldn't believe his own watering eyes, fired some more of it at the man, who took it without comment, without visible effect. No pain, no inflammation, not even a grimace. Just those eyes boring into him.

Lazarus just smiled at the officer. Never, in 15 years on the force, had Ramsey ever seen somebody take something like that without so much as a flinch.

"I think you need something stronger, Officer," Lazarus said, wiping his face with the back of his hand. The policeman drew his service pistol, an automatic. A Glock. He flipped off the safety.

"Get down," Ramsey said. "What are you on, angel dust?"

He brought his other hand up, talked into his walkie talkie, called for assistance. "Code Eight. I'm at the boat slip at the river bridge, at Sixth and Beech."

"Angel dust?" Mal asked. "You might say that. The Light in the Dark. I'll show you, if you like."

"Get down!" Ramsey yelled at Lazarus. His call would bring anybody in radio range running. Ramsey didn't want to think that this skinny freak was somehow beyond him, but anybody able to take a face-full of pepper spray without flinching was trouble.

Lazarus shook his head, kept walking toward Ramsey. Ramsey fired a shot at the man's leg, his left thigh, the pistol punching a hole in his flesh. He didn't even flinch. There was just the physical jolt of the shot passing through him. At this range, the jacketed rounds would simply perforate him. He'd had his warning shot. The next one would be to kill.

Ramsey gave him one more chance. "Get down!"

Lazarus held his arms out to Ramsey, and Ramsey fired a shot into his chest, where his heart ought to be. The bullet went right through him. At point-blank range, it was all it could do. He actually saw the bullet hit the river water behind Lazarus.

"The Light in the Dark," one of the boys said.

Lazarus grabbed at the handgun, and, to Ramsey's amazement, the man was strong. He strained against him, tried to use his weight and size to his advantage. The others would be here soon.

While Ramsey was huffing and puffing, Lazarus didn't even look like he was breathing. The bullet had been a heart shot. Ramsey could see the point of entry. He'd hit the man's heart. But there wasn't a drop of blood; there was nothing.

Lazarus pivoted hard, prying the handgun out of Ramsey's hand. Ramsey couldn't believe how strong the man was, for his size. Not even PCP could account for the absence of bleeding. He wasn't wearing body armor.

Ramsey spun on his heel and ran for his cruiser. There was a shotgun in there. Let's see the fucker take that. But Lazarus caught his feet as he'd turned, and Ramsey fell forward, striking the ground hard on his face, before he'd even gotten his hands up to break his fall.

He saw stars, was reeling. Felt Lazarus dragging him to the river's edge, toward the water, the cold of the water soaking his legs, then his chest, then his face. Then down they went into the water, Ramsey clawing at the slick river stones with his hands, trying to kick his way free of Lazarus. The man's grip was like a ratchet cranked tight, inexorably drawing Ramsey into the river, blood pounding in his ears, the waning light of the day going to watery hues, Ramsey trying to pull himself up, his arms finding no purchase.

Deeper they went, Ramsey panicking as he felt his lungs burning.

I'm going to drown.

This crazy fuck is going to drown me.

He kicked hard in the dark, where Lazarus ought to be, hating the man, not believing this could be happening to him, wondering what his wife would think, wondering what kind of funeral they'd give him.

Down and down into the river's muddy depths they went, Lazarus crawling along Ramsey's body like a crab, holding fast, standing on his back. The red pinwheels in his gaze had gone to black blobs, and Ramsey was forced to exhale, his lungs working like a bellows, drawing in the water, killing him. Drowning him. The ultimate bodily betrayal, his lungs feeding him muddy, filthy water, his brain flailing in its bony cage, his body twitching, and in the dark, the pale of Lazarus's smiling face. No smile in the eyes, but there was light in them.

The Light in the Dark.

8.

Three days. It always took three days. Mal would watch the police officer emerge from the water after three days. It had been a near thing, drowning the man, getting to the cruiser and driving off with it, leaving the Ludlow Police Department wondering what had happened to one of their own. The other officers had gotten there, but there'd been nothing to see.

Mal and the boys had abandoned the cruiser several blocks away, as the sound of sirens filled the air. They looked for their lost piggy, they huffed and they puffed, but they didn't find him.

They found his cruiser, but they didn't find him. Witnesses said they'd heard some shots fired, but weren't sure where, because the valley bounced sounds around.

Mal had put the boys to work, told them to work at night, taking homeless to the river. Under cover of night, not in broad daylight, he explained. Take them to the river and drown them in it, he told them. Hold them down and let them breathe the river's water. It was so simple.

He'd wanted to conduct all of the baptisms himself, but realized that there was a lot to do, and it paid to delegate. He was still the Messenger. Let them take the poor and the indigent and feed them to the river.

Meanwhile, Mal waited for Ramsey to emerge. Three days, he waited. He saw on the news how authorities were on the lookout for a "Mal Lazarus" who was believed to be implicated in the disappearance of Officer Don Ramsey.

He should have been bothered to see his name floated out in the local media, but he felt nothing at all. It didn't matter. A name was nothing. He was more than a name. Just the same, he thought it would mean the First Church of Lazarus was stillborn. He'd come up with a new name for it.

The New Life Church? Maybe "church" was putting too fine a point on it. The New Life Prayer Center? Something like that? It was hard to know what was inspirational, anymore. Inspiration seemed so passé to Mal. Then inspiration came to him.

The Light in the Dark. That was it.

While he thought about that, he stitched himself back together. The policeman's bullets had punctured his flesh. No blood, no pain, but there had been damage to his flesh. He was glad the officer hadn't shot him in the face. That would've been complicated.

The wound wouldn't heal. The river brought him back from death, but couldn't heal him. He took a needle and black thread and sewed up the wounds on his chest and leg, tugging on the stitching, watching without emotion as he punctured his flesh and pulled the thread through. It wasn't going to be perfect, Mal didn't know if it was even right, what he was doing. There wasn't even a need for it, he thought, but something in him compelled him to go through the motions. Perhaps it was a vestige of his former self, this sense of biological propriety that moved him to sew himself up. He neither knew nor cared. When he was done, he looked at the skin, pulled tight against itself, forced together in ugly black stitching. There was nothing to be done about the exit wound. He didn't want to rely on Eugene or Zitface or Pigeyes to take care of it. They were better-used going after the bums. Like water, each of them flowed to their own level.

Some were destined for greater things. Others were destined to drown vagrants in the river at the command of their master. Such was the way of the world.

Others, like Officer Don Ramsey, had far greater uses. Mal waited by the shore, wearing a new black suit, a new black tie, a new black shirt. He waited for Ramsey to emerge, reborn.

Sure enough, Officer Ramsey walked out of the water, covered in mud, his face half-obscured, water pouring off of him, out of him. The miracle once again, like all of the other times.

Beautiful, in its way.

Resurrection was always beautiful.

Water ran from the man's ears, out of his mouth, down the front of his shirt. He looked at Mal without emotion, though with understanding. He had seen the Light in the Dark, he had understood.

"Go home," Mal said. "Get cleaned up. Spread the word. Bring your friends. Show them. One by one, show them."

The big policeman looked down at Mal. "They'll wonder where I've been."

"Tell them you were lost," Mal said. "Lost in the wilderness, chasing Mal Lazarus, but that you found your way out again."

"They'll ask about you," Ramsey said.

"Spread the word," Mal said. "Let them come."

He thought that made him sound like a prophet. He'd taken the Bible and skimmed through it, looking for words.

Isaiah 41:22: "Let them bring them forth, and show us what shall happen: let them show the former things, what they be, that we may consider them, and know the latter end of them; or declare us things for to come."

He thought perhaps he was the "thing" referred to. Prophets spoke like that. Although he wasn't interested in being a prophet per se; he was merely interested in delivering people to the river, if "interested" even applied. There was a message to deliver in the rippling waters, a message clear to all who had partaken of it.

Mal thought this as he and Ramsey stood at the shore, watching a barge float by, weighed down with iron ore, most likely.

Ramsey walked off without comment, his wet shoes squeaking as he made his way, leaving big footprints on the river stones.

With numbers, all things were possible.

That was the gospel according to Lazarus.

Numbers made everything.

9.

Donna Ramsey couldn't understand what was wrong with her man. Don had gotten so cold. It was like he was another man. He had taken back-to-back duty shifts, was almost never home. She'd cook dinner and he'd not eat a bite of it.

She'd tried to talk to him, asked him what he was doing.

"Working," he'd always say, his face like it was cut from a quarry.

Don Jr. (aka, Donnie) and Dane, their boys, had noticed, too, said they were afraid of how serious Dad had gotten. They were big boys, likely to grow up to be as big as their old man one day, Donna thought.

She'd taken pride in his size when they'd dated in high school. She herself was only five feet five inches tall, so six-foot-six Don was a real treasure and pleasure to her. She enjoyed the mountainous expanse of his strong back, his oxlike determination to do the right thing, his tremendous appetite for her all-American style cooking. Donna wasn't an innovative chef like Michelle Norris, always showing off her latest creations at parties, but Donna thought she covered American classics pretty well, added heartiness to the menu in lieu of fanciness.

So when Don passed on her short ribs, historically one of his favorite dishes, Donna stopped him in the hallway.

"Baby, what's wrong?" she asked. "Why won't you eat?"

"I'm not hungry," he said. "I've got work to do."

"Don," Donna said. "I haven't seen you eat in days. Days, honey. What is wrong with you?"

Her husband looked down at her, as if seeing her anew for the first time.

"Nothing's wrong with me," he said. "Everything's fine. Do you want me to show you?"

"Show me what?" she asked.

"The river," he said.

"What about the river?" Donna asked.

"There's something in it," Don said. "Something wonderful. The Light in the Dark."

"What is it?" she asked.

"You have to see it, before you can believe it," Don said. "I can take you and the boys. We can all go see it, Donna. We can take a family field trip."

Donna felt afraid of Don for the first time in her life. He was a legend of the police force, Big Don. But at home, he was gentle as could be. Even when they argued, she'd never felt any danger from him.

But today, in their hallway, Donna felt something, saw something dangerous in his slack face, in the look in his eyes.

"You'll see," Don said. "It's special. Get the boys."

Donna had no intention of taking the boys down to the river, had no idea what Don had in mind. She remembered some of those news stories where family members went crazy, killed all of their family and then themselves.

She never thought Don would ever hurt them. Even as a police offer, with so much stress in his job, Don had never, ever taken it out on them. He took "to serve and protect" close to heart.

Donna went to their deck out back, looked for the boys. She had this bizarre intuition that something terrible would happen to them if she went to the river with Don. What in the hell was he even talking about?

She thought she saw a flicker of Dane's orange jacket in the woods.

"I'm going to have to round them up, Don," she said. "Why don't I meet you down there in awhile?"

"Fine," Don said. "Drop by any time, Donna. And if you don't see me there, maybe go to the station. They'll know where to find me."

He went to leave, but Donna stopped him. "Don't I get a kiss goodbye?"

Don had lately been lax about that, about any kind of physical contact with her. In fact, Donna wasn't even sure if Don was sleeping in their bed at night. Since she worked in town, and Don worked most nights, she thought he was sleeping during the day, but when she'd get home, the bed looked untouched.

"I've got to go to work," Don said, walking out the door, shutting it behind him. Donna watched him get into his cruiser and drive away.

Donnie came in. "Did Frankenstein leave?"

"Don't call your father that," Donna said. "He really loves you very much."

The boy looked like his namesake, just smaller. The same lantern jaw, the big stride. Same hair. Donna felt great love for him, hugged him tight. He squirmed out of reach.

"No, he doesn't," Donnie said. "He just sits there sometimes, stares at the television. Like he's not even here. I think he's going mental."

"What makes you think that?" Donna asked.

"Mom, he's out to lunch," Donnie said. "Dane and I hide from him. He's just off. Ever since that day he came home all soaking wet, he's not been right. Ever since he got lost in the woods."

Yes, that was odd. She hadn't really connected it, but it was true that ever since he went missing those three long days, he'd left something of himself behind. It was like Don was walking around, but what made him Don was gone, or just a faded memory, like the contrast between a photograph and the thing that had been photographed. What was left of Don was just a reflection of him.

She'd tried to get him to talk about it, but he only spoke of this "Light in the Dark" that had led him out of the wilderness. She had urged him to take some sick days, maybe get looked at, but he'd refused, said there was no point to it.

It had left her confused. But seeing him this morning, that odd look in his eye, that had left her afraid. Afraid for her and the boys.

"Your father keeps going on about the river," Donna said. "Do you and Dane see anything?"

"Nobody goes down there, Ma," Donnie said, sneering. "It's not safe. You and Dad always warned us about going down there."

"Well, good," Donna said. "I want you to stay away from it. If anybody, even your father, wants to take you down there, don't you go. Do you understand me?"

Donnie's sarcastic sneer faded before his mother's concern. "Sure, Ma."

"Good," she said. "Just stay away from there, no matter what."

"You worry too much, Mom," Dane said.

10.

Somebody was cleaning up Ludlow.

Jolene Clevenger noticed when she went downtown to deposit her check from Big Star. Smith Street and Wallace Street had this old park and gazebo nearby, and some of the bums would congregate there, on the benches, within sight of the war memorial (which war, she never knew, never bothered to look). They were always there, more reliable than the Post Office. Usually a half dozen permanent residents.

She only thought about it because she'd have to park downtown to get to First Regional to deposit her check, and the shortest way to the bank was cutting across Wallace Park, which meant passing the bums, who'd usually just stare at her, reeking of human stink, alcohol, and cigarettes. She didn't know what they were doing in Ludlow, but they were always there. Sometimes, around Christmas, they'd even put on Santa hats and make festive, egg nog on their beards. Jolly Old Elves.

But they weren't there today.

Not a trace of them.

Cool.

Just the pruned shrubberies of the war memorial, the flapping of the flag, not a bum to be seen. She smelled the air, was pleased to just smell autumn-cinnamon smell of fallen leaves and a hint of pine from somewhere.

Maybe Ludlow had passed some law or something? She didn't know, didn't follow it. Her only concerns were the gambling laws, hoping that everything stayed legal with the Big Star. If they ever shut that down, she'd be fucked.

She cut across Wallace Park, the way she always did, when she saw Mal Warner sitting on the last bench before the intersection at Smith Street.

He was wearing all black, looked at her without expression. His face was terribly pale. She'd heard that he'd quit at Big Star, out of the blue. It hadn't meant a whole lot to her, but she'd been curious, wondered if he'd had a falling out with Bernie or something.

"Hey, Mal," she said.

"Hey, Jolene," he said. "Going to the bank?"

"Yeah," she said. "You know how it is."

"Not anymore," Mal said.

He just sat there, like he'd been sitting there all day. Maybe he had. She didn't know. Being the way she was, she just came out and asked him.

"So, are you working?"

"Nope," Mal said. "I'm done with that. I've found religion."

She laughed. "Yeah?"

Mal nodded. He didn't look serene, or even smug. He didn't look like anything. Mal just was there, like he'd been there since the dawn of time.

"Yeah," he said. "I remembered you bitching about the bums in the park."

"Yeah?" she said, clutching one arm with the other. It was chilly. Winter would be here before you knew it.

"Yeah," he said. "I remembered. So, I did something about it."

"Oh, yeah?" she asked.

"Yeah," Mal said. "They won't be back. Not here, anyway."

The way he said it made her shiver. His voice was so cold, so dead. It was like the words were just bubbling up from inside him, without anything attached to them. Certainly nothing she could relate to.

She'd never been particularly close to Mal. He was a weird guy, just sort of did his thing, but never quite like this.

"I hope you didn't hurt them," she said. "You didn't hurt them, right, Mal?"

"I helped them," Mal said. "I showed them the Light in the Dark."

Jolene didn't know what the hell that meant. "Is that like finding the good in the bad? Like finding the silver lining on a dark cloud?"

"Yes," Mal said. "It's just like that. Isn't that what an optimist is? Somebody who finds the good in the bad? I'm now an eternal optimist, Jolene."

"That's great, Mal," Jolene said, feeling a little uncomfortable. She felt like maybe Mal had become a born-again Christian or something, wanted to testify or whatever they did. She remembered working with a few at Jiffyburger when she was a teenager, how they'd have these big grins on their faces and be all blessed and stuff, and Jolene was thinking "We're making Jiffyburgers, for Christ's sake! Where's the blessing in that?"

"I could show you, too," he said.

"That's okay, Mal," she said, looking at her watch. "I've got to deposit my check before the bank closes."

"Alright, Jolene," Mal said. "I'll see you later."

"Sure thing," she said, giving him a half-hearted wave as she crossed Smith Street and went into First Regional.

Weird fucking guy.

She endorsed her check and got a deposit slip, looked out the big bank windows, saw Mal still sitting on that park bench, looking at her. She wasn't positive he was staring at her, but somehow she thought maybe he was, because she could see the bit of white of his face, and the black hair, him leaning on the bench. Yeah, he was staring at her.

Okay, fucking weird.

She got in line for the teller, reminded herself again to get direct deposit. She kept forgetting to do it, so she was always waiting in line on paydays, having to cash her check. Somehow, it felt more real to her to have to deposit the check. It felt good to have some cash in hand.

Working at the casino, she was surrounded by cash she couldn't have, watched fat, foolish people come in and blow endless wads at the Big Star. It was like being a cook in a kitchen, but unable to take more than a few nibbles when she could. Even if she just had $20 in cash from her check, it was her $20, and it made her happy to have it there, instead of always charging everything, the way everybody else did.

While the teller processed her deposit, she glanced back out to Wallace Park, saw that Mal was gone, felt some measure of relief she couldn't quite put her finger on. Mal hadn't looked right to her. It was him, but it wasn't him, too. He'd always been kind of shyly weird, but now he was just weird. Not seeing him made her wonder where he'd gone.

"Here you go, Miss Clevenger," the teller said. "Twenty dollars. How would you like it?"

"Two tens," Jolene said, and the woman counted them out crisply. "Actually, could I have one of the tens as a roll of quarters? Laundry, you know."

"Sure," the teller said, giving her a roll of quarters shrunk-wrapped in a plastic tube. Jolene took the quarter roll and put it in her purse. She got out of line and left the bank, standing curbside, breathing the air again. It smelled nice. Christmas would be coming soon. They would string up lights and put a Christmas tree in Wallace Park, and it would look nice. Seemed like Halloween was hardly over when stores would already be putting up Christmas decorations. She remembered hearing about people declaring war on Christmas, but thought that was stupid.

Who could hate Christmas? The Grinch?

A police cruiser went by, with two cops in it, and two people in the back. Jolene looked at it for a moment, one of the people in the back banging on the window, mouthing "HELP" to Jolene, who looked at the man for a moment.

It was a young man, brown curly hair, big nose. He was wearing a flannel shirt. The squad car turned toward Wallace Street, headed downtown.

Jolene shrugged, crossed the street into the park. Maybe they were junkies or something. It wasn't her responsibility to worry about it. She'd cashed her check, was momentarily squared with the world, at least until the bills came in.

She went to her car, a red 2002 Camaro SS, got in, drove out of there.

Her phone rang, making her yelp. She flipped it open. It was Stan Reynolds.

Her boyfriend.

Balding. Fit.

Arms like a bear.

She liked the way he held her.

She liked his soft voice.

He never complained.

"Hey, Jol," Stan said. "When are you getting home?"

"Soon," she said. "God, you know who I saw? Mal Warner."

"What's he doing?" Stan asked.

"Nothing," Jolene said. "He was just sitting on a park bench, being creepy."

"What was he doing?" Stan asked.

"Just sitting there," Jolene said. "Like I said."

She looked in her rearview mirror, but Mal wasn't there. Downtown was receding. Downtown Ludlow was relentlessly quaint. Main Street, Smith, Wallace, First, and Church Streets comprised it. It was like a woman who'd been cute as a girl trying to pass that off in late middle age. Something about Ludlow's downtown charm felt forced, the oasis of green trees and parks and Main Street USA feel contrasted with the industrial blight just beyond it.

"What'd he want?" Stan asked.

"I don't know," she said. "I think he's sick. Just not well. Something's not right."

Stan was quiet on the line a moment, processing. He worked as one of the bartenders at the Big Star, was a good listener.

A car passed Jolene, a big brown sedan. It passed her and swerved around the bend. Once you got past downtown, the roads twisted and turned, having to accommodate the lazy mountains. There was that point where you had to decide how much dynamite you wanted to use to build your city. The elders of Ludlow mostly gave up after creating their downtown. It took a lot of dynamite to persuade the mountains to give up Ludlow.

"You want to go out for dinner tonight? Basil's, maybe?" It was a nice Italian place on Vista Road. The old rumors had it that it was a moonshining outfit during Prohibition, owned by Basil DiCicco, area mobster. Whether or not that was the case, Basil's had the best Italian food in Ludlow, or in the Valley at large.

"No," Jolene said. "We can stay in tonight."

"Alright," he said. "Maybe you can stop for KFC or something?"

"Hah," Jolene said. "From Basil's to KFC? I'm easy, but I'm not cheap. I'll get us something on the way home. Not KFC."

"Alright," Stan said. "Talk to you later, Bunny."

"Love you," Jolene said, hanging up. She liked when he called her "Bunny."

A police cruiser rounded the bend behind her, kept pace with her, headlights on. Self-conscious, Jolene turned on her own lights. It was getting darker. She glanced at the speed limit. It was 45 miles per hour, so she kept it steady right at that. She always did that when a cop was on her tail.

She remembered driving like 50 miles in Florida with a police car behind her the whole way, and a column of cars behind her. She wasn't willing to speed to get ahead of the policeman, and he wasn't willing to pass her, for whatever reason (probably because she had out-of-state plates), and nobody behind the cop was willing to pass him, so it was like they were having this parade across Florida. It made her really nervous, and she was greatly relieved when the policeman turned and went another way.

However, this car stayed with her.

She stayed in her lane, despite the winding roads, and the police car stayed with her, not quite tailgating, but not giving her space, either. She wondered if both her taillights were good. She hoped so.

Jolene looked in her rearview mirror, could see one police officer in the cruiser, this shadowy shape, and it looked like one person in the back seat, although she couldn't be sure. She had to focus on the road.

She dialed up Stan again on her phone, but when she did, the police cruiser's siren went off, its lights flashed.

"Oh, Stan," Jolene said. "I'm being pulled over."

"For what?" Stan asked.

Jolene went to the shoulder where she could, where there wasn't a blind turn. "Probably for talking on my cell phone while driving, Goofy. God, I don't know."

"Were you speeding?"

"No," she said.

The policeman got out, walked alongside the car, had a flashlight in hand. A big cop. It was Don Ramsey, she realized, to her relief. He was the cop who'd gone missing the other week, everybody had been worried about. But he'd come back and said he'd gotten lost in the woods chasing a suspect, had been out there three days. People had been relieved when he'd come back, none the worse for wear. Pale, maybe, but otherwise fine.

"Officer Ramsey," she said, smiling up at the big cop.

"Miss Jolene Clevenger?" he asked. "Put down the phone, please."

Jolene put down the phone, set it down on her dash, moving slowly. She'd read enough about police mistaking cell phones for guns, shooting people down and such.

"Can you step out of the car?" Ramsey asked.

"Uh, sure," she said, unbuckling, opening the door, getting out. She could hear Stan on the cell phone, his voice tinny, tiny, a world away. What had she done? She hadn't done anything she could think of.

Jolene stood beside Officer Ramsey, acutely aware of how big the man was. She could've disappeared inside him. Her face went squarely into his chest.

"Do you want my license and registration?" she asked.

"That won't be necessary, Miss," Ramsey said. "I'm going to need you to turn around. Put your hands on the hood of your car, palms down."

Jolene was terribly frightened now. He was frisking her? Her bangle bracelets clattered against the hood of the car, as she was bent over it.

"What did I do, Officer?" she asked. "Please. I was just on my way home. I wasn't speeding, was I?"

She felt like she was going to cry. She couldn't even imagine what she'd done. Ramsey took one of her arms and put it behind her back. He was incredibly strong, his hands colder than ice. Then he took her other hand, brought it behind her back, until her palms were touching. Then he held her hands with one of his great paws, and got out some handcuffs, snapped them into place. Another pair of bracelets for her wrists.

"What did I do?" Jolene cried out. "Are you arresting me? What's the charge?"

"Come with me, Miss," Ramsey said, pulling her up.

"Stan!" Jolene cried, hoping he'd hear her. "I didn't do anything!"

Ramsey walked her to the squad car, Jolene trying to resist, but unable to free herself of his grip. The man might as well have been a mountain. He opened the back door and cupped the top of her head with his hand, helping her into the back, while Jolene protested, tried to fight him. He was immovable, irresistible.

She landed in the back of the cruiser with a yelp, and Ramsey shut the door. He went back to her car, turned off the engine and the lights, then came back.

Jolene screamed. "Let me go! I haven't done anything!"

Then she realized someone else was in the car with her. She looked and saw Mal Warner sitting next to her, in the back.

"Jesus Christ, Mal," she said. "Can you believe this? What'd he get you for?"

"Vagrancy," Mal said, smiling, although the smile didn't touch his eyes.

Ramsey got into the police car, turned off the flashers, and drove down the road. "Aren't we headed downtown?" Jolene asked. "What am I being charged with?"

"We're not going downtown," Mal said. "We're going to the river."

In that moment, Jolene realized that Mal wasn't cuffed. He was just sitting there, the way he'd been in Wallace Park. Just sitting there.

"The river? What the hell for?" she asked, straining at the cuffs. Ramsey had made them tight. She couldn't free her wrists.

"For you," Mal said.

II.

Stan Reynolds heard part of the exchange on the phone, when Jolene had been apparently arrested by the police. He'd heard her crying out and screaming, before everything got quiet.

He called her number again, got her voicemail. Then he called the Ludlow Police Department, but they said they had no record of arrest of Miss Jolene Clevenger.

So, Stan got into his car and drove into town, tracing back the way he knew she'd go to get home, but there was no trace of her.

Not even her car.

Nothing.

She'd just disappeared.

He went to the Ludlow Police Department, which was surprisingly busy, with lots of cops coming and going. He didn't think there were more than 20 cops on the police force, but you'd not have known it to see the activity at the station. It was an old WPA building, built maybe in 1937.

The policeman at the desk said they hadn't logged any arrest of Jolene Clevenger. Stan thought it over.

"What about Officer Ramsey?" He'd remembered overhearing her say his name. "Where is he?"

"He's on patrol," the desk cop said. The policeman's name was Murphy. Older guy, black mustache. He was sweating. "Everybody's on patrol these days. You'd think we'd had a crime wave or something."

Stan didn't know what to do. Jolene wouldn't officially be missing for another 24 hours, if he remembered right.

"So, do I come back in 24 hours or something?"

"Something like that," Murphy said. "Come back tomorrow."

Stan looked over at the big corkboard along the wall, where there were lots of Xerox bulletins and notifications. "Have You Seen Me?" asked many of them. All of those white faces, black hair. Pale, ghostly. They were ghosts.

Boys, girls, men, women. All races. All missing.

He didn't want to think of Jolene's sweet face going up on that board, too. But what else could he do? He'd file a missing persons complaint tomorrow. Meantime, he'd look up Officer Don Ramsey.

Stan walked out of the station, down the steps, noting the police cruisers coming and going. There were four leaving for patrol just then, each going a different way. One up Smith, one up Wallace, one down Main, one down First Street.

A lot of activity, for sure. What was going on? Stan took out his phone and looked up Officer Don Ramsey on it, found his address.

127 Oak Forest Lane.

Stan decided he'd drive out there, see what he could see. Not like he had any desire to confront a cop about anything, but thought he should do it, anyway. The cop had done something with Jolene. He wasn't sure what, but he'd done something.

He dialed up Max Paulsen, a photographer friend of his, got his voicemail. "Max? Stan," he said. "Something weird happened tonight. Jolene got pulled over by a cop, and now there's like no record of what happened to her. Like no arrest report, nothing. She just disappeared. Anyway, I'm going to check it out. The guy's at 127 Oak Forest Lane. That Officer Ramsey, that guy who was lost in the woods the other day. I'm just telling you that so you'll know, alright? Something weird is going on. I'm telling you this, and I know it's crazy, but I'm telling you this in case anything happens to me, alright? Like if I fucking vanish, it's Don Ramsey who did it, okay?"

He hung up, could only imagine what his friend would say when he got that message. Max was a raging paranoiac, anyway. He'd eat this up. Stan hoped that it was nothing, that they'd laugh about it later, but he didn't know. He only knew that Max would believe him.

Oak Forest Lane. That was on the North Side, off Quarry Road. Fair enough. Stan drove up Quarry Road, mindful of the trees and the twists and turns. It was maybe a 15-minute drive from downtown, a solid enough neighborhood. He pulled into it and drove down it, noting the nice houses. Not the old ones or the mansions on the mountains, but still good, honest houses. Not the claptrap that was further downriver, in the valley, where Ludlow really looked like shit.

He stopped in front of 127 Oak Forest Lane, looked at the dark house, looked at his watch. It was 8:00, but the house was dark. He remembered seeing Officer Ramsey's wife and kids on the news, when the cop had been missing. Two boys. The wife was pretty enough. Red hair, he remembered.

There were two cars in the driveway. Guess Ramsey was well-paid enough. Then Stan realized that one of the cars was Jolene's Camaro.

"Son of a bitch," he said, biting his lip. He drove down the lane and then rounded the cul-de-sac, parked across the street.

He didn't know what to do about that, so he just sat there in the dark. The street had the same old-style streetlights that lit most of Ludlow, part of a city ordinance, which did more to keep everything dim and atmospheric, didn't do much to keep things illuminated. He was fine with that, as maybe the cop wouldn't notice him watching from up the street. Or maybe he would. Cops noticed things like that.

Maybe nobody was home. Maybe Mrs. Ramsey had the kids out late. Would Don Ramsey risk bringing Jolene here like that? He didn't know.

But a sure way of getting wasted was breaking into a cop's house, so there was no way Stan was going to do that.

Why was her car in his driveway? Ordinarily, he might've thought she was screwing around on him, but it hadn't sounded like that. And he doubted the cop would've brought his mistress's car right up to his house.

No way.

Stan gripped the steering wheel in his fists, watched his knuckles go white in the dark, and then let go of the wheel.

His phone rang, and he dug it out, hoping it was Jolene.

It was Max.

"Hey, Max," he said.

"Hey, Stan, what the fuck?" Max said. "Are you baked?"

"No," Stan said, whispering. He felt vulnerable in his car, slouched down in the seat. He didn't know how to do a stakeout. "Everything I told you was for real. I'm across the street from his place, and Jolene's car is in his driveway."

Max paused a moment on the line.

"You sure it's hers?"

"Yeah," Stan said. "It's hers."

"Okay, so what are you going to do about it?"

Stan didn't have a clue.

"I don't know. I'm not sure about the Ludlow PD."

"There's no FBI in town," Max said. "You'd have to call up Pittsburgh for that, I think."

Stan didn't know what to say. If he called Ludlow PD and told them that one of their own had his girlfriend's car in his driveway, they'd probably want his name, and then they'd tell Ramsey that this Reynolds guy called, and before he knew it, he'd get a knock on his door, and it'd be his turn to disappear.

"It's weird," Stan said. "She got pulled over, and Ramsey arrested her, and that was it. But I checked at the station, and they didn't have any record of her arrest."

"Maybe Ramsey's late on his paperwork or something," Max said.

"Wouldn't he have to call that in or something?"

"I don't know," Max said. "I'm no fucking cop."

That was for sure. Max was about the furthest thing from a cop.

The two of them had been buddies in high school, and Max had been mainly occupied with photography and growing pot in the mountains. He maintained that if you grafted hops plants onto pot, you'd get weed that looked like hops, yet smoked like pot. Stealthweed.

"What should I do?"

Max sighed. "What can you do? Wait it out, see if Jolene comes home."

A car came up the street, and Stan slouched even lower. It was a police cruiser.

"Holy shit," Stan said. "It's him."

The cruiser rolled into the Ramsey driveway, sure enough, and out came the big policeman. The guy was huge.

"Is he alone? Does he see you?" Max asked.

"I don't think so," Stan said. "I mean, he's alone, but I don't think he sees me."

The cop went into his place, turned on the front porch light. Some lights then came on in the place.

"What's he doing?" Max asked.

"Just walking around in there, I guess," Stan said. "Doing house shit, I don't know. Whatever a cop does after his shift's up."

The policeman came out of the place again, carrying a bag, left the porch light on, went back to his cruiser. He cast a mammoth shadow across his lawn, this Ramsey. He had to be the biggest guy Stan had seen. Unbelievable.

He got into his cruiser and started it up, then backed out of the drive. Then back down the street he went, disappearing red taillights.

"He's gone," Stan said. "He went to get some shit from his place."

"So, you know he's gone, then," Max said.

"I'm not going into his place," Stan said.

"Sure," Max said. "Look, do you have a spare set of keys to Jolene's car?"

"Yeah," Stan said.

"So, you pick me up, and we go pick up her car," Max said. "We drive it to your apartment building, since you guys have that parking deck, right? Leave the car there. Or someplace with a garage, so we can hide it."

"You're saying we steal back Jolene's car from the cop who stole it?" Stan asked.

"Sure," Max said. "I mean, if it's her car, it's her car. It's not like he can report it."

"You're crazy," Stan said. "That's fucked up. That would get us fucking killed. What's more, Ramsey could just make up anything he wanted, and that would be that. Our word against his. And that's assuming we did it without him blowing us away."

Max hummed when he thought on the phone.

"Look, fuck him," Max said. "He's breaking the fucking law, right?"

"He's a cop," Stan said. "He is the law."

"It's the principle of the thing, here," Max said. "If a cop kidnaps your girlfriend and steals her car, what are you supposed to do, just take it?"

"Well, no," Stan said.

"That's why they call them 'police states,'" Max said. "Because the police end up running everything. The official police, the secret police. Everybody tiptoeing around because they're afraid of ending up dead. Or disappeared."

Stan laughed. "There's a reason why people are afraid of ending up dead."

"Yeah, yeah," Max said. "Look, if you're afraid to steal back her car, give me the keys and I'll do it."

"For real?"

"Sure, why not? I'm not afraid of him," Max said. Max always talked a good game. Stan doubted he'd be so cocky if he'd seen Ramsey up close. Stan was a lot tougher than Max, but Max had that craziness that let him punch a bit above his weight class.

"He'd break you in half," Stan said.

"Look, in America, we don't fear the cops," Max said.

"Yeah, we do," Stan said. "They've got the guns."

"Okay, just pick me up, Stan. You get your keys, then pick me up, and we'll do this," Max said.

Stan felt his hands sweat.

He didn't want to risk it.

"No, forget about it," Stan said. "Maybe she's alright."

"Did she sound alright?" Max asked.

"Well, no," Stan said.

"Right," Max said. "Pick me up."

12.

Stan got Max, who was wearing his black Chuck Taylor sneakers and a black hoodie and some olive green pants, his glasses perched on the end of his pointy nose. He smiled at the sight of Stan, who was sweating and looking nervously around them. To Stan, it felt like everything was watching them, even though it was so dark.

"Got the keys?" Max asked. Stan held them up without comment. Max snagged them, pocketed them. "Look, this'll be a snap. We pull up, I get out, I grab the car, we get the hell out of there."

"It's fucking nuts," Stan said. "There has to be a reason why the car's there."

"Okay," Max said. "What are the possibilities? Jolene's screwing around with this Ramsey guy."

"Yes," Stan said. He didn't want to think about that one. But why stage that arrest scenario if it was that?

"Or Ramsey locked her up someplace other than the Ludlow PD for some reason," Max said.

"Yes," Stan said. He hoped it wasn't that, because where the hell would she be? And what's more, why would Ramsey have done that out of the blue like that?

"Or Ramsey's a serial killer and murdered her or something," Max said.

"Yuck," Stan said. "You are sick, man."

"Hey, I'm just laying out the possibilities. You always have to think of the unthinkable."

Stan laughed. "Is that a fact?"

"Yep," Max said. "The unthinkable is the unthinkable for a reason—it's because nobody thinks of it."

"Except you."

"Except me. It's called imagination."

"It's called paranoia," Stan said.

"Paranoia is right up there with ignorance as an American virtue, my man," Max said. "Anybody who's not paranoid isn't paying close enough attention."

Stan laughed at his friend, shook his head. Max would always be this way.

Max pushed his glasses up his nose, rolled down Stan's window, leaned into the breeze as they drove their way back to Oak Forest Lane.

"I'm just trying to lay out the possible reasons for why that cop has Jolene's car," Max said. "Don't kill the messenger, man."

Stan sighed, looked at his friend, who was sporting some stubble. Max's dark hair and pale complexion made him look like a ghost. A smug-ass ghost he would be, with this appreciation of the irony of an afterlife, no doubt.

"I think this is fucking nuts," Stan said, but Max waved a finger at him.

"What is fucking nuts is a cop arresting Jolene and stealing her car," Max said. "I bet she's dead."

"She's not dead," Stan said. "Don't even say that."

"Why else would he take her car? And why drop it off in his driveway like that? What's he thinking?"

"I don't pretend to know," Stan said. "Not a clue. Okay, here it is."

Max was all business, a joint tucked behind his left ear, looking out the window. They cruised up the street.

"Let me out on the approach, and then just go up the cul-de-sac and turn around. I'll have her car out of there."

"Okay," Stan said, slowing the car down, feeling like the whole neighborhood was probably watching them. The neighborhood was so quiet, with the dead-end street and the mountain up against it. There was no place to go. He liked where he and Jolene lived, near the river. The choice between the mountain or the river was an easy one for him, especially when winter came. The people who lived on the mountain had a hell of a time in the winter, while down in the valley, everything got prettier in winter. Winter was kind to Ludlow, made it scenic. Even the industrial parks looked scenic when fresh-looking snow fell on them.

"Now," Max said, dramatically jumping out of the car. The internal light came on when he opened the door, and Stan rushed to turn the thing off, feeling like he had a spotlight on him, lit up like a Roman candle, for all to see. Max crouched as he ran to the car.

Thankfully, Ramsey's cruiser hadn't returned.

Stan passed up the street, taking his time without going too slowly. Whatever made him seem less conspicuous. He couldn't believe how chickenshit the whole thing had made him, but the evening was just too bizarre. It made him bitterly amused to think that his biggest worry several hours ago had been what they were having for dinner.

Now he and Max were stealing Jolene's car from a cop's driveway. It was the kind of thing they'd have done as teens, not 30-somethings.

He rounded the cul-de-sac and already saw the red lights of Jolene's Camaro. Max rang him on his phone.

"It's done," Max said. "See? No problem."

"Yeah," Stan said. "No problem. Now what?"

"Not on the phone, Stupid," Max said. "Just follow me."

And they made their way down Quarry Road, worked their way down to Mercy River Road, which ran along the river of the same name. Max drove the car down to his place, his photography studio, which had its own garage, and parked the thing in there, while Stan pulled up behind him.

"There," Max said. "No fucking sweat, right? See how easy that was?"

"What if the car was being kept for evidence?" Stan asked.

"Then it would have been at the police station, right?" Max asked. "Look, you go in tomorrow and file your missing persons report, see what you can find out. I'll chill out and we'll see if she turns up."

His friend looked so smug, but Stan hugged him, anyway. "Thanks, man. I can't believe you sometimes, Max. That was fucked up."

"We should check the car for evidence," Max said. "Not like we'd know what to look for, anyway."

They went through the car, front and back seats. There wasn't any sign of a struggle. Jolene's cell phone was on the dashboard, closed.

"No blood, nothing," Max said.

"Somebody closed the phone," Stan said. "She'd left it on. That's how I'd heard stuff. Ramsey did it."

"Okay," Max said, leaning on the trunk of the car, arms folded. "So, Ramsey's a bad apple. This we know. Do you think it's maybe tied to the casino?"

Stan hadn't thought of that. He was glad Max was his friend. He was sharp. He and Jolene weren't big fish at the Big Star, though. It was perhaps possible that maybe Ramsey was on the take, had shaken her down or something. But if he wanted real casino money, she wasn't the right person to go after.

"Could be," Stan said. "Although I kind of doubt it."

Max closed the garage, dusted off his hands. "If she turns up, you can come get the car."

"And if she doesn't?" Stan asked.

"Then we've got a big fucking problem," Max said. "Then I have no idea. We could always park the car in your apartment complex or something. The problem isn't us having the car; the problem is Officer Ramsey."

Stan nodded. "You're right. Alright, I'll stay in touch, okay?"

"Sure," Max said. "You do that."

Stan pocketed Jolene's cell with his own, waved goodbye to his friend, then drove out of there. His mind was reeling. He was kind of glad that Max had come up with that whole car-stealing thing. It made him feel good to imagine that cop seeing that, shitting his pants, realizing he'd been caught.

Then again, maybe the cop would immediately suspect that Stan had been the one who'd done it. Maybe he'd be implicated. Christ. Maybe Officer Murphy would mention to Ramsey that some guy had come looking for Jolene Clevenger. It all made him sweat. He wasn't used to thinking like this. He was a bartender—sure, he dealt with people's problems every day, but not something like this.

If the cop turned up, he'd just play dumb.

Then again, maybe that wouldn't be enough. He just wasn't sure. He almost called Max again, to ask if he could crash on his floor or something. But if Jolene was missing, and the cop had something to do with it, then the worst thing he could do would be to not be home. It would make it look like he'd done something with her.

To her. Whatever.

Stan got back to their Hidden Valley apartment complex, parked in his spot, leaned his head on the steering wheel for a moment, to clear his head. He had work tomorrow night. He and Jolene had planned on enjoying the day together.

Now it was just him, alone.

The parking deck was dark and silent, the soundproofing they'd sprayed on the ceiling doing its job. It was a weird sensation. The place should've been full of echoes, but the whitish-gray stuff they'd sprayed on the ceiling just ate up the sound. Not even his footsteps made noise.

In five years living at Hidden Valley, Stan had never seen another tenant in the garage at the same time as he was. Sure, there were cars there, but he never saw the people come and go. He knew they were there, knew there were plenty of tenants and neighbors, but he just never saw them in the garage when he was. It was just one of those weird things.

He got to the apartment lobby and hit the elevator button after greeting Darryl, the security guy. Middle-aged black man. Wore a maroon suit.

Then he went upstairs to their apartment on the 13th floor, keyed in, hoped that Jolene was somehow there. But she wasn't, of course. It was dark, just him and their dog, Pepper. The black standard poodle ran up to greet him, licking his hand.

"Hey, baby," he said. "I should probably take you for another walk, eh?"

The dog heard "walk" and wagged her tail excitedly. He'd walked her before dinner, before Jolene was supposed to show, but he always walked her before bedtime.

His mind was whirling as he was walking Pepper. He and Max had just stolen Jolene's car. But the cop had stolen her car and abducted her to begin with. It wasn't something he was used to thinking about. Things like that didn't happen in America. Or did they? It was like that line about treason never prospering, because if it did, nobody would dare to call it treason.

He went through the neighborhood, the hilly streets, letting Pepper do her thing. Ludlow was pretty quiet tonight. From where he was, he could see the river in the distance, upon which a barge traveled for parts unknown. They never stopped, those things. The lights on it were green and white and red, and the thing moved with inexorable smoothness, like an iceberg, maybe.

Pepper stiffened on her leash, began to growl. Stan looked around.

"What is it, baby?"

She saw a homeless man walking toward them. He looked homeless, anyway, wearing a long, dirty overcoat and a tanker hat. Stan realized that the overcoat was soaking wet, that the man was dripping. He was soaked, left a trail of water behind him on the sidewalk.

Pepper began barking, but the man didn't flinch, just kept walking toward them.

"You alright, fella?" Stan said. "Fell in the river, huh?"

The man started to speak, but water came out of his mouth, splashed on the sidewalk.

"I saw the Light in the Dark," the man said. Pepper was snarling, straining on her leash. He'd never seen her react like that. "I can show you."

Each step of the man's shoes made a squishing sound.

Squish.

Squish.

Squish.

Squish.

The man was soaked from head to toe. Then Stan realized there were three other homeless guys walking up the sidewalk, all of them drenched. What the fuck, was it Bathe-The-Bums Day or something?

Squish. Squish.

Squish.

The bum's face was bearded, his face terribly pale, his eyes flat like lumps of coal, eyes not on the furiously-barking Pepper, but on Stan.

"The Light in the Dark, huh?" Stan said. "Sounds great, but I'm just walking my dog."

Stan tugged back on the leash, but Pepper went crazy, snapping at the man, who nonetheless kept approaching. Stan actually backed away, having to yank back on Pepper's leash to do so. She was a good dog, a nice animal, and never went at people like that.

"Your loss," the man said. "They don't let dogs into Heaven."

There were more bums on the sidewalk. Like four more. So that was eight soaked vagrants, walking up Stan's street. Christ.

Squish. Squish.

The one talking to him was just a few paces from Stan. Stan turned and compelled Pepper to go with him up the street, away from the bums. She was going crazy, trying to get at them.

"Baby, no," he said, looking over his shoulder. All of them were soaking wet. What the hell had they been doing?

Squish.

Pepper yanked so hard on the leash that she slipped free of his hand, and took off after the lead bum, running at him and biting him on the leg.

"Oh, shit!" Stan said, running back.

The man didn't even yell when Pepper bit him. He just looked down at his leg, watching her savage him, and then bent down, grabbing her by the collar.

49

"Sorry, Mister," Stan said.

Then the man lifted Pepper up off the ground by her neck, pried her off his leg, and held her there. Pepper yelped, afraid, now. Stan could see the guy tightening his grip on her neck, and Pepper whimpering, yelping.

"Hey!" Stan said, shoving the man in the chest. "Let go of her."

The man fell backward, landing on the ground with a plop. He didn't even try to break his fall, just landed right on his back, like he'd been a bowling pin knocked over. And he didn't let go of Pepper. If anything, his grip on her throat was tighter. Pepper was flailing, eyes bulging.

"Let go of my dog!" Stan said, kicking the man. "Let go of her!"

The man didn't even flinch when Stan kicked him, he just stared impassively at the writhing dog.

"Son of a bitch, let her go!" Stan yelled. He grabbed at the man's cold, wet, filthy hands and tried to pry them loose. He used every ounce of strength he possessed, but couldn't break his grip. Stan heard a crunching sound, and Pepper went slack in the man's arms.

While this was happening, incredibly, the man had no expression on his face. There was just nothing. It was like he was made of stone. It was like he was dead.

That thought rattled around in Stan's head like a marble in an old tin can. Like he was dead. The bum let go of Pepper, just tossed her aside, and the sweet poodle just twitched on the boulevard.

Then the man grabbed for Stan with white fingers. Stan pulled free before the guy could get a lock on him.

"Motherfucker," Stan said. "You killed my dog."

The man sat up, then stood up, and Stan realized that while this had been going on, the bum's buddies had walked up to them. They were all staring at him, these soaked things, these fucking homeless apparitions, in swollen down vests and ratty wool overcoats, fingerless gloves and stocking caps. All pale-faced and hollow-eyed, all those dead eyes on him.

And as the first bum got to his feet, Stan realized something else: he was the only one breathing. He was panting from his struggle to save Pepper, but the first bum was just standing there, silently. They all were, not a breath between them.

They were fucking dead men.

Walking dead men.

Fear gripped him in the belly, and Stan backed away from them, almost tripping. As he backed away, the men walked toward him. Stan turned and ran up the street.

Zombies?

They were like fucking zombies.

But they talked.

He heard running behind him, the squishing sounds on the sidewalk, coming up fast. Running?

Stan risked a look over his shoulder, and, indeed, saw them chasing him. "Holy shit!"

Stan ran for his apartment, which was at least a block-and-a-half away. He was reasonably fit, thought he could make that. Sure as hell could beat a bunch of bums, right?

He rounded the bend, grateful he didn't have to run all the way up the valley to get to his place. But the bums were running hard for him. Eight of them, running after him. And only Stan breathing, his heart beating hard in his ears, the rest of them silent except for the squishing sounds of their shoes and the water spattering the sidewalk.

His lungs were burning, and he fished out his keys as he ran, grateful that his building had a security door.

A block to go. His legs were hurting, his quads, which would always hurt if he hadn't stretched them. He wasn't planning on having to sprint for his life. He risked a backward glance, and saw that the vagrants were right behind him.

Almost arm's length from him.

Gaining on him?

Stan gasped and ran harder, mindful of broken chunks of sidewalk that hid in the shadows. It was tricky running in the dark in Ludlow, where the shadows played tricks on you.

He realized he wasn't going to make it. Somehow, those bums were faster than he was. They weren't getting tired, they were just staying on him. So, Stan hearkened back to his football days in high school, cut hard to his right, just past an oak tree, going between some parked cars, just as one of the bums tried to grab for him. He could hear the air displaced as the man's arm went for him.

His was panting, couldn't keep this up for much longer. He'd cut to the right and bought himself a few moments. The bums turned and crossed into the street. Now they were between him and his home. Everybody stopped for a moment—the bums standing silently, and Stan pitched forward, hands on his knees. Stan's mind was whirling.

"What do you want?" he wheezed.

"To show you the Light in the Dark, Breather," the first bum said. The others all said the same thing, murmuring. "To let you drink the river."

Stan couldn't outrun them. His only chance was to get to his car, somehow. The parking deck was maybe 50 yards away. Could he make that? His legs felt wobbly, he wasn't sure if he could.

But the bums were walking toward him again, driving him back the way he'd come, toward the river. And there was no way he was going there. No way in hell.

He ran across the street, sliding across the hood of somebody's car, his ass denting the hood, setting off the car alarm. The car started honking, lights flashing, but Stan was glad for that, hoped somebody would look out their window and help him. He ran toward the parking garage, the bums running after him like before.

"Fuck," Stan said. Fight or flight. It was funny how everything boiled down to that, in the end. You either fought, or you fled. Nature left you those choices. But here was something he could neither fight nor flee, apparently. That was the problem with the supernatural: it never played fair. He wasn't going to make it.

One of the bums grabbed at his collar, but Stan leaned away from him. He had an idea that took him back to football again. He abruptly stopped, pitching himself low, right at their knees. Three of the soggy bums tumbled over him, crashing into the hedges that lined the Hidden Valley complex, and the others overshot him. It was a good move, a one-shot deal. Physics still worked against them.

It bought him a few seconds. Stan ran to one of the balconies at Hidden Valley and jumped, catching the guardrail with his hands. He pulled himself up as the bums ran for him. The metal of the guardrail strained against him, but Stan nearly got himself up. If he could get onto the balcony, he didn't think they'd be able to reach him, didn't think they could jump as high, since he was taller than most of them were. And even so, he could fight them better there.

But one of the bums managed to grab his ankle as he was climbing up, and pulled down hard on him. The cold grip of the vagrant almost dislocated Stan's ankle. He hooked his right arm around the metal railing, grabbed that wrist with his other hand. In the distance, he heard the car alarm turn off.

"Help!" Stan yelled, as loud as he could. "Help me!"

More bums' hands grabbed at his legs, tugging hard on him. He felt his arms straining. There were too many of them. He felt his grip slipping.

"Help me!" Stan screamed, as the railing gave way, taking him down into the waiting arms of the vagrants, who restrained him, one of them clamping their filthy hand over his mouth.

In no time at all, they had him pinned, and were walking him toward the river, held over their heads, like a funeral procession.

Stan strained in their arms, but there were too many of them. He saw one of the apartment dwellers in a robe, looking on from the balcony. And the place where he'd tried to climb the balcony, they turned their lights on.

"What the hell?" the man on the balcony said. Stan tried to squirm free, but they held him fast, marched him down the street. Past lifeless Pepper, laying there on the boulevard.

All Stan could hear was his own muffled breathing and the squish of their shoes.
Squish.
Squish. Squish.
Squish. Squish. Squish.

"Call the motherfucking police!" Stan screamed at the guy, who just stared. The fucking man just stared at them. "Asshole, call the cops!"

The man on the balcony just gaped, holding a drink in his hand. That look on his face was the last thing Stan saw as the bums rounded a bend, and the apartment was concealed by trees.

The guy had just stared. All he had to do was dial 911. Three fucking numbers. That's all he had to do. And it was too much?

"Help!" Stan screamed. "Somebody help me! Anybody! Call the police!"

He tried to remember what they said to yell when you needed people to react. Something Jolene had told him once. Something like if you yelled "Rape!" nobody would do a damned thing; but if you yelled "Fire!" then people might react.

"Fire! Help! Fire!"

Stan screamed it until he was hoarse, but if anybody did anything, he didn't see it. Fucking people.

The bums took him down to the boat slip at the foot of their street, past the railroad tracks, past everything. Stan struggled until he was spent, until he had nothing left.

His cell phone rang in his pocket, and even in the horror of the moment, he felt compelled to answer, wondered who it was. It was driving him crazy. Was it Jolene? Was it Max? Who was calling him? He couldn't find out, couldn't get to it. The phone rang and went to voicemail. He'd never know.

The fucking zombies were taking him to the river.

Into the shadows they went, their feet turning over stones, the river water black to Stan's eyes, like ink, flowing thickly. There were lights across the river, sodium industrial lights in the distance, and above him, looming like a giant, the Mercy River Bridge, itself with some lights upon it, to guide the barges.

He saw a cross looming on the shore, where still more homeless were gathered. They'd taken a trash can and put fire to it, were warming themselves by it. The fire made the cross cast a shadow across the proceedings—this ugly, unholy thing of fencing and barbed wire.

Then Stan realized that the bums weren't warming themselves. Rather, they were drying themselves off. The fire burned high, the bums were standing close to it, eyes blank, faces slack.

A man moved among them, a Man in Black, with black hair, and blacker eyes.

Mal Warner. It was Mal Warner, Stan realized. Walking back and forth between the assembled congregation.

"More drums, more fire. Get dried off. Can't have you lot leaving a trail."

"You there," Mal said to the group carrying Stan. "What've you got?"

The first bum seemed to speak for the rest. "A sacrifice for the river, Lazarus."

Mal walked up, looked close, smiled at the sight of Stan, held helpless. "Oh, my, yes. That's a worthy gift for the river, indeed. Get him down there and then dry yourselves off by the fires, Brethren."

Stan strained against the bums, but he had nothing left. He saw Officer Don Ramsey standing nearby, a hulking shadow.

"Goodbye, Stan," Mal said. "See you soon."

Stan tried to yell, tried to cry out, but the bums walked him into the river, a funeral procession it was, with zombie vagrants as his pallbearers.

13.

Max poured himself some grape soda and took his casual camera upstairs, went up
to his deck, sat there in the dark, taking in the sounds. Even though Ludlow was a
tiny, quiet little town, because it fed into Pittsburgh, had proximity to the Mercy
River and rail lines, there was always this sense of movement and noise, even if only
in the distance.

It was a sense of frenetic movement far away, and quiet and dark close by. The
Wallace Industrial Park across the broad river lit the night sky some distance away,
turned it a sickly pinkish-orange. And there were nearer smokestacks, hulking
monoliths with red lights that blinked upon them. Long ago, they had been mills
of some sort or another, but now they were silent, illuminated to keep low-flying
planes from crashing into them.

Max heard a dog barking, heard somebody scream something in the dark, far
away. He toggled the low-light function on his camera and panned around with
it, hoping to see something. Nothing jumped out at him, just the typical lame-ass
Ludlow evening.

He heard somebody running in the dark, followed by some others, then the
honk of a car. A car alarm somewhere. Max smoked his joint, drank his grape soda,
rested his feet on the railing of his deck.

His building was mostly cinderblock-constructed. He thought it was once a
storefront that sold cans of paint a long time ago. Now it was just a gut rehab, one
his dad had bought years ago, left to him.

Living rent-free was the best revenge.

There was a sound of breaking glass somewhere, a sound that made him lean
forward and look around, blind, in the dark. His deck, the construction of the
building itself, its position on the hill, it made him feel like he was in a tower, sort of.

Just above it all.

A police car went down Broad Street, flashers on, shining with a spotlight.
The cruiser rolled down the way, then turned onto Vine Boulevard, the spotlight
searching, sliding back and forth.

Max wondered if that was Officer Ramsey. He wasn't about to find out. Rather,
he just stayed up on his deck, smoking his joint. Hmm. Maybe not the smartest
thing to be doing, but where he lived, there wasn't anybody in the immediate vicinity
to spy on him, and from a distance, it'd not look like more than a cigarette.

The grape soda fizzed in the cool autumn air, and Max drank it down. He loved
that fake grape flavor. He was also a fan of that fake banana flavor. Just something

about those flavors that appealed to him. He wondered how food chemists arrived at things like that, deciding that Flavor X was close enough to grape or banana to pass for it, even though no banana or grape ever really tasted like those artificial flavorings. It was like there was a point when industry said "good enough" and went with it. The triumph of mediocrity.

The police cruiser disappeared down Vine Boulevard, rounding onto 5th Street. Likely headed back to the station, he thought. His phone rang, making Max jump.

"Yeah?" he said. He'd hoped that it was Stan, but it was Adrienne, his sometimes girlfriend. She worked as an art teacher at Whidmore.

"Hi, Max," she said. "What are you doing?"

"Just hanging out," he said. "Why?"

"Oh, well, I was wondering if you wanted to head into the city tomorrow night," she said.

"Why? What's going on?"

The pot had mellowed him, stuffed the alarm bells in his head with cotton balls. Sure, there was a stolen car in his garage. No problem.

"There's an art showing there," she said. "Duncan Brandt's work."

"Hack," Max said. "No-talent hack. Rich boy douchebag."

"He's dead," Adrienne said. "It's a posthumous showing. Some of his sculpture."

"Mmm," Max said. Adrienne he liked. She had impossibly long legs, severe brown bangs, big eyes like walnuts, colored mahogany. A long nose, wide mouth, kissy lips. Great tits. Adrienne posed for him a bunch of times, mostly portraits. The camera ate her up. He'd done tons of shots of her, black and white, color, it hardly mattered. Max often photographed women he liked. He found that was a good way of really seeing them.

"Oh, come on," she said. "Tomorrow night. It'd be fun."

"Where's it showing?"

"Pittsburgh," Adrienne said. "At the Concept Gallery."

"Fine," Max said. "But you're driving."

"Alright," she said. "You get dinner."

"Deal," Max said. "Hey, have you noticed anything weird lately?"

"Like what?" she asked.

Max heard a thump of some car doors, saw some people walking, laughing. Two couples. Somebody singing.

"I don't know," Adrienne said. "I don't think so. Why?"

"Just wondering," Max said. "I'm going to take some pictures tomorrow. What time did you want to head into town?"

"We can head over by five. That way we have time for dinner before going," she said.

"Okay, so why don't you pick me up," Max said. "At that café. Moxie's? I'll be out front."

"Fine," she said. "Don't be late."

"Not me," Max said. He said his goodbyes and hung up.

Adrienne was pretty great. It would be nice getting out of town for a bit, even if it was to see that shithead Brandt's work. He'd gotten a bit of fame after hanging himself in front of his last piece, some sculpture he did. Seems like that was the best way to get famous, if you were an artist. He had already joked to his folks about that, said that if he died, that they should be sure to print out his photographs, so they could get rich off of him. It sucked to think that death was the best career move he could hope for.

The world's priorities were all wrong. Or his were, anyway.

He yawned and finished up his joint. On a whim, he thought he'd go back downstairs and check out Jolene's Camaro again. There might be something of interest in there. Maybe it was some kind of drug deal or something. Not like he could honestly see Jolene doing something like that. She was nice enough, but devoid of imagination, the way Stan liked them.

He went downstairs and got his favorite digital camera, which he'd been charging up, then slung it around his neck. He poured himself some more grape soda, drank that down, wiped his mouth, and went into the garage, turning on the light.

The Camaro was just as he'd left it, shiny and fierce. Only a certain type of woman drove a Camaro or a Corvette. They were signature vehicles when driven by women.

It wasn't his most progressive of thoughts, but he was right, anyway. There was just something about a woman who drove a muscle car. They weren't his type of woman, but a certain type of woman was exactly the type to drive a car like that. The type who'd happily snort blow off the hood of their car, or give you a lawn job, or a blowjob on your lawn, or all of the above. Jolene was quietly wild that way.

Unimaginative, but wild.

He could easily see her getting mixed up in something with the casino patrons, or with some crooked cops. Stan always saw the best in everybody, that was his way. He was a good guy, maybe a little toolish, but otherwise alright. And he saw the best in Jolene, and so, thanks to his loving eyes, the best in her came out when he was around.

There was something sweet in that, Max had to admit. They'd probably get married sooner than later. They just had that way about them. But Max wasn't ever going to do that. Not for Adrienne, or Teri, or Emma. None of them. They were all great in their way, but Max wasn't inclined to settle for any of them that way. Not without losing something that mattered to him most: himself.

He fished out the keys from his pocket, opened the driver's side, then went to the tool bench along the wall, found a flashlight, came back and shined it in Jolene's car, looking for something, anything. They'd already done this, but he figured he'd check again, just in case they'd overlooked a clue.

He ran his hands underneath the seat, rifled through the glove compartment, checked in the back seats.

Nothing.

No sign of struggle, nothing.

Of course, there hadn't been a struggle.

Ramsey had arrested her without incident, without difficulty.

Max got out and closed the door, leaned on the car, then rounded the back of it, his foot encountering a puddle.

"What the fuck?" he said. There was some water on the ground. He looked up at the ceiling instinctively, shining the light on it, but it was dry. The light shined on the ground, revealing a puddle of water.

He knelt down and touched it, tried to see where it came from. He saw a bit of dripping from the bottom of the Camaro. It was water, not coolant or oil.

Intrigued, he put the key to the trunk and opened it, careful not to whack his camera with the trunk lid as he did so. Stepping back, he shined the flashlight in the trunk and gasped, dropped the flashlight, which rolled underneath the Camaro.

Inside the trunk was Jolene.

"Holy fucking mother of God," Max said, shaking. He dropped to his feet and grabbed for the flashlight, gagging, shivering. He managed to get an enervated hand around the flashlight and found his feet again, gasping, shined it in the trunk.

She was curled up in there, fucking dead. Her face frozen in this scream, her eyes blank and sightless, her arms locked behind her. Not cuffed, but frozen in this stiff-armed gesture, her wrists mangled and bruised.

"Handcuffed," Max said. "My god."

His knees buckled a bit, and he braced himself with an arm against the car, looked in again. She was fucking dead. It was her. Her skin was blue-white.

Fucking dead. Fucking drowned.

Her face was this mask of wonder and horror.

Oh, she was fucking dead, alright.

Even if Max hadn't held a hand up to her mouth, hadn't checked for a pulse, he'd have fucking known.

The unblinking eyes, that ghastly expression.

She was fucking dead.

Drowned.

Her body was wet.

There was a pool of water in the well of the trunk, there was mud on her shoes and pants legs. She'd been drowned.

This changed fucking everything.

He dialed up Stan, got his voicemail.

"Stan, this is Max," he said. "You fucking have to come here, man. My fucking God, will you pick up? Call me right the fuck back. Christ."

This upped the ante well beyond doing a solid for a friend, or sticking it to the Ludlow Police. He backed away from the car, dropped to the ground. He felt exposed, even in his garage.

"Fuck."

Max sat in the shadowy dark of his garage and he thought long and hard about it. Officer Don Ramsey had murdered Jolene Clevenger. That was the whole deal, that was the story, Morning Glory.

For some fucking reason, the cop had pulled Jolene over, arrested her, then drowned her. Then put her in the trunk of her own car, then drove her to his place. This while apparently on patrol.

Maybe it was a waterboarding gone wrong. An interrogation that got a little too intensive or something. It made sense maybe why Ramsey had the car at his place after all. He was probably going to take it someplace and have it crushed, or maybe drive it into the river, where nobody would find it for 20 years.

Cops knew how to do this kind of thing. They'd seen all the tricks, knew all the scams, all the hiding places, all of it. Ramsey was worse than a corrupt cop; he was a murderer. Maybe a serial killer? Why not? It was almost perfect—he could find his victims while on patrol, murder them, do what he wanted. He had a perfect alibi, even: "I was out on patrol."

Max wondered if his car had that camera in it, recording his activity. There'd be that record of him pulling over Jolene's car. He didn't know how that worked, but there'd be some kind of record, even if he hadn't called in to the station.

Max dug out his phone again, called Stan again, got voicemail again.

"Stan, this is Max. You need to call me ASAP."

He debated whether to mention Jolene or not.

"I know where Jolene is," he said, hoping to keep it cryptic. He wasn't sure who, if anybody, was listening, but damned if he was going to out himself on this. "Officer Ramsey knows, too. Look, call me, man."

He hung up, went back to the open trunk of the Camaro, looked in there. The mud on her shoes and cuffs of her jeans was probably from her struggling.

Holy fucking shit.

Max hefted his Nikon digital camera, snapped a bunch of pictures of Jolene. He never had done forensic photography, that wasn't his thing. He was an events photographer, did portraits, too, to pay his bills, while he did plenty of artistic stuff, his real vocation. But he'd never availed himself of the Ludlow Police Department, couldn't imagine photographing a crime scene, let alone a corpse.

Until now.

He snapped close-ups of her face, of her body, of her position in the car. It felt cleansing to him, letting his photographic eye blink and blink and blink at the scene in the car.

Evidence. It was evidence.

He was bearing witness to something terrible. He owed that to Jolene.

Of course, a crooked cop inquiry would have him as the one who drowned Jolene, of fucking course. He was the prime suspect, even though he hadn't done it. He snapped shot after shot, the shutter click of the camera soothing him a little, even though he had to steady his hands, they were shaking so much. He'd never been this close to death before, and certainly, not this close to murder.

He shot picture after picture, until there was nothing left to shoot, no angle left unclaimed. Then he closed the trunk and turned out the garage light, went inside. His place was a slice of industrial chic in Ludlow's River District, where bohemians, artists, dilettantes, and poseurs with a penchant for cheap living stayed. Or at least those who weren't sensible enough to move to Pittsburgh, or Chicago, or New York. But there was plenty of money to be made peddling shit art at fairs that drew wine cooler-guzzling Baby Boomers eager to look at bad art while they listened to smooth jazz or jangly folk music.

His place had two floors, with a living room on the main floor as well as a kitchen, wood floors and track lighting. It doubled as work space and gallery space, where he'd sometimes show off his work along the walls. Everything looked better when it was overlit. He used one of the closets downstairs as his darkroom, back when he did the majority of his photography in the pre-digital way. Nowadays, he spent most of his time crafting images with his computer.

Upstairs was a spiral metal staircase that led to the bedroom and a bathroom, as well as a little deck that faced the river. For Max, the place was ideal, as it was a fraction of the cost of other places, and, with the Internet, he could be as connected as he needed to be, just submitting photographs as he liked.

He logged onto his system and uploaded the photographs from his camera, eyeing the status bar as he called Stan yet again. He glanced at his watch, saw that it was 11:30 p.m., figured Stan would have called him by now.

"Stan, it's Max," he said. "Where the fuck are you, man? I am not joking: call me."

He hung up, set the phone on the desk, toggled through the images, deleted the ones that he didn't think were as good as the others.

Shot after shot of dead Jolene Clevenger came upon his large screen, and Max studied them. He'd never seen a drowning victim before, but weirdly, she didn't look like he thought one would look. He didn't have any frame of reference for what a drowned person actually looked like, but she didn't seem right to him.

What a way to go, Max thought. Terrible. A nightmare. But why would Officer Ramsey do that at all? That was the thing Max couldn't wrap his head around. There was just no reason for it. Unless the cop had flipped.

He was tempted to call the police station and inquire, but with Caller ID these days, didn't want to risk word getting out that somebody was asking around for Ramsey. Instead, Max thought he'd stake out the police station and take photographs. That couldn't hurt. He could just sit in the café across the street from the station, the Shaker Café, and take pictures.

He saved the photographs and finished charging his camera's battery, made another joint, sparked up. Normally he didn't smoke up if he was feeling weird, but this whole Jolene-in-the-trunk thing demanded it.

And where the fuck was Stan? Max wondered if Stan had already gotten caught by Ramsey. No way. Nobody worked that fast.

He took out his phone, called Adrienne, got her voicemail. "Hey, it's me. Sorry, I can't make it tomorrow. Something's come up."

Max hung up. He couldn't imagine staying the night in a place with a body, but he was afraid to go outside, too, in case that big cop showed up. He rang up Stan again.

"Stan, call me, for Christ's sake," he said, checking his doors to be sure they were locked. He turned out the lights, went upstairs, locked himself in his room, kept his phone nearby.

He'd wait for Stan to call him back.

14.

Mal was less than pleased that Jolene had gone missing. Ramsey reported her disappearance to him. She'd been special, an experiment. Mal had wondered when Ramsey had emerged from the river, whether somebody had to stay in the river or whether simply drowning them in the river was enough. When Ramsey had taken him and Jolene down there, it had occurred to Mal that what better person to try this out on than Jolene?

She'd been freaking out in the back the whole time, straining against her cuffs, trying to break free, but the ride to the river hadn't taken long, and Ramsey had dragged her out of the back, with Mal following.

Although Mal was content to have Ramsey walk Jolene to the water, he was not going to have him drown her. Because Mal had learned that whoever did the baptism gained some measure of control over the other. There was some kind of spiritual delegation that occurred in the process. He did not fully understand it, but there it was. And he was not going to have Jolene subordinate to Ramsey.

There was some darkling spark inside him that compelled him to think this. It would be unreasonable to say that he felt this way, but he did think that way.

Jolene was his, not Ramsey's.

He thought this as he told Jolene not to worry, that the Light in the Dark would restore her, would wash her fears away. She screamed and cried, cursed him out with her last breath, until Mal had no choice but to take her beneath the lapping waves of the river, hold her tight, until she kicked no more. She'd always been nice to him. Maybe in a sad kind of way, like she was doing him a favor by being nice to him, but she always had been. Mal thought that as he held her under, watched her eyes bulge and felt her body shudder and spasm, and finally, go still, curling into the fetal position.

In the dark they waited together, in the cold water. And then, when he was sure she was dead, when he was sure the Angel had visited her, when the Light in the Dark had reached her, he brought her back up, handed her to Ramsey.

"We'll take her back to her car, then drop the car off at your place," Mal said. As good a place as any. A safe place. There was a lot to do, and Mal found it hard to keep track of everything.

And for now, she was gone. But she would be back. He had faith.

Ramsey told him that as he'd presided over the bums by the river's edge, their rusting trash cans filled with fire to dry themselves. He'd had them bring logs near the burning cans, so they could sit and dry off. It was important to look normal as possible. With bums, maybe it didn't matter, but Mal had them do it, anyway. The Boys had been very good at rounding up the derelicts—and once that ball got rolling, they got more and more.

He sent Ramsey out looking for Jolene's car, was unsure what could've happened to it. He regretted that the Brethren had drowned Jolene's boyfriend; perhaps he'd know what had happened. Perhaps he was involved.

But it bothered Mal in a strange way, this matter. Not in an emotional way, but in a kind of rational irritation, this sense of being thwarted. He was Lazarus, he was the Messenger, the bringer of the new way.

Woe to him who crossed him.

And somebody had.

He would find out who. Once Stan was reborn, Mal would ask him, see what he knew, what he remembered, if anything. Until then, Mal would focus on what needed to be done. Ramsey had already made good headway into the police force, bringing about half of them to the river. Mal had been fortunate to have gotten Ramsey early. The hulking policeman had been a great missionary, although Mal thought all of his flock were useful in their various ways.

The key was for them to do a certain thing. The derelicts he mostly saved for the evenings, when they could roam about and find disciples, bring them to the water. The police he directed to take criminals to the river once the police station had been taken. Then he'd work on Mayor Frank Fikes. That would be easier. And the City Council. With the police in hand, the city government would fall quickly.

Then the churches and schools.

With Jolene and Stan Reynolds, he had inroads into the casino, which would be the next thing to go. The casino was useful because people came in from out of town, and that meant opportunities to spread the Light in the Dark far and wide.

The challenge for him was to keep people doing their jobs. He and he alone seemed able to pick and choose what he wanted to do, perhaps because he'd been the Messenger, the first to drink the river and to see the Angel.

He didn't know, wasn't one to think about it too much. The others did what they were told, by and large, although without the spark of life they had before. Mal had to keep them focused on their appointed tasks. He understood that it was perhaps difficult to go back to being what one was before, but for now, it was important that the Brethren walked in death as they did in life, until such time as they could be more open.

Until that time came, they had to go through the motions of living, and that meant doing their jobs. None of them argued with him, there were no emotions to get frayed, no egos to be bruised, but he sensed in many of them a reluctance to obey, an urge to stray. In some of them, there was a forgetting of who they were, precisely, a loss of self. These were more difficult Brethren to control, the ones more likely to run amok.

Once Ludlow was claimed, Mal wondered what he'd do, next. Perhaps send missionaries into Pittsburgh, Youngstown, Cleveland. Bring people to Ludlow. Or perhaps build something to bring people here.

He spent a lot of time at the shores of the river, staring into the water, hopeful for guidance.

Build me a temple, the River seemed to say in its ripples and eddies, in the Angel's bubbling whispers. Mal dipped his hands in the water and let it run through his fingers. A barge knifed slowly through the water, some distance away. The vagrants at the shore paused to watch the thing go by.

Mal did not know whether It was confined to this part of the river or not. He would have to conduct more experiments. He would have Brethren baptize people along the length of the river, to see who was born again, and who would simply die. He was pleased with this idea, with this application of scientific methodology to the miracle of the river, to the mystery of the Angel in the Depths.

Once he learned the dimensions of the thing, the breadth of the miracle, then he would know where to build his temple.

"Brethren," he said to the vagrants drying themselves by the fires. "Bring people to the shore, baptize them in the waters, under the cover of darkness. Along either side, to the north, and to the south, in a line."

He would have them go to Mace Hardware, fetch lengths of chain and rope, to tie down the converts. He didn't want to have the bodies washing downriver. That would defeat the whole purpose of his experiment.

He would have the Boys supervise it, explained it to them, told them what he wanted.

Mal would see how far Its tentacles extended, how long Its reach was.

The barge tooted its horn. Was it a greeting? Mal waved at the barge, a gesture the other Brethren imitated. The barge tooted its great horn again. Mal coveted the barge, wondered if he could make a floating temple to the River, in the spirit of the floating casino.

He stood up, dried his hands against his slacks. It was time for him to revisit the Big Star. Perhaps that would become his temple. He had one of the other police officers drive him to the Big Star.

Mal hadn't been back there since he'd quit his job. Bernie would probably want to give him his last check, if he hadn't mailed it to him.

The Big Star was as garish as ever, an ingot of gold and red, bedecked with lights that washed over the river. There was a hotel next to it, an eleven-story building with a grand lobby, where patrons could stay while getting their pockets picked by the Big Star.

A giant neon star was at the top of the hotel, visible for some distance around, bright red, pointed rays going off like points on a compass.

"Wait for me," Mal told Ramsey.

"Where are you going?" Ramsey asked.

"Inside," Mal said, leaving the cop on the curb. He sometimes sensed something from the big cop, like a trace of resentment. Whatever it was that bound them together hadn't totally rubbed away their past. It was like in the vampire movies, when the master vampire sometimes had to bare his fangs at his charges. There was, at times, some pushing on the part of Ramsey, and Mal had to push back. He and he alone was the Messenger. He was the one who the River spoke to first. It was not Ramsey's place to resent or to question. It was his place to obey.

Mal was greeted by the staff at the lobby, who recognized him.

"Mal," said Sheila (Mal looked at her nametag, couldn't remember her), one of the greeters. Pretty, hair up, blonde. "Mal Warner. We'd heard something about you quitting."

"Yes," Mal said. "I did."

"Bernie's upstairs," she said.

"Thanks," Mal said. He walked past her, past the gift shop, past the tourists, into the gaming room, which hummed with festive noise, this cavernous gold-toned room with red patterned carpeting. A thousand slot machines pinged and tumbled, and to the right, the Emerald Room, the table games, where the "real" gamblers went.

And beyond that, up a trio of steps, the poker room.

There were people everywhere, milling around, gaming. The nature of the gambling offered dictated who was there—old people dominated the penny slots, while somewhat less old people played the quarter slots, and plenty of young people worked the Blackjack tables and craps games. The poker players were not visible to him. They were the gambling royalty, out of sight, away from the noise of the main floor. Everything was in that main room, wheelchair-accessible.

"Hey, Mal," somebody said in passing. Mal didn't notice. He looked like a crow standing in the middle of a ballroom, this vision in black and white, amid the fat-fingered, sweating and wrinkled gambling multitudes, like pigs at a trough.

There was something he sought here, and he walked into the place, knifed across the floor toward the long row of shaded floor-to-ceiling windows that faced the River. The vista was really quite extraordinary, although the emotional bells such a place would have rung in him when he worked here, before he was reborn, those bells were muted, almost silent. Now he just gazed through the great windows at the River beyond.

The River flowed all around the Big Star, but this place did not move, was not even truly a boat. It stood on its great pontoons like it could ignore the River, like it had somehow conquered it. Craning his head, pressing it against the glass, he could see the Mercy River Bridge in the distance, red lights slowly blinking. He could not estimate the distance. Maybe a mile? Two?

"Great view, isn't it?" a man said. Mal glanced at him, a fat, balding man, sipping a drink, wearing a cream-colored golf shirt. "I remember one year, when we had all that snow, and the river got all swollen, surging. Flood, really. I just watched it churning, flowing, swirling. Hell, I went out to the balcony, so I could hear it. You can't hear anything in here."

The man nodded to the balcony entrance. These days it was to accommodate the smokers, as the Big Star had gone nonsmoking a few years before, when they had remodeled and expanded it.

Marketed it as a family place, a casino, a spa, a resort, even. Back massages and honeymoon suites.

"You look like you could use a little fresh air," the man said, gesturing to the balcony.

"Sure," Mal said, and walked out with the man to the balcony. The air did feel nice, the quiet. There were some smokers in the shadows, talking to one another, standing close. A man and three women.

"I'm Raymond Dunleavy," the man said, extending his hand. Mal shook his hand.

"Mal Lazarus," Mal said.

"Is that Jewish?" Dunleavy said. Mal shrugged. He didn't know what it was, had just liked the sound of it.

"I work in real estate," Dunleavy said. "I'm a developer. This whole river valley is just screaming for development."

Dunleavy pointed with a fat finger, like a bratwurst, it was. "There's good bones over there, those old buildings and empty factories could get torn down, and you put condominiums there, and shops. Put a footbridge over the river, so they can walk right across it, come into the Big Star. Could work up the shore, there, connect the park spaces and the greenways. Call it 'Riverwalk.' We put up a floodwall and they stay high and dry."

"Riverwalk," Mal said. "Sounds nice."

"Hell, yes," Dunleavy said. The man was red-faced, more than a little tipsy. "It's all there, just waiting. And Ludlow's just a stone's throw from Pittsburgh. Just go on down the river and you're there. You've got the airport over there?"

The thumb went over their shoulders. It wasn't in sight of the Big Star, but it was close to it.

"See what I'm saying?" Dunleavy asked. "You see it?"

"I see it," Mal said, glancing over the railing, where the River washed around the pontoons of the casino. "I think you should follow that dream."

He liked the idea of development in the area. More people, close to the River.

"What do you do, Mr. Lazarus?" Dunleavy asked. He was sweating a little, took another sip of his drink.

"I'm a preacher," Lazarus said. That made Dunleavy laugh.

"Yeah? Have you come to rail about this gambling Babylon?"

"No," Mal said. "I used to work here."

"No fooling?" Dunleavy said. Mal shook his head. "Then you found God? Had to quit?"

"I found the River," Mal said. "Or, the River found me."

Dunleavy nodded, tugged out a cigar from his pocket, offered it to Mal, who shook his head. Dunleavy acknowledged that, clipped his cigar, lit it, puffed on it.

"There's no future in God," Dunleavy said. "He had a great run, but look where we're at today? Those megachurches—shopping malls for the soul. Get yourself a Café Latte with Bible verses printed on the paper cup. Where's the spirituality in that? Seems like spirituality demands sacrifice, doesn't it? Or suffering breeds spirituality. Nobody in America suffers nearly enough for that kind of spirituality. Everybody wants to get rich quick, the preachers worse than anybody. No offense."

"None taken. I'm not rich," Mal said. "I don't even have a church. Not yet."

Dunleavy laughed, sucked on his cigar, the thick coal at the end of it glowing orange.

"I don't know," Dunleavy said. "You started out with people in caves, jumping around in skins, wearing paint and animal masks. Your first priests, right? Witch doctors? And then you got the whole industry going, temples to Apollo, and then you get Jesus and they're praying in the catacombs beneath Rome, eating their dead, drinking their blood. I mean, you ever wonder about that, the whole 'This is my body, this is my blood' thing? Ritual cannibalism, man. That's what it is! Eating Jesus!"

Mal hadn't really thought about that. Dunleavy was in full swing, now.

"So, then they're building great big cathedrals, the Church gets rich as hell, and then Martin Luther spoils the party with his Protestants, and then everybody's supposed to be poor again, and the Puritans are starving in the New World, can't even pray for crops to grow, because they don't know how to do it, and the Indians, not even Christians, they help 'em out, show 'em how to grow food, and suddenly we're a Christian Nation, Manifest Destiny, conquering from sea to shining sea, right? Only the churches are these little claptrap things. They don't have that sense of grandeur the Romans did, so now we get shopping malls that aren't even called churches, anymore. They're 'worship centers.' Like shopping for salvation."

He paused to suck on his cigar a moment. The other smokers had moved upstairs, leaving just the two of them on the balcony.

"McJesus," Dunleavy said. "Fatass shopping mall Christians, pulling up in SUVs and calling down their righteous thunder. The moneylenders have taken over the temple, Mal. Jesus had words about that, like DO NOT ENTER—with regard to the moneylenders, but they've taken over the business. They're selling salvation on television, not even a toll-free number. 'Call now, and get a free Bible reading light.' Where's the sacrifice? Where's the spirituality? No, they're better off in caves again. That's how it always goes—you start out in caves, build up to temples, then you're back in caves again. Anyway, God's been done to death. Christ came to these shores to die, my friend. And when He dies here, there's no coming back, because

He's gonna die ugly. I mean, we got Christian tycoons in this country, fella. That alone should disqualify them from the Gates of Heaven. But, no, not here. Not in America. Nah. God came here to die. This 'Christian nation' be damned."

"I don't have a cave," Mal said. "I have the River."

Dunleavy waved the cigar at Mal, cutting him off. "Oh, I know, I know. I've seen that. I'm from Louisiana. I know. You get'em on the riverside, baptizing the faithful. I know all about that."

"Yes," Mal said. He wondered if there were other Messengers, other rivers. The thought made him a little uncomfortable, an unfamiliar feeling lately. Were there other Messengers? Could that even be?

"Anyway, good luck with that, Mr. Lazarus," Dunleavy said, clapping him on the shoulder. He produced a business card like it was a magic trick, a sleight of hand, put the card in Mal's palm, after shaking his hand. "Good luck. I'm not saying there's not good money in God; Lord knows there is. Mammon works in mysterious ways, you know? In God We Trust, right? But it's Mammon that they're praying to on the back of every dollar, not God. Good luck with that."

Dunleavy walked up the stairs, stubbing out his cigar in a gold ashcan. Mal turned the card over in his hands, stuffed it into a pocket.

Mal had a message for the Messengers.

15.

Father Francis Knightley didn't understand. He'd coordinated the volunteers at the Trinity Shelter, had the chicken stew, the bread, and cherry Kool-Aid all set up, had a half-dozen students from Whidmore ready as servers, and yet, an hour after opening, nobody had showed up.

Ludlow didn't have a huge community of homeless, but there were at least 30 regulars who could be counted on to appear. Father Knightley checked his watch. It was 6:30 p.m. They should have been queuing up an hour ago.

But walking out in front of the place, he saw nobody.

One of the students, Pat Sullivan, came up. A good boy, always wearing rugby shirts. Today was green and blue stripes. "Maybe there's a new shelter in town, Father?"

"I don't think so," he said. Several of the volunteers had told him that the shelter was getting fewer and fewer visitors over the past two weeks. Father Knightley wondered if perhaps the indigent community had moved on, headed to Pittsburgh.

"What should we do?" Sullivan asked.

"We'll stay open until seven," Father Knightley said, glancing at his watch. Where had they gone? Heidi Campbell, another student, a feisty girl with retro black-framed glasses and a pert blonde ponytail, who routinely volunteered and organized the others at the shelter, had told Father Knightley in her nasally way about the diminishing attendance at the shelter. Heidi was invaluable at the shelter, but her voice never failed to annoy Father Knightley, although he never let that on.

He saw some homeless men walking toward the shelter, down the street. Apparitions, scarecrows, ragamuffins.

"Ah, here we go," he said. Then he saw several more, and still more. Walking purposefully toward the shelter. Father Knightley went back in. "They're coming."

It was too much to hope for that all of the homeless in Ludlow had somehow cleaned up their lives, gotten the help they needed. So long as suffering existed, the Trinity Shelter would continue to minister to the needy.

A thin man with black hair came in first, not looking like he was needy, his expression flat, his eyes dark, but lit with something deep inside Father Knightley could not quite place.

"Father," he said. "I'm Lazarus."

"Are you hungry?" Father Knightley asked. "We have food."

"I don't need food, Father," Lazarus said, looking around the room. The students were at their stations.

"Would you like a place to sit, then?" Father Knightley asked. Some of the needy entered the shelter, then more. They took their seats on the benches, at the tables, none of them lining up for the food. The volunteers looked to Father Knightley for explanation, but he didn't have any.

"I don't need to sit. I'm not tired, Father," Lazarus said. "I've cured hunger, Father."

He gestured at the men, who were silent, watching Father Knightley and this man, Lazarus.

"My Brethren no longer go hungry, have no fear of death," Lazarus said. "For they are already dead."

Father Knightley looked at Lazarus, and at the homeless men. There was something wrong about them, he could see.

A stillness to them.

"Your dead will live; Their corpses will rise. You who lie in the dust, awake and shout for joy, For your dew is as the dew of the dawn, And the earth will give birth to the departed spirits."

Lazarus quoted Isaiah 26:19 to Father Knightley, smirking at him without humor.

"You give them stew and Kool-Aid, Father," Lazarus said. "Day after day, week after week. I gave them something stronger, something worthier."

Heidi Campbell came up, her face creased with concern.

"Father, are you alright?"

"Yes," Father Knightley said. There was something dangerous in the stillness of the men in the shelter. Some palpable feeling of dread overtook him as he beheld them, and this man, Lazarus, in front of him. "Why don't you have the others run along, now, Heidi. I think I can handle things tonight."

"Father?"

"Be sure to take the trash out before you go," he said. He hoped Heidi picked up on that. He wanted them to go out the back door, versus having to pass this unholy rabble in the shelter.

And "unholy" was just the right word for them. There was something dreadfully wrong about them, and Father Knightley knew it. The stink of their evil was as apparent as the earthen stink of some of the vagrants.

Each of the men was known to him, he knew all of their faces, but in that moment, they were strangers to him, in the emptiness of their eyes, the slack expressions they wore like masks made out of wrinkled, ruined skin. The paleness of their skin, almost luminous, they were.

"Something worthier?" Knightley said, hearing the volunteers follow Heidi's lead, head into the kitchen. *God, let them leave this place safely.* This thing that walked like a man looked like it wanted to talk to him, so Father Knightley indulged it. "What is this worthy thing of which you speak?"

Lazarus held onto his dead man's smile like it had been carved upon his face. "Would you like to see it, Father?"

"I would," Father Knightley said. Anything to get these apparitions out of the shelter, away from the children. That was paramount. If it meant walking beneath the light of the moon with these dead souls, so be it.

This revenant's lifeless eyes looked over his shoulder, at the volunteers. Father Knightley followed his gaze, catching Heidi's eyes.

"RUN AWAY" he mouthed.

"Are you sure you don't want to make it a field trip, Father?" Lazarus asked. "Bring the whole brood?"

"No," Father Knightley said. "They have to run along home."

"We'll see them soon enough," Lazarus said. "Come along, Father. Let's go down to the River."

There was some profane cousin to reverence in the way Lazarus said "river"— something that filled Father Knightley with dread, made him reach into his pocket and touch his rosary for comfort.

The men weren't breathing. Not a one of them. Their pale, hateful faces, their dead eyes upon him. They were dead. They were undead. Unquiet dead. It was insane, and yet, there it was. Father Knightley felt this as he'd felt nothing else in his life. He was face to face with the living dead.

"'Then the Angel showed me the river of the water of life, as clear as crystal. It was flowing from the throne of God and the lamb,'" Lazarus said, again quoting from the Bible. "'Then said Jesus unto them plainly, Lazarus is dead.'"

"Are you a preacher?" Father Knightley asked, hoping to give the children still more time. The dead man shrugged.

"I am a messenger," he said. "I have plenty to show, and nothing to tell."

At a glance from their master, the vagrants rose as one, a wall of death between him and the children, who appeared to be going out the back of the shelter, as he'd instructed. Except for Heidi Campbell and Pat Sullivan, who were peeking from the kitchen.

"Have you heard about the Light in the Dark, Father?" Lazarus asked.

"No," Father Knightley said, quoting Isaiah 5:20, figuring he might as well throw a bit of Bible back at these monstrosities. "'Woe unto them that call evil good, and good evil; that put darkness for light, and light for darkness; that put bitter for sweet, and sweet for bitter!'"

Lazarus seemed amused by that. "Your God can't protect you, Father. I am His messenger, He has sent me unto you."

He put a cold hand on Father Knightley's shoulder. It might as well have been made of stone, that hand, as cold and implacable.

"I very much doubt that," Father Knightley said. "He would have no such thing to do with you. You are an abomination."

His knees felt weak.

"The Lord works in mysterious ways, Father," Lazarus said. "Shall we go down to the River?"

"What will we see?" Father Knightley asked.

"A miracle," Lazarus said. He opened the door to the shelter, made an exaggerated motion of his arm, like he was an usher.

Father Knightley followed him out. "What about the others?"

"They know what they have to do," Lazarus said.

"They have to leave the shelter," Father Knightley said. "I have to lock it up."

Lazarus seemed amused by this, spoke to his flock, who trooped out of the shelter, lining up along the sidewalk. They looked like scarecrows of singular malevolence.

Father Knightley took out his keys and locked the front door. He could see Heidi and Pat in there, watching still.

He would lead these things way from town. It was all he could do. And talk to Lazarus. They went down Ash Street, toward the river.

"What is in the river?" Knightley asked.

"The Angel," Lazarus said. "Dark and beautiful. Shining like radium. She came to me, gave me life again, when everything else was lost."

"Can I speak to her?" Knightley asked.

"Oh, she'll talk to you, Father," Lazarus said.

"Angels don't have gender, Lazarus," Knightley said. "They are spiritual beings, not bound to the dictates of the flesh. To say an angel is male or female is like pondering God's hair color."

"White," Lazarus said. "White hair, white beard, right?"

"I'm saying you are misled," Knightley said, as they made their way toward the river, going down Church Street. "It cannot be an angel you saw in the river."

Despite his companions, Father Knightley felt power in his faith, comfort in his assurance that God was with him, even in this moment.

"It was an angel," Lazarus said, undaunted. "You'll see."

The dead walked as they did in life, steadily, not lurching or shambling, no groaning. They were silent, however, except for the scuffing of their shoes on the sidewalk. His was the only heart that was beating, his lungs the only ones drawing breath.

"It's a demon leading you," Father Knightley said, amazed at the sound of his own voice. He had never given much thought of demons, in truth. Only in the sense of something individuals had to wrestle with, personal challenges, whether alcoholism, or a bad childhood, or an unloving spouse. Demons abounded in daily life, and he encouraged his parishioners to conquer them. But Father Knightley didn't literally believe in demons, at least until Lazarus came to the shelter with his congregation of ghouls.

Now he was faced with a demon, for sure, and he had no idea how to deal with it. He hoped that the children got away from the shelter, went home, took comfort with their parents. He didn't know if they'd seen what he'd seen, had that sense of doom that hung about these revenants like smog.

How had Lazarus done this? What black magic had he performed upon them? Another thing Father Knightley did not believe in. There was no magic, black or otherwise. Magic was the futile, fleeting will of man seeking to interfere with the Almighty. Magic was the usurpation of the natural order of things. It was the triumph of the irrational in the face of an uncaring world.

"Are you dead?" Knightley asked.

"Reborn, Father," Lazarus said. "Dead men tell no tales."

The vagrants gradually dissipated as they went down Church Street, past St. Vincent's, past the Jewish temple, past First Methodist and Third Presbyterian.

"Where are they going?" Father Knightley asked.

"Missionary work," Lazarus said. "Spreading the Word."

"And what Word is that, Mr. Lazarus?" Father Knightley asked. They turned down Third Street, toward the railroad tracks. A train was rumbling by, loaded with coal, car after endless car of it.

Lazarus pointed to the Mercy River, flowing silently, ripples and eddies in it. Mountains slouching in the background, the Big Star Casino shining brightly still farther, and the lights of the industrial parks, farther still. The River Bridge loomed to their right, in the distance, like a kneeling giant.

"The River is the Word," Lazarus said. "The final word."

"I see," Father Knightley said. It was just him and Lazarus, now. The homeless had filtered out downtown. He wondered what they were doing. It was clear to him that Lazarus was leading them, but to what end?

"You don't see," Lazarus said. "None of you preachers see. But you will. You'll all see the Light in the Dark, soon enough."

They went beneath a crumbling viaduct, while the train continued grinding along, that soothing clank-and-clatter of the steel train wheels on the steel tracks.

Clatter-clank, clatter-clank.

Father Knightley found the purposefulness of trains pleasing. He had a model of Ludlow at St. Vincent's, an electric train set he'd made over the years, perfect in every detail. He greatly enjoyed playing with his trains in the quiet hours between services. There was something very satisfying in the precision of a lovingly-rendered model. His Ludlow was a delight to the children of the parish, and he'd let them play with the trains when they visited.

He knew exactly where they were.

Lazarus turned and pointed to the hunchbacked cross that was buried in the sand, wrapped in barbed wire, surrounded by flaming barrels and vagrants warming their hands by the fires, by bundles of branches.

"What is this place?" Knightley asked.

"My church, Father," Lazarus said. "I've come to show you a miracle."

He gestured and they walked to the shore, while the train continued to rattle behind them, over the viaduct. The stones here were wet and round, like tortoise shells, broad, the kind of stones once harvested for cobblestones. Father Knightley realized that the stones were wet from footprints, that the trail went to the specters standing before the fires. What was this cult doing, exactly? What was Lazarus up to?

The figures by the fire weren't homeless, at least to Knightley's eye. They were men and women of the community. Muddy and disheveled, but otherwise ordinary. Some were wearing pajamas, others in tracksuits. They didn't look like vagrants, except that they were filthy and wet. Some of them looked like parishioners, like Mel Campbell, who ran Mace Hardware, and Monica Wilkins, the attractive schoolteacher, wearing a nightgown that was wet and muddy. She was backlit by the fires, and Father Knightley averted his gaze.

Lazarus could see him looking at them.

"They wandered through life without purpose, fearful of death," Lazarus said. "I have given them new life. They no longer fear death and decay, no longer suffer from the agony of aimless days. They move with singular purpose, now."

"The police will break up your cult," Knightley said, although he felt foolish, for the thing standing across from him was beyond the laws of God and Man.

Lazarus walked to the water, raised his hands. "Behold, Father. Behold the miracle. Behold the end of your world."

Knightley looked at the water, saw ripples appearing in contravention to the current of the river. Little circles appearing across the length of the waters, and then something bobbing to the surface. Many somethings. Heads, emerging in the darkness, lit only by the fickle flames of the trash cans.

Heads, then shoulders, and arms.

Emerging silently from the water.

Father Knightley recognized them. Meg Wallace. Don Lively. Sean Collins. Phil Hoffman. These were people from town, soaked to the bone, ropes tied to their necks, water streaming from their dead mouths, mud on their faces, on the clothing.

The priest clutched at his rosary, nerveless fingers gripping the beads tightly.

"My God," he said, mouth dry.

"MY God," Lazarus said, smiling. "And theirs."

"Free them," Lazarus said, and some of the others went to the water and freed the tethered corpses, the walking dead. The living dead. As far as Father Knightley could see, a great line. Lazarus had drowned them all the way up to the pilings of the Mercy River Bridge, and downriver, as far as he could see. There must've been 50 of them, maybe more.

Father Knightley took a step backward, and then another. His heart was beating heavily in his chest, pounding hard. Lazarus turned to him.

"You see? Do you understand, Father?" Lazarus said. "The end of your world. That is the message I bring, Father. Take that back with you to St. Vincent's. Your days are numbered."

It was not possible. Even in the face of it, even seeing it walk ashore, stinking and soaked, Father Knightley could not bring himself to fully accept it. The scale of it was monstrous, the ineffable nature of it, impossible to comprehend.

Father Knightley turned and ran away from that foul place. He ran like the Devil himself was chasing him. He didn't stop running until he reached St. Vincent's, collapsed in a heap on the front steps, chest heaving, no prayers coming to his lips, only ragged, desolate breaths.

16.

Max drove into town the next morning, after leaving a couple more messages with Stan. He'd dropped by his friend's apartment building, tried to get him on the intercom, but he wasn't home. Stan was fucking gone. Without so much as a word, his friend was gone. Max went to the parking garage, saw that Stan's car was still there.

The cops had to have gotten him. That was the only thing that made any sense.

He stared at the building awhile, shook his head, went to his car, then saw a couple of vagrants hunched over something on the grass. He saw blood.

"What the fuck?" he said aloud. He took out his camera and turned it on, using the telephoto lens. He did that almost on instinct, trusting his camera's eye to let him get closer than he'd otherwise dare.

There were three bums, one in a rotten orange parka, one in an Army-Navy surplus green overcoat, bursting at the shoulders, mud-stained. The other was wearing a cracked lifejacket and hunting boots. Everything was muddy. They had blood on their hands.

Max snapped a shot of them, then a trio of shots, catching them in motion. Had they found themselves some roadkill or something? Either way, it was fucked up. Their faces were bloody, their eyes were dead. They were eating something.

The camera showed some animal torn apart on the grass, black fur, body shiny and red where it had been torn up. A fucking dog.

Max felt himself get queasy as he beheld it, snapping shots with his camera. They were eating a motherfucking dog. Raw. They had blood on their beards.

And not just any dog, Max noticed, zooming in, catching the poor animal's face. Pepper. It was Stan's dog. He was almost sure of it. He could see the dog's tags on the grass, the head almost untouched, compared to the indignities done to its body.

They were eating it. Out of their fucking minds. They tore the dog to bits, and then went walking back down the street, leaving bloody footprints in their wake. Max followed them, camera in hand.

He went to the dog, took a couple of shots of it, and knelt by its collar, steeled himself, reached for its tags. Pepper Reynolds. Stan's phone number. His fucking dog.

Stan wouldn't have let those freaks have his dog. Max looked up, saw the bums had crossed the street, were headed toward the river.

He went along with them, feeling terribly exposed in the daylight, going from tree to tree, great oaks and sycamores, heedless and huge.

The three bums walked without comment, went under the viaduct, toward the river. Max stayed with them, stayed well behind. There were a lot of people by the river. Muddy people. Some of them were bathing by the river. The bums went into the water, rinsed off. There were ropes in the water.

Max decided not to go through the viaduct. It didn't feel safe to him. Instead, he went up the railroad embankment, then crossed the dozens of railroad tracks, careful to look for any trains.

Then he got to the far side of the embankment, where there was a strip of green, where bushes and trees had grown thick and wild, gnarled by rusty fencing and weatherworn litter.

There was a trail up here that was about 20 feet above the ground near the river, the great bridge looming directly overhead. From here, he could spy on the goings on below without anybody being the wiser, assuming he was sneaky enough.

He dropped onto his belly and crawled over with his elbows, looked again with his camera, snapped pictures.

Dozens of people, all of them dirty, muddy. Dozens of barrels, full of burning trash and sticks and branches, where the people were apparently warming themselves. It was like some weird homeless community, almost out of sight of anybody, and yet right under the community's noses.

One of them walked back and forth through their ranks, a Man in Black, with black hair and an authoritative bearing to him. Max zeroed in on him and took his picture. He disabled his camera's shutter click function, so he could snap shots in silence. Whatever was going on here demanded silence.

And that was something that struck him. There was almost no noise, except for the people moving about. No talking, except for the Man in Black. Max recognized Devon Murphy, as he spent a lot of time at the library, always thought Miss Murphy was pretty hot, like a classic butterface—great body, but her face, not so much. And there she was in pajamas, her hair a wet tangle. She was combing out the tangles, and while her pajamas were mudstained, it looked like she'd cleaned herself in the river, the way the bums had. Those bums had emerged from the river, cleaner, now, for a trio of sick fucks who'd just eaten a raw goddamned dog.

Max snapped shot after shot of the gathering, tried to make sense of it. There was a cockeyed cross in the midst of this group, where the Man in Black seemed to draw people to him. He was talking, although Max couldn't quite make out what he was saying.

A police cruiser emerged from the shadows of the viaduct. Max halfway hoped it was a paddy wagon, but it wasn't. He saw Officer Ramsey emerge, a hulking presence. Max took shots of him, watched him pull some people out of the back of his car. It was Mayor Fikes, and two of his aides. They looked concerned, like perhaps Ramsey had caught them unawares.

Ramsey and another officer walked the Mayor over to the Man in Black. Max took pictures of this, as the Mayor and his aides—one a pretty blonde in a tight gray dress, and the other a young man with brown hair he was quickly losing, wearing a black suit and a red tie.

The Mayor shouted something, but the officers were unfazed, and were marching the Mayor and his aides to the water's edge.

"Holy shit," Max said. He didn't think anything could top seeing some bums eating a dead dog, but the abduction of the Mayor was something bigger.

The Man in Black had some of the others grab the Mayor and his aides, and they were plunged into the water, face-first. There was thrashing in the water. This, while Ramsey and the other cop looked on, while the Man in Black was talking.

Not abduction. Assassination. Holy shit.

Max kept snapping shots, glad as hell that he'd put a fresh memory card in his camera in anticipation of getting into town and taking pictures.

The others were just watching, everybody fucking silent, while the Mayor and his aides thrashed, and then finally went still. The Man in Black said something, and ropes were tied around the necks of the Mayor and his aides, keeping them immersed in the water.

Holy mother of fuck, Max thought, hands shaking.

Then his phone rang, the Peter Gunn theme chirping. He gasped, reached for his phone, saw some of the freaks nearest to him turn and look in his direction. Max looked at the phone, hoping it was Stan.

It was Adrienne.

He turned off the ringer, stuffed the phone back into his pocket. Two, then three of the muddy freaks, including Devon Murphy, walked in his direction. Max backed away on his elbows, keeping as low to the ground as he could afford to be. The problem was that there was almost no way he could go up the hill without them spotting him.

The freaks crunched fallen leaves beneath their feet as they walked up the bank toward him. There was a winding path that linked Max's perch with the edge of the river. There was the sound of a train whistle, some distance away.

Max backed up into a crouch, saw the first of them, Devon Murphy, looking at Max with dead eyes that bore into him, regardless.

"Hello, Mister Paulsen," she said. "What are you doing?"

"Taking pictures," he said.

"Of us?" she asked.

"Well, you know," Max said, mouth dry. Her pajamas were soaked through, her great body was there, almost in his face. Great tits, great everything, baby blue pajamas. "Shouldn't you be at work?"

"I'm getting there," Devon said. There were three others behind her, people he didn't recognize. "I think maybe you should talk to Mal."

"Mal? Who's Mal?"

"Mal Lazarus," Devon said. She turned and looked over her shoulder, calling down to the congregation. "Mal, there's a man taking pictures."

Max turned and ran up the hill, while the others with Devon ran after him.

He scrabbled his way up the embankment, careful not to turn his ankle, or to drop his camera. There was a train coming, sure enough, a big freight train with green and yellow markings.

Max made it to the top of the embankment, stumbled over the first set of tracks, the ones that went over the viaduct. The train blew its whistle, but Max wasted no time looking at it, nor looking over his shoulder. He just concentrated on crossing the tracks. One pair, two, three, four. The first two crossed the viaduct. The others were reserve lanes.

He risked a backward glance as he heard the train's horn blaring, saw three of the freaks and Devon Murphy just up the embankment, blocked off by the passing train, and a blaring horn.

Max slid down the embankment on the other side, ran up the street toward his car. The train rumbled over the bridge, and, lungs burning, Max wasn't about to look over his shoulder to see what was coming.

He got to his car, shoved the keys into the ignition, and backed out. He saw some of the freaks running under the viaduct, and he turned, tires squealing, and got out of there, eyes on the rearview mirror to see if anybody was after him.

It didn't look like anybody was.

Max tried to control himself, driving steadily, although his hands were shaking. "What the fuck was that? What the fuck was that? Drowning the motherfucking Mayor?"

Not like he was even a fan of Mayor Fikes, but nobody deserved to fucking die like that. What happened to Jolene made a lot more sense to him, now, although the why of it eluded him.

"Psychobilly Satanists?" he said, looking around Ludlow as he drove, trying to spot anything out of place. His nerves were frayed. "Some kind of Moonie cult? What the fuck was that? You don't just fucking drown people."

He reached his place, then thought better of parking in his driveway, just in case one of them had seen his car.

He parked down the street, gathered up his camera, composed himself a moment, forehead on the steering wheel, and then went down the street to his place. It was quiet in his neighborhood, but it usually was during a normal workday.

Everything made him feel like he was being watched.

The empty windows of the row houses, the abandoned industrial warehouses.

A thousand eyes on him.

Normally he'd have joked about the pot making him paranoid, but he had fucking reason to be paranoid.

They killed the fucking Mayor. Those freaks drowned the Mayor. And Officer Ramsey was in on it, and at least one other cop on the force. He wondered how many more were in on it, who he could fucking trust.

He keyed into his place and locked the door behind him, turned on his computer, uploaded the pictures from his camera, went into the kitchen while his machine was doing that, poured himself a grape soda and vodka, filled the glass with ice, hands shaking.

Then he sat down, dug out his phone, called Adrienne back. While her phone rang, he thought about Stan. Stan was fucking dead. He was sure of it. Those freaks had gotten Stan, had killed and eaten his dog.

"Adrienne, where are you?"

"I'm at work, why? What's with canceling out on our date?" she asked.

"Look, I can't explain. Not over the phone, anyway," he said. "You should come over after work. I have to show you some stuff."

She paused on the line.

"Ooookay. Cryptic much?"

"Please," Max said. "Just come by after work, alright?"

"Okay," she said.

"And watch out for freaks," he said.

"You mean like you?" she asked, laughing.

Max brought up the digital images on his computer screen, the pictures he took. It was surreal. The assassination of Mayor Fikes. Holy shit.

"I mean anybody who's not acting right," he said. "Just watch out, okay?"

"Alright, Max," she said. "Look, I've got class in a few, so I've got to go."

"Fine," Max said. "Just be careful."

"Alright," she said, sounding perplexed and concerned. They hung up, leaving Max alone with his photographs.

He had to do something with them, in case something happened to him. He had a photoblog where he kept a lot of his pictures. On a whim, he started a new one, called it "Shudderclick."

Then he uploaded the photographs on it. He didn't know exactly what was going on, but decided to let the pictures speak for themselves, except for a little caption indicating that the photographs were shot in Ludlow, so people would know.

"Homeless men eating dead dog."

"Cultists (?) warming their hands near fires by the riverbank."

"Mayor Fikes and associates being drowned in Mercy River."

"Officer Don Ramsey."

"The Man in Black. Mal Lazarus."

"This camp is near the Mercy River Bridge, just north of it."

He posted the pictures, then decided to do an entry with some writing in it.

Something's rotten in Ludlow. I don't exactly know what's going on. I think maybe there's some kind of weird cult or something. Fanatics. Freaks. You can see from the pictures. Some of them saw me taking the pictures, chased me. I got away, but just in case something happens to me, I want there to be some record of this.

It felt good to post those, so there'd at least be some record, in case he vanished.

Then it occurred to him that he had the pictures of Jolene Clevenger, and that Jolene was still in the trunk of her own car. That made him sweat even more. Then he decided to upload those, too.

"Jolene Clevenger, found dead in the back of her car. She was drowned."

"You can see she was handcuffed. I think she was murdered by the police."

"She was arrested by Officer Don Ramsey."

He hesitated, because if word got out that he had these pictures, they'd find him. He didn't post the pictures of Jolene, kept them saved on the computer. He could post them later. Then he reconsidered, since he already had Mayor Fikes shown, he might as well show Jolene. He posted those pictures, too.

I'm going to lay low. I don't want these freaks coming after me. The Man in Black is the one behind it. Mal Lazarus. That's his name. I heard one of the freaks say it. He's their leader.

He googled the man's name, got only a few hits, nothing that seemed to be the guy he saw. Max went back to the photographs he took that had Mal Lazarus in them, and cropped one, expanding the image, focusing on him.

Grateful for the large amount of megapixels he had with his favorite digital camera, Max saw that the resolution didn't get so bad when he zoomed in. He posted that picture with the others.

"Mal Lazarus," he said aloud, as he typed the caption.

17.

Heidi Campbell and Pat Sullivan had picked the Ludlow Public Library to talk about what they'd seen, to figure out what they should do. They had tailed Father Knightley and the creepy guy after they'd left the Trinity Shelter, had seen the crazies rise from the water, had seen Father Knightley run back to St. Vincent's. And they'd seen more than that. They'd seen some of the other religious leaders of the community brought to the creepy guy, had seen them drowned in the river. They'd seen this, even if they hadn't believed it.

There were a fair number of patrons in the library, old people, mostly, a few little kids with their parents. Heidi and Pat went to one of the back corners, where there was a table. It was near a window. The whole building had late 70s architectural styling to it, block-built, narrow windows.

"They drowned those men," Heidi said. "Rabbi Kaufman, Reverend Walters, Reverend Stiles."

"I know," Pat said.

"We should talk to Father Knightley," Heidi said. "We should go to St. Vincent's and talk to him. I mean, he talked with that guy."

"Yeah," Pat said, nodding. He had a boyish brutality to his features, a blunt handsomeness that called to mind country clubs, lacrosse, fraternity hazing and date rape. His hair was close-cropped, faded up from his ears into a spadelike thatch of red-brown up top.

"We should go to the police," Heidi said, pushing her glasses up on her nose. She had seen the men flailing in the water, drowned by multiple muddy hands, forcing them downward. And the creepy man, just hanging back, watching it without moving.

"My Uncle Larry is a sheriff's deputy," Pat said. "I could talk to him, tell him what I'd seen. He might believe me."

Heidi nodded. That seemed a good route to go. She couldn't imagine walking into the Ludlow Police Department and telling the policemen about what they'd seen.

"What do you think it means, those guys coming out of the water?" Pat asked.

"I have no clue what that means," Heidi said. "Maybe it was some weird ritual? I mean, it's tied to the water, right? Something about the river."

"Maybe they're insane Baptists," Pat said, scratching his nose. "I mean, maybe that's what it was."

"A forced baptism?" Heidi said. "How medieval."

It was clear that the Rabbi and the other preachers hadn't wanted that, had fought against it, but there were too many hands on them, forced them under against their will. It had been horrifying. The men had been held under until they'd drowned.

"What else could it be?" Pat asked. "Their leader grabs the other religious leaders, the rival sects, right? And he drowns them. It's like what they would do to Muslim prisoners—they'd make them touch pork, or eat it, sometimes before they would kill them, so they'd know that they'd go to Muslim Hell before they died. Maybe that's what the guy did to them."

"You need to talk to your uncle," Heidi said. "I'll talk to Father Knightley."

"And then what?" Pat asked.

"We can meet here again," she said. "It's a safe place. I have your cell phone number." She wrote her own number down, gave it to Pat.

"There, you have mine, too. You can call me after you talk to your uncle, and I'll hopefully have talked to Father Knightley, if he's still alive. And we can plan from there."

"Okay," Pat said, pocketing the number. He liked the clarity of a plan, even if he wasn't sure what the hell was going on. The whole evening had gotten bizarre. He'd only volunteered to get closer to Tina Prosser, who was always volunteering at the shelter. She was gorgeous, he wanted her bad. When he'd found out about her volunteering all the time, he thought it was the perfect in.

He'd been gearing up to talk to her, she of the big eyes, the cute lil' nose, the caramel-colored curly hair, of the incredible ass and perfect tits. His whole plan had been to serve fucking soup to the hobos next to Tina Prosser, to chat her up, maybe work something out.

And then the whole evening had gone just wrong. Those creepy people came in, stinking of the river, and their leader, that Marilyn Manson wannabe all in black, talking to Father Knightley, and just screwed the whole plan. It was weird, Pat thought, like how Knightley and the guy looked alike, all in black like they were.

Now he was stuck with Heidi Campbell, Ms. Know-It-All, Pushy Pushington. Fucking awful. Yeah, what he'd seen had been colossally fucked up, he admitted that, but he kept thinking about Tina Prosser's fine ass as she'd left with the others, while Heidi was grabbing his arm and telling him to come with her to see what those guys were going to do to Father Knightley. He'd just gone along without thinking, the way he always did.

Not like Heidi Campbell was bad-looking. She had bleached-blonde hair and dark eyebrows, a nice enough body she habitually hid in preppy sweaters and jeans. Those fucking glasses were too much. She'd look better without them, her blue eyes and freckled cheeks would work better without the distraction of those hipster glasses. She couldn't even pass for a hipster, so like why did she even have those? It bugged him. She bugged him. But he'd gone along with her because that's just how Heidi was; she'd bend the whole world to her will one day. Like he could totally see her being president. It was just fucking inevitable.

"So, you call me after you talk to your Uncle Larry, Pat, okay?" she asked.

"I said 'okay,'" Pat said. "No problem."

"Be careful, Pat," she said. "Those weirdoes are out there."

"You, too," he said.

They split, Pat watching Heidi's ass as she walked quickly away. She'd been wearing a plaid skirt and penny loafers, the skirt a little tight, but he wasn't sure if that was from design, or whether she was a little teensy bit plump. He'd like the big brass safety pin she'd used to pin the skirt shut. He imagined unpinning that thing, seeing what Heidi had going on down there. She always tried so hard.

He fished out his phone and looked up his Uncle Larry, dialed him up. "Uncle Larry? It's Patrick. Would you mind if I stopped over?"

"What's going on, Patrick?" Uncle Larry asked.

"I'd rather tell you in person, Uncle Larry," Pat said, watching some vagrants walk across the street.

PART
TWO

1.

Heidi reached St. Vincent's without incident, although she took pains not to be noticed, without drawing attention. This time of the day, downtown Ludlow quieted down considerably, except for a couple of restaurants. Ludlow was a town best enjoyed by day, or, during the holiday season, early evening, when they'd strung up lights along Main Street.

As she'd walked, Heidi thought about what she and Pat had seen, wondered what it meant, and what she should do. She was glad that Father Knightley had run, although she didn't know what he would be able to do about the fanatics by the riverbank.

That's all they could be, in her estimation: some rogue splinter group, some radical fundamentalists or something. A cult, centered on that creepy guy, who had some kind of Svengali-like control over the others.

But to drown people like that? That took a special kind of coldness. And the others had just watched. She'd looked at some of the pale faces, and had seen no reaction from any of them. Not wincing, no shudders, no revulsion. Just watching, perhaps with a hint of interest, but otherwise, just the coldest, most clinical of observation going on. If she hadn't known they were alive, she'd have thought they were statues standing there, in some ghoulish modern art piece, some monstrous tableau.

Of course, the first order of business was to report it to the police, but Heidi had to talk to Father Knightley, see what he had said to the creepy man.

She came up to St. Vincent's, the blackened cathedral, the wrought iron fencing around it rusting in places, but still strong. The doors to the cathedral were made of thick wood. Vaulted doors, with big wrought-iron rings hanging on them for door handles.

Heidi tugged on the doors, but they were locked.

She rapped on the door with her palm.

"Father Knightley," she said. "It's Heidi. Are you in there?"

She waited, knocked again, repeated, then walked over to the rectory, rang the doorbell.

"Father Knightley, please," she said. "It's Heidi."

She saw some stirring behind mullioned windowpanes, a stirring of curtains, and saw Father Knightley peek at her. Then he came over and opened the door.

"Heidi," he said, looking over her shoulder, eyes panning back and forth across the street.

"Father, may I come in?" she asked.

He nodded, let her in, shut the door, locked it.

"You should be home," he said, peering out one of the windows. His lodgings were stately yet spare. A dining room table, a conservative living room with a coffee table and ample books along innumerable shelves, a little kitchen off to one side. There was a bay window in the living room that overlooked a green courtyard that was fenced off. Heidi recalled playing in that courtyard when she was little. There were a couple of apple trees there. Father Knightley had been younger then, too, would tell the children stories from the slate patio that connected the rectory with the courtyard. With the cathedral on one side, the rectory on the other, Father Knightley telling stories, and the wrought-iron fencing, it always felt like the safest place in the world to her, a place where evil could find no purchase.

"Father," Heidi said. "We followed you to the river. Pat and me. We saw everything."

The priest's face paled, and he walked her into the living room, gestured to the sofa, went to the bay window, closed the curtains on it.

"We saw more than you did," she said. "They drowned the other preachers, Father."

"What?" he said.

Heidi repeated herself. He sat down across from her, leaning forward, resting his elbows on his knees, steepling his fingers. He told Heidi about what he'd seen, and she'd shared everything she'd seen.

"Who are they, Father?"

"A cult," he said, although he seemed to be holding something back.

"We have to call the police," she said. "What else can we do?"

"Yes," Father Knightley said. "You're right. That's the least we can do."

His manner threw Heidi off. Something was affecting him. He was holding something back.

"Father, what is it? What's wrong?"

He bit his lip, shook his head. "You'd think I was mad, my dear. We need to get you home. Your parents are probably worried."

"First, the police," she said. "Look, what if we just called and reported a disturbance by the river. Said something about a mob down there or something. That way, they know something's up, but we're not tied down trying to explain what's going on. I mean, they might not believe that there's some murdering cult down there, whereas they might be inclined to investigate a mob gathering by the river."

She was used to nobody believing her. Part of it came with being a kid, the other part came with being a girl. All she had to do was say she'd seen some cultists drowning townsfolk to have them not believe her, or think it was somebody playing some kind of prank. Stuff like that didn't happen in Ludlow.

Father Knightley picked up his phone, dialed the police station, reported the disturbance, noted the street, what he'd seen. He gave his name. Heidi saw a bottle of brandy on the stand next to the phone, and an empty glass.

"Yes, Officer," he said. "Thank you. Goodbye."

Then he hung up, looked at Heidi, who was peeking out the bay window, through the curtain.

"Well, it's done," he said. "Come here, Heidi, let me show you something."

He walked her into his study, where she saw a model of Ludlow, she immediately recognized it, perfectly rendered, with little electric train tracks cutting across it. There was the country club, and Mountainview, where the big estates were, and the River District, and downtown. Everything was there. It was amazing.

"They're down here," he said, pointing to the spot at the foot of Beech Street, which fed into the river. "Right along here."

"Yes," she said.

"I wish I'd detailed that area more. I was busy dressing up the town," Father Knightley said. "Not the forgotten places. The forsaken places."

His voice, something in the tone, made Heidi look up. "What is it, Father? Please tell me."

She could see the man aging before her eyes, his face full of fear. "I walked with them, Heidi. But I tell you this: they weren't living."

"What?"

"They were undead," he said. "The unquiet dead."

She'd have thought he was joking, but for the grave expression on his face. He was serious. He had also been drinking. It was unclear to her whether one had compelled the other, where one stopped and the other began.

"That's not possible," she said. "The dead can't come back."

"I tell you, that's what I saw," he said. "I saw them rise from the water, not a breath on their lips. None of them breathing, no hearts beating. Lifeless. You saw them, Heidi. Don't tell me you didn't sense something off about them."

She had to admit there was, in fact, something odd about them. Motionless, like human marionettes they were. That supreme stillness they possessed when they weren't moving around.

Somewhere in the distance, she heard a police siren's lonely wail. She hoped the police brought a riot van. They'd need more people.

"The cathedral door was locked, Father," Heidi said.

"Yes," Father Knightley said. "To keep them out."

"They couldn't set foot in St. Vincent's," Heidi said, but the priest shook his head.

"Why not? What's stopping them? If what you saw was right, they grabbed the others handily enough, didn't they? No, I think this place is no more of a sanctuary than any other. It's just a building, just bricks and stone and mortar."

"Father," Heidi said. "It's a church."

The police siren got louder. There might've been a couple of cars, by the sound of the sirens, or else the siren echoed in the valley.

"They'll come for me," he said. "A sure as they came for the others."

"Father, how do we stop them?" she asked.

"We can't," he said. "We don't have the means. I wouldn't even know. What, garlic? Stakes. Shotguns? Chainsaws? I don't know."

The police car stopped in front of the rectory, and Heidi and Father Knightley went to the window. Why had they come here?

"Shouldn't they be down at Beech?" Heidi asked.

There was a loud knocking on the door, and Father Knightley grabbed Heidi's shoulder. "Hide. Don't make a sound."

He handed her a keyring. "What's this?"

"Keys to St. Vincent's," he said. "Keep them safe. Go hide."

The knocks came to the door louder, harder.

"Father Knightley," came a policeman's voice. "Are you in there?"

Heidi ran into the study, where Father Knightley's train set was. She ducked beneath the table, which was screened with a green ruffle that went to the ground. There was a stack of boxes beneath it, which held extra trains. She made room.

Father Knightley opened the door after unlocking it. "Officer Rice, what can I do for you?"

"You called about a disturbance," Rice said, his voice low, but not melodious to Heidi's ears. There was a flatness to his voice, an absence of affect.

"Yes," Father Knightley said. "By the river. Not here, Officer Rice."

"I'm going to need you to come with me, Father," Rice said.

"Whatever for, Officer Rice?" Knightley asked. "I haven't done anything. I'm not even causing a disturbance. Those people down at the river are causing the disturbance."

Heidi heard the sound of a gun being drawn, heard a click of the thing, like she'd heard on television.

"Come along, Father," Rice said.

"No," Knightley said. "I will not go with you. I'm not afraid of you. He got to you, too, didn't he? Mr. Lazarus?"

"He'd just like to talk to you," Rice said.

"No," Knightley said. "He and I already talked. I have nothing more to say to him. You tell him that, why don't you?"

There was a scuffling sound, Father Knightley grunting after there was a thumping sound. Heidi wanted to say something, wanted to help him, but doubted she could do anything to stop what was going on.

She couldn't just hide, though. She came out from beneath the table, looked around, found a thick wooden candle holder, almost like one of those big pepper grinders she'd see at some of the restaurants her folks would take her to.

Heidi ran into the living room to see Father Knightley wrestling with Officer Rice. Rice was a portly police officer, with a sand-colored mustache.

At least that's what it looked like at first glance. In truth, Officer Rice was throttling Father Knightley with both hands, and the priest was struggling to free himself, face turning red as he grimaced. There was no expression on Officer Rice's face, no trace of strain or emotion. Just the coldest indifference was there. Heidi saw his pistol lying on the ground, and ran up to grab it, throwing the candle holder at Officer Rice.

The thick baton of wood struck the policeman on his temple, clattering to the ground. Then she held up the pistol, pointing it at him. Rice turned and looked at her, again, without a trace of emotion, and let go of Father Knightley, throwing the priest roughly to the ground.

"Put the gun down, Miss," he said, standing upright. He held out one of his hands.

"Stop, Officer Rice," Heidi said. "Don't move."

Father Knightley was coughing, hunched over, trying to catch his breath. The paunchy policeman lunged at Heidi, who squeezed the trigger of the gun. The pistol flashed, the thing nearly flew out of her hand. She saw a chunk taken out of Officer Rice's shoulder by the pistol. There wasn't any blood.

Rice kept after her, as if he hadn't even felt the bullet wound he'd just received. Heidi pulled the trigger again and again and again, right in the policeman's face. The first bullet took off a chunk of his forehead, the second bullet pierced his face, exploded out the back of his head. The third bullet went into his jaw, taking several teeth with it, blasting away part of his neck.

The policeman staggered, looked at her with one good eye, the rest of his face a meaty ruin, brought his arms up to touch his ruined face, then dropped to his knees, pitching forward, face smashing into Father Knightley's coffee table.

Heidi was shaking, dropped the pistol, stumbled backward, falling on her butt. "Oh, my god," she said. "I murdered him."

"He was already dead," Father Knightley said, kicking shut the door to his dwelling. He massaged his bruised throat, which had angry red marks on it where the officer had tried to strangle him.

Knightley went over to the body and rolled it over. "No blood, see? Not a drop."

Sure enough, there was no blood. Just the ruined expanse of Rice's face. "There's something in the river," Father Knightley said. "That Mr. Lazarus has tapped into something awful there."

"What do we do about this?" Heidi asked, her voice shaking as much as her hands. She couldn't believe she'd shot someone. But she couldn't believe a policeman was trying to murder Father Knightley, either.

"We can try to put him in his car, I suppose," Father Knightley said. "We should get him out of here, sure enough. I hope nobody heard the report of the pistol, or there'll be more police here, and they won't take kindly to one of their own being shot."

"What was he, some kind of zombie?"

"Something like that," Knightley said. "I think so. Something in the river, something to do with the river."

Father Knightley grabbed Officer Rice's feet and pulled him, grunting. "I may need your help with this, Heidi."

"Okay, Father," she said, tears coming to her eyes. She'd shot a man. She took his other leg with shaking, nerveless hands and tugged as hard as she could. He weighed a ton. They tried for a bit, only managed to get him a little bit across the floor before pausing.

"Let's just take his car someplace," Father Knightley said. "We'll figure out what to do about him later."

He turned out the lights in his place and locked the door, then went to the police cruiser. Heidi got in the passenger's side, and they drove the car through town, Father Knightley listening to the police radio with a grim set to his face.

"Thank you for saving me, Heidi," he said. "You're a good girl. Don't beat yourself up about what just happened. Officer Rice's soul fled his body days ago. You didn't murder anyone."

Father Knightley knew Ludlow perfectly, from his model work. He knew a good place to put the car. He drove up the mountain a bit, came to Sturgis Park, where a lot of the community came at different times of the year. It overlooked Ludlow, had a great view. And best of all, if he and Heidi went cross-country, down the mountain face, on some of the horse trails and footpaths around it, they could come out in the cemetery that was on the north side of St. Vincent's.

He parked the police cruiser in one of the lots, made sure nobody else was around, then turned off the motor. He fumbled through the keys to find which one would release the shotgun from its holder, and handed that to Heidi.

"There should be rounds somewhere," he said.

"What is this for?"

"For shooting them," Knightley said. "Of course."

He found a box of shells beneath the seat, handed them to Heidi. Then he got out, went to the trunk, opened it, looked in there. Heidi followed him out, acutely aware of how criminal they looked.

Father Knightley found a blanket, which he handed to her. "Wrap the shotgun in that."

Then he dug through the trunk, fished out some flares, stuffed them in his pockets. Then he shut the trunk. He went back to the police cruiser, took out his handkerchief, and mopped down the steering wheel, the doors, both handles. He left the keys in the ignition, wiped those down, too.

"This way," he said, pointing toward the woods.

Heidi followed, looking this way and that. Father Knightley had recovered some from his near-strangling, was moving with a sprightly step.

"Father," Heidi said, holding out the shotgun. "Can you take this?"

"Of course," he said. He took it, rested it on his shoulder.

The woods in Sturgis Park were full of brown, orange, red, and yellow leaves, the trees shedding their leaves quickly in anticipation of winter. From up here, Ludlow looked idyllic, the even lines of downtown crosshatching the valley, with the other mountains around it seeming to nurture and protect it. The river snaked to the east, broad and winding.

A moment later, they were back in the thick of the woods, with only the crackle of leaves and their footsteps to mark their passing.

"What will we do about him?" Heidi asked.

"I've got the perfect place for him," Knightley said. "Where's the best place to hide a body?"

He gestured at St. Vincent's Cemetery, the endless rows of tombstones of white, gray, and black, generations of Ludlow's dead.

2.

Leon Granger never got lost. He and Ted Brin and Todd Rosser had all hunted in Fikes Forest for years without ever getting into trouble. The thing about hiking in the forest near Ludlow was that it really wasn't possible to get lost, because if you went west, you'd eventually hit the Mercy River, and if you went north, you'd start hitting some of the municipalities that dotted the Valley. If you went south, you'd hit the river again. Only if you went east did you really run the risk of getting into trouble, and even then, only if you were sleepwalking.

They had been hunting for bucks and had gotten separated. Fikes Forest was pretty thick, gnarled maples and oaks and birch trees all piling around one another, branches and deadwood all over the place, hilly ground, mountain rock jutting here and there, ready to catch a foot, break an ankle.

Leon wasn't lost, but he'd lost sight of the others when Ted had gone off after something he said was maybe a wild pig. Brin was obsessed about wild boars and feral pigs, wanted to bag him one. Leon thought that was stupid, especially with a hunting rifle. He had told Ted he wouldn't try to bag a boar with anything less than an assault rifle. With boars you wanted plentiful ammunition, just as insurance in case you just wounded the thing and pissed it off.

The trouble Leon found was that he'd lost his footing along one of the deer paths and had tumbled down toward the riverbed, and with the leaves all down and everything wet and slick, the clay-packed soil and all of that, Leon couldn't get back up the way he'd tumbled, and the guys couldn't hear him.

But he didn't want to be a sissy about it, firing off an SOS with his Remington .30-06. He'd never hear the end of it. No, he just planned to follow the river until he made it free of the ridgeline and found an easier way back up.

His wife would nag him about it, being too old to go out with the guys, would chalk it up to him being frail or forgetful or something like that. Sure, he was 65 to Rosser's 58 and Brin's 53. He was lean and fit, while they were both portly. It pissed him off to think that anybody would think he couldn't tramp through the woods with the best of them. He was a born sportsman, a natural woodsman. Fuck Todd Rosser and Ted Brin in the ear; he'd find them before sunset. He was sure of it.

He wasn't lost. Just looking out over the river, he could see that. The Mercy River Bridge, for Christ's sake, was looming into view. That alone told him where he was, where he needed to be. It was pretty steep on the eastern bank of the river, where it cut through the old limestone, where the mountains slumped in broken tree-packed greens in summer, and in golden hues in fall, and stark brown-black with salt-and-pepper snowfalls in winter. It was late fall, and Leon just told himself he was going for a stroll. He'd get back to their Bronco ahead of the others, tippling bourbon from his flask, like he'd been there all afternoon.

Across the river, he saw fires on the shore, along a patch just past the bridge pylons, where there was a bit of a bend in the river. There was a bunch of people there. He held up his rifle, looked through them with his scope. He could just imagine them shitting their pants, seeing this orange-vested townie with a rifle taking aim at them. Assuming anybody noticed him at all.

It was a bunch of bums, warming themselves by barrel fires. There must've been a dozen barrels there. Leon wondered how the township could let those people all gather there like that. The west side of the river always had shady stuff along the shores, sure, but this was like a damned bum revival. Leon imagined picking them off, one by one. Take care of the homeless problem quick enough.

They all looked unsavory, all pale and shiny-faced, dressed in muddy rags. Disgusting. Then he saw an old school bus roll down the boat ramp, oddly enough. He saw this junkie-looking driver and out came more weirdoes, dragging people with them. Like they were prisoners.

Leon wasn't sure what the hell was going on. The people leading the others were pale and had no expression on their faces, were just blank. And the prisoners were gagged, struggling against their captors.

A freight train rumbled by, blaring his horn, carrying scrap metal and timber, following track that paralleled the river. There were railroad lines on either side of the Mercy, always coming and going.

He saw that the prisoners had their hands bound with plastic bonds, and were being led to the water, where some of the bums were tying their feet with rope.

Then the prisoners were dragged into the river, up to their ankles, lined up along the riverbed. The gags were removed, and the people cried out.

"What in the hell is this?" Leon said, looking this way and that with his scope, panning around. It was like a prison camp. To his mind, he thought maybe there was going to be some kind of execution or something.

Sure enough, after the people were lined up along the shore, the bums took their feet out from under them and knocked the people down, face-first, into the water, and knelt on their backs.

"Son of a bitch," Leon said. The people being drowned by the bums were just ordinary people, good Ludlow people.

Without hesitation, Leon dropped to his belly, put the rifle out in front of him, steadied himself. There was no time to do anything else.

He took aim at one of the bums, a bearded man in a filthy John Deere tractor hat. Aimed right for his head. The man's face chilled Leon even from this distance, the lack of emotion as the man drowned his prisoner, who struggled in the water, bubbles popping to the surface.

A head shot. That's what it would take. He didn't want to risk shooting for the heart, given all the clothing the bum was wearing.

Leon didn't want to rush the shot, but he didn't want to wait, too, for the sake of the prisoners. There were dozens of them.

He had the man's head in his scope, dead center. Leon squeezed off a shot, the rifle crackling smoothly. The bum's head vanished in the scope, the bum tumbled to the ground. Smooth as he could, Leon chambered another round. His bolt-action Remington was lovingly maintained, but had only a five-round magazine before he had to reload. He wished he'd brought his old M-14, but hunting with that wasn't sporting.

Leon took aim at the bum next to that one, and the bum, a woman, seemed to be looking right at him, dead eyes, hair wild, face slack.

Another shot, right between the eyes, and she was blown clear of the prisoner. The two prisoners he'd saved had rolled over, gotten their heads above water, were gasping, screaming.

Leon took down another, and another, and another. They weren't reacting right, were just staring around, looking for him.

He reloaded his rifle, took aim again. Some of the bums were still trying to drown the prisoners, while others were wading out into the river, heading towards him. He smiled to himself, as there was no way in hell they'd be able to ford the Mercy River. It was just too deep, too broad, with uncertain currents. He didn't worry about them, focused on the ones trying to drown the prisoners.

Five more bums went down, and he reloaded again, while the train rumbled on and on and on. He wondered if anybody even heard the rifle shots over the rumble of the train.

The bums that had waded into the water had disappeared below the water. They'd just walked one by one until they vanished beneath the water. Leon couldn't believe what he was seeing. Where the hell were they?

He'd loaded his rifle again. Took aim again. Couldn't imagine why those bums weren't taking cover, why they kept trying to drown the prisoners, even in the face of Leon's deft shooting. He dropped five more.

The prisoners whose attackers Leon had shot were scrambling out of the water, running pell-mell along the shore, pursued by some of the other townsfolk. He didn't know whether he should try to help the ones who were being drowned, or perhaps to shoot the ones pursuing the ones he's already freed.

Fifteen, he thought to himself, reloading. He had one more magazine's worth of ammunition. Five more lives bought with his rifle. He rarely brought more than twenty rounds with him when he went hunting, not wanting to get bogged down with lots of ammunition. He remembered Joe Penske, who would show off his Uzi, his long 32-round clips. He'd go deer hunting with a submachine gun. Leon had always thought that was for shit, although today, of all days, he wished he'd had more bullets with him.

Five bullets, five lives. Or five chances for life. Several of the people he'd freed had been recaptured and were being dragged back to the water.

Leon took aim at another of the Drowners—that's how he saw them. They were Drowners. He dropped one.

Two.

Three.

Four.

Five.

Twenty.

Twenty shots, twenty kills. It was his finest hour, as he saw a couple more of the victims struggle out of the water. But not nearly enough. There was a whole line of them along the shore, the splashing diminishing, as the Drowners went about their grisly business. Not one of the Drowners had even taken cover while he was shooting them.

Leon didn't know what else to do, hoped Ted and Todd turned up. With Leon taking so many shots, it had to have gotten their attention. The freight train kept rolling by as before, the great steel juggernaut loaded with cargo, impassive, unrelenting. Right there, and yet, a world away.

Then Leon saw something closer, as the water near him rippled and broke, and he saw heads emerging from the water, eyes set on him. Five of them, stern-faced. Five Drowners—four men, one woman.

Leon's heart skipped a beat, watching these apparitions emerge from the water. They were ordinary Ludlow people, as bland and mundane as anybody else, except that they were covered in ooze and mud, soaked through, and were walking toward him.

"You Drowners stay back," Leon said, holding up his rifle. "I've shot twenty of you, I'll shoot more."

He hoped they understood a bluff when they heard one, but then he wasn't hopeful. How could one reason with people who didn't breathe? He was sure these were some of the ones he'd seen enter the river from the other side. Nobody forded a river by walking along the bottom.

Nobody living, anyway.

That thought curdled in his chest, made his heart pound hard.

"My God," Leon said, backing away from them. They were out of the water, now, had cleared the sticks and brambles, and were trying to cut him off. They weren't afraid of the rifle. They just looked at him impassively. They had forded the river, walking toward him underwater, without taking a breath. Nobody could do that.

Leon turned and ran from them, unwilling to leave behind his rifle. If nothing else, he could club one of them with it. The Drowners kept after him, running after him, their clothing squishing and slapping against their pale flesh as they came.

"Mal has a message for you," one of them said. The woman. "He wants you to see the Light in the Dark, old man."

Leon felt his heart pounding hard in his chest as he ran through the trees, oblivious to the sticks scratching his face, to the slip of leaves beneath his boots, the clods of mud thrown from his cleats.

"Todd!" he yelled. "Ted!"

They were gaining on him. The Drowners might've been soaking wet, but they ran well enough. Leon wasn't going to let them take him.

"Todd! Ted! Can't you sons of bitches hear me?" Leon called out, winded, as loud as he could. He was spent, could run no farther, leaned against a tree, chest heaving, sweat on his brow. He thought of his wife, his children, his grandchildren, hoped they would be okay. Then he thought of those Drowners getting hold of him and sending him into the river.

The Drowners caught up to him, grabbing him with outstretched limbs, gripping him tight with cold hands that might as well have been made of iron. They pried him from the safety of the tree, began frog-marching him down to the water. There was nothing Leon could do. Not with five of them to his one.

"Hey," Ted called out. "What the hell are you people doing?"

"Shoot 'em," Leon cried. "Just shoot them, Ted."

"We're taking him to the river," the woman said. She had mud-colored pigtails. Leon saw her hair was covered in mud, already caking on the strands of hair. "Wanna come?"

"Like hell," Ted said. Then over his shoulder. "Todd, over here. I found him."

One of the Drowners let Leon go and started toward Ted, who did not waver, his assault rifle pointed squarely at the Drowner's chest.

"You hear me, people? Let the man go," Ted said, but the Drowners kept heading for the river, except for the one heading toward him.

"Shoot them, Ted," Leon said. "What you think I've been shooting at all this time?"

Leon's boots touched the water, and Ted fired a warning shot ahead of the Drowners, while the other one kept heading for him. Todd appeared around a bend, took stock of the scene.

"For Christ's sake, will you shoot them, already?" Leon said. "They mean to drown us in the river!"

Leon's ankles were in the water. In a few moments the water would overspill past the rim of his boots, soaking his feet. Absurdly, the remembered that wet feet were death out in the wild. Like the worst of his worries were wet feet.

Todd fired first, shooting one of the Drowners that held Leon, catching him right in the back. The force of the high-velocity round sent the Drowner flying into the water with a splash. The others didn't react to it, just turned and looked at Ted and Todd, while not even breaking stride in their march for the water.

"Shoot them, you nits!" Leon said, trying to struggle free.

Ted blasted the Drowner that had come close to him, shooting him in the chest. There was an actual visible hole where the bullet had blown through him. But the Drowner kept coming on, kept reaching for him. No blood. Not a drop.

Todd concentrated on the ones with Leon, shooting at them in rapid succession. They made no effort to defend themselves, just took shots and careened into the water. And then got back up, came back for Leon.

"In the heads," Leon shouted. "Shoot them in their goddamned heads!"

He was free of the Drowners, splashed back ashore, keeping his own head low as his hunting buddies went after their targets. In short order, they had finished off the Drowners with a half-dozen head shots. Sure enough, as with his own effort, the Drowners dropped when they were shot in the head. Leon couldn't explain it, but there was no arguing with results.

Leon went to the others, gasping, still trying to catch his breath. "Those Drowners are piled up on the other side of the river. They're killing folk over there."

"Drowners?" Ted asked.

"Don't know what else to call them," Leon said.

"Zombies," Todd said, kneeling beside the one nearest them. "Motherfucking zombies."

"Alright, then," Leon said. "Zombies. Whatever. We can't go tell the police there's a bunch of zombies on the river's edge, drowning people. They'll think we're drunk."

Ted looked through his own scope at the far side of the shore. Sure enough, there were plenty of those zombies, or whatever-they-were, over there. More were entering the water, wading toward them.

"I think they see us," Ted said.

"They'll cross here," Leon said. "Cross right under the river. Walk right over to us. That's what those ones did."

"Like hell," Ted said, popping off shots. He was dropping the Drowners in the water, the ones wading toward them. He must've fired off fifteen rounds before his clip was spent.

"We have to get out of here," Leon said. "We have to warn people."

"We can patrol this side of the river," Todd said. "Shoot down the ones we see."

"Sure," Leon said. "But we have to get out of here, first."

"Right," Ted said. "Alright then. Let's go back to town and tell people about this."

Then they saw a police cruiser pull up, and a couple of police officers got out. The Drowners looked to be talking to the police, and then pointing. To Leon's eye, the police looked like Drowners, too.

"I think they're part of it," Leon said. "Look at them."

"Okay," Todd said. "We'll go to the lodge, tell the guys what we saw."

"That's a start," Leon said.

"I can't risk shooting a damned cop," Todd said. One of the officers went to his car, got to his radio.

"Let's get out of here, now," Leon said. The others agreed, at last, and the three men hoofed it back through the woods, Ted seeming to know where he was going. Leon kept looking over his shoulder until they were out of sight of the river.

"They got the cops?" Ted said.

"Seems like maybe they did," Leon said.

They reached their vehicles, stowed their weapons, and drove out of there, after agreeing to go to the Ludlow Elks Lodge Local No. 119. That seemed a safe place to go. They drove their three trucks out of Fikes Forest and worked their way to the Mercy River Bridge, headed into town.

From this vantage point, what was going on at the river was invisible, he realized. Nobody would look or think twice about it. They didn't know it was going on.

They drove up to the Lodge, parked and filed in. There were a half-dozen of the regulars there, hanging out.

"Gentlemen," Leon said. "We got ourselves a situation, here."

3.

Mal walked into the Ludlow Humane Society, to the sound of barking dogs and hissing cats. About four rows of double cages, full of animals.

There was an assistant at the far end, a portly young woman with a sand-colored ponytail and thick glasses.

Mal made his way past the cages, noting the animals watching him, their panicked way of dealing with the sight of him. They were not happy to see him, seemed to know something about him the woman didn't understand.

"Can I help you, sir?" the woman asked. Her nametag said her name was Marjorie.

"Yes, Marjorie," Mal said. "I'd like to buy some dogs."

"Take your pick," she said. "We've got all sorts. What were you looking for?"

"Something for security," Mal said.

She wrinkled her nose thoughtfully. "We don't really have guard dogs here, sir. Just strays and mutts and so forth."

"Hmm," Mal said. "I'll take all of them."

He held out a roll of money, and while Marjorie looked at it a moment, she looked longer at Mal.

"I don't think we can do that," she said. "Dogfighters often try to clear out places like this, use the dogs that way, like to test them on pit bulls and so on."

"I'm not into dogfighting," Mal said.

"Why don't we just start you with one, and then go from there?"

Mal didn't like that. He wanted all of the dogs. "You won't give them all to me? Even for this?"

He just set the roll on the table, this green column of money. Marjorie shook her head. "If anything, that makes me less inclined to let you have any of our dogs, sir. That you would throw money around like that makes me think you have bad intentions toward these animals."

Mal managed his smile, his practiced smile.

"That's interesting," he said. "I have only good intentions toward these animals. I want to show them the Light in the Dark."

"The what?"

"It's hard to explain," Mal said. "I could show you, if you'd like."

Marjorie looked uncomfortable. "I've got a coworker coming back in a few. She was just getting us some dinner."

The dogs barked furiously. Mal pocketed the money.

"I don't think so," Mal said. "I think you're here alone, Marjorie. Alone with all of these animals."

She backed away from him, glanced at the phone on the wall. An old phone, the color of canned peas.

Mal jumped past the counter and grabbed her before she could reach the phone. She struggled against him, her face full of outrage and fear. Mal restrained her with his arms, stronger than he ever was in life.

Then he grabbed the back of her hair in his fist, and slammed her face into the counter. Her glasses cracked, fell from her face. She cried out, grabbed at him with her fingers wriggling like spiders. Mal slammed her face again into the counter again, and again, until she was unconscious. There was blood on the counter, smeared from her face.

Mal let her fall. Then he walked out the front door. In the parking lot, the school bus awaited, where the Boys were milling about.

"Take all of the animals," he said. "Load the cages into the bus. Be quick about it. Get the woman, too."

The Boys got out, along with some of their bum helpers. In no time, the bus was loaded, the Humane Society emptied of cages. Zitface hauled out Marjorie, threw her in one of the seats.

Satisfied, Mal turned the OPEN sign in the door to CLOSED, and got on the bus, headed toward the river.

The bus bumped and rolled it way through town, until they reached the boat launch, the driver backing the bus up expertly. Then they opened up the back doors and hauled out the cages.

There were a bunch of bodies on the shore.

"What happened?" Mal asked. One of the tramps pointed across the river.

"Shooters," the tramp said. "We went after them, but you can see that they shot a bunch."

"Okay," Mal said. He pointed to some of the biggest, burliest of Brethren. "Cross the river. Go to the far side. Anyone you see, you kill. Drag them to the river and drown them. If they have guns, hide and ambush them."

He sent a dozen of them into the river, then looked at the bodies. He gestured at them, drew the attention of some of the bums.

"Get rid of the bodies," he said. "Get them out of here."

The cages were stacked on the shore. The Boys lurked nearby. "Drown the animals. Put all of the cages into the water, where there's room. Do it by hand."

It was bothering him, these shooters. That his enclave had been discovered. He took out his phone, called up Officer Ramsey.

"Somebody's been shooting at us," Mal said.

"I know," Ramsey said. "One of my officers told me."

"Set up patrols on the far side of the river," Mal said. "I've got Brethren at the shore, but anybody showing up over there should be brought to me."

"Right," Ramsey said.

Mal hung up. It was getting hard to keep all of the details right in his head. His plan was simple enough, but the execution of it was more complicated. And the more Brethren he made, the harder it was to control them all. He felt himself losing track of things at the margins.

He alone of the Brethren had free will, because he had no sponsor (as he put it), except for the Angel in the River. He answered to the Angel alone. All of the others answered to the one who'd made them, in a long and inexorable chain of command, a great, pale pyramid with himself at the top of it.

Mal found that some of the Brethren were more functional than others. That some were as hapless in undeath as they had been in life. The less intelligent of them very soon lost a sense of themselves, were given over to baser urges.

The dogs barked and the cats hissed and clawed as their cages were delivered to the water.

These Brethren he sent away from his church, to do missionary work. He didn't want them drawing unwanted attention to the church. As he watched the bums hauling the bodies of the dead, all shot in the head, he knew that unwanted attention would ruin everything he'd worked toward. He wondered what would have happened if he had been at the riverbank when the shooters had struck. Perhaps he would have been among the dead. And then where would they be?

He watched Pigeyes drown Marjorie. The River was getting crowded, packed with the dead. They had been very busy, he'd had them going night and day, delivering souls to the River. But it was a great River, could handle the burden. The Angel did not complain, welcomed the sacrifices.

Mal had even changed tactics, doing what he'd attempted with Jolene, which is drowning them and taking them out of the River, in hopes that they would awaken. He had them in buses and vans throughout Ludlow. The buses were all parked at the bus lot, while the vans were parked everywhere.

He'd thought about having them delivered back into their homes, but knew that was quite beyond most of the Brethren. It was easier just having them in the vehicles. They would awaken soon enough, would understand what was required of them.

But the prospect of the shooters bothered him. He thought about them as he watched the animal cages sink into the water, bubble, and fall silent.

Peace at last, Mal thought.

He could not afford to have more shooters come. He called up Officer Ramsey again, instructed him to impound the guns sold in Ludlow, and the ammunition. That seemed sensible. Ramsey said he'd take care of it.

Mal wondered if he'd been too aggressive too early, if he should have worked slower, sneakier. But he brushed that aside. He had so much work to do. That demanded working quickly. He admitted that he hadn't given thought to defending the church. He had been so consumed with playing offense that he hadn't thought about playing defense. He'd remembered the old adage about the best defense being a good offense, had taken that to heart.

That was why he'd sacrificed the animals to the River. The librarian had told him about the man with the camera, the Camera Man, taking pictures, spying on them. And Mal thought that it might be useful to see if the Angel took animals under Her wing, if they could be Brethren. Then if anybody snuck too near the church, they would find themselves attacked by Mal's menagerie.

He had been pretty proud of himself for this idea. He thought perhaps some of his animals could be placed across the river, too, in case the shooters returned. They would not find it so easy the next time around. His mistake had cost him Brethren. Mal would not be caught unawares again.

Mal watched the bums begin to eat the bodies of the dead. He had told them to get rid of the bodies, and they were honoring his command. Although it was not what he'd had in mind when he had instructed them, he did not correct them. In a few hours, the bodies were gone, well-hidden in the bulging, undead bellies of the Brethren.

4.

Adrienne looked at the pictures, while Max paced back and forth. She took her time, toggled through them, one by one. Max's photography was always excellent, the images clear, the colors rich. What was in the pictures, however, left her cold.

"I don't understand," she said. "How'd you do this?"

"What?" Max asked, stopping his pacing. "What, you think I faked these?"

"Wouldn't you have to? What's this for?"

Adrienne had come from school, as he'd asked, wearing jeans and some clogs, a peasant blouse of dove gray. She brushed at her bangs a moment, as she absently leaned on her elbow.

"I didn't fake these," he said. "These are for real."

"Okay," she said. "So they're real. What next?"

Max sat down next to her. His face was shadowed with stubble. He looked scared. Adrienne wasn't used to that. She'd seen a lot of expressions on Max's face, but fear wasn't one of them. It wasn't like he was brave; rather, he just didn't give enough of a fuck about anything to be afraid. Seeing Max afraid made her more than a little uneasy.

"That's the question," he said. "I think the police are in on it. I think they're compromised. I mean, look at those two cops there. They fucking drove the Mayor to this Lazarus guy."

"Okay," Adrienne said. "You think the whole force is compromised?"

"I don't know," Max said. "I'm afraid to find out. I don't want to end up in the back of a cruiser, on a one-way trip to the fucking river."

"It's too crazy," Adrienne said. "Why are they drowning people?"

"I don't know," Max said. "Some cult ritual? Look, I just took pictures. I don't pretend to know what's going on with these whackos. I haven't set foot outside since I saw this stuff."

Adrienne scrolled to the pictures of Jolene Clevenger.

"She's in my garage," Max said. "In the trunk."

"What?"

Max told her about what he and his friend Stan did, how they stole the car back from Officer Ramsey's place, and how Stan was gone, now, and Max stumbled across the body in the trunk.

"Let me see it," Adrienne said. She'd really thought Max was playing some kind of prank with her, some elaborate scam, but the pictures of Jolene made her think otherwise.

"You want to see the body?" he asked.

"Yeah," she said. "Let me see it."

Adrienne had taken the whole thing a lot better than Max had thought she would. She'd taken it better than he had, for sure. But then, seeing it in pictures wasn't the same as seeing it in person. That's what Max told himself.

Max led her to the garage, to Jolene's car, to the trunk of her car. There she was, as she'd been the day before, and the day before that.

Adrienne looked at the body, actually reached out and touched it with an extended finger, recoiled from the touch.

"She's not rotting," Adrienne said. "Shouldn't she be rotting?"

"What?" Max asked.

"Look," Adrienne said. "She's dead, alright. But she should be decaying by now. I mean, how long has it been since she disappeared? I mean, since she was, well, murdered?"

"Two days, maybe three," Max said. "I haven't kept track."

"Well, she should be stinking up the place," Adrienne said.

"She stinks," Max said.

"Yeah, but it's river stink," Adrienne said. "She smells like the river. Like mud, rust, and water."

"So, what's your point?" Max asked.

"I don't know," Adrienne said. "It's just weird."

"There's probably enough pollution in the Mercy River to pickle anybody soaked in it," Max said.

Adrienne studied the look on Jolene's face, that frozen look of horror and wonder, mouth agape, eyes staring blankly, arms behind her back, body hunched forward. What a horrible death she'd had, this poor woman. And for what? Some crazy cult leader? It was too bizarre.

"Okay, so this cult is drowning people in the river," Adrienne said. "That's what you've got, right?"

"Yeah," Max said.

"So, I guess that means we should talk to the FBI," she said. "We should call them up, tell them about it. At least tell them what we suspect is going on. If nothing else, it's odd enough that maybe they'd send an agent or two down here to check things out."

"See, you should call them," Max said. "You could explain it in a way that makes sense. They'd just come lock me up if I tried explaining it."

Adrienne smiled, as Max shut the trunk.

"You want me to call them?" she asked. He nodded. They left the garage, Max turning out the light, locking the door.

"Get me the number, and I'll do it," she said. "I don't care. I'll tell them. You are so paranoid, Max."

Max found the local number for the Bureau, and Adrienne dialed it, sat down, crossed her legs. She never had a problem talking to people. Max was more comfortable with his camera, always got flummoxed when he had to deal with authority.

"Hello? Yes, I'll hold," she said, looking at her nails a moment. She'd been working with clay with the students today, and had gotten some clay under her nails. She wondered absently where the clay had come from. Was it local? Had it come from the riverbed? No, that was too polluted. No doubt the school imported its clay from someplace else. The phone clicked, and she was connected. She spent several minutes getting herself connected within the FBI's system before she actually reached an agent.

"Hi, this is Adrienne Morse," she said. "I live in Ludlow."

"This is Special Agent Holliday. What can I help you with, Miss Morse?" A man's voice, middle-aged by the sound of him.

"I wanted to report something odd," she said. "I think there's a cult in Ludlow. I think they're drowning people in the Mercy River."

"Really?" Holliday said. "You witnessed this?"

"Yes," Adrienne said. It was a little lie, but it was easier than the truth. Lies were the grease on the wheels of life. "I saw them drown the Mayor."

She held up a finger as Max looked on.

"I have pictures," she said.

"Could you send those to me, Miss Morse?" Holliday asked.

"Sure, Special Agent Holliday," she said. "I have a bunch of photographs. They seem to be ritually murdering people in the Mercy River. Near the Mercy River Bridge. Near Mercy Gorge. Oh, and I'm calling you about this because I think the Ludlow Police Department are compromised. You'll see in the pictures. A couple of the officers were at least accessories to the Mayor's assassination."

"Assassination by drowning," Holliday said. It sounded like he was writing things down.

"Yes," she said. Holliday gave her an e-mail address to which she could send the photographs. "I think it's some kind of ritual for them. Like a ritualized murder."

Adrienne was surprised at how calm she was, given that Max was pacing again, looking afraid.

"Are you in any immediate danger?" Holliday asked.

"No," Adrienne said.

"Alright," Holliday said. "Send me the pictures, Miss Morse."

"Sure, Special Agent Holliday," Adrienne said, hanging up. She set the phone on the desk with a cocked eyebrow. "There, was that so hard?"

Max stopped pacing. "I can't even believe how cool you are."

Adrienne smiled. "Hey, I work with kids all day; you think a corpse in a trunk and a doomsday cult is going to throw me? Hopefully the Feds'll look into this, and that's that."

"They'd better bring a lot of people," Max said. "A squad of agents, a fucking busload. Helicopters. Gunships. Helicopter gunships."

5.

Heidi and Father Knightley had buried the dead police officer in one of the open graves that Mr. Treece, the undertaker, had unearthed. The priest had been careful to tamp down the earth where Officer Rice was buried, so when the grave was given its proper occupant, nobody would notice, hopefully.

It had taken some doing to get the man out of the rectory. Father Knightley had gotten a hand truck and had rolled the officer up in a blanket, then wheeled him out the back door, toward the cemetery, hoping nobody would see. Then he chose an appropriate site and, with Heidi's help, buried the man.

Then he did a little service for Officer Rice, between himself and Heidi, the two of them a pair of shadows in the greater shadow of the woods around Sturgis Park.

"Father, I don't pretend to know what is happening in Ludlow, what your design is for us. But I ask you to commit this man to Heaven, and to give us the strength to fight this evil that has infected our town. Officer Rice was just a victim. Let his soul find peace by your side. In Your name we pray, amen."

"Amen," Heidi said. Father Knightley tossed a handful of dirt into the grave, crossed himself, which Heidi did, as well.

Then they took the shovels and dropped them off at the shed, and went back to the cathedral in silence.

Father Knightley knew that all roads led to Lazarus. He was the source of the evil, he was the one who had to be confronted. He'd known it when that apparition had appeared at the shelter. He knew it as clearly as he knew that he doubted he had the strength to face him, let alone kill him. And yet the killing of Officer Rice showed him the way.

"A shot to the head," Knightley said. "I'm no good with guns, however. And I don't think a policeman's riot gun is going to let me get a good shot."

Heidi's phone rang. It was Pat. "Just a moment, Father. Yeah, Pat?"

"There's nobody here," Pat said. "The Sheriff's office is empty, Heidi. I'm standing in the lobby. It took me forever to get down here, because there were those things stalking around. Anyway, I got there, and nobody's here. What now?"

"Come back to St. Vincent's," Heidi said. The line cut out. "Pat? Pat?"

She did the redial, got Pat's voicemail. "Pat, we got cut off. Come to St. Vincent's, okay?"

Father Knightley looked on with concern. "What happened?"

"He said he was at the Sheriff's, and nobody was there," Heidi said. "Then the line cut out."

"Lazarus already got to them," Knightley said. "He's taking over the town."

Knightley took the shotgun from the table, turned it over in his hands, studied it. Then he opened the box of shells, took some out. They were red-capped. He held one up, shook it. It was silent.

"Slugs, I think," he said. "That's good. That would take off one of their heads."

He envisioned putting the shotgun in the face of Lazarus, harbored a most uncharitable, un-Christian thought of violence for the man. That was the crux of it: he was no longer a man. He was a thing. Lazarus represented a usurpation of the natural order of things, a contravention of God's will.

But then he wondered what it was that had given Lazarus this dark gift. What was it in the river that did this thing? Therein was the true source of the evil. Lazarus was, as he said, just a messenger.

Father Knightley thought about the old Thoreau quote: "There are a thousand men hacking at the branches of evil to one who is striking at the root."

Heidi tried calling Pat again, while Father Knightley pondered this. The root of this evil was somewhere in the river. That was the source.

"Pat's gone," she said. "I can't reach him."

"It's in the river," he said. "Somehow, we have to go to the river and find this thing."

Heidi shivered. "I wouldn't want to go down there on a good day, let alone with those things walking about, Father."

"I know," he said. "Lazarus spoke about the Light in the Dark. That's what we have to find. We have to find this Light in the Dark, and we have to draw it out of the river, and we have to destroy it."

"But what is it? How would we know?" Heidi asked.

Father Knightley closed his eyes, imagined it. A graven idol? The heart of a demon? A toxic meteorite? It could be anything.

"One thing at a time, I guess," Knightley said, loading the shotgun, one shell at a time. Five shells. He pocketed the rest of them, felt the weight of them, felt sorrow.

I am the Angel of Death, he thought.

He took the shotgun and put it in his golf bag, like it was a driver. Why not? He put a cover over the butt of the shotgun, looked at it. It looked fine. Not something to arouse suspicion. Then he hefted the bag, tested it out.

Heidi looked on, amused. "A good disguise, Father. Although folks will wonder why you're golfing at twilight."

Knightley took the two clublike candlesticks and put them in the bag, too, took out several of his other clubs, to lighten the load. He tested it again.

"It's all I can think of," he said, putting the extra boxes of shotgun shells into the pockets of the golf bag.

Heidi dialed up her parents, got her mom's voicemail.

"Mom, it's Heidi. I'm going to be home a little late. We're cleaning up at the shelter." She hung up.

"That buys us some time, I guess," she said. "But what are we going to do?"

Father Knightley shook his head.

"You're going to go home. I'm going to take you there. After that, I'm not sure what I'm going to do, to be honest."

She tried to call Pat yet again, but got his voicemail.

"I think something happened to Pat, Father. I think they got him."

Father Knightley fetched his car keys, his bag slung across his shoulder.

"Come along, then. To home with you, then I'm going to do some golfing."

6.

Max heard the thumping from the garage. He thought perhaps the cops had come for him, after all.

Thump thump thump-thump.

He and Adrienne had been sitting on his futon in the living room, were talking about what they should do next, when the thumping began.

"What the hell is that?" Max asked. Adrienne shook her head. They got up, went to the garage door.

Thump-thump thump.

"Christ," Max said, his ear to the door. He took a breath, unlocked the door, opened it, turned on the light in the garage. Jolene's car was rocking on its shocks. The thumping was coming from it.

"Jolene," Adrienne said.

"She was dead," Max said.

"Not anymore," Adrienne said.

Max's hands were sweating. He had no idea what to do.

Jolene was back from the dead.

She was a fucking zombie.

Not some crazed cultist; she was a zombie.

Thump thump thump thump.

"We should open the trunk," Adrienne said.

"What the hell for?" Max asked.

"To see what she's become," Adrienne said.

"She's a zombie," Max said. "You saw. She was fucking dead. You know what zombies do? They bite. They make more zombies."

Thump thump thumpity-thump.

"So, we won't let her bite us," Adrienne said, like it was that easy.

Zombies were always getting the drop on the norms. Max knew this.

Thump thump thump.

"What if we just took the car out of here, drove it someplace?" Max asked. "Just get it the hell out of here?"

"I want to see," Adrienne said.

"Christ," Max said, shaking his head. "Are you serious?"

Thump THUMP thump.

Adrienne looked around the garage, found a snow shovel, picked it up, held it up, like it was a weapon. "Yeah."

Max ran back inside, got his camera, put it around his neck. Then he went to his toolbench and put on some workgloves.

"This is fucking nuts," he said. Adrienne nodded, focused, serious, shovel held up.

Thump thump THUMP.

Max fished out the keys, put them in the lock.

"Hey, zombie," he yelled at the trunk.

Thump—

"Jolene, can you hear me?"

"Yes," came a muffled reply. Max looked at Adrienne.

"Zombies can't talk," Max said.

"Zombies aren't real, Max," Adrienne said. "You're talking about them like there's rules to them."

"I'm just saying, they can't talk," he said. "They're mindless."

"So, you're saying she's alive?" Adrienne asked. "We checked her. She was dead."

"Maybe she's a vampire," Max said.

"Max?" Jolene asked. "Is that you?"

Her voice was dead. The words were there, but there wasn't much behind them. They were just words, dreadful, empty words.

"Yes," Max said.

"Let me out," Jolene said.

Max backed away from the trunk, looked at Adrienne, whose lips were a thin white line, taut, the shovel still upraised.

"Max, let me out," Jolene said.

Thump.

The keys jangled from the impact of her fist on the inside of the trunk.

"Max, let me out," Jolene said.

Max didn't know what to do. Right now, she was confined in the trunk, and couldn't apparently get free. He and Adrienne were safe. He could just take the Camaro out of there, drive it someplace, and hope that Officer Ramsey didn't find them, and just leave it.

Then again, Jolene knew it was Max who was keeping her. As far as she knew, it was Max who did it. She could just tell the police about it.

"Max, let me out," Jolene said.

Thump thump.

He looked at Adrienne, who nodded, steeled herself.

"Okay, Jolene," Max said. "I'm going to open the trunk, now."

He turned the key, and the trunk latch popped. The trunk flew up with a punch from Jolene, knocking Max back. He hit the garage door and fell on his ass.

Jolene tumbled out of the trunk, just as Adrienne took a swing at her with the snow shovel. The shovel passed harmlessly over her head, clanging against the trunk lid, while Jolene fell on top of Max.

Her skin was no longer blue, was just ghastly pale, her eyes were dead, her mouth opened wide, her knuckles were raw. She bit Max on his upraised forearm, just past his glove. Clamped down on his arm.

"Auuuuuuugh!" Max said, prying free his bleeding arm.

"Max," she said, without a trace of emotion, his blood on her lips.

"Fuck me," Max yelled, shoving her off him. Jolene looked at him with that bloody mouth, those pie-plate eyes boring into him.

Adrienne recovered herself, readied the shovel. Max scrabbled away from Jolene, clutching his arm.

"You fucking BIT me," Max said. "She bit me! Fucking Christ."

His forearm had a ragged crescent shape where Jolene had gotten him. Max was sweating.

Jolene got to her feet, looking around. "Where am I, Max? Who's this?"

Max was reeling. The cunting zombie had fucking bitten him. He knew what that meant. He couldn't believe it had even happened. He wanted to puke.

"Adrienne Morse," Adrienne said, holding the shovel ready. "What do you remember?"

Max couldn't believe how calm Adrienne was. He got to his feet, looked around for something to pour on his arm. Something antiseptic.

She fucking bit him.

"I remember the river," Jolene said. "The Light in the Dark. I remember Mal."

"Mal Lazarus?" Adrienne asked. Max found a can of lighter fluid, popped the plastic cap, poured it on his arm, fished out a lighter, ignited it. The lighter fluid went up with a whoosh, and Max watched it sizzle, felt the burn, did nothing to stop it, just whimpered, gritted his teeth.

"I'm infected," Max said. "Goddammit, Adrienne. I told you we should have left her in there."

Jolene stepped toward Adrienne, eyes only on her. Black eyes, her face slack.

"I'm so hungry, Adrienne," Jolene said. "We should go to the river. There's fish down there. Plenty of fish to eat. Fat fish. Frogs. Worms. A feast, just out of reach."

"Jesus, Max," Adrienne said.

Max patted his arm out, the scent of petroleum distillates and burned hair in his nose. He didn't know if he'd cauterized it enough, didn't know the protocol for zombie infection prophylaxis.

Jolene took her keys from the trunk, closed it.

Then she walked toward them.

"Max," Adrienne said, backing up. Max turned and saw Jolene crowding Adrienne, Adrienne backing away, half-swinging the shovel.

"I have to see Mal," Jolene said, without expression.

Max looked around for something, anything. He didn't have much in the way of weaponry in his basement. He grabbed his camera in nerveless fingers and snapped pictures of Jolene walking toward them. The flash strobed in the basement.

Adrienne swung the shovel at Jolene, catching her on her forearm. Jolene didn't make a sound. The only sound was the clang of the shovel, and the snap-pop of the camera flash.

Jolene opened her car door.

"Do we stop her, or what?" Adrienne asked. "What do we do?"

Max grabbed Jolene. "Fuck it."

He yanked hard on her, amazed at how strong she was. Max threw his weight against her, pried her back, then got her in a headlock. He didn't know why he did it, except that he thought it might be useful to talk to her, to learn what they were up against.

Fucking zombies.

His arm throbbed as he tried to restrain her.

"Max," Jolene said, stepping back, shoving him against the edge of the toolbench. Max brought his legs up and around her, clamping on tight.

"Duct tape," Max said to Adrienne. "Kitchen. Top drawer next to the fridge."

"Let me go, Max," Jolene said. "I saw Stan. I saw the Light in the Dark. I saw Mal."

She stank of the river, of dark things, pollution, muck. Max just held on, while she reached for him with her dead limbs. She was so cold to the touch. Max heard Adrienne rooting around in the kitchen. It horrified him, this dead thing moving.

"Top drawer, next to the fucking fridge!" Max bellowed.

"I got it!" Adrienne yelled back.

Bleach. Bleach killed everything. He needed bleach for his wound.

Jolene grabbed for Max, tore at his shirt, sank her fingers into his arms, tore at his skin.

Adrienne reappeared with the duct tape.

"Get her feet!" he yelled.

Adrienne ran up and wound the tape around Jolene's legs, forcing them together. Jolene fell backward, Max taking most of the fall, landing with a grunt, his camera hitting the ground with a crack.

"Fuck!" Max shouted, kicking at Jolene.

Jolene strained at the duct tape, flopped onto her hands and knees, crawled toward Max, dead eyes upon him.

"Max, I'm hungry," she said. "Let's go to the river, Max. Stan's there. He's waiting."

Max kicked her away from him, while Adrienne fumbled with the tape. It rolled under the Camaro.

"Jesus," Max said, while Jolene grabbed for him. He scrambled to his feet, while she struggled with the tape.

"Max," she said, looking up at him with lifeless eyes. "I'm hungry."

Adrienne grabbed the snow shovel and scraped the tape back into reach, while Jolene grabbed at the duct tape at her ankles, tugging on it, arms straining.

Max grabbed a broom and forced it across her arms, in the crook of her elbows, bringing her arms back.

"Tape her!" Max shouted, while Jolene strained against him. "Around both wrists."

Adrienne caught Jolene's wrist and taped it, then went across her chest to her other wrist, tying it as well, until the tape was taut across her chest.

Then Max hoisted Jolene up by the broom handle, while she fought against it, without a trace of emotion or exertion, just silently struggling to free herself.

"Max," Jolene said. "I have to see Mal."

Max half-dragged, half-pushed her from his garage into his living room, set her down on one of his kitchen chairs. Then they duct taped her to the chair, winding the silver-gray tape around her over and over again, until she couldn't struggle so much.

Jolene just looked on impassively as this happened, talking in that dead voice of hers.

"Max," she said. "Mal is going to come for me, Max."

Max sat down on the floor, lighting a cigarette with a shaking hand. He offered the pack to Adrienne, but she waved it off.

"Your idea," Max said. "I wanted to keep her in the goddamned trunk."

He looked at his arm, flexed it. The wound was raw.

"Sorry," Adrienne said.

"Max," Jolene said. "I saw the Light in the Dark."

"What is that?" Adrienne asked.

Jolene looked at her, that chilling gaze, those dead eyes somehow seeing. It wasn't possible. Max couldn't believe what he was seeing.

This dead thing, moving, talking.

Thinking, even.

He went to his laundry room, grabbed a bottle of bleach, opened it, poured it on his arm.

"Fuck!" he shouted.

The sting of it was unbelievable. Motherfucking bleach killed everything. That was assuming that the zombie pathogen hadn't already infected his bloodstream, wasn't already slowly turning him into a zombie.

After pouring about half a bottle of the bleach on his wounded arm, Max went to his bathroom and rinsed the ugly wound out, then sprayed it with Bactine, then put gauze on it, then wrapped it with a bandage and some medical tape.

He looked at himself in the mirror, thought he looked pale and ragged. He didn't know how long he had. He was sweaty and pale.

Max opened his medicine cabinet and took out a Klonopin, popped it with a swig of water. Then he ran a hand through his hair, went back downstairs, where Adrienne was talking to Jolene, like they were having a normal conversation.

"Nothing fucking rattles you, does it?" he asked.

"She keeps talking about that Light in the Dark," Adrienne said.

"Beautiful," Jolene said. "I can show you. Mal can show you."

"I'm fucking infected," Max said, sitting down. "How long do I have?"

"Not long," Jolene said. "Mal will find me."

Max grabbed a camcorder from his a/v shelf, checked it, turned it on, recorded Jolene sitting there, looking at him with that dead face.

"What's your name?" Max asked.

"You know my name, Max," she said. "Jolene Clevenger."

"What's the last thing you remember?" Max asked.

"It doesn't matter," Jolene said. "Everything's different, now."

It made Max uncomfortable, watching her not breathe, watching her talk to him without breathing. How could she even make a sound?

"I remember the river," she said. "Mal held me down, made me breathe the river, Max. Made me see it."

"See what?" Adrienne asked. "What did you see?"

"The Angel," Jolene said. "The Angel in the Depths."

Max kept the camcorder on her, steady. There was, perhaps, something useful in this. Evidence of some sort.

"What does the Angel look like?" Adrienne asked.

"Shiny, long arms reaching," Jolene said. "I have to see Mal. Max, let me go."

She strained against her bonds, and the broom handle creaked a bit, dimpling the skin on her arms. There was no sign of strain on her face, just the mute contention between undead flesh and taut bonds.

Max kept the camera on her. The dead eyes bored into him through the viewfinder. Seeing, but empty.

"She's not breathing," Adrienne said. "She really is dead."

Max just let the camera record it. He would post it on YouTube, put it someplace where people could see. Put it on his blog. People had to see.

"What is the Light in the Dark?" Adrienne asked.

"I can show you," Jolene said. "You can't close your eyes to it. It washes over you."

"You're dead, Jolene," Max said. "Do you know that?"

"I'm hungry, Max," Jolene said. Her lips had a tinge of blue to them, and his blood, drying on her lips.

"You bit me," he said. His arm throbbed beneath the bandage. He wondered how much time he had left.

"I'm so hungry," Jolene said.

Max kept the camera on her, talked to Adrienne as he did it. "Those freaks I saw eating Stan's dog the other day. Zombies. Motherfucking zombies."

"Pepper?" Jolene asked. "My dog. Not Stan's."

"Pepper's dead," Max said. "Somebody killed your dog."

She didn't react to it, there was no emotion to her. She may have been talking, but she was dead inside, it was so clear to Max. Not like he knew Jolene very well, but she was at least animated in life. This Jolene was a ghastly reflection of the real Jolene, a revenant.

"I'm hungry," she said.

"Her mind seems focused on that," Adrienne said. Jolene strained at her bonds, making the broom creak, making the chair squeak.

"Hungry," Jolene said.

"I may have some cold cuts in the fridge," Max said, nodding in the direction of the fridge. Adrienne got up and walked over, nosed around in there.

"There's ham," she said, waving the pinkish bag of meat.

Jolene followed Adrienne with a turn of her head, with her eyes. Max's blood was on her cheeks, on her tongue. Adrienne took out a wet slice of ham, held it out. Jolene snapped at Adrienne's hand, ignoring the ham. Adrienne dodged her open mouth.

"She wants your hand," Max said.

"Hungry," Jolene said. Something close to fire appeared in the blank recesses of her gaze. Her mouth snapped, the teeth clacking. The broom strained again, Jolene's hands flexed, clawlike.

Adrienne put the ham back in the baggie, put it back in the fridge. "I don't think she wants it."

"Yeah," Max said. His forearm was itching. "What should we do with her?"

He turned off the camcorder, set it down. Jolene watched his movements, followed him with her head.

"Max," she said. "I'm so hungry, Max."

"I have no idea," Adrienne said. "Maybe get her to Ludlow General?"

"She needs a morgue, not a hospital," Max said.

Jolene rocked in the chair, flailing back and forth, knocked herself to the ground. The chair creaked.

"I wanted to keep her in the trunk," Max said again, righting the chair again. Adrienne just looked on, thinking. She was always a thoughtful woman. That's what Max liked about her.

"Hungry," she said, baring her teeth. His blood on her teeth. She had no saliva he could see, there was nothing to wash away the blood.

"I have no idea what we should do," Max said. Adrienne tapped her cell phone.

"I could call back Special Agent Holliday," Adrienne said. "He should've gotten the files we sent by now, right?"

"And tell him what?" Max asked. "That she's a zombie? He won't believe it."

"We could just tell him we caught one of the cultists," Adrienne said.

"I don't think he'd be too happy about that," Max said. "Vigilantism, that kind of thing."

They sat there, thinking, while Jolene writhed in the creaking chair, working her mouth. Max could hear the tape ripping, reapplied a layer, while Jolene snapped at him. His arm throbbed.

"I don't want to end up like this," Max said. "You'll have to kill me."

Adrienne laughed. "No way, Max. It's on you."

"You won't kill me?" Max said. "You never do anything for me."

She laughed coolly, shook her head. "Life's a bitch, Max."

Jolene again pitched over the chair, this time falling forward, her face hitting the floor. She looked up at Max.

"Let me go, Max," she said, snapping the broom handle.

"Crap," Max said, fetching the duct tape again. He wound it around her, tied her tight. He didn't know what to do with Jolene. It wasn't her, he kept telling himself. She had become something he didn't understand.

It was tied to the river, to what he'd seen. He thought of the Mayor, of the others. Who knew how many others?

"He's taking over the town," Max said. "That's what Lazarus is doing. He drowned the Mayor. The Mayor'll come back like this, too. They all will."

"Ludlow'll be born again. So will you," Jolene said.

Adrienne looked down at the struggling Jolene, her eyes settling on Max's. "Maybe we should get out of town, after all."

"Yeah," Max said. "Although I can't just leave her here."

"We can drive to Pittsburgh," Adrienne said. "Show her to Special Agent Holliday. That might do some good. Better than us trying to explain it over the phone."

Max thought that wasn't so bad of an idea.

"Alright," he said. "We'll put her in my car, like in the trunk, and drive to Pittsburgh."

"Good enough," Adrienne said. "You get the car, I'll keep an eye on Morticia."

"Jolene," Jolene said. "I'm Jolene Clevenger."

Max scooped up his keys, ran out the door, clutching his arm. It tingled. He could feel it tingling where she'd bit him. Christ. How long did he have? He was already feeling a little zombie-like. He could feel it.

Outside, the air was cool and breezy, the evening eerily quiet. He looked up the street one way, then the other. The other buildings were dark and empty, just lit by sodium lights.

He listened to Ludlow, heard cars driving around, some gunshots. There looked like there was a fire burning somewhere. He couldn't be sure, just saw flickering lights. Heard police sirens, took no solace in those. It was happening.

Then he went to his car, unlocked it, warmed it up. His arm ached. He didn't know how long he had. Not long. It was too much to think about.

He drove up and left the car running, then ran in to help Adrienne with Jolene. They put tape over her mouth, which was difficult, because she kept snapping at them.

"This is fucking insane," Max said, while they did it. Jolene looked at them with those flat eyes, seeing, unseeing. It gave Max chills, made his stomach turn. What the fuck was she?

"Yeah," Adrienne said. "Nobody plans for the apocalypse, Max."

They carted her out to the car, put her in the trunk. Max put a blanket over her. He prayed nobody stopped them. No cops. Nothing. He locked his place up, took his cell phone, went back to the car.

Adrienne was warming her hands by the car heater. Max gripped the steering wheel. "We can take Route 65 down to Pittsburgh."

"Sure," she said, impossibly cool.

"I can't believe how well you're taking this," Max said. He was impressed, and maybe a little horrified. Then again, he'd been the one who'd been fucking bitten.

"What can I say? I roll with things," she said. "What am I supposed to do? Go hysterical?"

They could hear Jolene squirming in the trunk, could hear her gnawing at the tape gag. Even with everything that had happened, it felt wrong to Max. It made him feel bad, treating this person he knew this way, even though she was just a shadow of what she was. Not like Jolene was a great person, but she deserved far better than this.

Max started driving through town, keeping an eye out for things. He could see people walking around, looking at them with pale faces. Under the orange of the sodium lights, he couldn't tell friend from freak.

They went past the police station, which was busier than ever, with cruisers coming and going, paddy wagons.

"Fuck," Max said, trying to be nondescript. A couple of police officers stood curbside, watched them go by. Their faces were shadowed. They could be anybody. They could be living, they could be dead.

He drove carefully, cautiously, while Jolene chewed through her gag.

"Max," she said. "Max. Mal's going to find you, Max."

Then he worked his way toward State Route 65, heading southbound. As he got near the edge of town, he saw there was a roadblock set up, several County Sheriff cars and roadside flares.

"Fuck me," Max said, putting on the brakes.

"Why are they blocking the road?" Adrienne asked.

"Lazarus doesn't want anybody to leave," Max said, scratching his forearm. He was sure of it. Motherfucker really was taking over the town. There were several cars by the roadside, not Sheriff's cars, either.

"We should turn around," Adrienne said, and Max didn't hesitate, did a U-turn, started driving back toward town.

"We could cross the Mercy River Bridge," Max said. "Then take 51 down. We could reach the Interstate, then."

"Sure," Adrienne said.

"Max!" Jolene said, insistently, from the back seat. "We're near the river. Can you smell it? Can you see the Light in the Dark?"

He took them toward the bridge, but there was a roadblock there, too, halfway across, in the middle. More Sheriff's deputies, more flares, more cruisers.

"Fuck," Max said, pausing. "Alright, we could go back through town, head toward the Heights, then work our way to I-79. I don't think they could've cut off the fucking Interstate, could they?"

"I don't know," Adrienne said.

"I'm hungry, Max," Jolene said. "So hungry."

Max wondered how Lazarus was doing all of this, if he was as thick-headed as Jolene was. Obviously, he wasn't. He'd been pretty fucking busy.

Mountainview and Ludlow Heights was where all the mansions were, up in the mountains. Winding roads, dark and peaceful, removed from the industrial glut and postcard town in the valley.

There were two on-ramps for I-79, two points where people from Ludlow could go, one in the Heights, and the other back toward town. If Lazarus had those covered as well, then they were well and truly fucked. There would be no way out of town, short of stowing away on a barge, or hiking the mountains on foot. They weren't big mountains, but they were bigger than Max, and that was big enough for him.

Max glanced at his gas gauge. Quarter tank. He wanted to fuel up, to be safe. He pulled into a Safeway and gassed up his car, hearing Jolene struggle in the trunk, beneath the blanket. Nobody else was out, except for the clerk working at the store, keeping an eye on him, no doubt wary of him stealing gas.

He clutched at his wounded arm. It was all too incredible. Zombies? Not fucking possible. Insane. They were all losing their minds. Maybe the government had done a night flight over Ludlow, sprayed something that was making them all trip. Even that made more sense than some kind of supernatural coup d'état. A police cruiser went by, lights flashing, disappearing around a bend.

So many fucking cops, Max thought. The whole fucking force looked like they were out and about. What were they doing? Rounding people up for Lazarus? Key people in the town? When was it Max's turn? Adrienne's?

The gas pump clacked off, and he replaced the cap, got his receipt, got back in his car.

"She won't shut up, Max," Adrienne said. "She's getting, I dunno, agitated. She says Lazarus is looking for her."

"For real?" Max asked. Adrienne nodded.

"We have to get out of here, Adrienne," Max said. "Seriously. If those on-ramps are barricaded, I don't know what we're going to do."

"We could run them," she said. "Take our chances."

Max had this image of spike strips and shotgun blasts. He shook his head, while Jolene called out in the back.

A van pulled up behind Max's car. Out came some men with slack faces, walking toward Max.

He turned on his car and cruised away from the gas pumps and the van. One of the men went to pump gas into the van, while the other walked into the convenience store.

A moment later, the man came out with the clerk, flat on his back, unconscious. The man who'd grabbed him was dragging him by his heel. The freak was wearing a flannel shirt and a down vest, had sandy blonde hair. He looked like a hunter.

The clerk's head clonked on the pavement as the man walked across the parking lot to the van.

"Fuck," Max said, from the vantage point of his car. He'd been about to drive off when he'd seen that. "Did you see that?"

"Yeah," Adrienne said.

Max reached under his seat and got out a tire iron, opened the door.

"Max, don't."

"Look, he's one of those freaks," Max said. "Fuck him."

He walked toward the men, one focused on filling up the van, the other opening the back of the van.

No words. Max was scared shitless, but he couldn't just let those freaks just grab somebody like that. The brazenness of the assault pissed him off.

"Hey," Max said, to the guy at the back of the van. The guy turned to look at Max, and Max smashed him in the face with the tire iron.

The man didn't cry out; there was no blood. There was just Max gasping as the shock of the impact went through the bar, into his hand. Max could see feet in the back of the van, just as the man with the smashed face grabbed at his throat.

Max bashed the man back and forth with the tire iron, until his face was unrecognizable. Still the man reached for Max, sightless, unthinking.

"Bob?" the man pumping the gas asked. "You finished back there?"

Max bashed the man in the head again, then ran around the far side of the van, coming up behind the other guy, hitting him from behind as hard as he could. This man was broad-shouldered, middle-aged, wearing a rough-hewn leather jacket and a trucker hat.

The tire iron cracked the man's skull, and he turned toward Max, only to get the tire iron in the face. Max smashed him again and again, knocking him to the ground, striking him over and over until he stopped moving. The other man

129

staggered around, searching for him with his hands. Max hit him in the head again and again, until he fell, too.

Max checked the clerk, who was unconscious, but seemed otherwise okay. He had no choice but to leave him there. He felt too exposed under the lights. The men…the zombies he'd attacked just laid there, heads smashed in. There was no blood. Not a drop.

In the van, it looked like there were a dozen people in there. Max shut the door in the back and ran to the van, turning it on. He wheeled around the gas pump island, drove up to Adrienne.

"Take my car," he said. "Let's go to my place, I guess."

"What about the Interstate?" Adrienne asked.

"You can try for it, maybe," Max said. "Try to get to Pittsburgh. But if there's a roadblock, you come back to my place, alright?"

He didn't know what else to do, his hands shaking. He couldn't believe he'd done what he'd done. He'd never killed anybody, never had even gotten in a fight.

"I'm going to my place," he said. "We'll see what we can do for these people."

Adrienne got out of the car and put her hand on Max's, giving it a squeeze. "That was really brave, Max. Crazy, but brave. Crazy-brave."

She smiled at him, and Max smiled back. He was breathing heavy, winded from the exertion. Killing zombies took a lot out of a man. The rest of him ached almost as much as his arm.

"Look, you be careful, alright?" Max said.

"Sure," Adrienne said. "I'm careful."

Max leaned out and kissed Adrienne, and she kissed him back, holding his face with one of her hands.

"Call me when you get there," Max said. "K?"

"Alright," she said. "Bye, Max."

Then she hopped back into his car, looked at him a moment with a smile, and headed toward the Heights.

Max drove the van through town again, toward the industrial strip, where his place was. He parked and opened the back of the van. There were twelve people stacked in there, hands tied with plastic bands, behind their backs. Some of them were moaning.

He ran into his place and got out some shears, then climbed back into the van, cutting the bonds, after checking that everybody was alive and breathing.

The victims were young men and young women, all about the same age, something like 18 to 24 years.

"Hey," he said. "Wake up, you guys."

It took some doing, but he roused them all. They all had stories about being waylaid by those guys, who just ambushed them and put them in the van, without word or explanation.

Max explained what he knew, telling them that there were freak cultists trying to kidnap people and drown them in the river. He left out the zombie part, not wanting them to think he was nuts, and figured warning them about the freaks was hopefully enough.

"They all look the same," he said. "Dead faces, dead eyes. Just blank as can be. If anybody you know is like that, they're one of them. You can just tell. No emotions, no pain. Nothing. They're like walking dead. All of the cultists are like that. Just stick with the people you know, okay? And if you run into those freaks, just get away from them if you can. Oh, and it seems like the police are in on it—they've barricaded routes into and out of town. I've already tried those. Get weapons if you have any."

Part of him wanted to tell them everything, but they were already pretty shocky. Max told them they could take the van, get themselves back home or wherever they needed to go.

Max felt some pride at having done something foolish and heroic, the first time he'd stuck his neck out like that. He had just acted instinctually, hadn't really thought it out so much.

Max lit a smoke, sat down on the steps leading up to his place, scratched at his arm. He hoped Adrienne got where she needed to be, made it to the Interstate. He had been afraid to leave her to her own devices, but was sort of confident that she would make it through. Adrienne was very enterprising. If anybody could do it, she could. He was impressed at how coolly she'd taken the night's events.

He walked up to his place, keyed in, and locked the door, then sat at his computer, waking the thing up. His camera was where he'd left it. He hooked it up to his computer, uploaded the latest round of pictures, looked through them.

Jolene's dead eyes stared through the monitor at him, his blood in her gaping mouth.

Max peeled off the bandage and looked at his wounded arm. His attempts at prophylaxis had left the wound savaged and raw. It looked like hell, stung like fuck. He turned on the camcorder, pointed it at himself, then reconsidered, went to his webcam. Fuck it. Put it on the webcam.

He turned it on, recorded. "I got bitten. One of the zombies got me."

Max held up his forearm, turned it so the webcam could see it, then set it back down.

"I don't know how long I have," he said. "I wasted a couple of zombies. They were driving a van, had a bunch of people in it, victims. It all revolves around the river, drowning people in the river. The police are in on it. They have barricaded the streets. There's no way in or out of town, as far as I can tell. There's something in the river."

He uploaded the video, turned off the webcam. At least a testimonial like that might get some attention if anything happened to him.

Then he went to his medicine cabinet and took some more painkillers, then sprayed Bactine on his arm again, put fresh gauze on it, and another big bandage.

He finished up his cigarette, then washed his hands. His hands were bruised from where he'd bashed the zombie dudes.

Then he poured himself a vodka and grape soda, walked upstairs, went to his balcony, listened to Ludlow talk to itself.

7.

Heidi had not wanted Father Knightley to drop her off, wanted to stay with him, felt like he was about to do something dangerous and drastic, but she knew that her parents might be worried, and that she had to get home. It bugged her to be so conscientious. Seemed like her little sister, Lisa, was always being bad, always getting into trouble, but it was Heidi who got the third degree if anything was awry. It was like because their expectations of Lisa were so low, they gave her an unfair amount of liberty, relative to her sister.

If only they'd known that she had helped bury a dead man. That she'd shot that dead man in the face. Heidi had washed her hands repeatedly in the sink, scrubbed the dirt out from under her fingernails.

Her father, Allan Campbell, was a lawyer in Pittsburgh, would make the commute home every night. Her mom, Monica, worked part-time at City Hall.

Neither of them were home when Heidi got in. There was just Lisa, sprawled out on the sofa, watching television, eating popcorn, one popped kernel at a time, held pincerlike between black-lacquered fingernails. Lisa with her whole Goth thing, all in black, pancaked face, dyed black hair.

"Where are mom and dad?" Heidi asked. Lisa looked disdainfully at her big sister. With Lisa, everything was overturned. She was insolent when she should've been respectful of her sister's good example, she was lazy when confronted with the tireless industry of Heidi.

"I don't know," Lisa said. "They didn't call."

"And you didn't think to call them?" Heidi asked. Lisa shrugged.

"I called Matt, but he wasn't home," Lisa said. Matt Wallace was one of her Goth boyfriends, this pathetic scarecrow of a boy with hair in an unruly spray of black, and staring blue eyes that he bracketed in black mascara.

Heidi gave her sister a reproachful stare and whipped out her phone. She called their mom, first, got her voicemail, and then their dad.

Her dad picked up. "Hey, Pumpkin. I'm working late tonight. I'm sorry, I should've called. I'm buried in this personal injury case I'm working on. Tell your mother that I'm going to be late."

"Mom's not here, Dad," Heidi said, glaring at Lisa, like this was something Lisa should've done an hour ago.

"Did you call her?" Mr. Campbell asked.

"Yes, of course," Heidi said. "I got her voicemail."

"Huh," he said. "I'll call her work line, see if I can reach her. Will you and Lisa be alright?"

"Yeah, Dad," Heidi said, wanting so badly to tell her father about what had happened, but knowing that there was no way she could. Parents could only handle so much information. It was best to filter it to them in small doses. Reality was deadly to parents.

"Have your mother call me if she gets home, okay?" Her dad asked.

"Sure, Dad," she said. "When are you coming home?"

"Late," he said. "I'm sorry."

"I love you, Dad," Heidi said, wishing she could hug him.

"I love you, too, Sweetheart. Hugs to you and your sister."

"Yeah," Heidi said. Lisa looked like she was ignoring the conversation, like she was just watching the television, but she was totally eavesdropping. That was her way. Lisa was like a cat. It bugged Heidi. "Bye, Dad."

She hung up, then took her phone to its jack, to recharge.

"Dad said I'm in charge while they're gone," Heidi said.

"Hah," Lisa said, not even as vehemently as Heidi had hoped she would. Rather, it was colored with an inscrutable, familial disdain.

Heidi wanted to rest, wanted to lie down. But she was too jittery. Where was mom? Had THEY gotten to her already? It was possible. THEY were out there.

She looked at her sister, blithely eating her popcorn, one piece at a time, like a metronome set at its slowest rhythm.

Tick…tock…tick…tock.

Heidi wanted to tell her that she'd shot a man in the face, buried his body at St. Vincent's. See how she took that. It made her almost giddily amused to think that she'd done something her sister never would, for all of her Goth posturing.

There was a knock on their front door. A single, loud rapping. Then more.

"Expecting anybody?" Heidi asked.

"Only Matt," Lisa said, putting the popcorn bowl on their coffee table. "Why don't you see if it's him?"

"Why don't you?" Heidi said. "He's your skanky boyfriend."

"He's not my boyfriend," Lisa said. "He's just a boy friend. I've got a lot of boyfriends."

"Yeah, I know," Heidi said. "Everybody knows."

The knocking came again, louder.

"Alright," Lisa said. "Haven't they heard of doorbells?"

Lisa went to the peephole, looked out. "Eeew, it's Brian Auckerman."

"Who?" Heidi asked.

"Oh, a total creep," Lisa said. "Icky boy. Pizzaface."

Auckerman banged on their door again. Lisa backed away from the door.

"You get it," Lisa said.

"You're right there," Heidi said. "I'm sure he wants you."

"Lisa," Auckerman said, from the other side of the door. Muffled.

"See?" Heidi said, gesturing.

"What do you want, Pizzaface?" Lisa said.

"I want you, Lisa," Auckerman said. "Let me in."

"Uhhh, no?" Lisa said.

The knocking came harder. "Come out and play, Lisa. I want to show you something."

"Yeah, I'll bet," Lisa said. "I'm going to call the cops, you creep."

"Go ahead," Auckerman said. "Call them."

"I'm serious," Lisa said.

"So am I," Auckerman said. He hit the door harder. Heidi was in their kitchen, looking down the corridor to the foyer. Their front door was stout oak, banded and solid. She felt a splash of fear in her, a conviction that Auckerman was one of THEM.

Another knock on the door.

"Go away," Lisa said. "Not interested."

"Is the door locked?" Heidi asked. Lisa checked, nodded. Heidi went to the door, looked through the peephole.

There was Auckerman, his shiny face pale and lifeless, the acne landscape looking almost lunar in the moonlight. He seemed to look right at Heidi through the peephole, dead eyes boring into her.

"Fuck," Heidi said, making her sister snort.

"What?" Lisa asked.

"Liiiiissssaaaaaa," Auckerman said in a sing-song. "I'm coming for you, Lisa."

"Ohmigod," Heidi said. "He's one of them."

"What are you talking about?" Lisa said.

Heidi ran upstairs. "Do NOT open that door, Lisa."

Her sister looked at her like she was insane, the way she always did.

"Uh, no dangers there, Heidi. Where are you going?"

She didn't answer, just ran through upstairs, looking for their father's guns. Her father had a hunting rifle he kept locked away. It was in their room. Heidi went to it, tried the door, cursed. Locked, of course. Inside was a rifle and a shotgun, just inches away.

The knocking on the door became hammering, like a drumming sound.

BAM! BAM! BAM! BAM!

Lisa yelled something at Auckerman, then stomped away from the door, yelled that she was calling the police.

Heidi picked her brain. Mom and Dad had the keys to the gun locker, of course. There was no way of getting into the thing. Well, she could break the glass to get in. This was an emergency, in her view.

BAM! BAM! BAM!

"Liiiisaaaa," Auckerman called.

Two people in one night? Heidi thought, as she looked at the guns. She'd be a regular Bonnie Parker. Good God.

Thou Shalt Not Kill.

But then Father Knightley had already absolved her.

You couldn't kill what was already dead.

There came a loud thump on the door, a splintering sound. Heidi could hear Lisa downstairs on the phone, could hear her yelp in fright at the breaking of their front door.

Home invasion. It was a simple case of self-defense. Heidi drowned her Catholic Guilt in adrenaline, grabbed one of mom's throw pillows on their bed and put it against the glass of the gun case. Then she kicked hard at it, smashing it.

Another kick came to the door, and the splintering of the wood was louder. Lisa cried out.

"Heidi, what the fuck?!" she said. "Where are you?"

Heidi used the pillow to push away the glass, stuffing flying from the pillow as broken glass shards cut at the fabric. When enough was clear, Heidi reached in and grabbed the shotgun. It was the sensible choice.

A double-barrel thing. She broke the breech, gazed at the empty barrels. There was a box of shells on the shelf beneath the firearms. Heidi took out two shells, dropped one, picked it up, loaded the thing.

Then she grabbed the box of shells, wished she'd had some pockets. Heidi ran to the top of the stairs.

"Heidi!" Lisa cried, as the door crashed inward. Heidi half-ran down the steps, as Auckerman lurched into view, looking down the hallway at her sister with dreadful, dead eyes. He looked just like the police officer.

"Hi, Lisa," he said. "I want to show you something."

Lisa screamed, almost directly underneath Heidi. Heidi came down the steps, pointing the heavy shotgun at Auckerman. She pulled both triggers, and the shotgun roared, catching Auckerman in the chest, blasting him off his feet, nearly sending him out the front door.

Heidi, for her part, was knocked back, slipped down the stairs on her butt, her penny loafers slick on the carpeting.

Lisa screamed. "Jesus fuck, Heidi! You shot him!"

Auckerman was on his back, the shotgun having blasted a pair of holes in his chest. Smoke rose from the wounds, where his clothing had been singed. He wasn't breathing, but Heidi wasn't fooled. She'd seen this.

"You killed him," Lisa said, staring at her sister in disbelief. Heidi ignored her, kicked off her loafers, ran back up the stairs, where the box of shells was, right at the top of the steps. She broke the breech and expelled the empty shells, grabbed for another pair with tingling fingers. The shotgun was a 12-gauge, the buckshot, double-O. She was grateful that their father, in his lawyerly way, had pedantically instructed his daughters in use of the guns.

Auckerman sat up, smiled at Lisa. Lisa screamed. Then Auckerman looked up at Heidi. He stood up. Not a drop of blood was spilled.

"Naughty, naughty," he said. Heidi ignored him, stuffed the shells into the shotgun, closed it again.

Auckerman ran and grabbed Lisa, who was losing it in the foyer. He just scooped her up over his shoulder. Heidi took the box of shells with her as she went down the steps, while Lisa fought to get free of Auckerman.

"I'm going to show you the Light in the Dark, Lisa," he said.

"Put her down," Heidi said. Auckerman turned, whacking Lisa's head on the doorframe.

"Ow!" Lisa said, pausing in her screams.

"You wouldn't want to hit your sister, right?" Auckerman said.

Heidi lowered the shotgun, aimed at his legs, and fired. The shotgun blew off one of his legs at the knee, sent it spinning off into a corner, by their umbrella stand.

Auckerman tumbled, dropping Lisa as he fell. He didn't even really catch himself, but just fell. Lisa cursed as she hit the ground, then kicked away from him. There was no fear in Auckerman's eyes, nor pain. He just kept crawling for her sister.

Heidi reloaded the shotgun once again, as Auckerman crawled for her sister, who was cursing and wailing.

She leaned over the railing, pointed the shotgun right at Auckerman's head, and pulled the trigger, without a word. The shotgun exploded his head, and at last Auckerman stopped moving.

There was no blood. Heidi reloaded again, went down the steps, shoved the front door as shut as it would go. She could only imagine what the neighbors were thinking.

Lisa was crying, mascara running down her cheeks. Heidi slipped on her loafers again, her ears ringing from the shotgun blasts. She could barely hear, and the smoke from the gun filled their foyer.

"You murdered him," Lisa said.

"He was dead," Heidi said. "Didn't you see?"

Absurdly, the leg she'd blown off was standing in the corner. Heidi could hear the sound of police sirens.

"The police are coming!" Lisa said.

"We have got to get out of here," Heidi said. "We have to hide."

"What? Why?"

"Trust me," Heidi said. "Please. For once."

8.

Mal had requisitioned two charter buses. One of the Brethren worked at the Travelot Bus Company as a manager, and Stuart Robinson had been one of the first to end up in the Mercy River. This mustached, mildly fat man had come out of the River with a keen sense of his place in the order of things, had mentioned the buses to Mal, who had a vision.

Maybe "vision" is too strong a word—Mal had an invasion plan. He had gathered his biggest, burliest Brethren, and he had them pile into the buses. Then he had some of his other Brethren cross the River, make their way to the Big Star Riverboat Casino, to wait in the shadows of the thing, in the water, in the dark.

Then he had the police who had been Brethren escort the Travelot buses to the casino, itself, Mal riding at the front of the first bus.

How odd it was to be coming back to his former place of employment, which had been like a second home to him, this temple to American commerce. It was like holding something at arm's length, this faraway life he used to live, when he breathed and sweated and fretted, before he found the peace of a stilled heart, before the Angel had come to him and delivered him from fear and death. They all felt that, he knew, that communion of spirit that compelled them. The Angel was in each of the Brethren. Mal was aware of his good fortune at being the first, but he would have gladly joined, regardless. To go from what he had been before to this, it was altogether extraordinary. It was miraculous and magical, and he knew this like he knew nothing else.

The Big Star was now an alien place, a vestige of his past life, like the cast-off skin of a snake or a spider. He had shed this past, and this place which had held him fast now had no power over him. But he could remember.

The parking lot had been full, as it always was. Rain or shine, in good times or bad, people came to the Big Star, in vain hope of finding their fortune.

As the buses made their way into the lot, Mal had specific instructions for the Brethren. They were to mix and mingle, to wend their way into the casino. He knew just where to send them, because of his years working there.

The bright star shined on the windows of the buses as they came to the offloading area, and everybody got out, walked in, Mal at the head of them, like he was Genghis Khan. The forced opulence of the place, the studied decadence of it. If he were still capable of feeling it, he would have been impressed by the colors, by the thick carpeting, by the musky scent in the air, the thick stands of cut flowers that were brought in daily. So much money spent baiting the traps with what they thought the no-brow locals would consider worldly and sophisticated. But it was a trap, just the same.

And that's all a casino really was—a trap. Mal liked that notion. One massive lure, intended to draw people in and part them with their money. That was how he knew he had to do this, why it was so central to his scheme, so vital to the Angel's interests. Take the casino, make it his.

He had Ramsey and his men take out the staff, first. That was the easy part. Not the servers, not the dealers—the management. The security. The cops came in and trotted them out, starting with Bernie Ross, Mal's former supervisor, but getting all of them. All of those petty, powerful men who ran things behind the scenes, who were hidden behind secrecy and security, who watched the casino run through camera eyes that bulged in arachnid black from the ceiling, unobtrusive but intruding in everyone's lives. Those camera eyes made him think of the Angel, that sense of glossy observation, devoid of anything that could be understood as emotion. Eyes that saw you for what you were, and nothing more. Eyes that saw right through you, and never blinked. Ever.

Mal had them all walked out to the balcony out back, and, without fanfare, thrown over the side, into the River, where the other Brethren waited to receive them. One at a time, over they went, while Mal watched.

There was no point in delivering a sermon to the Breathers. They would understand soon enough. Mal was never one for theatrics. He just did the Angel's bidding, and fed the sacrifices to the river, one after another, watched them cry out and splash into the water, to be pulled down by the waiting Brethren, who held them under, as the water boiled and churned from their struggles.

Somewhere, deep within the water, the Angel watched, and he could feel that It approved of this, welcomed the sacrifices. Deep within the river, there was light. It was the Light in the Dark, the blessed tidings of the Angel.

When it came to Bernie's turn, he gazed at Mal without comprehension.

"Mal, what the hell do you think you're doing?"

"I'm taking over the Big Star, Bernie," Mal said. "New management."

And over he went, right over the side. Mal watched them get drowned in the River, without a care in the world. Nobody had seen that coming, he was sure. For all the things that the Big Star was ready for, invasion wasn't one of them.

Once the management had been taken care of, once Security had ended up in the River, Mal turned and went back into the Casino, and had the other Brethren go to work, dragging people off their games, hustling them to the balcony, as he'd instructed them, and sent them over the side. Their faces would have been comical, if Mal still had a sense of humor. They all looked the same, that moment of anger and stunned outrage as they were ejected from their game, that trace of fear and confusion as they wondered what they had done wrong, what rule they had violated. The fearful fury as they were tossed over the side, into the dark and waiting waters below. And, sometimes, wide eyes and wider mouths, crying out, reaching for the blinking light of the Big Star, as they were drowned by unseen hands of the waiting Brethren, themselves dark and drenched shadows, grasping and silent.

With the Big Star light going on and off, bathing the river in a warm yellow-gold glow for a moment, then the contrast with the darkness and the sodium lights across the river making more shadow than they banished, it was entrancing to Mal, watching the passing of these Breathers as if under a very slow strobe light.

Splash and grab.

Darkness.

Light.

Struggle and gasp.

Darkness.

Light.

Hands upraised.

Darkness.

Light.

Churning water, shadow-soaked.

Darkness.

Light.

Light in the Darkness.

And, at the center of it, Mal, watching it all transpire. He had been very careful, had wanted it to go smoothly, had used what was left of his knowledge of the place to allow the Brethren to effectively empty it of patrons and employees. The great thing was that he had them take people out area by area, table by table, so it didn't cause an immediate distraction.

In all the noise of the casino, the flashing lights, patrons didn't notice until it was too late, until their number had come up. Sure, some of the dealers noticed, because dealers were paid to notice things. Mal had the police take out the dealers and the pit bosses, while the others, the burly Brethren, would march the patrons to the balcony.

It was almost like the Casino has become a giant slot machine, and, instead of disgorging coins, it was spilling people over its balcony, feeding souls to the Angel. Mal rather liked that image. Jackpot.

He watched the Breathers splash into the River, saw the Brethren pulling them under, watched the water churn and ripple in that flicking golden light and deep, nourishing shadow. It was beautiful. The water was like a tapestry. Mal could not be moved, but it was stirring, just the same, to see the Angel so well-fed, the shimmer in the depths.

Officer Ramsey approached him to one side, watching the Breathers drown. Did he find it as transfixing as Mal did, this massive sacrifice? His lieutenant was not prone to seeing the grander scheme of things the way Mal did. He was more of an operations man, focused on clear-cut action items.

"I don't understand this," Ramsey said. "Why the Big Star?"

"We need it," Mal said.

"We can't run a casino," Ramsey said.

"The management can," Mal said. "Three days hence, they will."

"No one will be fooled," Ramsey said. The hulk of a man would have been threatening to Mal, but no longer. He gazed up at his lieutenant.

"Let me worry about that," Mal said.

The last of the patrons were being dragged from the casino, including ones taken from the hotel, in various states of undress. All of them were confused and protesting, struggling against their captors, angry and confused, some afraid, most of them indignant and uncomprehending. The Brethren, to their credit, were unfazed by this. Not that Mal had any reason to feel concern about this. The Brethren knew what was required of them. Unlike Breathers, they never shirked, never questioned, never doubted, never faltered. The covenant of the Angel kept them on the path that had been made for them.

Ramsey didn't say a thing, just watched the people being drowned below them. Mal watched, too. It was compelling. They had all made that journey not so long ago. The memory of the Angel remained, that sense of deliverance, of transcendence. There was divinity in those depths. Mal knew. Ramsey knew. All of the Brethren knew. All of the Breathers would know, eventually. The Angel would enfold them all in its silvery, luminescent arms, and hold them fast, until all were one.

"Have someone put up signs that say 'Closed for Remodeling' until we get everybody back in place," Mal said.

"Right," Ramsey said, turning away from the balcony with some sense of reluctance.

"Have you fed your wife and boys to the Angel, Ramsey?" Mal asked.

"No," Ramsey said. "They were gone when I came for them."

"We'll find them," Mal said.

"I know," Ramsey said.

"You can give them to the Angel," Mal said. "Of course."

"Of course," Ramsey said.

Mal could not tell whether this prospect appealed to Ramsey or not, and, in truth, he didn't even care. He only cared that their souls would join everyone's, in the river.

9.

Special Agent Frank Holliday looked at the pictures from Ludlow, had pored over them. He didn't know what to make of them, in honesty. If it wasn't a hoax, something bad was happening in that town.

He'd called the Ludlow Police Department, but had been put on hold. The County Sheriff hadn't answered.

That didn't leave him much to go on, so he called back Miss Morse, to confirm that he'd received the photographs.

He got her voicemail.

"Miss Morse, it's Special Agent Holliday," he said. "Just letting you know we got your pictures, and we're going to have them analyzed. I'll get back with you, but if you could call me, I'd appreciate it."

He left his number, his direct line, then hung up. Then he tried the Ludlow PD again, and the County Sheriff. Again he didn't get through. Something was going on. It might not've been what Miss Morse thought it was, but something unusual was happening, if those photographs were to believed.

On a whim, he called the Mayor's Office, but got their voicemail. Apparently nobody was answering their phone in Ludlow.

That also made him wonder. Ludlow was about 45 miles north/northwest of Pittsburgh. That was a doable drive, of course. Even if what he really wanted to do was go home.

But it couldn't hurt to take a look, as he saw it. Just see if everything was alright. So, he left a message saying he was going to Ludlow to check things out, told Special Agent Robert Maxwell where he was going, and then took a little road trip.

The drive to Ludlow didn't jump out at him in any particular way. The river corridors that fed into Pittsburgh were a blend of Rust Belt industrial overproduction, the thumbprint of wartime expansion, urban blight, and post-industrial decay, with green mountains folded in like moldy rolled dough.

Special Agent Holliday didn't know what to expect in Ludlow, frankly. He thought Miss Morse was a credible witness, judging from his talk with her.

As he went further along the river roads, toward the Mercy River, he saw the industrial pipelines become more patchworked, rail lines and industrial parks set between green mountain hideaways, where he imagined moonshiners and meth labs were tucked, just out of sight, if not out of reach.

He thought about the bizarre apocalyptic cult Miss Morse had mentioned, the photographs of the victims. Assuming there were any victims. He thought he would get to the Ludlow Police Department and make some inquiries, see whether there'd been a spike in missing persons reports.

Holliday's eyes went to the street signs, showing about 18 miles until Ludlow. The Mercy River flowed thick and insolent near the road, a gray-green snake that was part of the river network that fed the valley and merged into the Ohio River.

Then a ribbon of green blocked his view of the river on one side, with civilization represented by strip malls and fast food restaurants.

He tried calling Miss Morse again, again got her voicemail, again left a message with her.

Then he pulled into a gas station, refueled his car, stopped in the restroom, got himself a Diet Coke. His wife had been insisting that he wean himself from coffee, but he still needed a good caffeine fix, and thought diet cola was a good substitute, not so strong.

The clerk was a young man of uncertain ethnicity, tanned, bearded, with big eyes. Holliday took his soda and went out, got back to his car. It would be evening by the time he got home, assuming nothing kept him in Ludlow.

He went toward the exit ramp off the interstate, saw that it was closed. Detour information indicated there was a route at Quarry Road that was accessible.

Holliday drove to the next exit, saw that it was closed, too, and pulled off at the side of the road.

There was a Sheriff's cruiser parked at the end of the exit. Holliday drove around the blocked exit and worked his way to the second barricade, where a pasty-faced sheriff's deputy stood, wearing aviator sunglasses.

The man was watching Holliday, approached with his hands out.

"Road's closed, Sir," he said. His nametag had him as Tibbs.

"Special Agent Holliday, FBI," Holliday said, holding up his ID. "What's the problem, Officer Tibbs? Anything I can help with? The other exit was closed, too. I hadn't seen any word of closed exits on the traffic reports."

"Chemical spill," Officer Tibbs said. "Very dangerous. Something got out of one of the train cars, Special Agent Holliday."

The man's demeanor was flat, his voice unexpressive, compared with the information he was conveying.

"Really? I hadn't heard anything on the radio," he said.

Officer Tibbs shrugged. "They don't tell me anything. The Hazmat guys just told me to keep this exit clear. They don't want people coming into town and coming right in the middle of it."

Holliday looked past the man, saw a few other cars parked on the roadside, leading up to the barricade.

"What happened to them?" Holliday asked.

Officer Tibbs shrugged again. "We had to impound their vehicles. They tried to get past the barricade. There was a bit of a panic when the accident happened."

"Sounds serious," Special Agent Holliday said. "You wouldn't mind me looking into it, would you?"

Tibbs held up his hand. "I'm sorry, Special Agent Holliday, but I was ordered to keep everybody out. That means everybody."

Holliday was familiar enough with the jurisdictional pissing contests that went on between local law enforcement and the Bureau to not be put off by this. Being part of the elite end of law enforcement earned Agents a mix of envy and admiration and resentment from the locals.

"I don't know, Officer Tibbs," Holliday said. "A hazardous spill sounds like something the Bureau might want to look into. Could have been a terrorist incident."

"We've got people looking into it," Tibbs said.

"I could get a Hazardous Materials Response Unit here in less than a half hour," Holliday said. "No offense to Ludlow's finest, but we've got experts. Physical Security Specialists, that kind of thing."

"No one, Special Agent Holliday," Tibbs said. "I'm not supposed to let anyone past."

There was no way Ludlow had better personnel than the HMRU people in Pittsburgh. No way. Holliday was only willing to allow a local so much leeway. And what's more, he didn't think the man was being honest. He thought Officer Tibbs was lying to him.

"Alright," Holliday said. He went back to his car, got in, dialed up Pittsburgh. "Bob, it's Frank."

"What's up? You find anything in Ludlow?" Maxwell asked.

"In a word, yes," Holliday said. Tibbs watched him from the barricade, without expression. "Something about a hazardous materials spill in town, something with one of the trains. I suggested an HMRU come down here to look into it, but the local law enforcement wasn't going for it. I think something's up."

"Do you want me to have an HMRU down there? I can check to see if there was any accident reported," Maxwell said.

"That's just it," Holliday said. "I don't think there was a spill. I think there's something going on here. Have you looked at the photographs I sent you?"

He had sent Maxwell the files he'd gotten from Miss Morse, just to get a second opinion. Bob had been busy with another case, hadn't looked at them before he'd gone.

"Not yet, Frank," Maxwell said. "I'll get to it."

Deputy Tibbs walked up to Holliday's car, taking his time. Holliday entertained the notion of running the barricade, but instead turned on his car and backed out of there, away from the pale sheriff's deputy.

"Where's the sheriff's office around here?" Holliday asked. "Can you look it up for me?"

"Sure," Maxwell said. "It's at 127 Delmont Avenue, across the river. East side."

That was fine by Holliday, who was already on the east side of Ludlow. Holliday pulled past the first barricade, leaving Tibbs behind. The deputy still watched him, the aviator shades making him look like some kind of bug. Holliday looked for traffic on the Interstate, then accelerated, was on his way.

"Tell me how to get there," he said.

10.

The Big Star was dead tonight. Lincoln Booth thought that sourly as he walked around the place. The lights were on, sure enough, but nobody was home. He'd never seen the place so desolate. He'd cashed his check and was looking to play some blackjack, but he couldn't find a dealer to save his life.

Where the hell was everybody?

He'd put on his worn jeans and his worn cowboy boots, and his nice white shirt, had his lucky gold nugget ring he wore, big and thick on his thick fingers, and the turquoise and silver ring on his other hand. He'd come prepared to win. He was hoping to win big and get himself one of those sweet complementary rooms for the Gold Star patrons. Maybe find that Suzy Mayweather, the waitress with the hair bleached to gold and the fake boobs and year-round tan, have her come up there with him. He was pretty sure the Big Star frowned on that kind of fraternizing, but on the other hand, he didn't care. What was the point of winning if you didn't get to savor your prizes?

The banks of slot machines chirped and flashed, unattended. Not a grandma in sight. And the craps tables were similarly unattended.

The concierge had been rather blank-faced, the brunette named Sandee—he couldn't remember her last name. She'd ushered him in without her usual smile, so he knew the place was open, but where the hell was everybody?

The whole point of a casino was its life and activity, all the frenzied energy, the faces of the patrons in that delicious place between hope and fear, anticipation of reward and dread of punishment, a Pavlovian play acted out at row after row, table after table, with Lincoln Booth to work his leathery charm on the staff. He wasn't handsome enough to be Robert Redford, but put himself somewhere in the neighborhood of Nick Nolte, maybe in the 70s, before his lifestyle caught up with him. Booth kept a principled tan as an arbiter of his good health. Maybe a bit retro, but it was part of his charm.

Blackjack was Lincoln's game, and he meant to play it. Only wusses clung to the slots, and cowards played craps; the real action was, as always, at the proper table games. And there were a baker's dozen of blackjack tables, a handful of poker tables, and even a baccarat table. Ludlow was a small town, but it took a lot of pride in its casino, raked in a lot of money from it.

Booth worked as a forklift operator at the Riverworks Industrial Park, loading and unloading freight that came in on some of the trains, or up from the barges. He worked hard at that, and when he wasn't busy slinging tons of freight, making other men rich with his work, or paying support checks for his ex-wife Marjorie, Lincoln was at the Big Star, where he felt like he could actually be somebody. He mattered here, because he was actually good at blackjack. He could play.

He got himself a thousand dollars' worth of chips from the unsmiling cashier and strode through the Big Star like he owned the place. He wasn't yet confident enough to head out to Atlantic City or Las Vegas, but he felt like he was probably one of the top 50 players in the Tri-State Area, and could definitely give as good as he got.

So, striding through the banks of unattended slots, on to the Emerald Room, where all the table games were, Lincoln was confident that, regardless of how slow a night it was, he was going to come out ahead.

Pushing past the gold and green doors that led into the Emerald Room (which was, itself, lit with bright green argon letters), he was dismayed to see a handful of souls in there. Two big guys at either side of the door, and this pale-faced ghoul sitting at one of the blackjack tables.

Lincoln recognized him. He worked at the Big Star. Malcolm something or other. He'd seen him around. He wasn't a dealer.

"Where's Joe Stiles?" Lincoln asked. Stiles was one of his favorite dealers.

"Stiles has the night off," Malcolm said. He had a deck of cards on the table in front of him.

"Did Cohen make you a dealer, now, or what?" Booth asked.

"Cohen works for me, now," Malcolm said. "Did you know that, Mr. Booth?"

That was not possible. Malcolm was some kind of bottle washer. He couldn't remember what the kid did, just remembered seeing him lurking around, like some kind of fucking waif. The kid had dead eyes. So did the burly guys who lurked by the door. Booth had the uncomfortable awareness of being the only one in the room who was breathing. It was a subconscious thing, surely his imagination.

"You like to gamble, don't you, Mr. Booth?" Malcolm asked.

"Sure," Booth said.

"Well, let's play a game, then," Malcolm said. He dealt out the cards to Booth, like they were playing blackjack for real.

"What're the stakes?" Booth asked.

"Your life," Malcolm said.

The guys in the room, the guys by the door, came over, stood near Booth. Big, big guys who smelled like the river. What the hell was this?

"My life?"

Malcolm nodded, unblinking, unsmiling.

"If you win, you can walk out of here," Malcolm said. "If you lose, then I show you something in the River."

"Are you fucking kidding me?" Booth asked. He moved to go, but the big guys stood nearby, ready to grab him.

"This is no joke, Mr. Booth. Let's play. Bets?"

"I want to talk to Cohen," Booth said.

"I told you, I'm running the Big Star, now," Malcolm said. "You deal with me, or with nobody. You understand me, Mr. Booth? Mr. High Roller?"

Booth laid down a $100 chip. The kid was out of his mind.

He was dealt 17, while the kid showed a 5.

"Double down," he said.

Malcolm laid the cards down, showed another 5 and a ten to Booth's 3. They matched at 20.

Booth felt a trickle of sweat at the nape of his neck. He threw down $200 on the next bet, with the kid showing a Jack of Clubs to his 2 of Spades and a Jack of Spades.

"Hit me," Lincoln said, and was rewarded with an 8 of Diamonds. A good, solid 20.

The kid turned his cards over. A 6 of Diamonds, then an 8 of Spades.

"You lose," Lincoln said. "Dealer busts."

Malcolm looked down at the cards, icy-cold, not a lick of emotion on his face. Completely unreadable, like stone.

"Congratulations, Mr. Booth," Malcolm said. "Well played."

Booth slid the chips over to his pile.

"So, I can go now?" Lincoln asked.

"No," Malcolm said.

"But you said that if I won, I could leave," Lincoln said.

"Best two out of three," Malcolm said.

The burly guys behind Lincoln weren't moving, so Booth took a gamble. It wasn't his first time, by any means. This kid couldn't play.

Where the hell was Cohen, anyway? The fat man should have been walking around, glad-handing everybody. The place should've been hopping.

He bet $100, and the kid dealt, giving Lincoln an 8 and a 6 to his Jack.

"Hit me," Lincoln said, and got another 6, giving him 20. Good enough. He gazed across at the kid, who gazed at him without expression.

Down came a 2 of Clubs.

Then an Ace of Clubs.

Malcolm dealt another card.

Queen of Spades.

"Dealer busts," Lincoln said. "I win. Again."

The kid set the deck down, folded his hands in front of him.

"Get out of here, Mr. Booth. Get out of Ludlow. Do not come back," Malcolm said. "If I see you in town again, you're going to end up in the River."

Lincoln slid his winnings from the table, gave a nervous glance over his shoulder at the brutes, who stepped back when Malcolm nodded to them.

Booth stepped around the goons, because goons is what they were, pure and simple, and he trotted out of the Emerald Room, walked over to the cashier, looking over his shoulder, nervous as hell. The casino was making its usual noise, but not a soul was in this place, not a patron in sight.

"Cash these out for me," he said, drumming his fingers on the counter, while the cashier took the chips and turned them into cash.

"$2400, Mr. Booth," the cashier said. "Congratulations."

He folded the money in half and stuffed it into his jeans and walked out of there, mindful of that Malcolm kid standing at the entry to the Emerald Room, watching him from across the casino floor, with those unblinking basilisk eyes. Never in his life had Lincoln Booth ever wanted to leave a casino more than he left the Big Star that day.

He walked out of there, got to his pickup truck, and he got the hell out of there, and he never went back.

II.

Father Knightley hadn't known what he was going to do.

He had driven through town with his golf clubs, hoping that he would think of a plan of action as he drove. Part of him wanted to just drive to the Church of Lazarus and shoot him.

It wasn't the most Christian of impulses, but at the same time, he felt like he was something of a crusader, a holy warrior, with a very important mission. He could not fail in his task. Not if Ludlow was to be saved from Lazarus.

But when he'd driven down to that area, he'd seen several school buses parked in the viaduct, blocking the way. He'd have to go there on foot.

So, he parked some distance away from the viaduct, and put on his golf bag, and walked along the ribbon of wilderness that flanked the railroad embankment, found a break in the rusting fencing, and walked up the hill to the level railroad yard, admired the many paired stretches of tracks, the steel shiny from the regular use they endured.

He wasn't about to lug the golf bag across all of those tracks, so he took the shotgun and a nine-iron, and made his way toward the river, looking this way and that for trains. For the moment, it was clear, with only some empty boxcars lined on one of the extra lanes, silent, motionless. It was all very quiet, not even any traffic humming on the Mercy River Bridge. That seemed strange to Father Knightley, made him glance upward. But the bridge held onto its secrets. There was no way of telling what was going on up there.

Knightley crossed to the far side, slid down the embankment, and checked the shotgun. He'd already cocked it, but still checked to see if a round was chambered. It was.

He crept quietly through the brush, past the tangled thickets, toward one of the great concrete pylons that formed the foot of the Mercy River Bridge. The trees and brambles reached for him, having shed their leaves.

At the shore, there were hundreds of those things, standing by great fires, milling about. He could recognize some of them, despite the mud. The people of Ludlow. And there was Mal Lazarus, preaching to them, some distance away, like an oversized crow, dressed in black.

Father Knightley took out the shotgun, wondered if he could shoot Lazarus from this distance. He didn't think he could. He'd never shot a gun before. And this was a policeman's riot gun, not a hunting rifle. It surely wasn't intended for use at this distance. Still, he didn't know what else to do.

Then he heard something creeping in the bushes behind him. He turned and looked, saw a dog, a mutt, creeping toward him, ears flat on its head, teeth bared. A brown dog with white patches, matted fur.

Rabid? He thought. The animal looked sick to him, mud across its muzzle. And the way it moved struck him as wrong. The thing was stalking toward him, the way he'd seen dogs go after squirrels, that intent gaze, that furtive stepping, before the final spring.

This dog didn't have an intent gaze, however; its eyes were flat and lifeless, but the teeth and the snarl made its intentions plain.

"Go away," Knightley said to the dog, but the thing just snarled at him. Then he heard some crunching in the leaves around him, nearby, and saw a couple of cats stalking toward him, a calico and an orange tabby. They hissed at him, stalked toward him. The same dead eyes.

The ground around him was alive with crunching leaves and snarling animals, he realized, looking around. All of them stalking toward him.

Big dogs, small dogs, cats of every color, all snarling at him, all walking his way. Many beasts, one and all, like they'd been in the river. All of them with matted fur.

That gave him pause.

He hissed at them, quietly, but they didn't flinch, didn't startle. He looked around for something to throw at the animals, and saw more approaching up the hill. The animals weren't moving right. There was something wrong about them. Father Knightley didn't want to risk shooting the shotgun at them, for that would alert Lazarus and his infernal congregation.

So he set the shotgun down, raised the golf club. The animals were between him and the railroad tracks, were cutting him off.

He took as swing at the nearest dog, expecting the animal to leap out of the way, but the dog took the swing with a meaty thud, the golf club denting its flank. The dog snapped at him, but didn't yelp or otherwise react to what was surely a painful blow.

The animals kept advancing, and Father Knightley was faced with a choice of trying to vault over the animals, or perhaps sidestep them, or else slip down lower, near the riverbank. Knightley swung again with his golf club, dashing in the dog's skull. The dog fell over, but the rest kept on him, forcing him farther away from the tracks.

There was no blood spilled with the dead dog; just the emptiness of its stoved-in head, the ruin of bone and tissue that comprised it. Lazarus had turned these animals into his servants.

It piqued Father Knightley to have been outwitted by Mr. Lazarus. That this monstrous man had thought of a way of protecting himself that had not, could not have occurred to the priest.

Where was the justice in this? How could God countenance these unholy things, these sins against His natural order?

As he saw the animals stalking him, Knightley felt sorrow and pity for them, for all of the victims of Lazarus. They were simply pawns in some diabolical game. Maybe they all were.

It was how he lived his life. Knightley had always understood that God worked in mysterious ways, that His plan for mankind was ineffable, inscrutable. It was a blessing to know one's place in the order of things. From God to Angel to Man to Animal, a divine order.

God made the world, and everything in it. He made His angels to tend to it. He made Man in His own image, and some of His angels rebelled, perhaps jealous of the love God showed His creation.

That always stuck in Knightley's craw—the envy of the angels. All of them were God's creations; how could any be seen more favorably than another? How could envy and pride tarnish an angel's heart?

Perhaps God was not perfect, after all. The loss of Lucifer and so many of the angels. Hadn't Lazarus spoken of the Angel in the Depths?

Maybe this was one of God's own fallen angels at work here, in Ludlow. It gave Knightley pause.

The snap of animal teeth brought him back to this world.

Seeing their eyes upon him, those same lifeless eyes, Father Knightley knew that Lazarus had drowned the animals, had fed them to the same monstrosity in the river, that they were as lost as the other members of his infernal congregation.

Another dog appeared, a big mongrel, muscles rippling. The animals were driving him toward the river, pushing him toward it in a wedge of bared teeth. Knightley's feet slipped in the dead leaves as he was driven down the embankment in this slow clash of wills between man and animal.

Down the hillside Father Knightley went, the animals snarling after him. Dogs and cats of every variety, all orphans and strays, unwanted. One of the dogs snapped at him, and Knightley took a swing at it. As he did, the animals all pounced on him, sinking their teeth in him wherever they could.

Knightley howled, seeing stars, feeling teeth at his wrists, thighs, forearms, shoulders, knees. The animals clung to him, the cats sank their claws into his back, his chest, while the dogs shook their heads, leaned hard on him, forced him into the water.

Father Knightley fell backward with a splash, tried to cry out, but the big mongrel jumped on his chest, clamped down on his throat with its cold jaws.

The animals piled atop him, forced him under the water, and Knightley couldn't help but swallow the water as he thrashed. And worse, the water went into his lungs, making him cough and gasp.

The world blurred above him, the water filled with his blood, as the animals forced him deeper into the water.

He slid down piled rocks, gripping the mongrel dog with his hands, trying to get it to release him, but it was hard, as the other animals held onto his arms, like dozens of weights, holding him down.

It can't end like this for me, Knightley thought. *God, show me that Your mercy still holds sway in this wicked, wanton world. Not like this. Please, not like this.*

Knightley's burning lungs let go, and he inhaled the Mercy River, found his blurred vision overwhelmed with blobs of black, and, at last, saw the Light in the Dark, reaching for him with silvery arms, long, like ribbons, winding around him. It wasn't God who came to the fallen priest; it was the Angel in the Depths.

And It was beautiful.

12.

Stan Reynolds was at Max's door, knocking on it. Max saw him through the peephole, saw that dead face through the fisheye lens, those flat eyes.

"Max," Stan said. "Let me in, Max. I need to see Jolene."

His voice was flat, that lifeless rush of noise past his teeth, same as Jolene's had been. He thought of Adrienne driving off with her. Adrienne, who'd basically vanished with his car. He'd called her a half-dozen times, to no avail.

"Max," Stan said, hammering the door with his fist. "Open the door, Max."

Max was grateful that his place had a metal door, legacy of its industrial past. The pounding of Stan's fist just rang on the metal.

"Max," Stan said. "Mal knows you've got Jolene."

The hammering kept coming.

"I brought friends," he said. "Brethren."

And Max heard his garage door creak, pushed by unseen hands.

"Let us in, Max," Stan said.

He was in a tracksuit, his friend was, all muddy. Each time his fist hit the door, his image blurred.

Max didn't know what to do. He doubted he could take Stan in life, let alone in unlife, or whatever it was that was animating him.

The hammering on the garage door got more insistent. It sounded like two or three pairs of fists.

Max went to his computer, logged onto his blog, turned on his webcam.

"They're coming for me," he said. "I have to get out of here."

While he was doing this, Stan's voice could be heard clearly, calling through the door.

"Max. Let us in, Max."

And banging of dead fists on a metal door.

The front door wasn't the problem. The garage door would give before the front door did. That was the weak point.

"Ludlow's sick. Stay away from it," he said. "Or bring the Army. Something. Look, it's in the river. Whatever IT is, it's in the river."

He turned off the camera, turned off his computer. Then he took a handful of memory cards, got his favorite camera and its recharger, put it in a camera bag. Took his cell phone charger, put that in there, too. Then he threw a loaf of bread and a jar of peanut butter in there, and a bottle of water. Several cans of grape soda. A bottle of vodka.

The garage door was rattling louder, and the others seemed to have picked up Stan's chorus: "Max. Open up, Max."

He took Jolene's car keys and went to her car, opened the door. His garage door opener was a button on the wall. He locked the door into his place, thought about staying there. It had to be safer than going out and about.

And yet, what if it wasn't? What if they broke into his place and cornered him? Fed him to the river? He'd die, first.

Then he thought maybe if he left his place, the things would go after him, so maybe he could lead them away.

"Max," Stan said, nearby. Max turned, saw his friend looking at him through the glass block on the far side of his garage. His dead face pressed against the glass. "I have to see Jolene, Max."

He punched the glass block, his fist making a squishy sound against the glass. There wasn't so much give on that, versus Max's metal doors.

Max looked back at the door opener. He'd have to push that button, then run to her car, then start it. He didn't know how fast the zombies would be, but knew he had to be faster.

Their punching at the garage door made it sound like it was hailing. Max pushed the garage door button and ran to the Camaro, as the gears ground and the door came up. He saw four pairs of feet beyond the door.

Without waiting to see who Stan's "friends" were, Max ran to the Camaro and closed the door, locked it, and keyed the ignition.

The car didn't start, coughed and sputtered.

"Fuck me," Max said. Stan and the others came running in. It was him and a couple of townsfolk he didn't recognize. Muddy, though. They'd been to the river, sure enough.

They pounded on the car. Stan and three other people he didn't recognize, a woman and two men. Their faces devoid of expression, their fists pounding on the car.

Max turned the ignition again, got the Camaro to start, then put the thing in reverse, floored it, shot out of the garage, with Stan sprawled across the hood. The Camaro stalled out again, and they slid silently into the street, Max struggling to turn the wheel in the absence of power steering.

Stan's dead face, black eyes, were just inches from his own, separated by that thin pane of windshield glass. Stan punched the window, and the window rang at the impact.

Max restarted the car again, careful not to give it too much gas, and then raced down the street as the others ran after him. Stan was still gripping the hood, still banging on the glass, cracking it.

"Max," he said.

"Stan," Max said, scared by those shark's eyes looking through him. He slammed on the brakes, sending Stan tumbling in front of the car. Then Max floored it, ran his friend over, grimacing at the thumping sound.

In the rearview mirror, he could see the others were still running for him. Stan got up, looking a little messed up, but standing, anyway.

Then Max drove toward Ludlow Heights, where Adrienne had gone. He was acutely aware of being in Jolene's car, afraid that Officer Ramsey would pull him over if he saw him.

There were many people walking through downtown, pale, blank apparitions. Dead-faced. They were grabbing a townsperson out of Mace Hardware. It was a young man. He was being dragged toward a moving truck, the door in the back opened.

"Fuck," Max said.

He drove into the crowd with the Camaro, smashing into them, knocking them across the hood, running over a couple. The man was dropped.

"Get in!" Max yelled, unlocking the doors. One of the freaks was on the hood of the Camaro, some dead-faced man dressed like a postal carrier. His bushy gray-white eyebrows almost as gray as the rest of his face. Max threw the car in reverse, peeling out, knocking the man off his hood. Then Max shifted back to drive and pinned the man under the front of his car.

The clerk at Mace ran to the car, opened the door, dove in. Max hardly waited for him to get into the car before fishtailing backwards. He glimpsed other people in the back of the truck, trussed, eyes full of fear.

The freaks (Max still resisted calling them zombies) that weren't squished got up and ran after them.

"Thanks, dude," the clerk said. "Those psychos just piled in the store, grabbed the guns, grabbed the customers. Grabbed me."

There wasn't time to think, to do anything. Max couldn't, in good conscience, leave those people behind. But each moment he lingered increased the chances of getting caught, himself.

Max peeled out and whipped the car into gear and drove around the block, trying not to draw attention to himself more than he already had, although the dents in the hood of the car, the broken grille in the front, would telegraph what had happened to anybody looking. There was even a spider-cracked flower in the windshield where the mailman's head had hit on the first impact, where Stan had punched.

The freaks ran after them.

"What the hell is wrong with them?" the clerk asked. He was a young guy, goatee beard, skinny, thick-rimmed glasses.

"They're dead," Max said. He rounded the block again, took a left, then another left. He was coming back for the truck from the other direction. "Like zombies."

The truck was where it was, the bodies laid out in the street. Some people were looking, commenting.

"Try to get out of town if you can," Max said. "Just don't use the main roads. If there's a barricade, like cops or anything, avoid it."

"What are you going to do?" the clerk asked. His nametag said his name was Seth. White letters on black. Hi, my name is SETH.

"I'm going to drive that truck," Max said. "Get it out of downtown. Look, the cops are in on it. Anybody who's not right, they're in on it, alright? They're all fucked up like those people. You watch out, and if they get you, they'll take you to the river and drown you, make you one of them."

It was probably too much for Seth to take in at once, as he looked at Max like he was nuts, but Max gestured to the bodies laid out on the street.

"Look, who do you want to believe? Me or them?"

He parked the Camaro, grabbed his camera bag, then ran to the truck. Seth didn't wait around, drove back through town in a squeal of tires.

Max got into the cab of the truck, a Ryder truck, and turned it on, drove it up the street. Of course, with the door open in the back, there'd be all sorts of trouble. However, he had to get those people out of there.

He was sweating, breathing fast. The cops would turn up at some point. He was sure of it. His luck would run out. You didn't just run a bunch of people down with impunity. He looked at the wound on his arm. He didn't know how much time he had, anyway.

The freaks rounded the corner, came right at him. They'd chased him around the block, alright. Max didn't recognize them, was amazed at how many people in town he didn't know, but then he didn't get out as much as he probably should have.

He plowed into three men, caught them broadside, sent them flying, didn't bother stopping.

No blood, just the crunching compression of steel and plastic against flesh. They flew off, one crumpling against a mailbox, the others into a storefront, Miller's Bakery. One of the men mashed a wedding cake into oblivion with his undead ass.

Max could hear people rolling around in the back. He had to park the truck someplace. But not in town.

Instead, he drove up Quarry Road, toward the Heights, figured at least that would give them some breathing room. Downtown was looking more perilous by minute.

Glancing beside him, he saw some guns piled up: pistols, air rifles, shotguns, hunting rifles, and boxes of ammunition.

"What the fuck?" Max asked aloud, remembered what Seth the Clerk had said, like about the freaks grabbing guns and customers. It was probably some plan Lazarus had. Sure, why not?

A car came up behind him, and Max winced, thinking it was the cops. However, it was Seth, in Jolene's Camaro. He honked the horn, stayed behind him.

Max felt like a lemon-yellow target in that truck. He went to Stegner Field, the soccer field that served Whidmore, parked in the lot.

He ran out of the cab, went to the back of the truck. There were a half-dozen townsfolk trussed up in the back, arms tied with those plastic bonds the cops used. They looked terrified.

"Look," Max said. "You're okay, alright? I just rescued you from those freaks. Do you understand? We don't have much time."

"I was just shopping for hinges," a fat man said. "They just piled on me."

"I was looking for some eyebolts," a pretty blond woman said. "Rounded a corner and they grabbed me. Who are they?"

He dug into his pocket, fished out his Swiss Army knife, blue with a Star of David on it. A gift from a friend he had kept for years. He cut the bonds, deflected their questions.

Seth the Clerk kept lookout while Max freed everybody, talking while he worked. He explained what he knew, what he thought was going on, what he suspected.

"That's nuts," an older man said. A bald guy. He rubbed his wrists.

"You're free, okay?" Max said. "You go where you want, do what you want. But you go to the police and you're going to end up in the river. That's where they're taking them. That's where they'll take you."

The bald man just squinted at Max, shook his head. "You're crazy."

Max was sweating profusely, his eyes kept flitting to the horizon, looking for the police. He thought he could hear sirens somewhere.

"Look," Max said. "They're out there, alright?"

He ran to the passenger side of the truck, looked at the firearms.

"Seth," he said. "You know these, right?"

Seth the Clerk walked up. "Sure, dude."

"Match up the guns with the ammo," Max said. "Or better yet, let's just put them in the Camaro."

The other people were milling around behind the truck, unsure where to go.

"My advice to you is to try to get out of Ludlow," Max said. "Or get home and hunker down there, if it's safe, I suppose. Look, I don't know."

He saw a police cruiser racing up Quarry Road. Fortunately, it didn't appear to notice them at Stegner, because of the way the field sat relative to Quarry Road.

He had thought about ditching the truck. It was too obvious a target. But then again, he imagined using it to knock one of those cruisers off Quarry Road, thought that would be of use. But he scotched that, thought it was too obvious. Zombies maybe they were, but the freaks weren't stupid. It was bad enough driving around in a red Camaro, running people down.

"I can take you back to my place," he said. "Some of those freaks were trying to get me there, but they're probably gone, now. We can fit maybe three more in the car."

Three of the customers stepped forward. The blond woman, a thin middle-aged man, and a young man who looked younger than Seth the Clerk.

"We'll go with you," the woman said, tucking a stray lock of hair behind her ear. The other two, one man roughly Max's age, with curly brown hair, the other a slightly-older man with a thick blond mustache, talked to themselves, said they were going to take their chances with the truck. They wanted a pair of the guns, and Max had Seth the Clerk give them a couple of the hunting rifles, with corresponding boxes of ammunition.

Then he had the others get into the Camaro, and they parted ways with the Ryder truck guys. The car could hardly accommodate that many people. They fidgeted and complained as they tried to cram themselves in there.

"Why didn't you have them stay?" the woman asked. Max shrugged.

"They can go where they want," he said. "I'm not the boss of them."

He started up the Camaro, drove back toward his place, while Seth the Clerk loaded each of the guns, handed them back to the passengers. Max took sidestreets, avoided the heart of downtown, anxious to avoid detection. He'd wanted to go look for Adrienne, but with that police cruiser heading up Quarry Road, he thought it was perhaps unwise to do so.

They saw a trio of police cruisers with lights flashing, in front of the Elks Lodge.

"What's going on?" Seth asked, finishing loading a shotgun.

"I don't know," Max said. It looked like a standoff. Maybe that was why no police had harassed them when they'd gone after the truck.

He pulled near the scene, without getting too close. There were a half-dozen police cruisers arranged in front of the lodge, weapons drawn, and there were a couple of spotlights on the lodge.

Max took out his camera, his telephoto lens, and looked through it. "Keep an eye out, Seth. If anybody creeps up to us, show them the gun. If they keep coming, shoot them."

Then Max saw bodies in front of the place. Men who had been shot. He snapped shots of it, of the whole scene.

"Maybe those crazies are holed up at the lodge?" the woman said.

"I don't think so," Max said, trying to get shots of the policemen. Their backs were turned, he couldn't be sure. There was blood on the ground in front of the lodge, and from what he'd seen, the freaks didn't bleed.

"What should we do?" the kid asked, from the back.

"I don't think there's anything we can do," Max said. "I don't want to try to get into a shooting match with a bunch of police."

Tear gas was fired into the windows of the lodge. Max could see it, saw the plumes of gas coming out the windows. He just kept shooting with his camera.

Some men came running out of the lodge, hands up, coughing, gagging. They were grabbed by some of the policemen, quickly cuffed, put into the back of a police van. Maybe a half-dozen men came out.

Then the police took something else out and began shooting it onto the roof of the lodge. Fires sprang up. They were firebombing the lodge! He snapped pictures of that, too.

"Are you some kind of photojournalist?" Seth asked.

"I am, now," Max said. "I need to upload this stuff when I get the chance."

Max's phone rang. He paused with his camera to look at the number. He didn't recognize it. It was local.

"Hello?" he said.

"Max," Adrienne said. "I'm downtown."

"Where the fuck have you been?" he asked.

"Hiding," she said. "The Interstate was barricaded. There were some deputies there. I ran away before they could get me."

"Where are you?" he asked.

"At the library," she said. "I'm on a pay phone."

"Where's Jolene?" Max asked.

"With the car," Adrienne said. "I just ran. I could tell the deputies weren't right. They looked like she did."

THE car. With HIS car.

Max cursed.

He wanted his fucking car back.

Still, he was glad Adrienne wasn't dead. The fires rose above the lodge, great, towering plumes of flame. Perhaps with the police occupied with this, he'd be able to get into town and get Adrienne out of there.

"I'll come get you," he said. "Five minutes."

He hung up.

"Detour," he said. "We're picking up a friend of mine."

"Alright," Seth said.

Max stashed his camera and started up the car again and drove back the way he had come, carefully heading back into town, toward the library. He passed the spot where he had jacked the truck. The bodies of the dead were still there, but there were others hunched low around them, grabbing at the bodies.

He almost swerved the car off the road when he saw that the townsfolk were eating them.

"Oh, Christ," he said. The others looked, gasped, and moaned in turn.

"You've got to be fucking kidding me," Seth said. "Are they eating them?"

Max rolled down the window and took out his camera again, took shots of it. He wanted to document everything he saw. People had to know.

They were eating them, alright. A dozen or so townsfolk, bent over the bodies of their neighbors, feasting on them. Max saw blood on the ground, realized that some of the victims had been norms. He could just imagine them walking up, wondering what was going on, and being attacked by those freaks.

"Fuck," Max said, shooting a couple dozen photographs. He put the camera beside him, rolled on past. The townsfolk didn't even look up, so intent were they on their little roadkill feast.

The passengers in the back looked over their shoulders, craned their necks to see it.

"My lord," the woman said. "They're insane."

"The whole place is going crazy," the man said. "It's the End Times."

"Maybe the government sprayed nerve gas on us or something," Max said. "Like some kind of hallucinogen. Are we part of some kind of test? No fucking clue."

While he did have a bit of a clue, he wasn't going to try to explain it to these strangers.

Instead, he drove to the library, where he saw Adrienne in the lobby, by the phone. Max waved to her, and she came out, trotting to the passenger's side. As she came up, Seth sighed.

"Wow," he said. "That's Ms. Morse! I had her for art class."

"Yeah," Max said.

Adrienne opened the door, looked in. "Jeez, Max. A little crowded, don't you think?"

"Hop into our clown car," Max said. Adrienne did just that, sitting on Seth the Clerk's lap. Seth seemed at peace with that decision, and they managed to close the door. Adrienne looked tired, but otherwise okay.

Then he took off again, headed back home. It was the only thing he could think of doing. He just hoped the others were gone.

13.

Heidi got her sister into St. Vincent's through the rectory, using Father Knightley's keys. It was as it had been when she had been here with him earlier in the evening. It made her shudder.

She and Lisa had snuck out the back when the police had arrived at their house. It had taken some persuading for Heidi to get Lisa to listen to her, but she'd complied. They crept to the woods behind their house and watched the police stalk through their house, walk around the place. Heidi had taken her father's guns, put them in an athletic bag.

"Why are we hiding?" Lisa whispered in her ear.

"Because they're in on it," Heidi said. "I saw a policeman try to murder Father Knightley this evening."

"For real?"

Heidi nodded.

The policeman stood on the deck, seemed to be looking out at them. He talked into his radio. She couldn't understand what he'd said.

"It's not safe here," Heidi said. "We'll go to St. Vincent's."

She and her sister had crept through the woods, worked their way downhill, avoiding cars. Across the cemetery they went, toward the cathedral. While they traveled, Heidi told her sister about what had happened.

"I can't believe you blew that guy away," Lisa said. "And you shot a cop? My God, Heidi."

"It's not my fault," Heidi said, checking the curtains before turning on the lights. She locked the door. "Something terrible is happening."

Lisa walked around Father Knightley's rectory, checked out his train set.

"Where is Father Knightley?" Lisa asked.

"I don't know," Heidi said. "He said he was going to try to fix things."

Lisa knelt down, leveled her gaze at the tiny Ludlow. "This is amazing."

Heidi walked over. "Yes, he made it exact. Lazarus started it all down here."

She pointed at the boat launch. An aluminum pushpin had been put there.

"But I think it has spread," she said.

Lisa sighed. "What can we do?"

Heidi didn't know for sure. She thought of calling their dad, but didn't want him stumbling into the midst of anything. When he got home, that would be bad enough. He'd freak out.

She called their mom, but got her voicemail again. "Mom, it's Heidi. Call me back."

She hung up. Mom should've been home when all of that stuff went down at their house. City Hall didn't stay open after hours in Ludlow. It was their dad who worked irregular, long hours. The prospect of something happening to her mom filled Heidi with fear and worry, but she had to be strong, lest Lisa pick up on it.

"Where is Father Knightley?" Lisa asked. "This is too weird, hanging out here."

"He should be back," Heidi said. "Unless they got him."

"They," Lisa said. "That Auckerman was such a freak. What did he want with me?"

"He wanted to drown you in the river," Heidi said. "That's what they do. Something about the river."

"We should drain it," Lisa said.

"Yeah, that'll happen," Heidi said. "We can call the Army Corps of Engineers."

"Huh?"

"Never mind," Heidi said. "They can't dam the river. What's more, they won't. Too much traffic up and down it."

"Remember when the Mercy River caught fire?" Lisa asked.

"That was before we were born," Heidi said. Their dad talked about it a few times. Some kind of chemical spill in the 70s, the river going up in flames. "You don't remember it. You just remember Dad telling us about it."

"Whatever. The point is, there's nothing we CAN do, right?" Lisa said. It reminded Heidi of when Lisa complained that she didn't have a "can do" attitude. In truth, Heidi didn't know what they could do.

"We can wait to see if Father Knightley comes back tonight," Heidi said.

"Oh, that'd be rich," Lisa said, making her voice like she was *The Ludlow Sentinel*, the local paper: " 'Two Teen Girls Found Hiding in Area Priest's Rectory.' If that doesn't earn him a defrocking, nothing will."

"If he doesn't come back," Heidi said. "We can assume the worst."

Lisa picked at her clothes a bit. "We should've packed or something. We can't just camp out here. We have to go home. Mom and Dad'll flip out."

"They can call us," Heidi said. "The point is that a policeman attacked Father Knightley and me. I don't trust them. They're in on it, whatever IT is."

"You are so paranoid, Heidi," Lisa said.

"I'm also right," Heidi said. "I know what's going on; you don't."

Lisa shrugged, and Heidi fiddled with the shotgun. Her hands felt numb from using the thing. The noise of it had been incredible. The guy hadn't bled. None of them had. They didn't bleed, but you didn't even really need to see that to know when somebody had been changed. Everything about them was just wrong.

"God," Lisa said. "We'll have to go back to school, right?"

"I don't know," Heidi said. "Will we?"

"I mean, what if our classmates are all those things?" Lisa asked. Heidi hadn't really thought that far ahead. The thing about living in the moment was that it concentrated your gaze and your thoughts, distilled them. She hadn't been thinking more than moment-to-moment, at most, minute-by-minute. In her present mental state, an hour was a lifetime away. For all she knew, she and her sister didn't have more than a few hours until those things came for them, dragged them to the river.

Zombies. Ghouls. Something like that. She didn't really have the words for what they were.

"I don't know," Heidi said. "We should call around, see what people know."

Lisa brightened at that prospect, dug out her cell. Heidi held her hand before she started texting her friends.

"Just ask them if they've seen anything weird," Heidi said. "Don't tell them everything we've seen. And don't say where we are."

Lisa looked at her like she had just said the dumbest thing ever, rolled her eyes, scoffed.

"Duh. I know. I'll just ask around, see what people know."

Heidi thought she should do that, too, but she went to the other room, looked at Father Knightley's model of Ludlow, studied it, found herself lost in thought.

If it was an infection, the infection started at that point. She went to the spot where she'd followed Father Knightley. It seemed like forever ago, but it wasn't. Moment-by-moment, minute-by-minute. A lifetime in a matter of hours. That is what she felt she'd lived. Her day-to-day concerns were nonsensical in the face of what she'd seen, those things bashing down doors.

Walking dead.

Everything paled by comparison. School? She couldn't imagine even walking to school, pretending to give a fuck about Geography or French right now. She imagined looking out the window and seeing those things out there, dragging people away. Or worse, seeing them walking through their halls, looking for victims.

No, she wasn't going back to school. It would take force of will to get her out of St. Vincent's. She thought she and her sister could live on whatever food Father Knightley had in his place, and once that was gone, maybe go somewhere else. She wanted to go home, but didn't dare head back there. At least until their parents got home. Assuming they were both alright. She worried about her mom. It wasn't like her not to call.

It wasn't fair. This was supposed to be her golden year, the year everything clicked for her, when all of her studious hard work and volunteerism and everything just carried her out of Ludlow for good, out to the East Coast, to something better and brighter. She had worked hard to deliver herself from Ludlow, and that was coming to pieces right in front of her.

Ludlow bit back, clamped down, and held fast.

That future, her future, was gone.

No. It was delayed. This was just a speed bump. If she and her sister had encountered those things and triumphed, others must have, too. They couldn't be the only ones. They'd try to find others, try to attack this thing that had infected the town.

That was the proper response. Surrender was easy; fighting was hard. And if Heidi was anything, she was a fighter. Lisa wasn't, however. Lisa was a spoiled brat. But she was her sister, and that was something.

St. Vincent's felt safe to her. She thought of going up into the bell tower, and using it to spy on the town. St. Vincent's was the tallest structure in town, the spire of the cathedral offered a commanding view of the surroundings.

She looked around for binoculars, for anything like that. She found a telescope, a white tube trimmed with black, on a tripod, near one of the windows of the rectory. Then she unscrewed it from its tripod and put it on her shoulder.

"What are you doing?" Lisa asked, between phone calls.

"I'm going up into the bell tower," she said. "I want to look around."

"You're so Nancy Drew," Lisa said. "Are you going to leave me down here?"

"Well, yeah," Heidi said. "Unless you want to climb lots of stairs. Look, just keep the doors locked and don't draw a lot of attention. He has a television. You can keep talking with your friends, taking notes. Did they see anything?"

"Oh, I guess," Lisa said. "People are thinking the Rapture's begun, because people keep disappearing."

Even though her sister caucused with the freaks, she was certainly more popular than Heidi, who was involved with nearly everything but didn't really blend in with any of her peers. She was just a doer, didn't have time to really sweat popularity. She felt like being the go-to person for nearly everything at Whidmore gave her a good proxy for popularity. If she wasn't precisely the one that people wanted to invite to parties, at least she was the one who was involved with nearly everything of importance at school.

"I'm going up into the tower," Heidi said. "You just stay down here, try not to be stupid, okay? I'll leave you the shotgun."

Lisa recoiled from the shotgun.

"I'm not touching that thing."

"I'll leave it with you, anyway," Heidi said. Heidi didn't relish toting it up the bell tower, and it wouldn't be useful, anyway. She didn't know a lot about guns, but knew that shotguns were better at closer targets.

She set the shotgun on the coffee table, along with the shells. Lisa just stared at it in mute disapproval.

"If something's up, call me. Or scream, at the very least," Heidi said. "I'll be upstairs."

14.

Special Agent Holliday broke into the Sheriff's office when nobody answered the door. The place was dark, no lights on at all. He went in and turned on the lights, calling out.

"Anybody here?" he asked. "Anybody?"

Row after row of lightswitches. He toggled them all, two at a time, index finger and middle finger, flicking them on.

What the hell was going on?

He drew his automatic, cocked it. At the very least, something highly irregular was happening. It comforted him to have his weapon drawn.

Holliday took out his phone in his other hand, dialed up Maxwell. Got his voicemail.

"Bob, I'm at the Sheriff's office," he said. "The whole place is shut down. Nobody's here. I'm going to look around. Call me when you get a chance."

He hung up, pocketed the phone, and walked into the place. The offices were empty. Room after room of putty-colored emptiness.

He checked them all, called out, hoping he'd hear somebody.

Even with the lights on, the place was haunting to him. It was like being in a morgue. Something about the artificial lighting, and the silence. This place was dead.

He went back to the jail, opened the security door, which was ajar. Then he went in, flicked on some lights there.

The jail cells were full of bodies.

"What the hell?" Holliday asked. He took out his phone and took some hasty pictures with it.

There were clearly bodies of inmates, people who'd been guests of the Sheriff. But there were others in there, too. Everybody just piled up in there, like they were stacks of lumber. He'd never seen so many bodies in one place.

Holliday went from cell to cell, looking. They were all dead. Nobody breathing except for him. He went to one of the cell doors and tugged on it. The thing was unlocked.

There was water on the ground. A lot of it. He looked at the other cells. There was water all over the floor.

He called Bob again, got his voicemail again.

"We've got some kind of mass murder thing going on, here, Bob," he said, trying to keep his voice steady. "Bodies are piled up in the jail. They look like they've been drowned. We need to get a team down here."

He took out his phone and took pictures of the stacked bodies, the people with their bluish skin, eyes wide. Young people, middle-aged, men, women. All types, all races, all dead. Holliday's hard-soled shoes squished the water on the floor.

There were ten cells here, and he did a quick body count, counting feet. He counted twenty bodies stacked in this cell. Two hundred dead. It made him want to gag. Two hundred murder victims. Mass murder. Holliday couldn't understand how the Sheriff's office could be party to something like this.

He hung up, sent the pictures to Maxwell, using his phone. He figured if anything happened to him, at least there'd be something to show that something bad had happened in Ludlow, something worthy of investigation.

Holliday remembered the phone call from Ms. Morse, about the river, and the photographs. The puddles made sense. These people had surely been drowned in the Mercy River.

There was a sound at the front door, the turning of a knob, a creak of a hinge. Holliday closed the cell door, went down the hallway, to one side of the jail entrance, gun at the ready.

Somebody was walking through the place. They must've seen the lights on, came to investigate.

His phone chirped, and, cursing inwardly, Holliday turned off the phone's ringer, glancing to see who it was. Maxwell.

Whoever had been walking in the other room stopped.

Holliday stood where he was, holding his breath, listening. There was no sound in the other room. Nothing.

He opened his phone and texted Maxwell:

See pix. Send HMRU. Many agents. Natl Guard?

Still nothing from the other room, just a cavernous silence. Then he heard a step again, and another, and another. It was the only sound he heard, along with his own breathing.

He was sure whomever it was in the other room was at least partially involved in what was going on.

Then he heard a splash from down the hallway, and a shuffling sound. And another. There was movement in the jail cells.

Holliday's mouth went dry as he saw people rising up, their shoes squishing wetly on the puddles.

Everyday people, rising up from the dead.

Not all of them, but some. The farthest two jail cells were full of activity.

A sheriff's deputy walked in through the door where Holliday was. Middle-aged, pale-faced and paunchy.

"This way, people," he said. "This way."

He hadn't seen Holliday.

The people, the dead people, looked in the direction of Holliday and the Deputy, walked toward them both.

"I'm going to need you people to come with me," he said. "Lazarus wants to talk to you."

His voice was as dead as he was, his manner not unlike the deputy Tibbs Holliday had encountered earlier. Holliday wondered if it was possible to fool these things. Could he pass himself off as one of them? He wondered what Lazarus had to say to them.

The Deputy turned and saw him. There was no surprise, no reaction. Just those dead eyes upon him. The Deputy went for his pistol.

"Don't," Holliday said, but the man didn't listen, kept going for it.

So Holliday shot him in the leg, but the Deputy was unfazed, had gotten his pistol out. Holliday shot him in the head as the man was bringing his weapon up. The Deputy careened backward, hitting the ground, was still.

Holliday took the man's pistol, a Smith & Wesson .357 Magnum combat revolver. He was grateful the man hadn't had time to shoot this at him. He put the pistol back on the man's gunbelt, then removed the belt, slung it over his shoulder. It would be useful having access to his radio.

The townsfolk just stared mutely at Holliday, looking at the corpse of the Deputy. Then they walked toward him.

Holliday took a step backward, holding up his pistol for emphasis.

"Special Agent Holliday, FBI. Slight change in plans. We are going to see Lazarus, but I'm going to take you."

15.

Max's place looked as he'd left it. Garage door open, no sign of Stan or the others. Good. He pulled the Camaro back into his garage and shut the door. He was glad to see that they hadn't been able to break into his place. When the garage door went down, he turned off the car, opened the door, and got out. Everybody filed out.

He'd gotten the other passengers' names as they'd gone through town. The woman's name was Elissa, the older man's name was Phillip, and the kid called himself Vin. When Max asked him what that was short for, the kid just said "Vin." So, Vin, he was.

He keyed into his place and let everybody else in, while Seth the Clerk hauled in the guns, put them out on Max's kitchen table.

He and Adrienne had told them everything they had seen and discovered, and while it sounded incredible when told that way, having seen what they had seen, the other townsfolk largely accepted it. They had seen things, themselves.

"We need to get out of town," Vin said. "That's what we need to do. This is too big for us."

Max nodded.

Phillip snorted, nodding at the firearms. "I don't think we've got enough guns to take on the rest of the town. I've never shot one of those in my life. I don't want to, either."

Elissa folded her arms across her chest, looked nervously from face to face. "This is our home. We're all from here. We can't just walk away from it. We can't just run away."

"True," Max said. "I get that, I do. Right now, I think we're just brainstorming a little."

He'd turned on his computer, was uploading his photographs. Vin stalked around the room.

"We have to take out that Lazarus," he said. "He's the guy behind it all."

"Yes," Max said. "We have to find him, first. I'm all for wasting him, if he's the source of it. But first we need to track him down."

"We could take the trains out of town," Phillip said. "The trains roll through here constantly. We could stow away aboard one of the freight trains."

Adrienne nodded. "That's a good idea, Phillip. We could ride right into Pittsburgh, assuming we're not caught first."

It was a good idea, Max thought. Lazarus may have blocked the roads in and out of Ludlow, but stopping the trains was another matter.

Elissa called her husband, went to a far corner to talk to him. Her voice sounded strained.

"Help yourselves to what you want in the fridge," Max said. "If there's much in there, I dunno."

He'd uploaded the photographs, was sorting through them. Then he posted them to his photoblog.

"Tried to get out of town," he wrote, speaking aloud as he typed, as was his habit sometimes. "Got sidetracked. I'm stuck back at my place. Picked up some refugees."

"Refugees," Phillip said, scoffing. "Survivors."

Vin jumped up, clapping his hands together once, startling everybody.

"The Armory," Vin said.

"What?" Adrienne asked.

"The Ludlow Armory," Vin said. "There's a National Guard armory. In the old part of town. The North Side."

Max knew what he was talking about. An old, squat building. He'd not thought about that place for a long time, since he was a teen, wanting to break in there and steal a jeep or whatever else he imagined was in there.

"That's not a bad idea," Max said. Adrienne looked at him. She looked tired. They all did.

"Fight or flight?" she asked.

Max didn't like to have to make a decision. It shouldn't have been up to him, anyway. Maybe it wasn't.

"Everybody should do what they think is best," Max said. "Seth and I helped free you guys; the rest is up to you. You know what's out there, now."

The others looked at him, awash in their own thoughts. Adrienne spoke first, as Max thought she would.

"We should stick together," she said. "You saw how they mobbed up on you. They come at us in groups."

"We should fight," Vin said. "That's what we're talking about, right?"

Phillip shrugged. "I just want to go home."

"My husband is coming to pick me up," Elissa said. "We're going to try to drive out of here."

"Not a good idea," Adrienne said. "Unless you know some secret way out. They've got the exits covered."

"We'll figure something out," Elissa said.

"I'm with you, Max," Seth the Clerk said. "I owe you my life, dude. We all do."

"The Armory," Vin said. "Machine guns. Tanks, maybe."

Seth scoffed at the younger man. "You know how to drive a tank?"

Vin looked ruffled, defensive. "How hard can it be? It's a snap on Playstation."

"Tanks, machine guns," Phillip said. "Are you honestly prepared to shoot down your neighbors and loved ones?"

"If they're part of it, yeah," Vin said. "What other choice have we got?"

"We can hide," Phillip said.

Max divided his attention between his computer and the others.

"You'll run out of food. I was thinking about this. These…things are disrupting Ludlow. That'll mean food will become scarce. There may be a run on the grocery stores in town if things get really fucked. Maybe it's already happened. We just don't know. But eventually, we're going to be out of food, and we'll have to get out of here. I say we should get out while we can, when we're still relatively strong."

Max used MapQuest to get a map of the area, printed it out on his printer. A nice terrain map, showing roads, routes, mountains, all of that. He printed out several copies, handed them to everybody.

"We could scavenge from the empty houses," Vin said.

"Kinda dicey," Seth said. "Maybe there are survivors in there, maybe they'd shoot us."

Max rubbed his eyebrows with his thumb and forefinger. He wasn't sure what was the right thing to do. It just wasn't clear. This kind of stuff wasn't supposed to be happening. They shouldn't have to make this kind of decision. He looked at Adrienne.

"'All that is necessary for the triumph of evil is for good men to do nothing,'" said Adrienne. "Edmund Burke said that."

"Who?" Vin asked.

"Never mind," She said.

"Whoever wants to stay, should stay," Max said. "Whoever wants to go, just go. Simple as that."

"How am I supposed to get home from here?" Phillip asked. "I live at the other side of town, in Willowbrook."

Willowbrook was the golf community in the toe of the Heights, where upper middle class folks lived downhill from the truly rich. Max always hated Willowbrook's endless beige pretensions, the bricks the color of baby puke, the rolling hills, the "neighborhood" integrated with the Willowbrook Golf Course, and nothing else.

"Oooh, Willowbrook," Vin said. "Yeah, that's a haul for you."

"Driving's dangerous," Max said. "Hell, everything is."

"My car is downtown," Phillip said. "You can just drop me off there."

Max hated to think of going out there in the red Camaro again. He felt like there was a big target painted on him. It was, in effect, a stolen car, although he thought the police had other things on their lifeless minds than law enforcement these days.

"Alright," Max said, ignoring Adrienne's shaking of her head. "I'll drop you off downtown, Phil. After that, you're on your own."

The man looked fearfully happy at that prospect, nodded in silence. Max's own hands sweated at the idea of going back into town. He felt safe at home, or at least safer. Out and about, anything could happen.

He glanced back at his blog, saw some comments readers had left. They were predictably perplexed by the recent cult/freak/zombie turn he'd taken, thought he was pulling some kind of gag.

Let them believe whatever they wanted, Max thought. *Just let them see.* That's all a photographer was supposed to do, anyway.

"Okay," Max said. "I'll drive Phillip to his car. Everybody else is fine with staying, then?"

They all nodded, Adrienne looking particularly worried.

"I figure I'll drop him off, then try to do a grocery store run," Max said. "See what's there."

"You want help?" Seth asked.

"No, it's okay," Max said. "You can keep an eye out upstairs. I have a balcony up there. Just keep a lookout for those freaks, and for Elissa's husband when he rolls up. While you're at it, be sure Elissa's husband isn't one of the goddamned freaks. Adrienne, you just hold things together. Vin, don't go shooting anybody unless you're sure they're already dead."

"Heh," Vin said, toting the rifle he'd picked from the stock Seth had liberated. "Right."

"Alright," Max said. "Let's get you to your car, Phil. When I come back, we can figure out what we want to do, next."

PART
THREE

I.

Lazarus looked at the assembled townsfolk, this great swelling of Brethren he'd gathered in the war memorial park downtown, with himself at the center. Ever since the shooting at the riverbank, he'd kept remote from the Others in town, knowing that they were his enemies, knowing that some of them intended him harm.

The priest was the least of them. There were ones with guns. Like the men at the Elks Lodge, who'd taken to shooting the Brethren as they passed by in their trucks. Lazarus had taken care of them, though. It was almost too easy, too simple to know who to target. The town was very nearly his. Not yet, but soon. The noose was around Ludlow's neck, but it had yet to pull tight. Or it had pulled tight, and the town hadn't yet stopped kicking.

Looking at all the pale faces, the dead eyes all upon him, Lazarus felt some strange kindling in his chest, some long-forgotten emotion stirring inside him, like a faint aroma calling back a distant memory.

Pride. He thought that was what it was. He was proud of what he had done.

"Brethren," he said. "We must sanctify this town. We must go door-to-door, bringing the Breathers to the River. We'll drive trucks down the street, and groups of you, my young, my strong—you will break down the doors and fish out the infidels. We'll take them to the River and show them the Light in the Dark. We must not stop until the whole town is purified."

There was no applause, no roars of agreement. Just silence.

The silent faces all upon him, drinking in his will. The way of it was so clear to him, the invisible puppets' strings upon them, leading to him, for he was the Messenger, the link in the chain between them and the Angel. He was the conduit. Though he had not made all of them himself, those he had made had made them, and in so doing, conferred power to him. He could see it, could tug on those lines and make them do his bidding.

It was a miracle.

"And once Ludlow is purified," Lazarus said. "Then we will reach the rest of the world. We will open our doors and let people come, and we will show them the Light in the Dark, and on and on, until all are one. It will take time. There are enemies afoot even now, who intend to bring us harm, who will try to thwart destiny. We must not let them. We must fight them with everything we have."

There was no fear in their eyes, nor fear in his own stilled heart. It was more an understanding of how things were, and how they would be. Destiny was not something best left in the fickle hands of Fate. No, destiny was something one had to shepherd about, guide with resolution.

He saw Ludlow drawing people from all around, stealthily, of course, taking them, bringing them to the Angel, to the River, changing them, and sending them off as missionaries, emissaries, always returning, like birds on migration. Always coming back to this, their place of spiritual rebirth. More and more visitors, more Brethren. Like a holy virus.

A sacred infection, spreading across the land.

First the tri-state, then the region, then the country.

Then the hemisphere.

Then other continents.

Then the world.

Lazarus could see it so clearly. He hoped the Mercy River could take such a massive migration of humanity. Maybe 13 million gallons of water for the entire United States. The number was humbling, staggering, but he thought the Mercy River could take it, was sure the Angel could.

The Angel wanted more.

In small doses, it was all doable. Every step mattered, that sense of inexorable progress. Toward a world united.

There were challenges: it was getting harder still, he found, to keep the Brethren in line. Though they were all bound through him, the lines blurred with distance, and it was difficult to find what strand to yank, and when.

"Door to door," he said. "Leave no stone unturned, no door unopened. Find them all, and take them to the River. You know what to do. Find the Breathers."

There were no torchlit processions, no fanfare, no tangled, angry murmur of the mob. There was only the shuffling of shoes, without even a breath from the lips of the Brethren. A great and silent army they were.

Lazarus watched them dissipate, until it was just him and his bodyguard, the biggest of the Brethren he'd culled from the ranks. They surrounded him, and Lazarus watched the Brethren go about their business. In a few days, the town would be fully sanctified.

Thousands of souls, unified in purpose.

The Big Star would be as close as the Brethren got to a cathedral, bright and shiny, enticing, luring the unwary and the unconverted. It would be the perfect trap. That's what casinos were, after all. This would just be a further refinement of the thing's purpose.

One of the problems Lazarus had encountered was that the Brethren no longer wanted to do what they had done before. It took specific intervention on his part to compel them to remain working in a grocery store, or at a library, or at a school. When the Angel claimed them, their old lives faded in significance—there was no point in their old lives when contrasted with the new life they had inherited.

He understood this, felt much the same thing. It had been one of the first things he'd done, leaving behind his job.

But in the face of his takeover of Ludlow, there was some value in keeping up appearances, and he found to his dismay that the Brethren were unable to truly keep up appearances, anymore. Slowly, the social fabric that made up the community was unraveling, and Lazarus was the source. He knew this, didn't care, except that the Breathers noticed it. It was apparent to them, and they fought back. But how could one compel one of the Brethren to flip burgers when they no longer had the need to eat them, no longer required money to live?

That was the primary challenge Lazarus was facing. The police had remained in their capacity because it was not so much of a departure from what they were in life, although he found even they were slipping a bit, taking less care about their appearances. It was something unforeseen, something Lazarus could not have imagined, and in truth, from his own biased vantage point, he could offer no solution for it.

Only one thing mattered: bringing more and more Brethren to the Angel. That was his purpose. That was all of their purpose, now. Nothing else mattered. And when the whole world was made one, what next? It was a flight of fancy he was unaccustomed to, for he knew that when all of the world was made one, there would be no rockets traveling in space, no colonization of other worlds.

Rather than progress, that hallmark of Breathers, there would be a final regression, the very darkest of Dark Ages, when all of the vanities of old would crumble and molder and fall by the wayside, while the world's multitudes would look skyward with the blackest, deadest eyes, gazing at the uncaring stars with pale faces, blank and empty as the void itself, and wait for the world to end.

He imagined them all watching a comet or an asteroid smite the Earth, great plumes of ash and fire taking the world, and an ocean of unbeating hearts meeting this celestial end without emotion.

He could not feel anything with this vision, but could see it all the same. It didn't matter. The Angel wanted what it wanted. It wanted more souls. It wanted all the world's souls. That was all it wanted. It wasn't his place to question the Angel's will. It had given him new life. He had been born again. It was his place to honor his rebirth.

A school bus rolled up, and a group of Brethren emerged.

"You're late," Lazarus said. "You must go from house to house, taking the unconverted. Take them to the river, take them to the Angel."

The Brethren parted, while one of them went back into the bus, turned on the engine, and drove it around the war memorial, then went downtown. Lazarus watched the bus drive away, then saw it turn again, heading back their way, picking up speed.

He watched the bus drive straight for him, accelerating.

"Officer Ramsey," he said. "Shoot that bus. All of you. Shoot it."

The armed Brethren drew their various weapons and began shooting at the bus, the weapons rattling the quiet of downtown Ludlow. The bullets tore into the front of the bus, shattered its windshield. Still, the thing came on, vaulting the curb, smashing into several of the Brethren, running them down.

Lazarus backpedaled away from the onrushing bus, which was tearing through the shrubs that flanked the war memorial. Officer Ramsey dodged to one side, and Lazarus was struck in the chest by the bus, falling beneath it.

But fortunately, there was room beneath the bus for him, and the thing passed over him without crushing him, even as the other Brethren fired at the bus until their weapons were empty.

The gears of the bus ground and the thing backed up, while Lazarus rolled out from under it. He saw an older man behind the wheel, nobody he knew. The man saw him, too, and pointed a pistol at him.

Lazarus ran in front of the bus as it was backing up, looking for Ramsey. The bus turned after him, while the officers were busy reloading.

"Ramsey," Lazarus yelled, over the sound of the bus. "Get me out of here."

Ramsey went to his car, while the other officers continued firing at the bus, which continued to pursue Lazarus. The man was an assassin.

The bus smashed one of the park benches at the war memorial, and Lazarus ran to his right, while the thing followed. He didn't want to get on the driver's side again, lest the man with the gun fire upon him.

Who had sent this assassin? Who was he?

The sound of gunfire was deafening, the bullets shredding the bus. Steam was rising from the engine of the bus, flattened tires spewed rubber on the street, but still the thing drove on, seeking him out.

Lazarus slid over the hood of a parked car, looking for Ramsey. He was calm, even in the chaos of the assassination attempt. He could not feel fear, only a heightened concern that his service to the Angel might be abruptly ended if the bus driver had his way.

Ramsey's cruiser pulled up, and Lazarus hopped inside. The police car peeled out, as the bus grazed its rear fender, before smashing into the parked car Lazarus had cleared on a few moments before.

"It's an assassin," Lazarus said. "He's trying to kill me."

"Yes," Ramsey said.

"Take me to the station," Lazarus said. "Someplace secure."

Ramsey drove through downtown, toward the police station. Who could the man have been? The bus had brought Brethren. The man had brought them. Who was he? It didn't matter. He had failed in his bid to assassinate him.

No one could kill Lazarus. His mission was too important. He resolved then and there to remain out of sight until Ludlow was secure. He had told his Brethren what they were to do.

Lazarus would ride it out in his bunker until it was done.

2.

Heidi watched the bus riding roughshod downtown, smashing through bushes and running over townspeople. She could see it from the church tower, could see it with the telescope. She saw the older man behind the wheel, a man she didn't know, saw him driving hard for Lazarus, almost running him down at one point. She saw Lazarus get away, too.

She saw the bus crash, saw the man force open the doors and run out, engaged in a running gun battle with the Ludlow police officers. Heidi shuddered at the memory of her own encounter with the cop, felt sympathy for the man, who seemed to know what he was doing, felled a couple of the policemen with carefully fired shots of his pistol. Shots to the head, she noticed.

The sound of the weapons fire was like firecrackers from where she sat.

Pop. Pop.

Pop-pop. Pop. Pop.

She took out her father's hunting rifle, took careful aim at the police officers. She didn't know who the man was, but he'd been trying to kill Lazarus, so she thought that meant he was a good man.

Heidi took careful aim with the rifle, adjusting the scope. One of the police officers was right in her sights, his head bisected by the crosshairs. She remembered what her father said, about holding her breath, squeezing the trigger.

"Take your time," he'd said. He'd taken her target shooting. He loved it, said it was relaxing. She kind of agreed, found a quiet satisfaction in hitting targets. But paper targets weren't the same as this.

She pulled the trigger, and the rifle bounced in her hands. The noise of it, the kick of the thing. Incredible.

It took her a second to reorient, to peer through the scope. But when she did, she saw the officer she'd targeted lying face down, his head a mangled mess. Not a drop of blood. They didn't bleed. That was how you knew. Although it took shedding of blood to see who didn't have any.

She chambered another round, took aim again. The officers were still intent on the man, who was pinned down between Moxie's and The Candle Shack. He was reloading, and appeared to be aware that somebody had helped him, as he was scanning around nervously.

It was odd to be in this situation, playing sniper. Heidi felt like the Angel of Death up in the tower, taking aim, deciding who lived, who died. It was frightening, humbling. She aimed at another officer, fired, this time careful to handle the kick.

The officers' head split, he fell lifeless. Now the other officers were looking around, dead-eyed, slack-faced.

One of them appeared to see her, and she shot him, knocked him off his feet. Another one down.

The man with the pistol fired at the remaining officers, trying to draw their fire. From her position in the tower, and the man's location, they had them in a crossfire. She took another officer out, and another. They didn't defend themselves properly, she noticed. No fear.

That was what hampered them. They didn't fully appreciate their danger; they couldn't. She shot one of the officers in the leg, and the man finished him off.

There had been a half-dozen Ludlow police officers after the man. Now there were only two left. Heidi shot one as he was getting to his cruiser, reaching for his radio. The man shot the remaining officer, then ran for the cathedral.

Had she been that obvious? Was she that easy to see? She didn't know, ducked down and reloaded the rifle with shaky hands.

It wasn't murder if they were already dead. It wasn't.

She peeked out, saw the man down below, breathing hard, looking up.

"Open the doors?" he said.

Heidi called up her sister. Lisa answered.

"What's with all the shooting?" Lisa asked. "What are you doing, Heidi?"

"Never mind that," Heidi said. "There's a man at the cathedral entrance. Let him in."

"Who is he?" Lisa asked.

"A friend," Heidi said. "I'm coming down."

She took one last look around, then set the rifle down to one side, ran down the steps. There wasn't much point in lugging the rifle up and down the bell tower.

When she got down, she saw her sister uncomfortably talking with the man, her arms folded across her chest.

The man held up an ID badge. "Special Agent Frank Holliday, Miss Campbell. FBI. Thank you for the assistance."

"Those men were already dead," Heidi said, hastily. She felt immediately guilty in front of the FBI agent. He held up his hand, stopped her.

"I know," he said. "I saw. I know."

He sat down, catching his breath, setting his pistol on the table. "That was some great shooting. Where'd you learn that?"

"My dad used to take me target shooting," Heidi said. "It helps that those things don't move right. They don't duck-and-cover, or whatever you call it."

"Evasion," Holliday said. The man was older than her dad, thin and obviously fairly fit, but still worn out from the pursuit.

Lisa looked at them both like they were space aliens. Just stared, a look of confused disgust on her face, a look she'd mastered since she was about 13.

"You were trying to kill Lazarus," Heidi said.

"Yes," he said. "I was sort of winging it, there. It occurred to me that the infection might stop and start with that man. I don't fully understand it, but couldn't let an opportunity like that pass."

He reached into the pocket of his overcoat, then the other, looking concerned. "Crap. I lost my phone back there."

"You can use mine," Heidi said, holding hers out.

"Thank you, Miss Campbell," he said, dialing quickly with his big-fingered old man's hands. Then he paused, frowning. "No signal."

He tried again, and again.

Heidi took the phone and tried, but the phone was dead.

"I don't know what happened, Agent Holliday," she said.

"Look, we have to get out of here," he said. "We have to get out of Ludlow. We have to warn people."

"How do we do that?" Heidi asked, still fiddling with her phone.

"The roads are barricaded," Holliday said.

"The river," Lisa said. "We can take a boat downriver."

Holliday looked at both of the girls. "Alright. Either of you ever drive a boat?"

They shook their heads. Holliday smiled.

"Me, neither."

3.

Max had dropped Phillip off and wished the guy good luck, then went to the grocery store, weirded out because while there were a few cars parked in the lot, there was nobody going in and out of the place. The lights were on, but nobody was coming or going. He sat there in his car, watching it for awhile, and then decided to risk it.

He opened the door, looked around. The lot was silent. The town was silent. Then he heard a shot somewhere. A rifle shot. An echo, distant.

Closing the door, locking it, Max walked up to the grocery store and peered in. Again, it looked like nobody was in there.

Max grabbed a cart and went to the doors, which opened automatically for him, letting him in. He went in and "Cherish" was playing on the Muzak.

No matter how much he wanted to, Max didn't say anything. He felt an odd compulsion to call out "Hello?" to the empty store, but resisted it. Instead, he filled the grocery basket with dried fruit and can after can of food. Boxes of crackers, boxes of cookies, cans of soup, all of that kind of long-term hunker-down stuff. He snagged a few cartons of cigarettes.

"Hey," a voice said, down the aisle from him. Max turned to see a fat kid in a butcher's smock, carrying a cleaver. The kid was big and fat, with pouchy eyes.

Black eyes, dead eyes. His mouth was bloody.

"What?" Max asked, trying to roll his cart nonchalantly. He wanted to see what information he could get from the freak.

"Store's closed," the kid said, walking toward Max. The cleaver he carried was bloody. The kid's apron was bloody.

"The door was open," Max said. "Where is everybody?"

"Out," the kid said. He had that little white hat on his head, askew. His face was pale, his expression, emotionless, and he kept stalking toward Max, cleaver at the ready.

"I'm not stopping by the deli," Max said, glancing around him. They were in the toy aisle.

"Mal told me to kill anybody who came in here," the fat kid said.

"That seems like it'd be bad for business," Max said. He grabbed a couple of bags of marbles. The kid was just out of reach. This close, his unblinking eyes, his lack of breathing, it was hauntingly apparent.

The kid swung at Max with the cleaver just as Max held up the bag of marbles to defend himself. The cleaver sliced through the bags and marbles spilled on the floor, clattering about around the feet of the kid, who slipped and fell with another step.

Max ran with the cart down the aisle, trailing the rest of the marbles, while the kid struggled to find his footing.

It was something that had always bugged him in zombie movies—no appreciation of physics. For all of the emphasis on guns, something as simple as marbles could deal with zombies. Or at least delay them a bit. They had to walk, just like anybody else. Make that hard for them, and you bought yourself some time.

He had seen some overturned grocery carts, spilled cans sprayed down some of the aisles. But no people.

Not a fucking soul. Had the kid taken them somewhere and hacked them to bits? Were there prisoners in there even now? He imagined people in the freezers or something. He couldn't know for sure.

He didn't want to wait, however, as he heard the kid stumbling out of the toy aisle, having found his footing again.

"Hey," the kid said, running after him. Max ran out of the aisle, as "Send in the Clowns" came on the Muzak, next, which set Max's teeth on edge. Then his phone rang.

Max cursed and wheeled the cart through the store, past the empty checkout counters, while Fatbody came charging after him.

He knew as he ran out of the store that he had a real problem, here. The kid was one of the freaks, the walking fucking dead—in this case, the running dead. Whereas Max was out of shape and a smoker. He was already wheezing as he was trying to make the car, while the kid kept after him, gaining.

Not knowing what else to do, Max shoved the grocery cart toward the car, and then threw himself at the legs of the kid, which sent the kid tumbling over him, landing on the pavement with a horrible crunching scuffling sound.

Max ran over and brought his foot down on the kid's hand, the one carrying the cleaver, while the kid fought to free himself, clawing at Max's leg.

There was a sound of breaking finger bones beneath Max's foot, but the kid didn't squawk, didn't so make a sound, just pummeled Max, trying to free his hand, while Max drew the pistol from his belt, a Medusa Model 47, pointed it to the kid's head, and fired twice.

The kid stopped moving, and Max fell to the ground, ears ringing. No blood, as ever. The kid just stared sightlessly at the ground, the holes in his head smoking a little, the stink of singed hair and gunpowder in the air.

The little paper hat the kid was wearing was still on his head, now with two holes in it.

"Fuck," Max said, backing away from the body. He put the pistol back in his waistband. He'd never shot anybody before. He'd never even fired a gun before. The kick from the thing had hurt his hand.

He opened the trunk of the car and loaded the groceries in there, then shoved the cart away, keeping an eye on the kid, who hadn't moved from where Max had shot him.

At least then folks can go to the store without being attacked, he thought. He lit a cigarette and walked back into the store. He had to know for sure that nobody else was in there. He drew the pistol again and walked the aisles.

"Hello?" he said. "Anybody?"

In the back, near the deli, he saw the blood. There were four people there, chopped into pieces. They looked like disassembled dolls. Max retched, threw aside the cigarette.

The floor in the deli was covered with blood.

"Anybody?" Max said.

He wanted to check the freezer, just in case. He carefully crossed into the work area, mindful of the blood. The heads were missing from the bodies. The kid had taken the heads.

Max stalked carefully to the freezer and opened it, peering in. There were no bodies in there, just stacks of cold cuts and cheeses. He got out of there, shutting the door and leaning on it, gazing at the bodies. Where were the heads?

He walked out of there, hands shaking. The freaks were worse than zombies; they weren't mindless. They were something else. Words failed him.

"Hello?" he said, one last time.

The Muzak had changed again, he noticed, to Bread's "Baby I'm-a Want You." That made him want to retch all over again.

Then he saw something at the corner of his eye, and turned to see that the kid had put the heads behind the glass, in a row, like they were up for sale. Four heads, in a row.

"Fuck," Max said. Nature abhorred a vacuum; this was something else, a sense of filling the void within with blood.

He felt bad for the poor folks who'd been killed by that thing out there.

"Goddammit," he said, then remembered his phone. He tugged it out of his pocket and saw that the call had been Adrienne. There had been no message.

He tried redialing Adrienne, but it went to voicemail.

"Hey, what? Are you okay? Call me back if you are."

Max hung up, pocketed his phone.

He walked up to the front area again, and went to one of the cashier microphones, toggled it on. Jim Croce's "Time In a Bottle" played on the Muzak.

"Is anybody alive in here? You've got like two minutes to make it up to the front. I'm not one of the freaks; I just shot that crazy fucker with the cleaver," Max said. Then he ducked down, gun at the ready, wondering if anybody would show. Nobody did.

He waited the full two minutes he gave them, listening to that fucking song, watching the time pass on the store clock, and then he got up and walked out of there. The kid was still where he was. Still dead.

Max got in the car, keyed the ignition, and got out of there.

The town was empty but illuminated. The streetlights were all on, but nobody was about. Not even the freaks.

Where the hell was everybody?

4.

The Brethren went from house to house, grabbing whomever they could find, and carting them down to the river. It took many arms, duct tape, fists, but they dragged the Breathers down to the river and made them take communion there, one by one, five by five, ten by ten. All of them held in the water until they took it into their lungs and found peace, at last. Every last one of them, all the ones the Brethren could find, until their bodies were piled high on the banks of the Mercy River, and truck after truck was requisitioned and the bodies placed in there for safekeeping, until they awakened again.

Only then did Mal emerge from the safety of the police station. Only then did he face his flock. Each day, there were more, as the Brethren returned to life, bound inextricably to him in a tarnished silver causal chain of events, from drowning to drowning, each one meeting the Angel in the Depths, the Light in the Dark.

It was preternatural, the silence. This assembled mass of people, his Brethren, all standing there, silent, waiting for him. There had to be hundreds. In a few days, thousands.

"How many people lived in Ludlow, Mayor?" Mal asked.

"Around five thousand," the Mayor said. Since his rebirth, the formerly affable Mayor had emerged as a grave and joyless specter, not that Mal minded. His role was a formality, now; Mal ran Ludlow, now.

"Five thousand," Mal said. "Five thousand of us, Brethren. Now, I know we haven't gotten everybody, I understand this. But we will. In three days, nearly five thousand of us will walk these streets. Do you know what that means?"

No one answered.

No one knew.

It was for Mal to know, for he was the Messenger.

"It means that Ludlow is our home, now," Mal said. "It means that we can bring things back to normal. It means that we become a town again. We can welcome people here with open arms—Breathers—we can let them come to our town and we can take them to the Angel. One by one, two by two, and take them to the River, make them see. We must be welcoming, we must be inviting. People will come and they will see our peaceful streets and our calm demeanors, Brethren. They will see the peace of this place and they will come. And we will take them to the River, and we will send them on their way. And they will bring more and more Breathers to our fair town. And we will take them all to the River. Every last one."

There was no cheering. There was only silence. Mal accepted this. This was the face of the future, the Age of the Angel.

"But we must be careful, Brethren. Beyond Ludlow, the Breathers outnumber us, and will try to stop us if they realize what we are doing, so we must be so careful. We must make Ludlow a model community, a place people would be happy to visit. So, I want you to go and clean up our town. Go to your jobs, and do them. If you see messes, clean them up. Make our town peaceful and presentable, so when Breathers turn up, they'll not see what they are not prepared to see. Take the people you've fed to the Angel and put them in the gymnasiums of the schools. Mind them until they are reborn. You are the vanguard of a new age. An age without hope or fear or uncertainty—you breathed the last of those empty things in the River. A deathless age. Go, Brethren."

Again, not a cheer was offered, nor did Mal expect or require one. Breathers cheered. Brethren knew everlasting life and everlasting peace. The Breathers would breathe their last and the Brethren would claim them all.

Mal was pleased with the pace of everything so far. His flock had done what was required of them, and only a few Breathers remained in Ludlow, now, he was sure. In fact, some of the last of them were being brought in to him right now. Jolene had told him about them, and he wanted to see this group.

He didn't recognize the woman at the head of them.

"Where is this 'Max' that Jolene mentioned?" Mal asked.

"He's not here," the woman said. She had been crying, and they all looked disheveled.

"And who are you?"

"Adrienne," the woman said.

"I don't know you," Mal said. "I don't know any of you. Where is Max?"

"He took off," Adrienne said. "Tried to get out of town."

Zitface came up. "They shot a bunch of us. A whole bunch."

"How many?"

"Fifteen," Zitface said. "But we got'em."

"Yes," Mal said. "Max left you in his place and just skipped town?"

Adrienne nodded.

"I don't believe you," Mal said. "I think he's still around. Feed them to the River. Give them unto the Angel."

Mal rather liked the way that sounded. It felt biblical.

The Breathers wailed and struggled, but too many of the Brethren were holding them. Mal relished watching them hauled to the back of a pickup. He directed one of the police officers to drive him to the River to watch.

As they drove through town, Mal admired the silence of it, row after row of silent, dark, empty homes. Many of them already with their owners lain to rest upon their beds, waiting to reawaken. The image of all of those bodies, the

Brethren, at peace, to be reborn and find everlasting life in the service of the Angel—it was as close to beauty as Mal could comprehend.

The convoy of vehicles reached the shore of the River, the ramp that fed into the dark waters.

Mal got out, everybody got out, and they watched a barge loaded with ore slide its way down the river. The crewmen on board watched the group of townsfolk without comment, looking like dolls aboard the massive ore barge.

Mal held up a hand in greeting, but the wave was not returned. The men just watched. The Brethren had sensibly muzzled the Breathers.

Standing among the stones, watching the water lap along the shore, the restive wake from the barge making waves, Mal thought something would have to be done about the River traffic eventually.

There seemed to be an opportunity there, if he could perhaps commandeer one of those boats. There were always boats on the River. That would allow traffic to come and go with ease. But the Angel lived only here, in this part of the River.

All Breathers had to be brought to this place. Still, the River offered another way into and out of Ludlow, and sooner or later, he'd have to reckon with it.

The Brethren waited until the barge had slipped down the River, out of view, before forcing the Breathers down to the water. There, Mal looked at them all in turn, and spoke unto them.

"You're fighting against something that you cannot vanquish," he said. "You will see the Light in the Dark and you will be born again. This is a joyous thing, Breathers. You will never know fear, or pain, or hunger again. You will know only everlasting life, and everlasting peace. All of your lives, you have known turmoil, you have wandered about without purpose, lived in confusion. Without spirit, without direction. You have moved liked barges down the River, rudderless, purposeless. The Angel will give you purpose. You will be as you have always been, only renewed. You will move as gears in a great clockwork mechanism that will reach unto the heavens, each with a discrete role to play. Like musicians in an orchestra, with me as the conductor, making the most beautiful music. Unity of spirit, unity of purpose, unity of mind."

The Breathers struggled against the Brethren, and Mal grabbed Adrienne and pulled her to him. Her eyes were full of rage and fear.

"No one's going to rescue you," he said. "You know this, yes? You're absolutely alone right now. I'm going to make you myself. Would you like to see the Angel? You will. Soon."

He grabbed her and walked her into the water, with the other Brethren following his lead. The Breathers fought and failed, but with at least two Brethren holding each of them, there was only so much they could do.

Mal took off the gag on Adrienne's mouth and she immediately shrieked in protest, as loudly as she could, which Mal knew she would do, for he thrust her into the water, cutting off her scream. It made everything easier when they screamed.

Her cell phone rang, and Mal yanked her out of the water, sputtering, choking, while he fished the phone out, answering it. He thought who it might be, and he wanted him to hear this.

"Hello?"

There was silence on the line.

"Max, is that you?" Mal asked.

Adrienne was coughing.

"Why don't you come down to the River, Max?" Mal asked.

"Max," choked Adrienne. Mal gave her a shake.

"There's nothing you can say, is there, Max?" Mal said. "You know what I'm going to do, you know her fate, and there's not a thing in the world you can do to stop it."

"I can shoot you," Max said. "I've got you in my sights right now."

Mal looked around, tried to see, but all he saw was woods around them.

"Let her go," Max said. "And I won't put a bullet through your skull."

"You're bluffing," Mal said.

"You really want to find that out for sure?" Max said. "I can put an end to your little crusade right now. You let Adrienne go. You give her back her phone, and you let her go. You let them all go."

The other Breathers were already churning the River water into foam, as they went from living to dead, from Breathers to Brethren, taking the water into their lungs, their movements becoming spasmodic, then ceasing altogether, all the while held fast by the Brethren.

And below, in the depths, he could feel the Angel uncoiling, receiving this latest sacrifice, with its unquenchable thirst for souls, this marvelous thing in the water, touching each of the Breathers in turn, as it had touched Mal, himself.

What a glorious spectacle, this miracle in the mire, the Light in the Dark, that would bring these wayward spirits back as Brethren, reborn. The Angel had graced them all, and retreated back into the depths. All of them, limp and lifeless, the spiritual unborn.

"It's too late," Mal said. "But you know that, don't you?"

"Let Adrienne go, or it ends for you right here, right now," Max said.

Mal scanned around them again, but he couldn't see anybody except the Brethren. The trouble was, the terrain was such that Max could be telling the truth.

"I'm a photographer by trade," Max said. "But the funny thing about photography is that it's just another form of shooting. You get the subject—the target—in your sights, and you frame the shot, and when you have the shot, you take it. A good photographer takes the best shots. You ready for your close-up, Mr. Lazarus?"

Mal shoved Adrienne away from him, while she sputtered, splashing in the water. Some of the Brethren went to grab her, but Mal stopped them with an upraised hand.

"This doesn't change a thing, Max," Mal said. "I've taken the whole town. You and Ms. Adrienne, here, you think you can stop all of us? I'm going to feed you to the River myself."

"Give her back her phone," Max said. "We'll talk again."

The bodies of the Breathers floated in the River, still held by the Brethren.

Mal tossed the phone to Adrienne, who caught it and put it to her ear. She looked at Mal with terror, and nodded. Then she started running, going up the concrete precipice, her sneakers squishing wetly as she ran. The Brethren watched her go, then looked to Mal for spiritual guidance.

"A Judas Goat," he said. "She'll lead us to the Other. Finish up here. Take them home."

Mal exited the water, stalked to the police cruiser. Adrienne had already vanished from sight in the woods.

"Get some of the Brethren," he said. "Clear this brush. I want all the scrub within 100 yards of this spot gone. Just clear it all. And across the River, too. I want a clear, unobstructed view of the surroundings. And I want Brethren at the perimeter at all times. No one is to get near this holy place. And Sheriff? Get every gun you can, every rifle. I want them all."

5.

Special Agent Holliday and the girls had managed to evade the mob that had gone street-by-street, house by house. They had simply gone to the cemetery and hidden there, watching as the townsfolk went through St. Vincent's. The irony of the living hiding from the living dead in a cemetery was not lost on any of them.

They had seen people carted from their homes and put into vans and buses, and seen them driving for the river.

Holliday had wanted to do something for those people, but by himself, he couldn't. Instead, they focused on getting down to the river, as stealthily as they could, in hopes of finding a boat.

The older girl, Heidi, had an encyclopedic knowledge of Ludlow, and navigated them down to the river, past the railyards, where they saw hundreds, if not thousands of people, being forcibly drowned in the river.

The scale of it was monstrous, unlike anything Holliday had seen in his career as an agent.

"Girls," he said. "I have to do something, here."

"What'll you do?" Heidi asked.

"I have no idea," he said. "But look at this."

It was an efficient operation, if an ad hoc one. A vehicle would come up and they would remove the victims, who were then drowned in the river. Once verifiably dead, they were then carted to a waiting vehicle and driven off.

Everybody was being fed to the river: man, woman, boy, girl. Old and young. Every ethnicity. All of them were being drowned.

Something had to be done.

"Girls," Holliday said. "You find yourselves a boat, and get out of here. Go down the river, tell somebody, anybody what you've seen. Get out of town."

"What are you going to do, Agent Holliday?" Heidi asked.

"I'm going to try to put a stop to this," he said. He had Heidi give him the hunting rifle she'd used to save him earlier. "If nothing else, I can delay them a bit."

He left the girls with some numbers they could call when and if they got out of town, and then he crept along the railroad tracks. There was a train sitting there, a length of cars just motionless, for one of those unknowable reasons of the rail industry.

Holliday climbed one of the ladders that led to the top of one of the train cars, where he'd be able to look down on the townsfolk, without them necessarily finding him. At least not at first. The rifle's report would carry in the river valley. It would be hard to pinpoint just where he was, at least at first.

Dropping to his stomach, Holliday army-crawled on his stomach, then made sure the rifle was loaded. He had two boxes of 25 rounds apiece. The rifle chambered five rounds.

If he could get Lazarus, maybe he could put an end to this insanity.

It was bad enough looking on at the mass murders taking place. But through the scope, which magnified the atrocity, it was even worse. The fearful faces, the implacable blankness of the murderers.

This was unvarnished evil, right before his eyes.

Holliday took careful aim. The rifle was high-powered, and at this range, could likely bring as much harm to the victims as the perpetrators. He had to shoot carefully.

So, he scanned the killing ground, wondered who he should shoot first. The police seemed the most logical targets. After all, they had guns, themselves. There was the immediate threat of civilians being drowned, but Holliday knew that the police posed the greater threat at the moment. He hated having to make that kind of life-and-death decision, but had to target the most dangerous of the cultists.

He got one of the deputies in his sights, and pulled the trigger. The man's head exploded into a cauliflower of flesh and bone, and the man went down. Before his partner could react, Holliday had chambered another round and fired, tearing off this man's head, too.

The report of the rifle rang out, startling the victims, while the cultists looked around, trying to determine the origin of the sound. Many hadn't realized that two of their members had already been slain.

Holliday took advantage of that to fire off three more shots, killing two more of the cultists, and badly wounding another. He rolled onto his back and reloaded the rifle.

An assault rifle would've been much better, but beggars could not be choosers. He hoped that the commotion he was causing here would buy the girls time to find a boat. He was not sure how thorough Lazarus would be about locking down the town. The man had been pretty damned thorough.

Rolling back onto his stomach, Holliday fired another shot at one of the cultists, and two more. Then he rolled to his side and ran across the top of the train car, keeping himself in a crouching posture, to hopefully evade detection.

He set up again for another round of shots, reloading the rifle as he did so. The cultists were now under cover, while bodies floated untended in the water, and victims screamed and fought to free themselves.

There were shots being fired willy-nilly, but it was clear that they didn't know where he was, yet.

Holliday took aim again. With the scope, it was so much easier. Even the hidden ones sprang into view. He fired, downed another one.

And then another.

And another.

They were fanning out into the trees, searching. Holliday wondered if he could risk heading down to the boat slip and rescuing some of the victims. Or, he could run down the long ribbon of steel that was the train and perhaps end up in the next town, or at least get past the barricades that way. Since he was sure that Lazarus would not be stopping any trains. It was too risky.

A clear moral choice existed for him: he could risk his own life and try to save some of the Ludlow residents, or he could save his own life and try to get out of town and bring in more agents, bring in the Army, whatever it took. Where the hell was Bob, anyway? He had put the call through hours ago.

He fired three more shots, taking down three more cultists, then reloaded the rifle and crept down the side of the train, reaching the gravel below. Then he ran for the patch of scrub trees just past the railroad tracks, down the embankment, toward the river.

Holliday pushed past the tangles and the brambles, past the piles of litter, made his way to the sloping ground, huffing and puffing.

One of the cultists saw him and pointed, and Holliday fired a shot from the rifle, knocking the thing on its back.

I will not call them zombies, he thought, working his way down.

He fired at another one of them, taking his head off. Then he took a bullet in the shoulder, which sent him careening into the water, landing on one of the floating dead. Sputtering, he tried to bring up the rifle, but the throb in his shoulder prevented it. Several of the cultists were now clamoring for him, leaving Holliday no choice but to swim for it.

He rolled to his side, doing a sidestroke, leading with his good arm. Glancing back, he saw the cultists watching him, no longer shooting, standing before a mass of bodies, some of which had floated downriver already on the lazy currents of the Mercy. He wondered how deep the river was, his clothing getting soaked, weighing him down as he swam.

Shooting at killer cultists, swimming a river, wounded in a business suit. Just another day in the Bureau. Looking upriver, he saw the girls. They were in a canoe. They'd done it. He was glad. They would make their way out, could tell somebody.

He stopped swimming and floated in the middle of the river. Maybe they would pass him. He could hook his good arm on the canoe, and they could paddle each other to safety. He just had to wait.

The cultists were still watching him, although some of them had resumed their ghastly enterprise, drowning people in the river. Holliday felt awful. He had failed those poor people.

The girls were getting closer in the canoe. He hoped none of the cultists would shoot at them. The Mercy River was broad, and it would be a challenge to hit a moving target at that range.

Soon, they'd be close enough to see him. He just had to wait.

The Mercy River Bridge loomed high above him, an impressive feat of engineering, with its green metal spans and the arcing concrete and steel holding it together. A beautiful thing, really.

The girls were maybe a hundred yards away, now.

"Girls," Holliday yelled. "Girls!"

He held an arm up, and one of them saw him. He thought it was Heidi.

Then Holliday saw the water around him, the dark waters of the Mercy River, light up from within, a silvery color that shimmered in the lapping waves.

He felt something grab onto his ankle, something long and sinuous, coiling up his pants leg.

"My God," Holliday said.

Then something grabbed onto his other leg, too. Once it had done that, it began to pull down on him. It was impossible to resist.

He saw the girls watching, their horrified looks, and he gazed below him, and he saw IT, the Angel in the Depths. It had to be. And he screamed.

The thing pulled on him again, and Holliday bobbed like a cork. It would drown him, like it had the others. He drew his service pistol, knowing full well that the weapon was useless against the thing below him. The size of the thing was unbelievable.

It pulled him down with it, and Holliday's face broke the surface of the water for the last time, and he went down, seeing the silver barrier of the water, the luminosity in the depths, the shadow of the girls' canoe above him.

Down, down it went, securing its hold on him with more arms that braided around him, holding him fast, while his lungs burned.

The Light in the Dark. This was it. The cold radiance of the thing, the ghastly glow.

All around him was the darkness of the river, even the light above vanishing— the canoe, the bridge, the bodies, everything. There was only this monstrosity down here with him, and his lungs, throbbing.

He had failed. He prayed the girls got downriver, got out of there. There was one last thing he could do. One thing he must do. He would not become the plaything of this demon.

Holliday opened his mouth, where his waning air bubbled out of him, and thrust his pistol in, and pulled the trigger. There was air enough in his mouth for a parting shot.

Thunder in the depths.

6.

Max picked up Adrienne just off the train tracks and they drove up into the Heights, Adrienne sobbing soggily into her hands.

His own hands were shaking on the steering wheel.

"They're all dead," she said. "Lazarus drowned all of them. He was going to drown me, too. My fucking God, Max."

"Yeah," Max said. "I bluffed him. Those things can be killed. You shoot'em in the head, and they die."

Adrienne turned. "What do you mean, you bluffed him?"

"I told him I was going to shoot him if he didn't let you go," Max said.

Adrienne wailed. "I saw it. I saw that Thing."

"What did you see?"

"It was in the water," she said. "This glowing thing. Like a cold light. White, like, I don't know, an overcast sky in winter. That kind of leaden white. It was in the water, Max. I saw it touch all of them."

She cried, and Max tried to comfort her.

"They have the whole town," she said. "We're alone."

"No," Max said. "We'll find a place."

"They'll find us," she said. "There are more of them than ever. They keep rising out of the River."

"We'll find someplace," Max said.

"How?" Adrienne asked.

"Lazarus leads the whole thing," Max said. "It starts and ends with him. We take him out, the rest'll fall, just like dominoes."

"No," Adrienne said. "It's that thing in the water. That is what is behind this. That is what we have to go after."

Max chewed his lip as he drove.

"We can't go up this way, Max," Adrienne said. "They have the exits covered."

"I'm not looking to leave," Max said. He turned up one of the driveways, one of the estates, and drove his car down it.

"What are you doing?"

"Finding us a safe place," Max said. "This'll do."

They drove up the long, winding driveway toward the beautiful French manor house that eventually came into view, with a great view of the river valley below, elegantly screened by stands of willow trees and poplars.

Max parked the car beside the garage, then got out, pistol drawn. Adrienne got out with him, shivering in the chill autumn air.

The great house, the slate-roofed thing, sat silently before them. Max didn't know who lived here, was surprised Mal Lazarus hadn't requisitioned it for himself.

Max went to the door and tried it. It was unlocked. He went in, with Adrienne behind him.

"Anybody in here?" Max asked.

They were in a kind of mud room, with slate floors. Adrienne's shoes squished as she walked.

"Sorry," she said.

"No worries," Max said.

They walked into a cavernous kitchen of dark hardwood and granite or marble countertops (Max couldn't tell for sure), with mullioned wooden cabinets and a big, broad butcher's block and Wolf appliances.

"Nice place," Max said. "Who lived here?"

"I don't know," Adrienne said. "I never got up to the Heights so much, what with being an art teacher and all."

The kitchen fed into a long dining room, which itself opened into a grand living room that had a wall of window that had that same view of the valley. That window, broken into three long pieces of glass, itself overlooked a cut stone deck.

There was an almost feudally large fireplace in this big hall, and Max saw a couple of cavalry sabers hanging over it. He nodded toward those, handed Adrienne the revolver while he took them down, drawing them.

They had brass scabbards, and looked to be Civil War era. One was Confederate, the other, Union.

"They look real," Max said. "Great!"

He handed the Confederate one to her, and kept the Union one for himself, taking back the pistol.

"What, am I supposed to use this?" she asked.

"You want to be fed to the River again?" Max asked. He put the saber on his belt, wanting to laugh at the image of it, but too worried to do so. "We have to check this place. Every goddamned room."

"This place has to be like 30,000 square feet, Max," Adrienne said.

"And we're going to check every inch of it, Adrienne," Max said. "I'll be damned if one of those things is going to sneak up on me."

They found the family in their bedroom, everybody laid on their beds with apparent care.

All of them dead.

The mother, three children.

All dead.

The mother was young and blonde and willowy-tall, stunning, beautiful. The kids were teenagers, all looked like the mom.

Adrienne cried again.

"Who would have done this?" she asked.

"Whomever," Max said. "It hardly matters. All that matters is that they're dead."

"But why bring them back here?" Adrienne asked. "Why take them home?"

"I don't know," Max said.

"I think this is Lucy Balfour," Adrienne said.

"Dr. Balfour's wife?" Max asked. He was a surgeon at Ludlow General.

"Yeah," Adrienne said.

"Look, we have to, uh, dispose of them," Max said. "We can't have them coming back on us."

"You're sure they're dead?" she asked.

"Yes," Max said. "But you can check if you like."

Adrienne did, one by one, while Max took them out back, laid them out on the perfectly-kept lawn. They looked so pale.

"Lazarus probably took out the civic leaders first," he said. "Then worked his way up the Heights."

He drew the saber, but was stopped by Adrienne.

"What are you doing?"

"I'm sure as hell not shooting them," Max said. "Too noisy."

"So, you're going to cut off their fucking heads?"

"Thought I would," Max said. "We can't have them waking up, Adrienne. Look, if it's a problem, you just go inside and keep watch. I don't want Dr. Balfour turning up here and surprising us."

Adrienne turned on her heel and crunched away on the gravel, leaving Max with the bodies. He checked the children again, and Mrs. Balfour, Dr. Balfour's trophy wife.

"Just meat," he said. "Dead meat."

He lopped their heads off, one by one, with smooth cuts of the saber. There was no blood, because, as he knew, they were fucking undead.

Each time the saber cut, Max winced. The smooth power of the sword was marvelous, the way it transferred the energy of the stroke down the length of the blade, making the severing of a head almost seem easy. Each time it struck, the saber gave off a metallic ring.

And yet, each time he did this, he felt horrible. It had to be done, but it was horrible all the same. He did not hesitate, and the dirty work was done. He blamed Lazarus. This was his doing. All of it was.

He cleaned off the saber, although there was only water and flesh on the blade, no blood. Then he put the saber back in its scabbard and lit a cigarette, his hands shaking.

Dr. Balfour would likely be back. He wondered how Mal had put him to use. Maybe administering tranquilizers to whatever Breathers were still around, so they could be put into the River without much difficulty.

All the same, despite the circumstances, Max felt a stab of something like remorse. "I just killed your family, Dr. Balfour."

He wondered if the Good Doctor had drowned his family himself? Max shook that off, threw away the cigarette, went back inside.

Adrienne wouldn't look at him, was just gazing through those big windows, looking at the valley below them.

"Would you do that to me if I'd been…taken?" Adrienne asked.

"Yeah," Max said.

"These people," Adrienne said.

"They're not people, Adrienne," Max said. "Not anymore. Look, don't you even start mindfuckng yourself or me on this. Lazarus killed all of these people, turned them into things that only look like people, alright? They died in the river; they all died there."

"But they talk," Adrienne said. "They think, even."

"They don't feel," Max said. "They're not who they used to be. Honestly, Adrienne, you can't do this to yourself, or you're going to be dead. I saw some fucked up shit today."

"You think I didn't?" she said.

"I saw a kid putting severed heads on display at the deli counter," Max said. Adrienne winced, didn't offer a rebuttal. "I think there's something else going on, here. Those things get a little squirrelly when they're not on Mal's leash."

"They're people," Adrienne said, but Max cut her off.

"They *were* people, Adrienne," Max said. "Lazarus took that away from them. That thing in the river did that. They're not people, anymore. They're things that won't hesitate to make us one of them, or, failing that, to kill us. You understand that?"

"Yes," Adrienne said, tossing aside the Confederate saber. "I do. But I can't kill them."

"Then you're already dead," Max said. Adrienne glowered at him, but Max just shrugged. "We're at war, here."

Adrienne fretted, knitted her fingers. "We can't win. Not just you and me."

"We'll regroup," Max said. "We'll find a way out. The River's the key to everything. Maybe we can destroy it. Or just slip out of Ludlow by raft."

"Destroy the River?" Adrienne asked.

"Something like that," Max said. "Still working on it."

She was going to say something when they saw a car driving up the winding road to the mansion.

"Oh my god," Adrienne said. "They're coming."

Max watched the car, then grabbed his camera, put on the telephoto lens, zoomed in on it, tracking the car as it came.

"It's the doctor," Max said. "He's alone. Look, he doesn't know we're here. We have surprise on our side. You go upstairs or something. I'll try to deal with him."

He put down the camera and drew the saber, while Adrienne just stood there, shaking.

"Upstairs," Max said. He grabbed the other saber, so he had one in each hand. That should do it. Adrienne went up the stairs, while Max waited in the shadows. It seemed to take forever for Dr. Balfour's car to reach the house. It was a gray Jaguar sedan.

He got out and walked to the back door of the place, while Max waited in the shadows of the kitchen.

He keyed in and walked in, silent. Max was acutely aware of his own breathing.

"Lucy?" he said. "Are you up there?"

He paused, waiting. Then he checked his watch.

"Lucy? Kids?"

Max walked toward the doctor, who was about to go up the stairs, when he saw Max coming and turned, gazing impassively at Max with black, soulless eyes.

There was not a trace of fear in the doctor's face, nor anger. Just emptiness. It disarmed Max a moment, even though he was poised to strike.

"It won't make a difference," the Doctor said. "Lazarus has claimed the valley. He has claimed the town. You're too late, Breather."

He had not moved. He just stood there, one of the walking, talking dead.

"I killed your family," Max said, but the thing still didn't react to it.

"They are with the Angel, now," the Doctor said. "As are we all. I don't fear you, I don't fear death. Lazarus has shown us the Light in the Dark. He'll show you, too, Max."

"How do you know my name?" Max asked.

"Lazarus told us all about you," the Doctor said. "He wants to take you to the Angel himself."

"What is the Angel?" Max asked. He figured if the zombie was feeling talkative, he might as well indulge it.

"Beautiful," the Doctor said. "More beautiful than anything you will ever know. True peace, harmony, understanding."

Clearly, not all of the freaks were operating at the same level. The Butcher Boy had been barely there, whereas the Doctor seemed almost normal, but for those black eyes gazing blankly at Max.

"What is it?" Max asked.

"Luminous, transcendent, life-giving," the Doctor said. "Arms enfolding you. There is peace in its embrace. The most marvelous peace. The stilling of the heart, the calming of the waves."

The Doctor took a step toward Max, heedless of the upraised sabers.

"Look at you," the Doctor said. "Sweating, afraid, heart pounding, lungs gulping air. And for what? Biology is a dead end. All that lives must die. But the Angel in the Depths brings life eternal."

The Doctor again stepped toward Max, who was forced to take a step back. He pointed one of the sabers at the Doctor's heart.

"The entire culture is built upon avoidance of Death," the Doctor said. "My career was based on that. Prolonging life. And here, Lazarus came across the cure for life itself. No one in Ludlow will ever die again. Will ever feel pain."

"Or love," Max said.

"Love is pain," the Doctor said. "Love is the word we attach to our mating instinct. And the love we bear the Angel outshines anything we have within our sorry species. Words are blunt and insufficient instruments for the task at hand. You cannot explain an epiphany, nor dissect a miracle. There simply is the Light in the Dark. And you will see it, and you will know."

The Doctor pressed against the point of the saber, right over his heart.

Max thrust the saber through the Doctor's heart with a lunge, and the Doctor actually smiled at him, unfazed by it.

"You see?" the Doctor said. "No death for the dead. Only the living need fear it. What a sad thing it is to live in fear, yes? What a sorrowful spectacle."

The Doctor shifted his stance, yanking the saber from Max's grasp. He stood there, run through, and looked at Max.

Then Max struck him with a slash of the other saber, which the Doctor managed to deflect with an upraised hand, which was severed at the wrist. The hand fell to the ground, motionless.

There was no blood.

Then the Doctor pulled the saber from his chest with his remaining hand, only to have that limb lopped off at the elbow by another saber cut from Max. The saber and arm landed on the floor with a clatter.

"Sure you're not feeling fear now, Doc?" Max asked. Incredibly, the Doctor just gazed at his severed limbs impassively.

"Such is the way of all flesh," the Doctor said. "But the spirit endures."

"Right," Max said, cutting off the Doctor's head. His body collapsed to the ground, while his head tumbled along the floor, landing in the living room.

"Max?" Adrienne called from upstairs.

"It's alright," he said. "I got him."

"Jesus Christ, Max," she said.

Max pried the Doctor's fingers from the other saber, and went to get the head. He nudged it with a foot.

"Maybe you should stay up there a bit," Max said. He fished the Doctor's keys from his pockets, took his wallet, took out the money he had.

Then he dragged the Doctor's corpse out and put it with the rest of his family. It was horrible, but he tried not to think about it. Clearly, some twinkling of consciousness stayed with the freaks. A smart person would make a smart freak; a stupid person would make a stupid freak. Maybe the rough edges smoothed out, but there was still a vestigial self, there. No sense of self-preservation, but the intelligence remained.

He went back inside, poured himself a scotch, while Adrienne made her way back down the stairs.

He'd done the work, but she was the one who looked haunted by it.

"I can't believe it," she said. "He just let you kill him."

"You have to stop thinking about them being alive. Something in the river is giving them life. Now, we're thinking about Lazarus all this time, but really the so-called 'Angel in the Depths' is what we need to go after. You were right about that."

"I'm not swimming in that river," Adrienne said.

"Me, neither," Max said. "But I have an idea of maybe how we can take care of that thing."

7.

Heidi and Lisa had paddled away from the boat slip after they'd seen the Thing claim Agent Holliday. They hadn't known precisely what they had seen, only that it had illuminated the river, and that it had tentacles. They had seen that, sure enough, as the Thing had wound itself around the FBI agent and dragged him under.

They'd paddled hurriedly over where he had disappeared, seeing only a rash of bubbles where the agent had been.

"Did you see that, Heidi?" Lisa asked.

"Yes," Heidi said. "Keep paddling."

"What was it?"

"I don't know," Heidi said. "Something awful."

They kept at their oars, Lisa pointing out the bodies that had floated downriver, some of them snagging on fallen trees, some still floating along. There were bodies piled up on the Ludlow side of the riverbank, being loaded into trucks by the lifeless, bloodless others.

"We have to get to the next town."

"We should've gone upriver," Lisa said. "Smithton's not so far."

"We're going with the current, Lisa," Heidi said. "It's quicker. Less work."

Heidi was terribly afraid that whatever had drowned Agent Holliday was going to come after them, so she kept paddling, trying to make up for her sister's lackluster efforts. Lisa half-assed absolutely everything, and even their escape was somehow too much work for her.

"Did you see those white eels grab him?" Lisa asked.

"Not eels; it had tentacles," Heidi said. "I saw them grab him."

She had no words for it, for she'd seen it, too. The thing had snaked up his body, dragged him under. They'd seen a glimpse of it, these silvery-white appendages, wrapping around him, like worms.

"Tentacles?" Lisa asked. "Are you fucking kidding me?"

"I saw," Heidi said.

"It's an alien," Lisa said.

"It's a demon," Heidi said. That felt right to her. Some monstrous abomination from the netherworld that had made the Mercy River its home.

"A demon? What the hell are you talking about?" Lisa asked.

"It's some kind of soul eater," Heidi said. "It takes those people's souls, and somehow brings them back."

"What, it's magical, then?" Lisa asked.

"Yes," Heidi said. Not like she knew, but she had to call it something she could comprehend.

They paddled past the Big Star Riverboat Casino, which brightly illuminated the river, that big star flashing on and off. For a second, Heidi thought maybe they could stop there, but she could see some of those others there, on the balcony that overlooked the river, watching them. The pale faces, silent. Lifeless apparitions. She pointed to them, and Lisa looked up, gasping.

"It's spread across the river," Lisa said. "It's spreading. What if they're in the next town, too?"

"Then we keep going."

They kept paddling, the green mountains flanking them, now, Ludlow gliding past them. They were nearing the old industrial quarter, the abandoned mills, which hung like rusting specters, silent and huge.

"How do we fight something like that?" Lisa asked.

"We don't," Heidi said.

"It got Mom and Dad, didn't it?" Lisa asked.

"I think it got Mom," Heidi said. "Dad, I'm not so sure. He may still be in Pittsburgh. At least I hope he is."

That pained Heidi more than she could possibly admit. She could see her parents fighting the zombies, her father arguing with them, trying to reason with them, and her mother, she was probably one of the first to go, if Lazarus went after the Mayor early on.

"Maybe they're alright," Heidi said.

"They're dead," Lisa said. "Or worse than dead. Undead."

Her sister started to cry, had stopped rowing.

"Lisa, not now," Heidi said. "We have to get on, here. I can't paddle us both."

"We're going to die, too," Lisa said.

Up ahead, Heidi saw a police boat sitting on the river, some distance away. It was Ludlow Police, she could tell from the colors, the black and blue of Ludlow.

"Oh, dammit," Heidi said, which stopped Lisa's snuffling a bit.

Heidi steered them toward the shore. In the dead industrial park, there was a lot of cover. Scrub trees and bushes.

"Do you think they spotted us?" Lisa asked.

"We'll know soon enough," Heidi said.

They brought the canoe up to the shore, Heidi stepping out and urging Lisa along. Together, they were able to muscle the canoe to the shore.

"What are we doing?" Lisa said. "This place is horrible."

"We can't hope to run a police blockade with that thing," Heidi said. "They'll scoop us out of the water and will drive us back to that spot."

Lisa dug out a cigarette, sat on a rock, and lit up.

"Oh, what the hell, Lisa?"

"I'm exhausted," she said, puffing on the cigarette.

"You're exhausted because you smoke," Heidi said.

Her sister looked at her like she was insane, like she always did.

"Are you kidding me? These are what's keeping me alive," Lisa said, flipping her sister off with a cigarette standing between her middle finger and ring finger.

"Right," Heidi said.

They had been heading north, toward Edgewater, the next town up from Ludlow. It was right there, down the river, with just a police boat between them.

Heidi grabbed their backpacks and tossed hers to her sister, who just smoked in the shadow of a sumac tree.

"We can't walk it from here," Heidi said. "We'd have to cross the river."

Railroads bracketed the Mercy River, carrying cargo to and from Pittsburgh. If she were only bold enough to risk boarding a moving train, she'd risk it. But Heidi doubted Lisa would be up to it.

Her sister stubbed out the cigarette she'd been smoking, ran a hand through her hair, and looked up at Heidi.

"Alright, Sis, what next?"

She gazed at the Big Star, which was like a miniature sun, going off and on. It even illuminated them, before plunging them into shadow. Golden light. Darkness. Golden light. Darkness.

"I don't know," Heidi said. "I really don't know."

"Wow, that's, like, a first."

Heidi ignored her sister. They could head south, but that would mean having to go past the crazies in the water, and past the Thing. No thank you.

"We can't camp out here," Lisa said. "Way, way too creepy."

It had to be the trains. The trains were the only way out.

But she didn't know which trains went which way. Then again, maybe it hardly mattered. She doubted that even Lazarus could keep the trains monitored.

"We're going to hop a train," Heidi said.

"Where?" Lisa asked.

"Anywhere," Heidi said.

She tried to get her bearings. Across the river, there were two sets of tracks. On this side, there was one. One of the sets across the river had a train on it, a lengthy snake of steel, which was not moving. She wondered why.

They could try walking on the tracks on this side of the river, just take it down to Edgewater, although there wasn't another bridge for a number of miles. Or, they could risk a river crossing and detection by the police boat, and then get aboard that motionless train and take it from there.

"Hey," Lisa said. "The boat's moving."

Heidi instinctively hunkered down behind one of the scrub bushes, and, sure enough, the Ludlow Police boat was moving. She hadn't even known Ludlow had a river patrol boat. It was probably tied to the casino, like there to fish out drunken tourists or something.

The boat just cruised up the river, taking its time. Was it looking for them? Heidi looked at the canoe.

"We have to hide this," she said.

"Um, how?"

"We drag it in the bushes," Heidi said. "Quickly."

She stepped carefully amid the river stones, trying to reach the canoe without turning an ankle, while keeping an eye on the boat. It would be able to see them once it got a bit nearer.

Heidi struggled to pull the canoe up the hill, while her sister watched.

"Help me, Lisa," Heidi said. Her sister joined her and the two of them managed to muscle the canoe up out of the water, but it was hard and awkward.

And the boat kept drifting nearer.

Upriver, Heidi saw a barge gliding downriver. Maybe that was why the police boat was moving. Maybe they hadn't been seen, after all.

She tried to gauge whether the police boat would be nearer to them or farther away. If the barge ended up between the girls and the police boat, then they could perhaps take the canoe and travel downriver with the barge, using it to screen their movements.

"What are you staring at?" Lisa asked.

"The barge," Heidi said.

Lisa followed her sister's gaze, shrugged. "So what?"

"It's a way out for us, maybe," Heidi said.

But the police boat had moved closer to where they were, rather than more on the Ludlow side. She could see three police officers manning the boat, while the barge was getting ever closer.

Heidi could see one or two people on the barge, tiny moving figures on the massive thing. She wondered if she could get their attention.

With the shotgun, she certainly could. But that'd have the police boat on them. And there was no guarantee the barge would even stop.

"Sis!" Lisa hissed. "They're coming."

Heidi looked and saw the police boat was, in fact, moving toward them. Had they been spotted after all?

She grabbed her sister's arm and moved away from the shore, heading into the cover of the trees that filled the long-abandoned grounds around the steel mills. They weren't big trees, but were large enough to hide the girls, anyway.

The boat pulled right across from where they had landed, and she saw two of the three police officers take a little launch and drive it to the shore, while the police boat floated nearby, shining a spotlight around where they were, back and forth.

Heidi didn't even have to see their faces to know that they were zombies. They saw the canoe, walked up the embankment.

"Fuck," Lisa said. "They're onto us."

"Shhh," Heidi said.

One of them shined a flashlight around, although it wasn't fully night, yet. In the overcast light of the day, though, with the mountains blocking what light there was, it was dark enough.

"Come on out," one of the officers said. Heidi thought she recognized him. It was Officer Peter Compton, who had come to the school and lectured everybody on Stranger Danger or something, when they were younger.

Now he was stalking around, flat-faced, empty-eyed, and dead-voiced.

"We know you're around here," Compton said. "You have to know there's no way out of town."

"We're here to give you the good news," the other officer said. "About the Light in the Dark."

The police officers were maybe 100 feet away, while Heidi and Lisa were hidden behind some trees. Behind the girls was some rusty fencing that bracketed the dead mill. They could run along that, but wouldn't be able to climb it without exposing themselves.

"In a few days, you're going to be the only Breathers left," Compton said. "Think about that. Everybody you knew, everyone you loved—all Brethren. You'll be all alone and afraid. But we won't be afraid. Fear dies in the depths. The Angel takes it away."

Heidi could see from her sister's expression that Compton was getting to her. She looked like she wanted to mouth off to him. Heidi held a finger to her lips.

The police officers were walking slowly, deliberately, a number of paces apart. Heidi would not be able to shoot them both at once. Maybe they had planned that.

The great ore barge slid by, a handful of tiny figures gathered at the railing, watching. Perhaps they had seen the bodies stacked upriver. Perhaps they knew.

"You know, we can literally stand out here all night," Compton said. "Unlike you, we don't need to breathe or sleep or eat. We can just stay here, as long as it takes, to find you. In three days, all of Ludlow will be like us. Can you imagine that? Thousands of us. All looking for you."

Lisa was biting her hand, glaring at Heidi, while Heidi had the shotgun ready. Even if they dispatched these two officers, there was the third one in the boat to contend with.

It wasn't fair. Ludlow deserved better than Lazarus, better than this. She thought of all of those people drowned in the river and got angry. Sure, she was going to move out of it one day, but today, it was her world.

The officers kept stalking around, Compton still talking, his voice lifeless, though words kept flowing out of him.

Lisa met her sister's gaze, something crossed her face, a resolve that Heidi had never seen before.

Then she stepped out, hands up. The boat's spotlight froze on her, casting the shadows of the officers across Lisa's body. Lisa squinted into the light.

"You got me, Officers."

It was all that Heidi needed. Just a momentary distraction, the turn of a head, the turn of an eye, the turn of a back.

She popped out from behind her tree and gave the officer one of the barrels of the shotgun, which sent him flying.

Officer Compton saw this and leveled his service pistol at Heidi, only to have Lisa throw her backpack at him, spoiling his shot.

Then Heidi aimed her shotgun at Compton and fired, catching him in the head. The police officer actually flipped onto his back. The other one was recovering himself, since Heidi had only caught him in the chest.

Lisa grabbed Compton's pistol and fired a handful of shots in the other officer's face, the flash of the pistol catching her terrified expression in still images, like a strobe light.

Heidi emptied the shotgun and reloaded. She grabbed the other officer's sidearm, a Glock pistol.

"That was brave, Lisa," Heidi said. Lisa just smiled sickly, her hands shaking. "Stay here."

She ran for the boat, hoping the third officer didn't see her approaching. The gunfire had certainly caught his attention. He was talking into his radio, likely trying to get Compton or the other officer to answer.

Heidi got as near to the boat as she dared, without revealing herself. It was maybe 20 feet from the shore, just out of range of the embankment rocks.

Taking aim at the wheelhouse of the police boat, Heidi let loose with both barrels. The officer inside took both shots, which punched right through the windscreen of the boat, hitting him in the chest. She had been using slugs, assuming that peppering the zombies with buckshot wasn't the way to go.

The barge had moved downriver, Heidi noticed, as she reloaded. She had not killed the third officer. If he'd been human, he'd have been dead. But he wasn't.

He also wasn't surfacing, but was remaining protected within the boat. Heidi didn't know how to drive a police boat, but assumed it was just a motorboat, which should have been easy enough to deal with.

Lisa called to her sister, and Heidi reluctantly followed her voice, as the police boat moved away from the shore.

"What?"

Lisa held up one of the walkie talkies.

"This is Otter 1, we have shots fired, here," said the radio. "Requesting backup."

"Dammit," Heidi said. "I didn't finish him off."

"Roger, Otter 1, we're sending someone over," said the radio.

"Okay, take the belts and the radios. At least we can hear what they're doing," Heidi said. "We need to get that boat."

"Forget that boat," Lisa said. "We need to just get out of here."

Heidi led them to the shore, and then she remembered that the police officers had used a launch to reach the shore. Sure enough, it was sitting there.

"There's our boat," Heidi said. "Get in."

Lisa made her way down to it, got in, while Heidi watched to see what the police boat was doing. Would the officer give chase? Either way, he was pointed the wrong way, facing upriver, so that might give them enough time to get a head start. They only needed to reach Edgewater.

Heidi handed her sister the shotgun and yanked on the pullchain for the motorboat launch. The engine sprang to life, and both of them fell over in the launch as the thing started, as Heidi got her hand on the tiller and adjusted the throttle. Once they were facing the right way, she gave the launch some gas, and the launch took off.

As they sped away, the police officer in the boat fired at them with his pistol. The shots whizzed by as Heidi zigzagged, while Lisa cowered in the bottom of the launch.

The officer fired thirteen shots at them, before stopping. By then, the girls were a hundred yards away from him, maybe more.

Heidi throttled the thing as far as it would go, and the launch cut a jouncing line through the water, as they raced toward Edgewater.

"What are we going to do when we get there?" Lisa asked. "What are we going to say? We're minors. Won't they just take us back to Ludlow, like to our parents?"

That was something Heidi hadn't considered.

"We just need to find a phone," Heidi said. "To call those people Agent Holliday told us about."

"Oh, yeah, the Zombie Management Authority," Lisa said, dripping with sarcasm.

"Whatever," Heidi said. "He gave us numbers to call."

"Do zombies qualify as bioterrorism?" Lisa asked.

"Why the hell not?"

The police boat lurched in a long circle, pointing toward them. Heidi tried to stay focused on the way they were going.

"Keep an eye out behind us," Heidi said. "Don't let him sneak up."

"Alright," Lisa said.

Heidi's main concern was not hitting a log or some stray rocks. Her mind wandered on what she'd even tell the people on the other end of the phone, assuming they reached one.

The launch bounced in the wake of the barge, which was ahead of them, too. That was another opportunity for the girls, if they took it.

Suddenly, something struck the launch's outboard motor, shattering it in a flash of sparks as the thing sputtered and died. It was faster than Heidi could react.

The motor simply died.

"What happened?" Lisa asked.

The motor had been killed.

"Got'em," said a voice on the radio.

Heidi gazed at the motor. Someone had shot it. There was a bullet hole in the motor.

"Oh, my god," Heidi said, looking around.

"Put your hands up," brayed a voice on a bullhorn, unseen. "Or we'll shoot you."

Lisa looked at her sister, her eyes full of fear.

"Goddammit, Heidi," she said.

"Put down your weapons," the voice said.

"The engine's dead," Heidi said. "They shot it. Some kind of sniper."

Heidi stole a look, and the police boat was coming for them. The train would've been better. Edgewater was tantalizingly in view, in the distance. Maybe a mile away, at most. The barge was closer, still, but was still hundreds of yards away.

"Put your hands up," the voice said.

"They aren't going to shoot us," Heidi said. "They want us for their river."

Lisa's eyes got bigger as she processed that. "What do we do? Fucking swim for it?"

The police boat would be there in a minute or two. There wasn't much time to think, not much time at all. Heidi wanted to cry. She'd tried so hard. It wasn't fair. None of this was fair.

"We should shoot ourselves," she said.

"No fucking way," Lisa said. "I'll swim, first."

"They're going to drown us, Lisa," Heidi said. "We're going to be like them. We have to jump."

There was no choice. Heidi understood this. There was only life. She dropped the shotgun and jumped overboard, into the river, swimming for the nearer shore. Snipers be damned.

Lisa went to follow, but a bullet from the sniper caught her in the arm, knocked her over. Her sister shrieked, unseen, hidden in the bottom of the launch.

Heidi could not abandon her sister. She would not. She swam back for the launch, got behind it, then began kicking the water, trying to propel them to the shore.

"I'm sorry, Heidi," Lisa said.

"Not your fault," Heidi said, gasping. They weren't going to make it. The boat was nearly there, and she could see shapes gathering at the shore, shapes that only looked like people, but weren't, anymore.

"I don't want to be like them," Lisa said. "I'm not going to be. I'm not going to weigh you down anymore, Heidi."

"Stop talking like that," Heidi said. There had to be a dozen shadows at the shore, waiting. In the growing dark, their eyes seemed almost to shine with a spectral light. "It's all my fault. We should've tried for the train."

The boat was there, and a spotlight was shined on them, like they were escaped convicts.

"Hey, Breathers," said one of the shapes from the shore. "We'd have shot you dead if you'd have tried the train. There's no way out of Ludlow."

8.

Max had managed to persuade Adrienne to risk a jaunt into town in the Doctor's Jaguar. The streets were barren, except for the periodic police car patrolling, which Max tried to avoid as nonchalantly as he could.

"In a few days, everybody that Lazarus has drowned is going to come back," Max said. "The whole fucking town is going to be run by those things. Right now is the time to act, while things are still in flux."

He had tried to access the Net from his phone, but Lazarus must've done something to the local service towers, because he wasn't getting any signal.

They were on their own, now.

The idea had come to him when he was reflecting on the scene at the river. There was, perhaps, something to be done, after all. But it hinged on him getting some dynamite, and that involved finding a place that sells it. There was an excavation company right in Ludlow, on Briar Boulevard. Max knew this because sometimes he got tapped to photograph sites they were surveying. It was Sturm & Drang Excavations. They had to have dynamite, plastic explosive, something.

They pulled up to the place, which was, like everything else in town, closed. Max parked the car, and waited a second, looked around.

Adrienne, for her part, looked petrified.

"You'd kill me before they drowned me, right?" she asked.

"In a heartbeat," Max said.

His deadpan expression, which he held for a beat or two, broke her mood. She smiled uneasily, giving him a punch on the shoulder.

"You creep," she said.

Max just smiled. "Look, we have to break into there. I'll try to climb the fence and open the gate. When I do, you just get the Doctor's car in the lot, and we'll break into that place and try to steal enough explosives."

"Enough for what?" Adrienne asked.

"Enough to take care of this," Max said. "If anybody comes, anybody bad, you just take off, alright? Don't worry about me."

"Alright," Adrienne said. "I won't."

It was Max's turn to smile. He picked up the Union saber and hung it from his belt. As far as he was concerned, he was taking that with him everywhere, until this was over.

Then he went to the fence and attempted to climb it. There was razorwire at the top of it, and that immediately discouraged him. Looking up and down Briar

Boulevard, Max then went to the trunk of the car, where he'd raided the Doctor's tool shed. Out came a pair of bolt cutters, which he took to the chain on the gate to Sturm & Drang, laughing to himself at not having just started with that.

Climbing fences was for action heroes; Max was no action hero.

He pushed open the fence, and waved Adrienne through, who drove the Jaguar past him and parked it in the slot marked "Employees only."

Max closed the gate, replacing the chain so it didn't look so obviously hacked, then put the bolt cutter back in the trunk.

Adrienne got out, and the two of them looked around the place. The main office building was mostly a glorified shed which contained some dump trucks, with an earth mover off to the side. A Sturm & Drang white pickup truck. The office had an awning and vinyl siding.

Max walked around to the back of the place.

"There are probably alarms for this place," he said. "I don't know how much time we'll have."

"Where would they store the explosives?" Adrienne asked.

"No idea," Max said. "I mean, part of me thinks the office would be a bad place for it, but maybe they want to keep it under wraps. Or maybe they just keep the blasting caps here. Maybe the explosives are in a shed on-site, away from the detonators."

"I still don't see the point in this," Adrienne said.

"We go to the bridge, or I go, anyway, and start lobbing dynamite into the river," Max said. "You said there's something in the water, right? Well, let's depth charge the Angel in the Depths."

"We don't even know what it is," Adrienne said. "Or whether it'll work."

"I'm willing to try," Max said, walking around, searching. There were several sheds on the lot. He walked back to the Jaguar, got out the bolt cutters again, and opened each of the sheds, in turn.

He didn't care what the damned thing was. Some dynamite would get its attention, he was sure. The explosives were in the third shed he checked, stacked carefully in wooden crates. Nearby was a wooden spatula, which Max assumed was to open the crates. He remembered something about that, like not opening dynamite with anything metal.

Opening one of the crates, he saw sticks of the explosive, all with fuses.

"Sweet," he said.

He grabbed three crates of the stuff, carefully walked it over to the Jaguar, put it in the trunk, while Adrienne kept lookout.

Once it was loaded, they drove out of there, replacing the gate.

"Okay, so now what?" she asked.

"We get to the Mercy River Bridge," Max said.

"And?"

"And you drop me off," he said.

"Aren't there police guarding it? Like sheriff's deputies or something?"

Max hadn't thought about the roadblock.

"Yeah," he said. As they drove down Briar, they could see some dead-eyed people emerging from their homes, heads turning, watching them. He drove past them, and they watched, without expression. "Look, you drop me off near the bridge, and then take this car back up to the Doctor's and hunker down there."

"You sure?"

Max had kind of hoped she'd offer to help him out, but Adrienne kept quiet.

"Uh, yeah," he said. "What we really need is for you to distract the freaks at the checkpoint, and, you know, have 'em chase after you."

Adrienne wrinkled her nose at this. "I don't like that idea, Max."

"I need you to draw some of those freaks off," he said. "I just need that. If this goes the way I planned, it'll all be okay."

"But you don't have a plan, Max."

Max smiled. "I have enough of a plan. Now, are you going to help me or not?"

9.

Mal watched as Ludlow came back to life around him, in waves, as the Brethren awoke, house by house, body by body. In three days, almost the entire town would be as it was, only better. Unified. He had monitored the radio broadcasts by his police, had seen that a couple of girls had tried to boat to Edgewater, no doubt to get help. And a federal agent had gone to his death in the River, itself, by the Angel, no less.

By his count, over 2600 Brethren now occupied Ludlow, and he had taken pains to put the rest of the town in the River. The Angel was gorged and growing, all the souls it could ever want, coming to it.

Looking at his map of the town, Edgewater and Acropolis would go next, Ludlow's neighbors on either side. Then Fairwater, south of Acropolis. And Winterdale, north of Edgewater. Smithton, too. By then, there'd be 25,000 Brethren.

Mal was bound to the Angel, as all Brethren were bound to it, but since he was the first, he felt his bond was closest, felt the Angel's hungry satisfaction at all of those souls, could feel it coiling and uncoiling in the dark of the Mercy River.

With his acolytes in charge of things—the Mayor primarily occupied with conversions, Eugene working on restoring order, and Ramsey in charge of fighting the remaining Breathers, Mal could concentrate on the big picture.

He sat in the Mayor's office, poring over a map he'd laid out on the desk. The rivers were the key. The rivers were the arteries and veins of America. All would flow from the rivers, guided by Lazarus and the Angel. The conversions would spread along those same arteries and veins.

Mal took a red pen and drew an X in the Mercy River, where the Angel lived. Soon, there would be more. By the time everything merged with the Mississippi River, Mal estimated there'd be over 600,000 Brethren, then. By the time it got to the Gulf of Mexico, a couple of million. A spiritual vanguard, all united in purpose, all ageless, hopeless, deathless, lifeless. Forever and ever, Amen.

There came a knock at the door.

"Come," Mal said.

It was one of the deputies. His deputies. A young man, already balding.

"Some Breathers are raising a disturbance in town," he said.

"Stop them," Mal said.

"I just thought you should know," the deputy said.

"How many?"

"One car," the deputy said. "I think Max Paulsen might be involved."

Mal gave the map a last look and then got up.

"Good," Lazarus said. "I don't want him killed. I want him captured. Make that very clear."

"Yessir," the deputy said.

It wasn't so hard being a leader. You just told people what to do, and they did it. Brethren could teach the Breathers a thing or two about good governance. Orders given, orders carried out, without question or hesitation. No debate, no discussion, no corruption. Just the cool efficiency of unchallenged authority.

Lazarus went to the window of the Mayor's office, which had a nice view of the boutiques and little cafes in the business district. Just past that was the River.

He was going to stay here, where it was safe. Until every Breather had been captured, he was going to remain here. He was the Messenger, after all. Without him, there was no Message, no direction.

Outside, he saw some of the Brethren hunched over the body of a dead Breather. Three women, bloody-mouthed, and a dead man. The women had taken bites out of the man's fat stomach. They huddled over him like buzzards, their eyes flatly wild.

Mal strode out of the Mayor's office and went down the hall, out the front doors of the place, to confront them. Almost without thinking of the danger to himself.

"Sisters," he said to the women, who were wrapped in pearls and shiny baubles, were wearing shiny sequined animal print dresses—one zebra, one cheetah, one tigress—they gazed up at Mal without recognition.

"Sisters," Mal said again, holding up his arms. "Whatever are you doing, here?"

"Hungry," one of the women said.

"There is no hunger, anymore," Mal said. "I cured your hunger."

"Hungry," another of them said, herself a fat woman with frosted blond hair.

"You never need hunger again," Mal said. "We have transcended the paltry needs of the flesh, Brethren."

"Hungry," the third woman said. Another Ludlow dowager, the kind prone to sporting overlarge hats and all-too-tiny dogs. She wore once-white gloves, which were soaked red to her wrists in Breather blood.

"That poor fellow belonged to the Angel," Mal said.

"Hungry," the women said.

"You have stolen that which was rightfully the Angel's," Mal said. He didn't understand why some of the Brethren did this. Were their wills weak? Were their makers less resolute? He did not know.

He also didn't know why none of his deputies had stopped them. There was a peril in rulership, in that one could not trust one's own flock to do their bidding in the manner intended by the ruler. It was like a game of Telephone, where seemingly clear messages got muddled the further down the line one went.

"Ladies," Mal said, trying to distract the women from their carnival. It wasn't that he objected to it per se—one less Breather was one less thing for Mal to have to think about. Rather, it was just contrary to the spirit he was trying to encourage in Ludlow. It would not do to have Brethren taking down Breathers and feasting on their entrails in the streets. There was no place for Brethren like these in his Ludlow.

In that moment, Mal understood something, had what might have been termed an epiphany, if Mal were a thinking man. These Brethren, the flesheaters, were heretics. They had found the Light in the Dark but clung to some aspect of their old selves, their old ways. Their hunger was a rejection of the infinite spiritual nourishment the Angel provided.

But heretics they were. And just as a bad apple could ruin a whole basket with its rot, so would these false-Brethren taint the flock.

Mal drew a pistol from his belt, a chrome Colt .45 ACP, and without hesitation, shot the ladies in the head, one by one, before they even had time to react. He just shot and shot and shot. The last one, the gloved one, merely looked up at him, chewing on Breather flesh, her eyes big and blank as unstruck coins. And he shot her.

One of his deputies ran out at the sound of the shooting, saw Mal standing there with the smoking pistol.

"Sir?" he asked.

"Get this street cleaned up," Mal said. "Have someone do it."

He put the pistol back into his belt, watching the brass casings shine brightly against the asphalt street.

Mal dug out a radio from one of his pockets.

"Ramsey," he said.

A few moments later.

"Yessir."

"How many of the Brethren have you seen feasting on the flesh of Breathers?"

"Sir?"

"How many?"

"Some," Ramsey said.

"A lot?"

"Many," Ramsey said. "Not all. I haven't been paying attention."

"I want you to have a couple of your deputies round these Brethren up," Mal said. "Put'em in a paddy wagon and bring'em to me."

"Alright," Ramsey said. "Did Smith tell you about that Breather Paulsen?"

"Yeah," Mal said. "Keep after him."

"Keep after him and fetch the Brethren, too?"

"Delegate," Mal said. "Have some of your deputies go after Paulsen, you round up the heretics."

Mal sat down at the curb, on the empty street. It didn't make him happy to think that he would have to put down some of the Brethren when he was busy making them. He could not have Brethren who were not amenable to the Angel's will, to his Message. He would not tolerate this.

Another of the Brethren, a fat middle-aged man, emerged from an alley, again with the bloodstained mouth, his fingers bloody.

That was the telltale sign of the heretics: bloody hands, bloody mouths.

The man looked at Mal without comprehension or recognition, and Mal didn't know the man, either. He was wearing a Postal Service uniform. He'd been a mailman.

"Brother," Mal said, standing up. The man gazed at him, knew him for Brethren, for they could always tell one another.

"Hungry," the man said.

"I know you are, Brother," Mal said, drawing his pistol. "I brought you something to eat right here."

He fired two shots, right in the head. The man's head exploded in a bloodless spray of flesh, brain, and bone, and he fell to the ground, lifeless once more. He had forsaken the Angel's gift, and had paid the ultimate price for it. No life everlasting.

Mal turned on his heel and went back into the Mayor's office, then went to one of the stacks of firearms that had been piled there by the Brethren. If this happened to some of his deputies, there would be problems.

He took an assault rifle, an AR-15 with a scope, and went to a nearby table, where boxes of ammunition had been piled. He found the .223 caliber rounds that matched the caliber of the weapon, and went up to the roof of City Hall, sat there on his elbows, watching. He set the radio next to him, listened to the episodic talk of his deputies, going about their business. Some of the chatter was about the bridge, and something happening there, a commotion. Trouble.

Mal got to his feet, pocketed the radio, and took the rifle with him. A prophet he was, but it seemed he had to attend to earthly matters as much as spiritual. The Angel required it of him.

"All available units, this is Lazarus," he said. "Converge on the Mercy River Bridge."

10.

Adrienne had tried to get the attention of the deputies at the Mercy River Bridge, gamely driving the Doctor's car around, but the deputies hadn't fallen for it. They just talked into their radios about a Breather going nuts in a stolen car, and put out a warning on it.

Max, who had been dropped off at the car dealership that was near the on-ramp for the bridge, watched with grim amusement as Adrienne drove off, without a soul giving chase.

There were three deputies at the barricade, which they had sealed off with their cruisers and some sawhorses, about midway through. The Mercy River Bridge was usually pretty busy, so they had been occupied with keeping folks from the neighboring communities out of Ludlow.

"Can I help you with something?" said a guy at the dealership, a balding dead guy in a suit with flat, beady eyes and glasses perched on the end of his nose.

Max turned to look at the guy.

"Breather," the man said. "BREATHER!"

Max took out his pistol and shot the guy in the head, then looked around, to see if there were any others who saw him. It appeared to be quiet, save for a train rumbling nearby, honking its air horn. The ground shook as the train approached. It traveled beneath the bridge, and may have been about a hundred yards from the dealership. He imagined the salesmen there trying to close deals with the noise of the train passing by, shook his head in amusement.

Then he had another idea, and took the guy's keys and walked into his dealership, which was empty of customers, of course.

The idea of a zombie car dealer made him snicker grimly. How would a zombie pitch a sale at a prospective customer? And would the customer be a zombie, too? How far would one go through the motions, in Mal's Utopia? Buy groceries for food you no longer needed to eat? Shop for clothes you no longer cared to wear?

So much of life was about buying and selling things, feeding needs—what would one do in an emptied world, where the overriding drive was eulogizing the Light in the Dark, where there was no need higher than feeding the Angel in the Depths? There was nothingness, and there was nothingness, he supposed—vacuous consumer culture didn't stand a chance against outright nihilism. You couldn't fight a void with a vacuum, or a vacuum cleaner, for that matter.

He found some keys for one of the cars on the lot, and then loaded the dynamite into the seat next to him.

The car, a BMW M3, bright red, started smoothly enough, and Max took it for a spin around the block, getting used to it. Murder, larceny, grand theft auto—just another feather in his cap these days. Desperate times required desperate measures.

He drove the M3 right up the bridge, right at the deputies, who were standing around, not lounging, just standing there. Two of them happened to be on Max's side of the barricade, while the third was talking with somebody who had wanted to cross the bridge, and was stopped by the barricade.

There wasn't time to be subtle. Max charged the M3 right at the deputies, who saw him coming and began shooting, shattering the windshield. Max lamented not bringing a camera or something to capture this moment. His whole life focused on filming things, and here he was without a camera in reach.

He let gravity and inertia do his dirty work for him, ramming both deputies against one of the cruisers, pinning them with the crunch of bone and flesh that had the M3's airbag deploy, shielding Max from the impact, only to deflate as the deputies fired on him.

Max opened the door and rolled out, having his pistol and saber at the ready. He fired on the deputy that had been talking to the terrified middle-aged man in an orange pickup truck, and was now taking aim at Max with a shotgun.

Max fired several shots at the deputy, knocking him off his feet. Then he reloaded, using the door of the M3 as a shield. One of the pinned deputies talked on his radio, reported the attack. Max thought it was amazing and terrible that the deputy was pinned to a car with two broken legs, and was still able to calmly relate the situation.

He popped himself up and shot the two pinned deputies, who were in the process of reloading, themselves. Four shots, and they both slumped against the hood of the M3.

The old man in the pickup was busy trying to dislodge a gun from the rack of his pickup truck, while Max ran over and shot the other deputy, who was getting back up.

"Don't shoot!" the old man said. "My God, don't shoot me!"

"I won't," Max said, grabbing the deputy's shotgun. "Look, get back where you came from, call somebody. Call the FBI, whomever. Tell them that there's a crazy cult running amok in Ludlow."

The man gaped at Max.

"You shot those police," he said.

"They're in on it," Max said. "Look, I don't have time, here. Just go. I'm not the bad guy, here. I mean, I could've shot you, too, right? But I'm not."

"They said there's a plague in Ludlow, that it's in quarantine," the old man said.

"Fine," Max said. "But they're the source of it."

"You mean I'm infected?"

"No, goddammit," Max said. "Just get to a phone, get out of here, alright? The cultists are going to be coming any minute now."

Max ran to the M3 and shoved past the mess of glass and torn airbags to pull out the boxes of explosive, which he then piled up behind one of the police cruisers.

The old man had turned his pickup around and got out of there with a squeal of tires.

Max wanted to follow him. It was striking—after all of the hiding and fear in Ludlow, he just had to head across that bridge and he'd be safe. But Adrienne was somewhere in Ludlow, and Max wasn't going to abandon her. And he didn't want to give Lazarus the satisfaction of having run away from this. And he couldn't. Too many people would die, too many more people would die, too.

He pried open the boxes of explosive, began twining the sticks by their fuses, creating 10-stick bundles he could hold with his hand. He duct-taped these together, made a bunch of them, hoping they'd be enough. He kept a few singletons on hand, too.

The police barricade extended to the pedestrian walkway on the bridge, too. That would serve Max well, once the freaks started coming up this way.

In Ludlow, he could hear police sirens getting louder. He went to the edge of the bridge and looked down.

At the shore, the freaks were there, as ever, drowning people, while other ones were gathering the bodies and piling them in the back of a tractor trailer. No more school buses, now.

The trees near the drowning site had been cut down. No more cover, there.

Then he gazed down into the green-black waters of the Mercy River, its unknown depths. But something was in there. Something squirmed in those dark depths. And Max was going to root it out.

Without fanfare, he lit one of the bundled sticks of explosive, then dropped it over the side.

"Bombs away, you fucker," he said, watching it fall. It splashed, disappearing into the water below.

Max counted to himself as it fell.

One.

The sirens were growing louder.

Two.

The train kept rolling by.

Three.

A crow cawed somewhere, unseen.

Four.

The police radios crackled with chatter.

Five.

Some of the victims below were screaming, trying to resist their captors.

Six.

There was a huge, muffled explosion that opened a white circle in the water that jetted skyward. Birds flew out of the trees, the bridge shook, the shockwave traveled out from the epicenter.

"Oh, hell, yeah," Max said. "Bet you that got your attention, didn't it, Baby?"

He lit two more, chucked them over the side, then ducked down again.

Then he saw dogs racing up the bridge, toward him. They weren't barking, however. They were silent.

Max grabbed the deputy's shotgun and took aim. There were a dozen of them, running hard for him.

The dynamite below detonated in two spectacular blasts. Plumes of water reaching even where he was.

The shotgun didn't have enough rounds to deal with the devil dogs, so he put that down and then grabbed a couple of the singleton sticks of explosive and lit them, trying to gauge it, letting the fuses burn down.

It was the silence of the dogs that was most odd to him, that communicated their wrongness.

When the fuses had burned down enough, he hurled the sticks at them.

"Fetch," he said.

The dogs ignored the sticks, which detonated in blasts that shattered the windows of the M3 and the cruisers, and had Max's head ringing.

There were no more dogs. They'd been splattered in the twin explosions on the bridge. He lit another two bundles of dynamite, peered over the side of the bridge, and dropped them.

At the on-ramp of the bridge, a half-dozen police cruisers had lined up, two by two.

They had seen the dynamite explosions, and were approaching warily. It was a curious thing to him. The freaks were fearless, but they understood that he could blow them to bits if they got too close.

Max peeked over the railing. Something was swimming in that water, something massive and white. Had he roused the beast?

He wanted his camera so badly.

Max lit a singleton stick of explosive and hurled it at the police cruisers. Let them chew on that.

The dynamite detonated, shattering the windows of the cruisers.

He lit two more singletons and chucked them toward them, laughing to himself. If Adrienne could see this, she'd be shaking her head.

One stick went off, then another.

They were trying to distract him, to delay him. He lit two more of the big bundles and threw them down at the amorphous white mass in the water. It almost looked whale-like to him, this leviathan, with a long, sinuous body and what could've been a fluke. It was hard to see in the murky water.

One of the stick bundles was flung back upward, landing near him, soaking wet, the fuse sparking fitfully.

"What the fuck?"

Max dove for it, grabbing it and tossing it back over before it went off. He ducked, covered his head, as both bundles exploded, one in the water, the other perhaps above it. He couldn't be sure, because his ears were ringing, his nose was bleeding.

Then he heard the thing below, some kind of roar, a horrible, unearthly sound that echoed in the river valley, calling to mind bull elephants crossed with groaning metal. A pair of silvery-white tentacles reached up and slapped against the metal trusses of the bridge, grabbing hold.

The thing was coming up here.

For him.

II.

Adrienne gunned the Jaguar's engine and tried to draw out the deputies, but they just wouldn't follow her. She imagined Max would be peevish at her for failing in what was, no doubt, in his mind, such a simple task.

All she really wanted to do was leave Ludlow entirely. Whatever was wrong here was something she was not equipped to handle. She was an art teacher, for god's sake, not a revolutionary, not a guerrilla fighter.

Townsfolk kept coming out of their places, just walking out and watching her drive by them with empty faces. And they kept coming, drifting into the streets. It made Adrienne bite her lip and whimper, just seeing how many people Lazarus had sent to the river. As a teacher, she was tied to the community, she knew so many of those people.

She had to swerve to avoid them, so many were heading out into the streets. Then she realized that maybe they were trying to stop her, and stepped on the gas.

Adrienne saw a police cruiser rolling down the street, using its PA: "Brethren of Ludlow, awake! The time has come to scour this town, to purge it."

Her car passed the cruiser, and the PA blared after her.

"Stop that car, Brethren."

And then she saw those townsfolk begin running after her, in her rearview mirror. Dozens of them, hundreds by the time she got down the end of the street. The police cruiser gliding down the middle of the street, with hundreds of Ludlow's breathless, deathless Brethren pursuing her. They were emerging from every house, now. Everywhere she looked, the streets moved, those dead eyes all on her and her car.

Adrienne banged the steering wheel of the Jaguar with her palm in frustration, unsure where to go.

She went down Oak Street, driving faster, until everybody was a blur to either side of her, although they were hemming her in, packing in closer.

She buckled her seatbelt and took a swerving turn onto Church Street, actually sliding into a number of Brethren who had been running for her. She broadsided them with the car, which made a horrible denting sound that sent the Brethren flinging over parked cars and into boulevards.

Then she sped down Church Street.

Getting out of the residential areas was better, although she still saw this seething mass of people running after her. They would never stop. They wouldn't get tired. She'd run out of gasoline before they got tired.

There was no place to go, no sanctuary.

The Brethren had taken Ludlow.

She turned down Third Street, which led to some of the business district, and slammed on her brakes.

Hundreds of Brethren were there, feasting on people that they had killed in front of the Home Depot. With their bare hands, by the look of it. To her art teacher's eyes, it looked like some ghastly parody of The Last Supper. Seeing her, all of those eyes, those bloody faces, they ran for her.

Adrienne could see the other Brethren in her rearview mirror. She floored the accelerator on her car and swerved to avoid the bloody Brethren.

There were just too many of them.

She cut a corner and winced as her car scraped against a stop sign, while the Brethren kept running, joined by their ghoulish peers from Home Depot.

Adrienne tried to keep her composure as she rounded another turn onto Fourth Street, only to strike one of the Brethren full-on, the body smashing over her hood and their face smashing into the windshield, forming an absurd impression of their face in the fractured glass before the body tumbled off to the side.

She fought to maintain control of her car, then brought it to a stop. The Brethren were still coming, still running. Hundreds of them.

"My god," Adrienne said. She didn't know where to go. Uptown? Downtown? The river was out of the question. Back to the Doctor's place?

Her hands were shaking.

Looking into her rearview mirror, she saw they were getting closer. Was she the last living person left in town? The last "Breather?"

She cruised down Pine Street, which led to the lumberyards, then kicked herself, because that would dead end at the river. The dead steel mills loomed in the distance, too.

Adrienne took a hard left and went up Vista Boulevard, which would take her uphill, up into the mountains.

But there were still more Brethren that way, blocking it. Throngs of them. So many.

She was trapped. She could take a right on Vista and end up down by the river, would become River Run Road. She could try to go up toward the mountains, and drive her way through the Brethren there, or she could turn back on Pine and run into the ones that had been chasing her. Were they herding her? Was that possible?

Gazing down Pine, at the blood-faced Brethren and their pale-faced peers, it didn't seem possible. What was going on?

Whatever happened, she would face her end with human dignity. She drove toward the river, fingers white on the wheel.

Adrienne drove toward River Run Road, speeding along, when she saw a blockade up ahead, a number of cars parked in a lengthy column. Gridlock in Ludlow? Impossible.

She slammed on the brakes. Ahead of her, Brethren, behind the mass of cars. Behind her, Brethren, racing downhill, toward her.

It wasn't fair.

She tried to dial Max, but he wasn't picking up.

Then she heard the explosions.

12.

Heidi and her sister had been at the riverside, grimly waiting for their end when the explosions had begun. Great blasts of water sprayed everybody on shore and left their heads ringing. The zombies clutched their heads each time the explosions occurred, and gazed about uncertainly.

Father Knightley had been one of the zombies who was supervising the drownings. He had personally taken Heidi and Lisa from the deputies, and was attending to them.

His dead eyes contrasted with her memory of the kindly priest, and Heidi cried. His hair was wild, his collar, askew.

"Father, don't you remember us?"

"Of course I do," Knightley said. "But it doesn't matter. I have seen the Light in the Dark, Heidi. You'll see it, too. As will your sister. It's so beautiful."

Then the first explosion went off, knocking them off their feet. Heidi kicked at Father Knightley, who did not react emotionally to her attack, but only turned his attention toward the water.

Lisa was mostly quiet, pale. The bullet wound to her arm, untended, had left her weak.

Two more great explosions erupted from the water. For a moment, Heidi had thought maybe the government had begun bombing the thing in the water, but then she could see that it was somebody on the bridge, dropping dynamite on it.

Father Knightley grabbed for Heidi.

"Come along, Heidi," he said. "The hour is upon us."

He grabbed for her, while Heidi kicked at him. His flesh gave, but he felt no pain.

There were more explosions higher up, smaller, on the bridge. Chunks of something landed on everybody below, bits of fur and flesh and bone. The remaining humans retched, while the zombies just kept trying to drag people into the river to drown them. There were huge piles of bodies in a semi truck's bed, the doors open wide, the bodies stacked high. Heidi would not go without a fight.

Father Knightley grabbed her hair and began to drag her down to the river.

"God, no!" Heidi screamed. "Lisa!"

But her sister had passed out. Knightley pulled her into the water, and Heidi coughed on a mouthful of it, sputtering. Then he paused, gazing toward the bridge.

They had all stopped.

Across the central span of the bridge, the Angel in the Depths had emerged, black ichor flowing from its damaged body. The thing was titanic, wormlike. Like a massive maggot, with a huge, distended, silver-white body. Long, long tentacles at one end, dozens of them, and it had grabbed ahold of the bridge with them.

"The Angel," Father Knightley said, dropping to his knees in the water.

It looked like a hydra, one of those things Heidi remembered seeing in a sample of pondwater. It looked like some kind of monstrous barnacle. Its tail ended in a kind of fin, something that grasped and flexed like a great mittened hand. The thing flailed and shook. Then the monster roared, and the sound was even worse than the explosions. It was like an avalanche of church bells, tumbling down a rocky hillside, clattering into the unsuspecting valley below.

It was the death of all that was good, and beautiful, and hopeful.

What was worse than that was all the eyes the monster had. She could see the things, these black bulbous eyes on eyestalks, like the eyes of a lobster, only there were so very many, turning this way and that, some gazing at the shore, most gazing above. Eyes like big, black bowling balls, polished shiny, devoid of sentiment or emotion.

Heidi cried out at the sight of this thing, this slithering abomination, as it wriggled and squirmed, trying to get its great bulk up to the bridge, slapping tentacle after tentacle onto the bridge frame to hoist itself upward.

She did not know who was up there, but she prayed for them.

13.

The explosions had taken Mal by surprise. He had not expected anyone to actually attack the Angel in the Depths. He had been preoccupied with the seizing of the town, had not accounted for someone actually going on the attack. The assassination attempts, he could deal with; this was something far worse. For an attack on the Angel was an attack on all of them, on Ludlow, itself.

"Stop him," he ordered the deputies. Ramsey and the others had run up the bridge, toward the blasphemer, only to be blown up by a couple of bouncing sticks of dynamite. It had been self-evident to Mal that they would dodge the oncoming explosives, but they had charged on, heedless, only to be destroyed.

Now, as ever, it was the Messenger and the Angel, working together. He toggled the AR15 to get it to fire in three-round bursts, his own holy trinity.

Then he gazed into the scope. He'd already emptied a clip into some more wayward Brethren he'd seen along the way, feasting on a handful of bodies. What was this world coming to?

He just needed a head shot. He used the Angel as his guide, could see where it was focused, the flurry of tentacles, the mass of the beautiful Angel, so shimmery white, as it heaved itself toward its attacker. There was such righteousness in this fight, were Mal's heart capable of beating, it would have been bursting with powerful pride at this noble endeavor.

He saw a man's leg, visible for a moment, and he took the shot, three shots—pow-pow-pow—and saw the rewarding blossom of blood and flesh that told him he'd reached his mark. His marksmanship had improved with death—not breathing, not feeling, he could simply take aim, carefully. It became simply a matter of physics and volition.

No more dynamite made its tumbling way down the street, so Mal began walking toward the blasphemer, rifle up and at the ready. He walked up the middle of the way, along the dotted yellow line, fearless, hopeless, ruthless, relentless.

He had become the Angel of Death itself. It would be his finest moment in an endless life. It would be his Waterloo, his Yorktown, his Little Bighorn. It was his Battle of the Bulge. The battle for the heart and soul of Ludlow started and ended here.

He would not fail.

14.

Max couldn't believe somebody had gotten a shot on him, even as the ghastly, bloody bulk of the beast loomed over him, tentacles reaching for him. The thing had grabbed onto the railing of the pedestrian walkway with its teeth, great black triangles the bent the metal. Max had cut at the tentacles with the saber, severed three of them with smooth strokes of the blade, its black blood spraying on him.

Its remaining tentacles had swarmed around him, as it searched for, then found him, black eyes turning on wretched stalks. First one, then four, then a dozen, then more. All of its eyes on him, black and shiny, water rolling off its wrinkled body.

Max lit the fuse on the last bundle of dynamite he had, although at this range, it would blast him to bits as surely as he'd hoped it would kill the thing.

Then the bullets caught him in the leg, making Max drop the dynamite, which the thing reached for with one of its tentacles. Max lunged for it, actually throwing himself atop it, while the creature coiled a tentacle around him. He hacked at it with the saber.

The bridge railing gave a groan to rival the roar of the beast, and suddenly the thing that had been boiling over the railing of the bridge was gone, subject to gravity. The jarring force of it had him drop the blade.

It fell down, but some of its tentacles were still wrapped around stouter sections of the bridge, drawing tight like rubber bands as they bore the strain of holding the thing up. The tentacle that held onto Max pulled taut, too, and he wedged a hand between a gap in the bridge, making it into a fist, howling at the strain on his body as the thing pulled on him.

He remembered the stories about baboons being trapped with little boxes with holes in them, a treat inside. The baboons would reach into the hole for the treat, only to find, when their fists were clenched, that they could not get their hands out of the holes. He was applying that principle to the section of bridge, keeping that fist clenched, letting it act as a kind of piton as the monster pulled at him.

Then he saw a shadow loom over him, the shadow of Mal Lazarus, carrying an M16 or something with a scope. He'd been the one who shot him.

Max felt his wrist dislocate from the strain upon it, and cried out.

In that moment, fueled by adrenaline and emotion, everything was like a snapshot to him, as if he were the camera—Lazarus above him, in silhouette, the sun behind him, a figure in black, eclipsing the sun, black hair slicked back, smooth and polished.

"Blasphemer," Lazarus said, pointing the rifle at Max. "Breather."

Max opened his hand, and the force on his body yanked him off the bridge just as Lazarus was shooting, the bullets sparking on the ground.

Max dropped the dynamite right as he went over the side of the bridge, as the monster roared at him. The force of the tentacles had Max flinging from the bridge, over the river, maybe 70 feet in the air.

He saw the dynamite he'd dropped into the mouth of the Angel explode, saw the Angel itself bulge, swell, and burst in a great plume of fire, he saw the tentacle that held him snap free of its moorings, felt himself fling farther from the carnage, saw himself skip like a stone on the surface of the river, then saw himself underneath the water, gazing up, the sound muffled by. In the water, he saw shining spheres flowing with the current, like garlands of golden grapes, carried by currents. Like little angels, brushing past his face, writhing in their golden globes, like tiny worlds carrying alien ambassadors.

Then he saw nothing—his mind had simply run out of film, and his vision faded to black.

15.

The explosion tore the Angel apart and knocked Mal off his feet. There was a crystalline crash, and the Light in the Dark, that which had sustained him and nourished him, was simply gone.

Mal made it to his feet, even as his body became like lead, his hands even number than they'd been before, his head like a balloon, tethered to the sinking rock of his body, while blackness closed in around him, he gazed at his own outstretched hands like they were strangers.

"No," he said. "Light?"

His legs buckled and he pitched forward, toward the River, and was gone.

16.

The explosion of the thing had been tremendous, had showered Heidi and everybody on the shore with gray-silver-white flesh and black blood. Blood poured from everybody's ears in the wake of the detonation, and in that gigantic flash and boom of the explosion, all sound ceased, and Heidi was momentarily blinded and deafened.

Then she saw all the zombies standing there one moment, watching the devastation above them, and then she saw them all fall lifeless to the ground, like unstrung marionettes. All of them fell at once. Father Knightley just pitched forward without a sound, floating out onto the river.

In that moment, in the wake of such thunderous noise, there was silence.

And Heidi saw a lone figure fall from the center of the bridge—a long, lonely descent into the river, landing with a splash, and vanishing from view.

All around them were the living and the dead. To be numbered among the living was a blessing, indeed. Heidi cried with relief and got herself out of the water, freed herself, roused her sister. And then went to work helping the survivors.

Bodies were piled everywhere. Bodies in the water. The dead, undead, and newly dead. The choking gasps of the living. Everyone oily-slick with the blood of the monster. The crooked cross in the river was garlanded with the flesh of the Angel, which turned this way and that. Smoke was everywhere.

Somewhere, she heard sirens, and a woman pulled up in a gray Jaguar. It was Ms. Morse, the art teacher at Whidmore. She ran down the boat launch, looking around.

"Where's Max?" she asked. She looked tired, her long hair a mess, although Heidi was not one to judge. She was sure she and her sister looked like hell. Although everything around them looked like hell.

"I don't know, Ms. Morse," Heidi said. "Can you help us? I'm trying to get people freed."

"He was up on the bridge," Ms. Morse said.

"I think he fell," Heidi said. "I saw someone fall, after the thing blew up. It was horrible."

Ms. Morse walked to the river's edge and looked, but with all the bodies around them, there was no way of telling who was who.

Around them, survivors were coming to their senses and were calling out for help, so Heidi went hunting for a knife or something to cut people's bonds, asked Ms. Morse to help.

Somewhere a helicopter was approaching, although it was unclear whether it was a news copter or something else, but the sound was very distinct.

"I'm thirsty, Sis," Lisa said, coughing. "What happened? Are we dead?"

"It's dead," Heidi said. "Somebody killed it."

"Max killed it," Ms. Morse said. "Max Paulsen did it. Max! Max!"

Ms. Morse called out, screamed his name, but nobody answered.

A military helicopter came into view, as did a news helicopter, and National Guard trucks rolled into Ludlow.

Heidi held up her hands.

"We're down here!" she cried. "Sis, we're going to be alright!"

Down came masked soldiers, rappelling down from the helicopter, carrying assault rifles. Down came trucks with soldiers wearing hazardous materials suits and gas masks. The soldiers walked from body to body, rifles at the ready, while Ms. Morse and Heidi held up their hands.

"Who's in charge, here?" one of the soldiers asked, his voice muffled by the mask.

"What?" Heidi said.

"Who's in charge?"

"Nobody," Ms. Morse said. "Everybody's dead."

17.

Max woke up in a white room, a square little cube with fluorescent bulbs whining overhead. He was on some kind of metal fold-out cot that appeared to emerge from the wall. There was a metal mirror on a far wall, over a basin, near a metal shelf. A toilet was next to that. The walls were white, except for one wall, at his feet, which looked like it was made of glass.

"Where the fuck am I?" he asked.

Silence.

He was wearing an orange jumpsuit, with the number 86-753-09 on it, and his last name, stenciled on a patch.

"Where am I?"

"You're in quarantine and observation, Mr. Paulsen," came a voice on a PA. "We're ensuring that you're not infected."

"I'm fine," he said, tapping on the glass. Thick. Lexan, maybe? He didn't know. "How long was I out? Where the hell am I?"

"That's classified, Mr. Paulsen. And you were unconscious for a week. Massive body trauma. You're lucky to be alive."

Max did feel sore all over. His shot leg throbbed, but appeared to have been bandaged. As was his wrist.

"I want to talk to a lawyer."

"Not necessary."

"I have my rights."

Silence.

"Nobody knows you're alive, Mr. Paulsen," said the voice. "Our recovery team found you downriver at the XCS."

"XCS?"

"Xenomorph Contamination Site," said the voice. "We need your account of what you think happened."

Max sat down at the bunk, scowled out the thick glass. "Not without a lawyer. I didn't do anything wrong; I fucking did your job for you, you pricks."

Silence.

"Seriously, why am I being held here? What have I done?"

His wrist ached. Slipping up his sleeve, he saw that blood had been drawn from him.

"Before I passed out, I saw more of those things," Max said. "Eggs. I swear they were eggs, traveling down the river. Eggs from that thing."

Silence.

"I'm not infective," Max said.

"That remains to be seen," said the voice.

"How long am I going to be kept here?"

Silence.

"You can't do this to me," Max said, but without much force, because he knew that they could. They could do whatever they wanted.

"You're being held until we can be sure there is no public risk of releasing you."

"Which'll be?"

"Indefinite," the voice said.

Max paced back and forth in the cell.

"I saved Ludlow," he said.

"Ludlow is dead," the voice said. "Nothing was saved. It's a ghost town, Mr. Paulsen. Now, tell us everything that you know about the Light in the Dark."

18.

In the town of Ludlow, over 4891 people had died in the course of a week in the fall of 2010, in what was portrayed in the media as the single largest episode of bioterrorism in the history of the United States, to date.

Eyewitness accounts pointed to some kind of millennial cult activity that had sought to forcibly drown nonbelievers in the Mercy River, led by the messianic figure of one Malcolm Lazarus, who apparently died at the scene. Ritual cannibalism was carried out throughout the community, as well as the mass drowning.

When government agents raided the town, a mass suicide occurred on the part of the cultists. News helicopters had filmed the masses of bodies along the banks of the Mercy River, and bodies piled in trailer trucks.

Although a number of survivors claimed to have seen what they described as some kind of monster in the water, government physicians and psychologists suggested that this was some kind of mass hallucination, prompted by the use of a nerve gas in the terrorist incident. Nerve gas was implicated in the suicide of the cultists, themselves.

According to authorities, blame could be placed at the River Rock Island Facility upriver from Ludlow, a Superfund site that had been shut down in the early 1970s, as the source of the bioterrorist arsenal. The exact identity of the nerve agent was considered classified, and was not revealed.

The group involved was an apocalyptic cult centered around Lazarus. The Lazarus Cult, as it came to be known, attempted to forcibly take over the town of Ludlow.

Ludlow was put under quarantine, pending further investigation, its surviving residents resettled elsewhere, under new identities, after they were processed and interrogated. River traffic along the Mercy was rerouted with the help of the Army Corps of Engineers, and now travels along the Ohio River, while teams of government zoologists and biologists examine Ludlow in detail.

The exits leading to Ludlow were blocked by armed military detachments, with traffic rerouted to neighboring communities. A razorwire fence has been placed around the entirety of Ludlow, with warnings of criminal prosecution if trespass occurs.

One missing Ludlow resident, Max Paulsen, had blogged about the events on the Internet, including a number of personal accounts and photographs of events leading up to the mass suicide, although there was considerable speculation that he had himself been infected by the neurotoxin used by the cultists, and his accounts of things highly suspect, the photographs doctored, the videos, staged.

Hackers disabled Paulsen's blog, Shudderclick, within 48 hours of the Ludlow Incident, although mirror sites of it continue to proliferate throughout the Net, as do accounts similar to the Ludlow Incident occurring in other communities.

THE END

ABOUT THE AUTHOR

D. T. Neal is a fiction writer and editor living in Chicago. He won second place in the Aeon Award in 2008 for his short story, "Aegis," and has been published in *Albedo 1*, Ireland's premier magazine of science fiction, horror, and fantasy. He is the author of *Saamaanthaa* (2011), and is currently working on several new works of horror and science fiction.

Made in the USA
Lexington, KY
20 June 2013